EMINENT DISDAIN

By

Alan B. Gazzaniga

*We at Trafford believe that it is the responsibility of us all, as both individuals and corporations,
to make choices that are environmentally and socially sound. You, in turn, are supporting this
responsible conduct each time you purchase a Trafford book, or make use of our publishing services.
To find out how you are helping, please visit www.trafford.com/responsiblepublishing.html*

*Our mission is to efficiently provide the world's finest, most comprehensive book publishing
service, enabling every author to experience success. To find out how to publish your book, your
way, and have it available worldwide, visit us online at www.trafford.com*

Trafford rev. 8/26/2009

 www.trafford.com

North America & international
toll-free: 1 888 232 4444 (USA & Canada)
phone: 250 383 6864 ♦ fax: 250 383 6804 ♦ email: info@trafford.com

The United Kingdom & Europe
phone: +44 (0)1865 487 395 ♦ local rate: 0845 230 9601
facsimile: +44 (0)1865 481 507 ♦ email: info.uk@trafford.com

The author wishes to acknowledge the special efforts of Linda K. Donoghue and my daughter Andrea for their work as both editors and contributors. A sincere thanks to my wife Sheila for her encouragement and critiques.

"The Constitution is a mere thing of wax in the hands of the Judiciary which they may twist and shape into any form they please."

Thomas Jefferson

Chapter One

The motorcycle sped north on Highway One. The driver, with his passenger clutching his waist, took a sudden left turn and then quickly banked right onto a dirt road. As the bike bounced along, its headlight flashed back and forth, lighting up the rows of grape vines behind a wire fence. After about a hundred yards, the road ended and Sean Casey slowed his motorcycle to a stop.

"Sorry about the sudden change of plans," he said over his shoulder, "I'm feeling lightheaded. I need to check my sugar." Sean was a seventeen-year-old juvenile diabetic familiar with the symptoms of hypoglycemia. Tiffany stepped off and stretched as Sean removed a black bag and blanket from his saddlebag.

"What's with the blanket?" she asked innocently.

Sean spread the blanket out on the ground next to the motorcycle and the five foot wire fence that enclosed the grape vineyard in front of him.

He glanced back at Tiffany as he spread his testing paraphernalia. Without answering her question he nodded towards the fence, "That's Doc Miceli's vineyard, if you're wondering. I've worked there a couple of times picking grapes during the harvest. Now that's work!" He shook his head slowly, as one who remembers hard labor of the past with a certain appreciation that comes from not doing it anymore. "Doc is my doc by the way," he added. "A great doctor. Saved my life once when I was in a coma. But kinda weird."

Tiffany, who was Sean's age, sat down and said, "Why would you go to a weird doctor?"

Tiffany was also a juvenile diabetic. They had met in a diabetic camp earlier in the summer and had been inseparable ever since.

"Not *weird* weird," Sean said, as he flicked on the penlight stored inside his test kit. He laid the light on the blanket, swabbed his left middle finger with an alcohol sponge, and then punctured the finger with a lancet device. He squeezed his finger hard until a small drop of blood appeared. He held the test strip, which was in the blinking glucometer, close and the blood was suddenly sucked up by the test strip. Within seconds the glucometer read 60.

"Shit," he exclaimed, "I knew it."

He stood and threw the test strip to the ground. "You should test yours. You took your insulin same time as I did."

"True. But, I didn't guzzle beer the way you did," she playfully mocked, not wanting to sound preachy. "It's a wonder you can drive this contraption," she said, nodding toward the motorcycle.

"Three beers won't do it. Sorry. Now test your sugar. Individual lancets are in the case. I'm climbing the fence. Those grapes look ready for picking and Doc won't care when it's for a good cause." With that, he easily scaled the fence and dropped to the other side. As he was doing this, he said, "Anyway, it's not that Doc Dan is weird like a serial killer. He's just old fashioned. He still believes in the constitution and listens to Rush Limbaugh and Roger Hedgecock. Enough said."

Tiffany shook her head as she prepared her left index finger with an alcohol pad. She inserted a lancet into her finger and soon a bead of blood appeared. She watched as the blood was sucked up by the test strip. The glucometer read 96. *Good.* She removed the test strip from the meter and also tossed it on the ground. She shut the penlight off and returned it and the glucometer to its pouch and zipped it up.

"Well, come over here," she heard Sean say. "I've got enough for both of us. Here, take them." He handed three bunches of grapes through the fence to Tiffany then climbed back over. He stretched out on the blanket and patted it for Tiffany to lie down next to him.

"Are you sure you didn't plan this detour," she said smiling. "Have you got something on your mind besides grapes?"

"No, I didn't plan this. Yes, I've got something on my mind." He reached into his front pocket and pulled out a condom.

"What time is it?" she sighed. "You know how my mom feels about us being together. She's afraid I'll get pregnant with you, thinking our kid would be diabetic. She's sorry she sent me to that diabetic camp."

They had been fooling around all summer, but now Sean wanted the real thing. They had come close a week earlier, an attempt that left Sean so mortified that nothing short of raging hormones gave him the courage to try again.

Sean glanced at his watch and said, "It's 11:15. I told your mom we'd be home around midnight."

"I'm not sure about this. I saw a car pulled off the road in the bushes back there."

"I didn't see no car," Sean said. "Besides, that's over a hundred yards back."

"Ok," Tiffany reluctantly agreed.

That was enough for Sean. He fumbled with his jeans and the condom. Tiffany slipped off her t-shirt, exposing her small, firm breasts. As juvenile diabetics, both Sean and Tiffany were skinny, unlike the fat teenagers they knew with acquired diabetes.

Although it was late August, the weather was cool. The ocean, only a short distance away, kept the nighttime temperatures lower than San Luis Obispo, where they had come from after watching a rock concert. Tiffany shivered a little, both from the cold and the anticipation. Sean's blanket did little to keep her warm.

With a few perfunctory kisses, Sean was more than ready, but just as he was about to slip inside Tiffany, there was a loud swooshing noise and the sky overhead lit up like daylight. "Shit," Sean stifled a scream as he rolled off Tiffany. There was a ball of fire at the end of the sloping vineyard approximately two hundred yards away. The light was so bright that he could see the eucalyptus trees encompassing the area where Doc Dan lived. Sean stood up and the full condom fell to the ground. He glanced down and shook his head in disgust as he pulled up his pants. Tiffany stood completely mesmerized by the fire down below them. She mechanically put on her t-shirt and pulled up her pants.

There was a loud scream and then silence as a second ball of fire rose up in the air. Tiffany was finally able to speak, "Is that Doc Dan's house?"

Sean watched for a moment as the initial balls of fire subsided and the light diminished. All that was left were sparks flying into the air and a loud crackling sound as dry timber burned. "That's Hector's house," he mumbled, "He's the caretaker. Doc lives up the road, over there." He pointed farther to the left of the fire.

"Should we go down there? Maybe someone needs help."

"We'd never even get close to a fire like that. I just hope Hector and Dolores got out in time."

Minutes later, as the light from the fire had nearly vanished, Sean heard a distant siren. "Shit, here they come. Let's get out of here." He gathered up the blanket and stuffed it into his saddlebag. He climbed onto his motorcycle and kick started it. Tiffany hopped on the back and Sean raced the bike down the dirt road. When he reached the driveway to the vineyard, he turned left and gunned the motorcycle up to Highway One.

"The car's gone," Tiffany yelled into Sean's ear.

"What car, for Christ's sake?" Sean's night was ruined and he really didn't care.

"The one I saw on the way in," she said.

Sean shrugged and said nothing. Moments later, two fire and rescue trucks raced past them heading down Highway One to the vineyard.

Dr. Dan Miceli had finished seven operative procedures and then saw twenty patients in his office. Dan practiced surgery in the City of Vista Del Mar, where he had grown up. Although known by reputation as a great surgeon, there were few who really knew him well enough to call him their friend. At 57, he was fit, standing about six feet tall and nearly 190 pounds. He had a full head of black hair with very little graying, dark eyes, and wrinkle-free olive skin. He could, when he wanted to, give a warm smile. Women described him as interesting and handsome, others described him as standoffish and unfriendly. No one described him as timid or unsure of himself.

He left for dinner long after the office had closed up and his staff had left. It was eight o'clock and a beautiful evening. He decided to have dinner at his favorite restaurant, *The Fun Thymes*, rather than microwave something at home. It was Friday night, and the restaurant was still busy. Most of the diners were tourists, so he didn't have to do much in the way of glad-handing patients. He had a dinner of poached salmon on Cajun creamed corn with a Caesar salad. Perfect, he thought. That's as healthy as it gets. After dinner, he drove home around nine o'clock. As he passed the garage of his caretaker's house, he noted there was no truck outside the garage door. He surmised that Hector and Dolores must already be in Fresno arranging for a grape picking crew to harvest next week.

A hundred yards or so beyond the caretaker's house, Dan turned into his garage and entered his house through the kitchen via a screened-in back porch. He turned on the light in the kitchen and opened the refrigerator. He grabbed a bottle of his own vineyard's pinot noir, with its distinctive label. The label said "Miceli's Noir" and had images of his grandmother and grandfather superimposed on a picture of the vineyard. He poured the glass of wine he had denied himself at dinner; he was careful not to drink in public. Vista del Mar was a small, seaside town of eleven thousand or so people, and he didn't want gossipers saying that the doctor was seen drinking, not when he prescribes so many of his patients to lay off the booze. He went to his den, which was next to the kitchen, sat down in his leather easy chair and flicked on the TV. Soon he was relaxing in front of the Dodger game.

At ten thirty, with the game in hand for the Dodgers and his wine glass still half full, he headed for bed. He was asleep before eleven, but twenty-five minutes later he was suddenly awakened by a bright light and the crackling, popping sound that could only be made by a raging fire. Dan leaped out of bed and rushed to the window. A huge blaze filled the area where the caretaker's house should be. He heard a scream and hurriedly pulled on his pants and slipped his feet into a pair of loafers he kept at the foot of the bed. He ran down the central staircase of the house and swung back toward the kitchen. Before he ran outside, he called 911 and told the operator he would meet the firefighters at the gate to his property. He grabbed the gate key off the nail by the back door and raced outside.

As he ran down the dirt road separating his house from the caretaker's, he was overwhelmed by the heat of the fire. Moving to his right, he used his left arm to shield his face while he sped past the burning buildings. Once out of the intense heat and noise, he ran up the hill toward the vineyard gate, which was about two hundred yards away. Halfway there, he heard a motorcycle gunning down the road in front of the highway and noticed its headlight turn up the road onto Highway One. By the time he got the gate open, the first of two Vista Del Mar fire trucks pulled onto his property. The first truck stopped when the driver recognized Dan.

"What have we got, Doc?"

Dr. Miceli had to catch his breath after all the excitement and running. "It looks bad, Bill," he said to the driver, who was also a patient of his. "I heard a woman scream about five or ten minutes ago. The caretaker's house and garage."

"Shit. Not good. I can feel the heat from here. You put in a hydrant near your houses last year, right?"

Dr. Miceli nodded his head while still catching his breath. "Soon as you turn left at the bottom of the hill you'll see it. Yellow."

"Thanks and keep back. There'll be a lot of guys running around."

With that, the truck took off with measured speed down the hill. Dan could see the truck stop after it turned left and soon he saw a stream of water heading toward the fire and surrounding trees. He thought about Hector and Delores. Hector's truck, which he never parks in the garage, wasn't there when he came home last night or when he went running by moments ago.

Hector may have gone to Fresno to meet his brother, but Dan worried that maybe Dolores decided to stay home.

Soon, the bright light from the fire disappeared and was replaced by high-powered lamps from the rescue truck. Dan read this as a signal he could return home. Bill Evans spotted him on the edge of the artificial light cast by the high-powered lamps.

"Bad news," he said, shaking his head. "It's preliminary, but we've got two charred bodies on the kitchen floor. Probably overcome with smoke and couldn't get out. Man and woman. I'm assuming it's Delores and Hector. I'm going to call the coroner in SLO Town."

"But, it couldn't be. Hector's truck wasn't here and he never parks in the garage. He keeps that as a workshop for all his tools and garden equipment."

"Does he keep gas there? Because there is definitely a petroleum smell here."

"Yes, but always in a safe place. There are no pilot lights in the garage."

Bill Evans looked back at the house and said, "If it was gasoline in the garage, how did it get over to the house so quickly? There's burned grass directly from the garage to the house. Looks like arson, but I'm not an expert on that. I'll have to bring up an investigator from Santa Barbara. Meanwhile, I'm taping this place like a crime scene." He was all business now.

"Do what you have to do," Dan said, shaking his head in disbelief. "I'll check the winery and see if Hector's truck is up there." Dan turned and trudged up the road past his house to the winery. He went to the machine shop, which housed his heavy equipment and also acted as a repair station. He unlocked the padlock to the door with the same key he used on the gate. He slid the door open and switched on the light. There stood Hector's truck with the hood open. Sitting on the counter was the truck's carburetor in the last stages of repair.

He knew Hector wouldn't take any long drives in the evening unless the truck was in perfect condition. Dan figured his very conscientious caretaker had probably decided to leave tomorrow. Today, he corrected himself, as he looked at his watch.

It was three o'clock in the morning when Bill knocked on the kitchen door. Dan was sitting at the table with a lukewarm mug of coffee. He looked at Bill and asked, "Want a cup?"

"No, thanks. I've had a few off the truck." He was still standing when he said, "The coroner removed the bodies. He took pictures and everything. He says it's a man and a woman. It's gotta be Hector and Dolores."

As if speaking to himself, Dan said, "I found his truck up at the machine shop. Carburetor out of it on the table," he sighed. "Thanks for your help. I'm going to call his two kids and his brother in Fresno. And my daughter."

"You could wait until the coroner identifies them for sure, but that could be several days."

"That wouldn't be fair. There is no other explanation. Thanks Bill, and thank the guys on the truck for me."

"You got it, Doc, and thank you for all you've done for me and my family. Let me know if I can be of any help."

After he broke the news to Hector's two children and his brother, he was wiped out. Talking to patients' relatives after a loss was never easy, even if medically you did your best when the odds were against survival. But, in this case, it wasn't an illness that took his caretaker and his wife, it was an accident. Or, at least, he hoped it was an accident. *Why would anyone deliberately set fire to a garage and house when the people living there were loved and respected by everyone in the community?*

Hector and Dolores had been working on the property since he was in college. Dan had been born on the property, in the very house where he was now living. Dan wondered if the fire was deliberately set by someone trying to scare him off his land? In the past few months, there had been a lot of talk floating around Vista Del Mar about the seizure of his property under the eminent domain laws. He had heard enough warnings from his patients and friends that the city council, in an attempt to stave off bankruptcy, was investigating the possibility of taking over his property and selling it to a private developer. It was a plan that would certainly increase the city's tax revenues.

With these thoughts agitating him, he dialed his daughter's number in Glendale. He had purchased a condominium for her while she worked as a Los Angeles police officer on the street gang task force.

"Hello," the sleepy voice said, "who is this?"

Dan couldn't recognize the voice on the phone, but he had his suspicions. "Is Debbie there? It's her dad."

He heard rustling and a "what?" then more rustling and then "Dad?" his daughter asked, annoyed at being awakened in the middle of the night.

"Yes, it's me. Who answered the phone?"

"Dad, I'm twenty-eight years old. It's my partner, not that it's any of your business. Why are you calling at this hour?"

Dan could have sworn when Debbie left home for U.C.L.A. that she was a conservative, straight, beautiful young lady who wanted to become a doctor. Instead, she ended up being a lesbian LAPD officer assigned to a gang task force because she spoke perfect Spanish.

"It's about Hector and Dolores. I'm afraid they died tonight in a fire at their house."

Dan could hear muffling of the phone again as he imagined his daughter sitting up in bed and adjusting the earpiece. "Dad, I don't understand. I can't believe it. Didn't they have smoke alarms?" she asked.

"It happened so fast, I don't think a smoke alarm would have helped. The fireman, Bill Evans, suspects arson and is treating the house and garage as a crime scene."

Softly now, she sobbed, "Dolores was like a mom to me."

Dan heard the pain and resentment in his daughter's voice. He knew she blamed him for never being around after Darlene, her mother and his wife, died. He had become used to the accusations that he loved his profession more than his family. A common criticism leveled at doctors, especially surgeons.

After she regained her composure, Debbie said, "I'm coming up there. I want to know what happened and why. What's that Frankie Valli song you loved so much, 'Big Girls Don't Cry?' Well I'm a big girl now. So, I'll see you later in the morning."

"I'd love that. I could use your help. But what about work?"

Debbie was silent, then she said, "I've been given two weeks of administrative leave. And in anticipation of your next question, I have done a lot to solve gang crime by overhearing things when 'bangers' think I don't know Spanish. Usually they are talking about my boobs or butt, yet they are so macho they can't help talking about their crimes. I also interview them well and get clues that way. Some of the male officers got their noses out of joint because I'm better at the job then they are. They have called for an investigation just to screw with me. Also, Margo, my partner, works in the LAPD crime lab and they say I get special treatment. And what's worse, they say I have kept cash from drug busts."

"Sounds like a set-up by your disgruntled colleagues. We can talk about it later. I'll look for you in the morning. Goodbye."

Debbie hung up without saying anything.

Chapter Two

When Debbie arrived the next day, it was nearly noon. She had stopped for breakfast on the way, and it had given her time to cool down. She thought about her Dad and how he was all alone now. Hector and Delores were his only companions and he loved talking to them after work to catch up on the happenings at the vineyard. The Miceli vineyard had been in the family for three generations. It was started by her great grandfather in 1918, after World War I. He had purchased the property years before when it was not a fashionable place to live. He had earned the money for the land while managing a small vineyard in Sonoma, which he later bought and sold. It was his idea to bring the pinot noir grape to the central coast where he knew the vines would flourish.

She decided to park her car near the entrance to the vineyard to stay out of the way of the fire and police personnel. She walked down the road to her old home, admiring the grapes and straining to smell their fragrance over the more powerful stench of charred lumber and plastic. As she walked by the burned out garage and caretaker house, she was suddenly hit with the realization that Hector and Dolores were gone forever. Debbie wondered if the vineyard would ever be the same without her surrogate parents around to run the show. She continued walking slowly toward the house, ignoring the three firemen who sifted through the burned out wreckage looking for evidence of arson. She called out for her Dad as soon as she entered the house.

"I'm here on the front porch," he yelled.

Walking onto the front porch, she was struck by how close the house was to the beach. She hadn't been home for nearly a year and the view of the Pacific Ocean through the eucalyptus trees was spectacular. "Wow. I almost forgot what a beautiful setting this is," she said, kissing her dad on the cheek.

"Can I get you anything?" he asked her. He felt awkward acting the host to his own daughter, but that was only one part of the awkwardness between them.

"No, thanks," she said, sitting down. "Do you have any more info on what happened?"

"Only that Bill Evans, the duty chief who put out the fire, thinks it was arson. The arson crew from Santa Barbara is out there now."

"Well, if it's arson then it's murder and if it's murder then the police should be handling it. At least that's my opinion. Fire will tell you otherwise. Anyway, what happened?"

Ok," he said, gazing at the porch's tongue and groove wood ceiling trying to recall all the events since yesterday. He went through the entire story, including the motorcycle he saw tearing down the frontal road next to his property.

"Do you think they were the people who set the fire and were trying to get away?"

"It's possible. Or it could just have been some teenagers having fun. That wouldn't be the first time people have used this property for their own private party. Or maybe they were stealing some grapes. That happens every year. Not a big loss. Do you want to go look around up there?"

"Sure. Let me change." She was wearing a pair of slacks that hugged her muscular thighs and narrow hips. Her gray tee shirt was thin enough and tight enough to reveal her sinewy back and six-pack abs underneath. Her hair was brushed back into a ponytail, exposing her strong neck, and on top of her head was an LAPD baseball hat with the ponytail poking out the back. Dan noticed his daughter's body for the first time since she had sat down. She had always been tall and slim, but now she appeared more solid and definitely more muscular.

Debbie noticed his surprised gaze. She said, "I've been doing a lot of strength training. I want to show the boy's club that a woman can pull her own weight. Literally."

"You look like you could pull an eighteen wheeler."

Debbie laughed, "I don't think I'm that strong, Dad. *Yet*, that is."

Dan said, "Well, one thing hasn't changed, and that's your old bedroom. Still the same as you left it. And no, no one else has been living here."

She smiled and pecked her dad on the cheek. "Same 'ol dad. I'll go put on jeans and sneakers. Be right back."

Dan watched her climb the stairs to her bedroom—it was like watching a ghost. She looked just like her mother, and she was just as beautiful. He always noted how men fell over themselves when they saw Debbie, and he sometimes was amused to think how those men had no clue their attentions were wasted on her. It also made him a little sad, too. He was uncertain as to why his daughter chose to be with women when she could have any man around. *I could drive myself crazy trying to come up with answers to that question. It's not my problem anymore.*

Minutes later they met in the kitchen. The gray tee shirt was now white and the pants were acid washed Levi's. She was wearing low top white tennis shoes with white low cut socks. They left through the back door and out the porch to the road running in back of the house, the winery to the right and the caretaker's house to the left.

They quietly walked past the burned out buildings and headed up the road. At the gate they turned left, since this is where Dan had first seen the motorcycle travel.

They walked slowly, scanning both sides of the road for any clues that might lead them to investigate. Debbie had retrieved an evidence kit from the trunk of her car. After a hundred yards, the road narrowed into a turnaround where the property fence and the edge of Highway One seemed to merge. Debbie stopped and looked around. Her senses alert.

"They stopped here. See the motorcycle tracks. Look on the ground here by the fence. There are several grape stems nearly picked clean."

Dan picked up the stem and sampled the grape. "These were picked recently. They taste like most of the grapes that are ready for picking."

"Look," Debbie pointed at the dirt below her feet, "Matchsticks." She picked up one and showed it to her father.

Dan gazed at it and then shook his head. "Those aren't matchsticks. They're diabetic test strips. Used diabetic strips."

Debbie put the strips into separate Ziploc bags. As she looked down, she observed that the weeds had been broken down. "Looks like someone was lying here. The weeds are flattened. Maybe a blanket. Oh yuck!"

"What is it?" Dan asked, moving over to his daughter.

"One of those men thingies. With semen in it."

"You mean a condom."

"Men thingies."

"Alright. So, we have a boy and a girl up here making out."

"Not necessarily a boy and a girl, Dad. Get with it," she smiled and placed the condom in another plastic bag. "Now we have one, maybe two, people who are possibly diabetic and one rides a motorcycle. Does that ring a bell?"

Dan thought for a while. "Well, if it was someone from town, there is only one I know about and that's Sean Casey. He's a patient of mine. Juvenile diabetic. My partners and I have been his doctor most of his life. If he was up here, it wasn't to cause trouble. Nice kid. A little misguided with the motorcycle gig."

"What, are motorcycles bad? Some day we'll all be driving them to stop global warming."

Dan stared as his daughter and shook his head. How did it happen? She not only bought into an alternative life style, but she has swallowed a scientific myth. "No comment. No, it's not that. It's just a dangerous way to get around, the way these kids drive."

She smiled; she knew she had jerked his chain. His conservative ideology would never allow him to have an open mind about the most serious issue facing the world. But, arguing with him was futile.

"Ok. Let me put these specimens in my trunk on the way back."

After Debbie closed the trunk of her car, they headed down the road. At the bottom, they turned left and slowly walked past the destroyed garage. She looked over at one of the firemen and saw that it was a woman. She looked familiar. Suddenly, the firewoman turned and looked at Debbie. For a moment they stared at each other then Debbie said, "Clare is that you?"

"Debbie Miceli. I'll be darned," she said as she walked over to meet her. "They told me this was the Miceli's vineyard, but I didn't put two and two together."

Clare took off her hat, exposing her short auburn hair. She was attractive even without makeup. Her face was streaked with soot and there were beads of sweat on her upper lip. They shook hands.

"Dad, this is Clare Longwell. Clare and I were in high school together. We got to know each other when we were on student council. I don't think you two have ever met, since I doubt my dad knew I was on the student council."

Dan shook hands with Clare and held back commenting on his daughter's jab at him. She knew perfectly well that he was aware of all her high school activities, even though the high school was twenty miles away in San Luis Obispo. It was just another attempt to play the role of the victim and recruit supporters to her side.

Clare looked at the two of them and decided to be neutral. "First off, it's Smith now, not Longwell. My parents still live in SLO Town." Becoming more serious she went on, "Well, I think we've found something here." She held up a transparent plastic bag in which there was a hunk of burned metal. "This is a light timer. Arsonists love these things. Cheap and they work. Also the favorite of eco-terrorists."

"So, you think this is a crime scene?" Debbie asked.

"We have to treat it as such. The dogs were here earlier and went crazy. They're trained on accelerants. Gas, kerosene, turpentine. We've collected wood, fabric, grass, and other objects for head space analysis. We'll know soon enough."

"Wow, Clare. I've lost track of you, but you sound like a real arson investigator."

"I am. Fully trained. Went to firefighting school then became an investigator. It keeps me busy. And you, I take it, are either married or going with a LAPD officer."

.

Dan chuckled out loud. Back at you, he thought. Debbie gave her father a withering look, recovered, then glanced at Clare, smiling, "Neither. I'm an LAPD officer. Gang investigator."

"Very good. We're sort of in the same business." As she finished, a police car with "Vista del Mar Police Department" stenciled on the sides pulled up.

Dan eyed the driver. He could see it was Chief Riley, and next to him in the passenger seat was Cal Lacey, the editor and owner of the Vista Del Mar Press.

Cal was tall and thin with a haughty look. He had a digital camera in his hand as he stepped from the car in his Birkenstocks.

Chief Riley approached and said, "Morning Doc. And is this lovely young creature your daughter? Hi Debbie. Long time no see." The chief eyed Clare, but did not recognize her. Debbie gave a thin smile in return.

"Chief, this is Clare Longwell, sorry, Smith, from S.B.F.D. Arson Investigations."

Just as he introduced Clare to Chief Riley, Dan noticed Cal Lacey raising his camera to take a picture. He walked over to him and pushed his arm down. "Who gave you permission to take pictures?" he demanded.

"Back off, Doc. Haven't you heard of freedom of the press?" Cal returned angrily.

"Yes, I have. And I have not given you permission to be on this property."

Debbie looked at her father, not believing what she was hearing. Clare stepped back several feet to stay clear of the fray. Debbie came over and poked her dad. She knew the importance of not getting on the bad side of the media.

"I'm sorry, Doc. I invited Cal to come with me. What's the big deal?" Chief Riley asked.

"You know damn well what the big deal is, Chief. Now, please escort him off this property. I'm still the owner."

Chief Riley sighed and directed Cal back into the car. "Mind if he stays there while I talk to Clare?" the Chief said.

Dan stared at the Chief for a while and then nodded his okay. "How long are you going to be?"

"Jesus, Doc, I don't know, but the quicker I get started the quicker I get out of here. Ok?" The Chief looked over at Clare, who moved toward the others.

"What have you found so far?" the Chief asked.

"This is all preliminary. But there is what looks to be a timer. And the dogs went crazy. So, most likely there was an accelerant." She turned toward the house and pointed in the direction of the lawn. "See the burn pattern of the grass between the house and garage? It looks like the ground was soaked with a flammable material then later ignited."

"That's it? A hunk of burned out metal and burned grass. I'll need more than that to start an investigation. It couldn't just be a gasoline explosion or something else that went off in the garage?"

Clare sighed. She had been through this before with police officers. "It's possible, but both structures burned nearly simultaneously. That indicates that both were soaked with something. I have head space analysis cooking on charred residue. We'll know by Monday if there was an accelerant used. I found an intact but burned gas container in the garage. We'll analyze that, too." She gave Debbie a quick look to try and gain support in her effort to convince the Chief.

Debbie decided to weigh in and asked, "How do you know that the buildings went up nearly simultaneously?"

"When Bill Evans arrived at the fire, both buildings were already nearly totally burned. Bill estimated that the time from the 911 call and their arrival here was eleven minutes. The buildings would have had to have been ignited together to be so similarly burned in that time frame. If we pick up some eyewitnesses, they could confirm that. Your dad awoke when both structures were burning, according to Bill."

Chief Riley wasn't convinced and shook his head. "Okay, let's leave it as a possible crime scene. I'll await your lab findings, but don't expect me to buy into everything here." With that, he gave Dan and Debbie a cursory wave and walked back to his car. He backed down the road, turned and then sped up the hill back to Vista Del Mar.

"Now, why is he so pissed?" Debbie said.

"I have an idea, but it's a long story and I'll tell it to you later," Dan said. "Clare, what is head space analysis?"

"Well, as I said, the dogs went crazy here. That usually means an accelerant was used. It's pretty obvious because of the odor. But, dogs can't go to court and testify. So, we need evidence. Collected samples from the fire scene give off vapors for a long time after the fire. When the samples are placed in covered metal containers, vapors are trapped in the space below the lid. We then analyze the vapors with gas chromatography."

"Accurate?" Dan asked.

"Very accurate, Dr. Miceli. We should know by Monday, as I said. Well, Debbie, it's been great seeing you. I'll call you guys on Monday afternoon and let you know where we are. I don't know about the chief though."

They both said thank you and headed for the house. Once in the kitchen, they sat down and just stared at each other. Debbie was puzzled over her father's outburst. She had known Cal Lacey for years, but only to say hello when she encountered him on the streets of Vista Del Mar. She considered him harmless, though a bit nosy. He gave off the appearance of a 60's Berkeley radical student, what with the Birkenstocks and long hair. Still living in the past, she decided.

"Do you want to tell me about it or are we just going to sit here and look at each other?" Debbie asked.

"Let's have a sandwich first. No breakfast for me and, despite everything, I'm hungry." He stood up and turned on a Panini grill. He took some home-grown tomatoes and a sprig of basil off the counter. He grabbed some mozzarella, prosciutto, and bread from the refrigerator. Pretty soon, he had a tomato, prosciutto, and cheese sandwich cooking on the grill. When the sandwiches were done, he sat down and gave one to Debbie.

While they were eating, Dan sat back and said, "The background of my current problem is the Supreme Court's Kelo decision in 2005. It allowed government to take over properties by eminent domain not only for public use, but that land could be sold to private developers as well. The upshot is that Vista is broke and the council wants to increase city revenues by selling my property for development."

"I'm shocked. Can't the law be changed?" Debbie asked.

"Did you vote in the June election?" Dan asked.

"Of course I did."

"How did you vote on Prop. 98 and 99?"

Debbie put down her sandwich and thought for a moment. "That was about the property rights. Yes, I remember. I voted no on 98 and yes on 99."

"How carefully did you inform yourself on these two propositions?"

"I'm embarrassed to say not much. I read the recommendations sent by the union and voted them. No on 98 and yes on 99."

"What you did was vote that people with single dwellings were protected from eminent domain, but people who owned businesses, churches, farms, as well as certain single dwellings were not. You fell for the propaganda put out that 98 was against taxpayers and was a covert move to protect businesses. You voted against me."

"Oh God. How could I be so stupid? You've got to be kidding me?"

"I wish I were. The 99 people cleverly put on an extensive campaign to trick voters into thinking 98 was deceitful, favoring landlords and businesses. Do you know who backed 99?"

"It must be the Democrats."

"Yes, but it was mostly homeowner's associations, public worker's unions, the ACLU representing prisoners, La Raza, people who benefit from the public coffers. Eminent domain use by cities for private development is an attempt to swell those coffers. Of course, Diane Feinstein and Barbara Boxer were for 99, since they receive so much union money."

"Dad, I'm sorry. I'm sure my vote didn't matter, but it shows how you can be fooled if you don't read the fine print."

"Lots of people were fooled. What else is new? The public worker's unions are organized and well-funded."

"That sucks. When did all this start? Going after your property?" Debbie asked, hoping to move away from the subject of her voting mishap.

Dan sighed in frustration and said, "Let me see. It was two years ago, during the beginning of summer. A bather who was swimming in the ocean near Vista Point, where swimming is not allowed, was swept out to sea. They never found his body. The area had been posted, warning swimmers there was no life guard on duty."

Debbie took a bite of her sandwich and reached for a paper napkin to catch the tomato drippings. "Got it so far."

"Needless to say, there was a big brouhaha over the fact that lifeguards weren't patrolling the beaches. There had been budget cuts because the city is nearly broke, and that's where they started to cut back."

"I thought they were county lifeguards."

"The county got out of the lifeguard business a long time ago and turned it over to the cities. Cal, who is only slightly to the left of Karl Marx, said it was because of the Gans-Jarvis tax initiative. Not enough new people moving in here to widen the tax base. Naturally, the city has no more room to spread. So, he started beating the drums to have, by eminent domain, Vista take over the vineyard and develop the land."

"Dad! How come you never told me about this?" Debbie put down her sandwich. She was clearly upset.

Dan took a bite of his and chewed slowly, thinking carefully about his answer. "First of all, it was so outrageous that I ignored it. The rantings of a 60's radical who never grew up. But, he kept at it with editorial after editorial, and he also ran stories about other communities facing similar problems. How they used eminent domain laws and so forth. Soon, people were asking me when I was going to sell my property to Vista."

"Where does it stand now? Has the City done anything?"

"Oh, yes. The city council sent me a letter saying they were considering the move and would vote on it at an open council meeting in September."

"September! That's the week after next. What are you doing to fight it?" she asked.

"Well, I've seen a lawyer. Some high priced eminent domain real estate attorney in Orange County. He's written several letters to the mayor, but of course it's nothing more than what they expected."

Debbie was silent. Her father was seemingly all alone, fighting the entire town, and she had been kept in the dark. Had they drifted that far apart where he wasn't going to include her in his problems?

Sensing her unease, Dan said, "Listen, Deb, you're living your own life now. To be honest, I didn't think you'd care one way or another.

You and I have had many differences over our approach to life. Let's just say you are far more liberal than I am. You look on people as victims, the solution to their problem is government. I thought you'd be in favor of this, tearing down the vineyard."

"Again, I'm shocked," she said. "We had those discussions when I was in college. I had to endure all the anti-capitalist and anti-American rhetoric at UCLA. Yes, it changed the way I looked at things. But, I've been an LAPD officer for three years, and my thoughts have shifted. You can't deal with what I deal with daily and not change your perspective. There's some real bad dudes out there."

"How far back? Because the last time I talked to you, democracy, in your mind, wasn't settled as the best way to go. I know that's code for more government control over people's lives."

"I don't listen to Rush Limbaugh or Roger Hedgecock, if that's what you mean. I'm sort of in the center."

"When I hear people say that, it means they have no core values. That's what bothers me. You can't cherry pick the things you like and be against other things. Anyway, enough of this. What concerns me now is that this fire may have been deliberate. At least you heard Clare say that's what she thought. The Chief's in bed with Cal and others in the town. I don't know how much investigating he's going to do. He's the leader of the local public worker's union and strongly backed Prop. 99."

"He sure didn't want to hear that the fire was deliberately set. I figured he was just being lazy. Or maybe a criminal act might throw their plans for the property into disarray. Anyway, I want to help. I'm going to snoop around myself. You said this diabetic young man has a motorcycle. I'll begin there."

Chapter Three

Debbie found Sean Casey's address in the phone book. It was as simple as that. He had a separate listing from his mother, and she called his number. Young Mr. Casey answered with a drowsy voice. Debbie introduced herself as Dr. Miceli's daughter and a LAPD police officer who wanted to speak to him about last night. When he heard that, the drowsy voice disappeared as he begged Debbie not to ask him questions in front of his mother. After some discussion, Debbie agreed to meet him at the McDonald's in town. The meeting was set for three o'clock.

Debbie then called her partner Margo to find out the most appropriate way to identify the individual or individuals at the scene. She suggested DNA analysis and told Debbie to have the kid drink a coke with a straw and then send it, along with the other evidence she collected at the scene, to a lab. Debbie liked that suggestion, but instead of sending the evidence to a lab, Debbie insisted that she hand over the evidence directly to Margo in order to maintain the evidence chain. After some discussion, they agreed to go half way, more or less, and meet for lunch in Santa Barbara the next day.

Debbie arrived at the McDonald's at a quarter to three and found the place nearly empty. She ordered two Diet Cokes. She tore half the paper off the straws and poked them into the lids. She picked out two seats in the corner and sat down. She waited for Sean to arrive and whiled away the time by reading the menu suggestions over the food distribution area. She noted that the McDonald's menu had changed since high school when she was a regular customer. Now, there were many healthy food choices being offered.

Her thoughts were interrupted when she heard a loud motorcycle pull up outside. She glanced out the window and saw a young male with spiked, brown hair and a ring in his left ear getting off his cycle.

He wore a tee shirt that had a local rock group's logo on it and blue jeans. He was skinny, somewhat pale, and did not appear happy. He entered the restaurant and looked around. He headed straight for her.

"You must be Debbie," he said without smiling. "You look like your dad."

"Hi, Sean," Debbie said and offered her hand.

Sean was surprised, but shook her hand and sat down opposite to her. He looked at the drink in front of him.

"It's Diet Coke. Dad told me about you. Nothing confidential, of course, only that you're diabetic."

"Everyone in town knows that. No secrets there," he said, pulling the remaining paper off the straw. "Now, what's this about last night?"

"I don't know if you've heard, but there was a fire at my father's vineyard last night. Two people were burned to death. Probably Hector and Delores," she said sadly. It still hadn't sunk in and she waited before she continued. Finally, she said, "Dad saw a motorcycle leaving as he was running to open the vineyard gate for the fire trucks." Debbie had been taught not to interrogate witnesses by asking leading questions. She stopped and waited for Sean to reply. He looked down at his drink then slowly sucked up some coke.

"Everyone knows about the fire and that the two people in the house were Hector and Delores. It's a bummer. I liked 'em. They were real nice to me when I picked grapes there a couple of summers ago," he paused and then added, "but about your dad seeing a motorcycle. It wasn't me."

"Well, the reason you came to mind was I found some diabetic test strips in an area where there had been a motorcycle. The strips looked fresh and some grapes had been recently picked."

Sean looked at her. He had never been the most honest person in the world. A juvenile diabetic had to learn how to get along in a non-diabetic world. That often meant dreaming up excuses to get out of commitments other kids took for granted. *I can't play baseball, my diabetes is acting up.* It had become second nature to him.

"So?'

"I just wondered if you might have been that person or knew some other diabetic motorcycle rider," she smirked, knowing he would understand how rare that would be. "I'm not suggesting the person started the fire. I just want to see if they saw anything that might help in a possible murder investigation."

"Murder?" Sean paled. "When did the fire become a murder investigation?" he stammered.

Debbie judged he was not as tough as he wanted people to think. He certainly did not act or look like an arsonist. In fact, he looked like he was in over his head. Debbie was experienced enough in interrogation that, despite the short interview, she was convinced Sean was at the scene.

"The arson investigator from Santa Barbara thinks it might be arson. She's not 100 percent, but when she finishes her investigation we'll know. Death as a result of an arson fire is murder."

"That certainly hasn't gotten around. I won't believe it until I hear it from Chief Riley. Nothing against you being a lady cop and all, but you don't have any authority here. I don't have to answer your questions, right?" Casey asked as he folded his arms on his chest.

Debbie noted his defensive posture and didn't want to make matters worse. "No, you don't, but Dolores and Hector were like parents to me. So, if I can help find out what happened I'd feel better about it. I appreciate you coming here to talk to me."

He looked at her, but wasn't convinced it was as simple as that. If he told her the truth then surely his mother would find out. Then Melody would get involved and that was more than he wanted. He took a long drink, emptying his cup, thinking about what he would say next.

"If you don't have anything more. I gotta go."

"You're free to go. This is strictly off the record and just between you and me, got it?"

"Yeah. Right." He stood up and gave her a mock salute. He went to pick up his coke, but she reached over and pulled it toward her. "It's on me. I'll toss it. Have a good day," she smiled.

Once Sean left, Debbie sat for a while wondering why he was so reluctant to talk to her. She could see his purple stained tongue when he spoke. It certainly suggested recent ingestion of grapes or a purple drink. She carefully removed the straw from the container and took it to her car and placed it in her evidence bag.

Sunday morning she awoke and prepared breakfast for her Dad, who had arisen early to inspect the vineyard. He had informed her, when she came home yesterday afternoon, that Hector's brother, Carlos, had called. He had not heard from Hector all day nor did he show up at his house. Sadly, it was becoming clear that Dolores and Hector had perished in the fire. Her dad also said Carlos was bringing a crew over next week to harvest the grapes. He would stay for his brother's funeral and as long as necessary after that to see things were going well. Dan had offered him the guest bedroom next to Debbie's and the crew quarters in the bunkhouse.

Debbie cracked six eggs into a bowl and added a splash of cream, bread crumbs, and parmesan cheese. She found a bell pepper in the refrigerator along with an onion. Soon she had them sauteing in the skillet. When the frittata was done, she called her Dad, who was in his den reading a special Sunday edition of the Vista Del Mar Press. Life had not returned to normal and they ate breakfast quietly.

Finally, Dan put down his fork and broke the silence by saying, "I haven't had such a good breakfast since your mother died. I'm glad you came home, even if only for a short while."

"Thanks. But, Dad, you've had plenty of opportunities to find someone else in your life. Why haven't you?"

Dan looked at her. In the past, he would have considered such a forward question to be intrusive, but times had changed. He was older and essentially without anyone.

"I always used the excuse that I was too busy when people tried to line me up with eligible women. And I was. I tore into my work after your mother was killed. We were so deeply in love that I can't imagine ever finding that again. It's easier to be alone."

"That's touching, but I worry about you. I can only remember Mom as a four year old would, but I'm sure she'd want you to find happiness again." Embarrassed, Debbie looked away. "Enough about this. What did Cal Lacey have to say in his special edition?"

Dan could see that Debbie had become more assertive than she had ever been. She was controlling the conversation much as she must do everyday in her job.

"He has somehow got this edition out since yesterday. He must have worked all night on it. He even has pictures of the burned out buildings. He said there is a possibility of arson. He must have got that from Riley on the way back to town or overheard us talking. Anyway, he says that this is further evidence that the vineyard presents a hazard to the town and should be condemned."

"What?" Debbie was shocked. "How can he conclude that from this incident?"

"Does he need to explain himself? He said the vineyard consumes a lot of the town water, which is getting less available, and doesn't provide any benefit to the area. No one living in the town is employed here. The same old criticisms of me and our family not having a tasting room or facilities for tourists. Therefore, people don't come here as a result of the vineyard. So, fewer tourist dollars."

"So, if this were a housing development or a resort area then the economic fallout would be great for the town."

"Exactly. But, that's not the story. The vineyard does benefit the town. All the profits that accrue from the vineyard go into a foundation and that money is used to pay salaries at the clinic and buy new equipment for our little hospital."

"Dad! I'm hearing this for the *first* time?! How come you've never told me this? No wonder no one understands you. You don't explain yourself. Everyone thinks you're a great doctor who is also a miserly, skinflint conservative."

"I take both those labels as compliments. Look, I keep my business to myself. It's no one's affair but mine what happens to my profits. I'm not about to go bragging about what I have done for this town."

"Don't you understand? This is a political battle you're in. The city council, for whatever reason, wants to take this land and you aren't fighting them. You've got to get the people living in town on your side."

"I understand that. But, if being a good doctor, underwriting the costs, and giving free care whenever it's necessary isn't enough, then it's hopeless to try and sell myself. Anyway, enough of this. When are you leaving for Santa Barbara and when do I get to meet Margo?"

Debbie stared at her father. She couldn't believe what she just heard. Rather than try to figure it out, she said, "When this is over— the fire investigation and the town issues and stuff—then I'll bring her up here. You'll like her."

"Good. Now, I'm going to take a walk in the vineyard and see what's up. I still have three people working here and with Carlos's crew we should have enough to complete the harvest on time. The fire hasn't stopped me and things are moving ahead."

Debbie drove down Highway One to San Luis Obispo and then turned onto Route 101. It was a lovely day in spite of all that had happened in the past twenty-four hours. She was certain that the fire had been deliberately started. The issue was whether it was related to the town takeover of her dad's property or not. Why would someone deliberately start a fire of that nature? Destroy two buildings and essentially murder two people? It was clear that a lot of people knew that Hector and Dolores were leaving for Fresno on Friday. They've been doing that this same time for years. Hector liked to hand-select the crew from Fresno. He didn't want amateurs picking his grapes and bruising them with rough handling. When she passed the University of California, Santa Barbara she knew she was near the end of her destination. It was a great University and close to her home. *Why didn't I go there?*

They met at a Starbuck's on La Cumbre road. Margo had already arrived and was sitting out front drinking a latte. Margo was the same age as Debbie. She was taller and thinner, wearing a gray LAPD sweatshirt, jeans, and white low-cut tennis shoes. Her hair was stringy, and she wore clear-framed glasses. No make up, since she had naturally pink cheeks.

They kissed discretely, and Debbie went inside and ordered a non-fat latte. She returned and sat down across from Margo. They looked at each other then laughed at finding themselves there rather than spending a quiet day at home.

Margo spoke first and asked, "How are you feeling and how's your dad?"

"He's holding his own, but there was a lot going on that I didn't know about."

"You mean other than the possibility of arson?"

"That too. But there's plenty more." Debbie then went on to tell her about the problems with the city council and the possibility that he might lose his property.

"Do you think this fire has anything to do with his legal problems with the city?" Margo asked.

Debbie waved her hand and shook her head while she sipped her coffee. "Don't know. I've only snooped around a little bit. I've told you about the possible reluctant witness. I'm sure he witnessed the fire. And he had a companion with him. Seems almost scared to talk." With that she reached into her shoulder bag and produced an evidence packet. She passed it over to Margo, who took it.

Margo looked at it and said, "Since you're on administrative suspension, I'm going to run this through a very good private lab. Okay?"

"Absolutely. You mentioned that yesterday. My Dad thinks it's a good idea and agreed to pay for it. I've left his credit card number inside the packet. Boy, he is behind the times on DNA analysis. He thought it would take two weeks or more."

"Not anymore. With the newer techniques, we should have this back in 24 hours. By Wednesday, at the latest."

"Can you date the age of the blood or semen?"

"Not with DNA, but we can look at the sperm to see how autolyzed they are. Should give us a good approximation."

Debbie thought about what Margo had just said. "One thing I.A. accused me of, because of our relationship, is preferential treatment in the crime lab."

"Ha. I did a lot of checking on that. They've got nothing. In fact, one of the officers accusing you of that has had a more rapid turnaround on his evidence submissions than yours. I've got all the data. They've got nothing."

Debbie smiled with relief and reached over and touched Margo's hand. "Thank you."

They talked for a while then said their goodbyes.

Chapter Four

On Monday morning, Dan entered his office and responded to Marilyn's questions about the fire and the fatalities. Marilyn had been Dan's secretary for twenty years and was sympathetic to his plight with the city. Still, she had decided to quit her job at the clinic and accept a job as an administrative assistant in the fire department. "Why do that?" Dan had asked upon hearing about her decision to leave. Her answer was simple: higher wages, better benefits, health care coverage and, last but not least, a better pension plan than the one she had with Dr. Miceli. It took Dan several days to deal with the news that she would be leaving him soon.

After answering her questions, Dan made it to his office. "Marilyn," he called from his desk, "how many patients?"

Marilyn walked back to his office and poked her head in the door. "Ten," she said, "The first one is in room one. Mrs. Chase and Davis, who had a hernia repair last week."

Dan looked up from the desk where he was poised to sign some papers. He could see the concerned look on her face and knew that it wasn't because of Davis.

"What is it?" he asked.

"I'm really bummed about Hector and Dolores. I've heard there is possible arson involved. Anything to that?" she asked in a hushed tone, glancing toward room one.

Dan sighed as he listened to her question while nervously tapping his pen on the documents before him. "Don't know yet. But some things are suspicious." Dan didn't want to get into this aspect of the tragedy, preferring to wait for the fire investigator's opinion.

Marilyn understood his reluctance to say anymore. "Room one."

"Okay. I'll be right there. By the way, how's your recruiting going for a replacement? Of course, that person will have to be a nurse, biller, typist, accountant and all the other things you've done by yourself over the years." Dan smiled to let her know there were no hard feelings.

"I'm sorry to say, but you won't find anyone like me. I'm old school. The available pool of prospects are all trained at these medical assistant schools. They know how to do their nails and make coffee," she tittered. "No. I've had a few who might be able to do half of what I do, but, as it looks now, you're going to need two people to replace me".

"Just what I didn't want to hear. How about you staying and we up the ante across the board?"

"Thanks for the offer, but, as I said before, it's more than money. This is hard work and you paid well enough. But, the kids are out of the house, my husband wants to travel and the fire job is a lot less stressful. The wages and benefits are actually better," she finished by looking down at the floor. She didn't want to embarrass Dr. Miceli. He had been very generous to her over the years. But, it was time to move on.

"Thanks for being honest. I won't bug you again about it. Now, on to Davis Chase and his mother." He dragged the last word out of the side of his mouth, indicating that he wasn't looking forward to meeting with her.

He walked down to room one, took the chart out of its slot, and opened the door. Mrs. Chase was sitting in the corner and Davis was sitting on the exam table. Davis was 12 years old and at the age when it was hard for him to greet someone older with any animation. Mrs. Chase was another story. She said hello through pursed lips and an insincere smile. Dan wondered if there was anything wrong with the surgery. He examined Davis and found everything just as he had hoped. His incision was dry and healing well.

"Looks good," Dan said to the boy, who was lying back with his hands folded behind his head.

He looked at Dan and without any change of expression asked if he could go swimming in the ocean.

"Of course," he said.

With that, Mrs. Chase stood up and told Davis to sit in the waiting room while she talked to Dr.Miceli.

Davis stood up and pulled up his pants. He glared at his mother on the way out. It was not hard to read the meaning of his expression.

"I asked Davis to leave so we could talk about his swimming in the ocean."

Mrs. Chase was one of many people who had moved to the area from a larger city. She still dressed like Vista Del Mar was Playa del Ray, where she had lived before her husband moved his law practice to San Luis Obispo. "Get away from the rat race" they had told everyone. She was dressed in expensive gray slacks and a pink blouse with a pearl necklace. She was trim and very businesslike. Dan was quick to notice the nasal spider veins and rosy cheeks. Standing near her, he wasn't sure whether he smelled alcohol or perfume.

"And?"

"Well, with the dangers of the ocean and the cutbacks in the lifeguard coverage, I'd think you'd be more cautious about recommending he could go swimming."

Dan looked at her and wondered if she talked this way at home to her husband. After all, she barely knew her son's surgeon and was treating him like he was her employee. Dan knew the worst thing a physician could do in this situation was get into an argument with the patient. There was no winning.

"I'm sorry," Dan said, "I only meant to say that as far as his surgery is concerned, he can go swimming. I wasn't recommending it one way or the other."

As if to signal that the discussion was over, Dan closed Davis' chart and placed his hand on the doorknob.

"Pardon me, Doctor," she said. "Where are you going? I have more questions."

Dan dropped his hand from the door and looked questioningly at Mrs. Davis.

"I'm not used to living in places where the city does not provide the basics in care and safety. The beaches in Southern California are always patrolled by lifeguards. Are we going to see a time when the city can afford this coverage?"

"I assume your question has something to do with the eminent domain issue concerning my land that is before the city council. I have no comment on that, and I don't think this is an appropriate conversation at the moment."

"I think it's a shame that we have to cut back on park maintenance and lifeguards. And now I hear they're going to reduce the level of personnel in the fire department!"

"From the tenor of your voice, I guess you think I should turn over my land to the city in order to provide more tax revenues. I would like you to think about what you're saying." Dan felt an up tick in his voice and cautioned himself to be careful.

"Well, that seems like the only solution to this money crunch. What with the lawsuit before the city on the boy who drowned last summer, it could be very serious."

"Isn't your husband the lawyer who's suing the city? What is his claim? There weren't adequate signs in the area where the boy drowned? It was only in English and Spanish and not in Vietnamese? And the signs were not large enough?"

"I'm not free to discuss the case, as you know. Let me just say that it's too bad a city of this size and reputation cannot afford to provide safety at the beaches."

Dan was not going on with this. When it comes to lawyers and their wives, it's never about money but some loftier issue. He couldn't even begin to count how many times he had heard the phrase "we need to send a message" coming from a lawyer's mouth.

"Davis is doing well, and there is no need to bring him back unless there is a problem." With that he waved goodbye to Mrs.

Davis and went to his office. She stood in the hall starring at his back as he walked away, then she marched out.

Moments later, Marilyn walked into Dan's office and said, "I don't think you'll see her in here anytime soon. Wow. What's her problem?"

"She wants me to sell my property to the city without a fight so that her son can swim safely in the ocean. I wonder how many beach drownings occur in the presence of lifeguards versus without?"

"Don't know. Maybe after I work at the fire department I'll learn about it. Anyway, while you were having a civilized conversation with the ice queen I put several more patients in rooms. Also, Chief Riley called with a bee in his bonnet about something. He wanted you to call him right away."

"Get him on the line after I see these patients."

When Dan finished seeing the second patient, he returned to his office and punched the blinking button. "Hello, Pete. How's everything? I'm sure this is not a social call."

"Not quite. Sorry about that dust up with Cal. I should've checked with you first. My bad."

"Don't worry about it. I'm sure you meant no harm. After all, you've kept the crime rate to practically zero with your preventive maintenance program," Dan chuckled.

"Well said and thanks. I need all the support I can get. This morning the county coroner called and confirmed that it was Hector's and Dolores' remains in the burned out structure. They worked all day Sunday on dental records. They're going to do DNA from the son, but the coroner says the dental I.D. was enough."

Dan thought before he responded. It was still hard to face the fact that his two long-time friends and employees were gone. He cleared his throat and said, "Thanks for letting me know so quickly. I am still in shock over it."

"Me too. It was devastating. Ex-marine, decorated, two tours in Nam. What can you say?"

"It's more than that. He was a caring father, learned the wine making business on the fly while he was running the vineyard. Took all those extension courses from Davis. Has to listen to negative stories about 'illegals' entering the country. This is, or I guess I should say *was*, a remarkable story," he paused and added, as if realizing it for the first time, "Debbie was practically raised by those two."

"Speaking of Debbie, that's the second thing I wanted to talk about. I got a call from Sean Casey's mom. She said Sean was forced to meet with Debbie yesterday and was asked questions about the fire. What gives?"

Dan didn't respond right away. He didn't want to tell the Chief about the motorcycle until he talked to Debbie first. "You know, I haven't really spoken to Debbie since Saturday. She was in Santa Barbara yesterday. Why don't you ask her about it?"

"I plan to. How about two o'clock in my office? She knows the way. Will you let her know?" he asked.

Dan didn't like being a messenger for the Chief, but he figured now wasn't the time to ruffle feathers. "Will do, and thanks for the heads up on Hector." He would break the bad news to Hector's brother tonight and arrange for the funeral at the vineyard's family plot.

When he arrived home later that evening, he told Debbie about his conversation with the Chief. She too wasn't happy about the Chief's indirect contact with her through her father, but she swallowed her pride and agreed to meet with him without further comment.

Chapter Five

The police station in Vista Del Mar was located on the edge of town and was situated on a plot of land carved out of the side of a hill. This afforded the station an excellent view of the town below and the ocean beyond. The building was one story and made from cement blocks painted a pale pink. Debbie could practically drive there in her sleep, since in high school she had spent time in the junior police program. She was allowed to travel with officers when they patrolled the city. At the time she did this, Pete Riley was Chief. Although he was a stickler for detail because of his military background, he was also very approachable and respectful to the students in the program. He had taken a liking to Debbie, but their paths hadn't crossed for almost eight years until they met on the day of the fire.

She parked in the lot above the police building and walked down a flight of stairs to the front door. Stenciled on the glass door was VDMPD. She pushed the door open and walked into a waiting area. To her left was a caged window. A middle-aged woman with glasses and gray hair sat behind the window, and the nametag pinned on her blouse said "Jan Casey." She was a civil servant and not in uniform. Debbie was beginning to get the picture.

"Debbie Miceli to see Chief Riley. Two o'clock," she said, forcing a smile.

Jan Casey brusquely told her to take a seat. She barely looked up to acknowledge Debbie then returned to her computer keyboard.

To Debbie, Jan Casey's reaction seemed over the top for something as innocuous as interviewing her son and buying him a Diet Coke. Ten minutes later, Casey picked up the phone, listened a few seconds, then motioned Debbie toward the double doors. Fortunately, Debbie knew the way to the Chief's office and didn't have to ask for directions. Clearly, Jan was not there to help.

Standing at the door of his office, the Chief smiled at her and shook her hand. He was not into hugging.

"It's been awhile since you've been back here. Does it bring back old memories?" the Chief asked.

"It sure does. This is where my police career began. I must have been impressed, since I like what I'm doing."

Pete Riley was in his fifties. He had a weather-beaten, rugged face with crow's feet creases at the corners of his eyes. He came to Vista Del Mar after a twenty-year stint in the Marine Corp. Debbie noticed that he hadn't changed a bit: no hair out of place and shoes spit-shined. The town had benefited from the chief and his crime prevention program. He maintained a strict curfew policy, rolling up the sidewalks at 9 p.m. His officers would stop anyone on the street they didn't recognize. If they were drifters, homeless people or teenagers from others cities, they were shown the way out of town.

"And I have checked up on you. You're with the gang banger unit doing an outstanding job. A little trouble with some male officers, but from what my friend at the LAPD told me, they are way off base. Sounds like there's support for you."

Debbie had forgotten how thorough the Chief was on every detail. It was good to hear she had some support. She was not surprised that the Chief had contacts in the LAPD It was rife with ex-marines, many of whom had been career enlistees. They made great cops because of their military training, but the LAPD bordered on a paramilitary unit, which was not always a good thing in this era of political correctness.

"Thanks for the kind words. Did your friend also tell you I'm gay? It has to be a factor. Some of my colleagues have a problem with it."

"I have no problem with it. The toughest marine in my unit was gay. Nobody fooled with him. It doesn't matter. Now, tell me about your encounter with Sean. I'm sure you noticed his mother out front."

Debbie knew Pete Riley was a good cop. He glossed over what might have been an awkward moment and moved on to the business at hand.

She couldn't tell him about the evidence she had collected or the subterfuge used to get Sean Casey's DNA. That would make things look worse than they were. She would go halfway.

"When you were at the house Saturday, we never got a chance to talk. Dad told me when he ran to open the gates for the fire trucks he saw a motorcycle speeding by. It was leaving the vineyard on the frontal road. We found some recently picked grape stems outside the vineyard where a motorcycle had been parked."

"That sound like good police work, but so what?" the Chief asked.

"Dad said it was teenagers. He rattled off several names of kids who owned motorcycles. Casey seemed like the best place to start. He had worked for my dad and knew where to park, though I think 'park' may be a euphemism in this case. There were two people on the motorcycle."

"So, you're talking about an investigation? We don't even know if the fire was deliberate yet. Aren't you jumping the gun?" the Chief asked in a doubtful tone.

Debbie didn't like the way this was going. "It seems to me that if there were witnesses to the fire, they may help us understand what happened. If this was accidental then no harm, no foul. But, if Clare comes up with it being arson, we're on our way."

The Chief eyed Debbie thoughtfully. Finally he said, "Okay, you can poke around. Let me know if you find anything. I think it's all a waste of time, but we, the police," he said, pointing his finger at his chest, "owe that much to Hector and Dolores."

Debbie was sure there were strings attached to that free pass she had just received from the Chief. There is no way he was going to let me solve a crime in his jurisdiction. At least it wasn't a cease and desist order.

"Thanks Chief," Debbie said, as she stood to leave. "You'll be the first one to know. By the way, how is Everett doing? I haven't seen him since high school."

Everett was the Chief's son who was in Debbie's class in high school. They had been friends and nothing more.

"If you find out, let me know," he smirked. "He never writes. I talk to him occasionally. He's a tree hugger up in Oregon. Works with some environmental group up there. Finished at State and got accepted to law school but never went."

Debbie glanced over at the bookcase along the wall behind the Chief and noted the picture showing the Chief, his wife, and Everett standing together. Everett was wearing a graduation gown and was clearly four years older than when she last saw him. He had the same serious look on his face like the woes of the world were on his shoulders.

"Well, if you hear from him say hello."

"Will do."

Debbie turned and gave the Chief a mock salute and left the office. On the way out, she passed Mrs. Casey, who was scowling but not at Debbie. Something on the computer screen was attracting her attention. She glanced up then waggled her eyes in an almost conspiratorial fashion. Debbie didn't know what to make of her actions though it was clear she wanted to say something.

She pushed open the glass doors and started up the steps to the parking lot. Suddenly, her cell phone rang with a musical sound that made her jump. She never liked the sound since, when on the job in L.A., it often meant trouble. She flipped her phone open and gazed at the caller id. A Santa Barbara area code.

Puzzled, she pushed the button and said, "Hello. Debbie Miceli speaking"

"Hi, Debbie. It's Clare Smith. Thought you'd like to hear what we found so far. It's not official because I have to run the stuff by my boss, but so far we know the hunk of metal is definitely a timer and the head space analysis on every specimen, about ten in all, showed E85."

"E85?" Debbie reached her car and stopped. She looked out at the ocean waiting for Clare's reply.

"That's ethanol gas—85% ethanol 15% gas. Used only in cars adapted for it. It's the latest environmental hot button. Remember Schwartzenegger was touting the purchase of vehicles for the state that ran on this gas. Trouble was there weren't that many gas stations carrying it."

Debbie jumped ahead and asked, "How many?"

"Eight or ten. Google it."

"So, what do you think about all of this?" she asked.

"What do I think? I think it's arson. Done by a person or persons who are good at it. Other than the use of a timer and the E85, we recovered no other forensic evidence. Unless there's an eyewitness or other clues, this will be tough to solve."

"And the hits keep on coming," she mused out loud. "I'm going to check out those gas stations carrying E85. I haven't uncovered anything here. A few things are cooking, but they look pretty thin. Thanks, Clare, and let's keep in touch."

Debbie hung up and climbed into her car. *Professional arsonists?*

Chapter Six

The Vista Del Mar City Council met on the first Wednesday of each month. The meetings were held in a town hall, which was nothing more than a two story, cinder block building with concrete floors. The agenda for the meeting was published online two days before the gathering and usually ten or twelve people showed up to argue over a public dispute or change in local statutes. A week before the meeting, usually on Monday, the city council members would meet at a restaurant and set the agenda. Of course, the dinner and wine were paid for by the taxpayers.

In anticipation of a very important council meeting, Mayor Adams insisted on publishing the agenda well in advance of the usual two day internet notice. This would assure him of a good citizen turnout and also get him off the hook if he was accused of being underhanded by sneaking issues past the voters. The preliminary council meetings were held at *The Fun Thymes* restaurant, the best restaurant in town. There was a meeting room in the back that could easily accommodate twelve people. While Debbie was at home on the computer looking for gas stations that sold E85 gasoline, the council members were gathering around holding glasses of wine, highballs of vodka gimlets or Manhattans. The mayor, as was his custom, went with a neat scotch.

Benjamin Adams had been Mayor for five years and was just beginning his second term. He was a realtor who had been only moderately successful. Vista wasn't the best market for real estate since turnover was very minimal; the people who left generally went via the undertaker. Also, there was no land for expansion, and businesses had been stable for years. In actuality, being mayor had been Benjamin Adams' most lucrative venture to date, increasing his personal income by 75,000 dollars a year.

"People," he said in a businesslike voice, pushing his wire-rimmed glasses up his ruddy nose, "Time to sit down." The din in the room had risen steadily as the drinks started flowing more generously. He could tell they were at the point when more booze meant a sloppy, unfocused meeting.

People began to sit. When most everyone had parked himself or herself in a chair, the mayor, who remained standing over his tribe like a kind patriarch ready to initiate some sacred ritual, began speaking.

"I want to begin tonight's very important meeting with some introductions. Some of you have already met Ted Schroeder, sitting to my right. Ted is the Vice-President of Property Development Incorporated and represents Richland International interests here tonight. Now, we've all heard of Richland and know it to be a respected company that builds and maintains resorts and golf courses around the world. Some of you have been to their main showplace in Palm Springs. Ted has worked for Richland for ten years and is the reason for its resurgence."

There was light applause as Ted remained seated and waved his hand at the group. He was a tightly wound, lean man in his early fifties with perfect brown hair and an air of self assurance that was impressive. Ted had reason for his confidence since he was ex-military, having served with Special Forces in Gulf War I.

Benjamin smiled with pride as he turned towards Ted and gestured to his tribe, "Now Ted, let me introduce you to the other members here. This is Sean Paxson from the first district. Sean owns the pet store in town. To his left is Police Chief Pete Riley, who I have invited here this evening to speak on certain matters of importance to us all. To his left is Mary Kelly, who runs the beauty salon from the third district. To my right and to your right is Jack Holmes, city attorney. Well, he's part time attorney. He is an estate lawyer in his other job. There is Jim Cravens from the second district to your far right. Jim is a retired airline pilot. Finally, Chief Bill Evans from the fire department's fourth district."

With the introductions done, Ben Adams sat down to find a plate of perfectly arranged food. A generous portion of poached salmon rested on a bed of mashed potatoes, with steamed carrots and broccoli framing the whole work of art. However, he first dug into a salad of baby spinach greens and tangerine slices tossed with a vinegar dressing. Everything was washed down perfectly with a crisp, coastal sauvignon blanc. When dessert was nearly finished, Ben tapped his water glass with his spoon, indicating that it was time to get down to business.

"Before we begin, I would like the Chief to bring us up to date on the status of the tragic fire at the vineyard."

The Chief remained seated and looked over his audience. He knew all of them very well, perhaps too well for their liking. Most people in Vista understood that he was not someone to be trifled with, especially when he knew your secrets. To a certain extent, he was more important than the mayor. He was head of the local chapter of the public workers union, which boasted 150 full or part time members. In a town of 11,000 plus people, this represented a powerful block of votes. Without the Chief's support, several of the council members would not have been elected. And they knew it.

Unlike the council members, the Chief never drank at public functions, making him the only sober person in the room. His sobriety came across in his voice as he addressed the group.

"I'm here to update you on the status of the fire at the vineyard. Sadly, two lives were lost, and they were two of the most solid citizens in this community." He paused to clear his voice. It was the first time anyone had seen even the slightest display of emotion from the Chief.

"Take your time, Pete," Ben Adams said, taking advantage of the moment to appear sensitive and understanding.

The Chief took a sip of water and continued. "I received a call from the arson investigator at Santa Barbara. The arson team was called in because Bill suspected something unusual about the scene. As it turns out, Bill may have been right, though that is strictly the opinion of the investigator in Santa Barbara. I myself am not so certain and am considering opening an official investigation after I receive and review the documents from the SBFD."

A low rumble of voices spread across the room immediately followed by a flurry of questions. The Chief merely held up his hand to stop the onslaught. "I know all the questions, but I don't know the answers. Here's what I do know, based on the lab analyses. The fire is believed to have been started using a timing and ignition device. E85 was the accelerant. Now, it still doesn't look like arson to me, but the investigation may go forward despite my own hunches on this one."

The council members fired off more questions for the Chief, but Ben Adams quieted the room down.

"If you have any further questions for the Chief, you may ask him personally. We have a lot more to cover here and not enough time to dwell on this one subject," the group mumbled amongst themselves as the mayor proceeded to speak above the low din.

"The sewer pipe leak on First Street will cost 90,000 dollars to repair. We can recover those costs by adding them to the property tax bill. The other item on the agenda for the council meeting next week is very important. The council must decide if the vineyard should be taken over by the city for private development. Now, in preliminary meetings with each of you, I find that most are in favor of it."

Jim Cravens raised his hand, but he spoke before being called upon, "I'd like to say, for the record, that I am opposed to it. I didn't retire here to see the city become larger."

"Thank you, Jim. I think the other members are aware of your position. But, unfortunately, growth is necessary in this case. We have a nearly red bottom line and cutbacks have cost us. The lawsuit over the drowning several years ago is proceeding to trial. I'm sure you're well aware that a settlement against us could wipe us out financially."

Mumbles of assent rippled around the tables. The Mayor continued, "Jack may want to comment on the status of the litigation later. Right now, I have received an environmental impact on the proposed take over and it is favorable to the city. Mr. Schroeder here was kind enough to underwrite the cost of the survey."

"Why wouldn't he? He stands to benefit from your reverse Robin Hood ploy," Jim Cravens nearly shouted.

"What do you mean, Jim?" the Mayor asked.

"Steal from the rich and give it to the richer." Everyone laughed, including Ted Schroeder to whom the quip was aimed.

"Okay. I think it's time to hear from Ted." Ben turned to the composed representative of Richland International.

Schroeder stood gracefully and flashed his best salesman smile to his audience—a combination of conspiratorial understanding and the merest hint of condescension. He had learned, over the years, that most people respond favorably to someone who makes them feel both special and just slightly inferior. It was true that none of the people he looked out upon was a threat to him educationally, politically or financially, but he didn't want to advertise that fact too aggressively.

"It saddens me when things come to this," he said in a distinctly squeaky voice, which may or may not have been the reason why he constantly cleared his throat as if it were parched. "Our company was approached by Ben several years ago after the U.S. Supreme Court Kelo decision. We were interested, but found the situation too politically charged. The owner of the vineyard was staunchly against selling any part of his property. When my company encounters this kind of resistance, we back off. However, in this case, the prospects for a successful venture was so great that we explored other avenues with Ben."

"What did you have in mind for the property? I hope nothing commercial like shopping centers?" asked Mary Kelly.

"Heavens, no," he reassured the anxious hair dresser. "Richland builds and maintains resorts. They have in mind an environmentally compatible hotel, golf course, and housing development. It should be very popular, particularly to people living on the East coast. Yearly revenues to the city in the form of tax and business revenues are estimated to be in the five to ten million dollar range."

"The city is practically broke right now. When could we expect to see some of this money?" asked Bill Evans.

"Well, the property has to be purchased by the city and then conveyed over to Richland. Realistically, that could take two to four years," Schroeder said.

"What's it going to cost the city for the land?" asked the pet store owner.

"PDI, with its equity, can assure bank loans to the city to purchase the land. For a fee, of course. Then we purchase the land from the city, which is then sold to Richland. All of that should only take the time of an ordinary escrow, so the city can afford the interest on the loan during that interval." The PDI representative and shill for Richland sat down. He didn't want to get too involved into the details of his business.

Ben Adams put up his hand to stop the questions. "I know what you all want to know. I've had the vineyard appraised by a well known Napa real estate firm that specializes in selling wineries. If it was kept as a winery, it's worth 25 to 30 million dollars. Now, the owner, who we all know is Dan Miceli, is a fixture in the town. We have all benefited from his care and excellent clinic. But, it's time to move on and expand our tax base to allow the city to survive financially as well as increase local business revenues."

The fire Chief said, "Excuse me, Ben, but I've known doc for 20 years. We can't just vote him out and be done with it. We'd be in for a courtroom battle if we do that. Why not take 225 acres and leave alone the 25 acres which includes his winery and home?"

Heads started nodding all around the table. The Fire Chief's plan sounded like an excellent out for the city, and it could even forestall a messy, lengthy lawsuit.

But Ted Schroeder shook his head resolutely and said, "The 25 acres you're talking about is prime real estate. Right on the ocean. Richland would certainly not entertain a purchase of land that leaves out the best part of it."

The room fell silent. Jim Cravens decided to toss in his two cents worth and said, "I would never be part of any scheme that takes away a man's home. God damn it! I flew missions off carriers in Vietnam to preserve something more than what we're scheming here."

Pete Riley eyed the old naval pilot. He had to work behind the scenes and couldn't counter this patriotic rant with what he thought. While Cravens was comfortably in the air in Vietnam, he was on the ground fighting the gooks mano a mano. He wasn't about to see this plan go up in smoke. But, he had to keep quiet.

With all the tact he could muster, Ben said, "Thanks for sharing, Jim. We all appreciate what you've done for this country, but the issue here is something separate. Do we go ahead and speak to the future or do we remain a sleepy seaside village?"

After a period of silence, Mary Kelly spoke up, "Given the future, I don't see any other choice. I say yes."

The fire Chief and the pet store owner also gave their agreement, and so it was decided to go ahead with the purchase. But, these were only words at this stage of the game. Everything depended upon these same people, perhaps in a more sober moment, voting this way at the open council meeting one week from Wednesday.

Ben adjourned the meeting and thanked Ted Schroeder for attending. As the Chief stood to leave, Ben caught his eye. When everyone had left, Ben sat next to the Chief and sighed. The room was empty.

"Well, you remained noticeably silent," Ben said.

"You know where I stand on this issue. If you'll remember, it was I who first suggested it to you. I can see what's happening to revenues and the pension fund. I didn't bust my ass for this town to retire without a penny." Pete was no longer taciturn. The Mayor had seen him this way before in their private meetings.

"I hear you. In your capacity as chairman of the city's pension fund, you have access to all the financial data. You of all people know we're strapped. If someone gets real pushy about an audit, they'll find out about our deal."

"Let's go over that again. I'm the head of the local public worker's union and as such draw a salary. So does Bill Evans. We both sit on the pension committee with Beth Truehart. Beth's tied up in her job, so she doesn't really know what's going on. When she was absent from a meeting last year we passed an amendment that would have never passed with her present. My salary and Bill's is now calculated on our combined salary with the city and union. Understood?"

"Yes, we agreed to that last year and I snuck it through the council by calling it a manager's proposal 3. In return, we under funded the city worker's retirement plan and you guys looked the other way. If we hadn't done that, more cutbacks would have been necessary, opening up a lot of messy questions from the voters."

"Right. I just wanted to be sure you remembered. What's done is done. Now we need to get on with this project with Richland."

"I'm going to need your help with that. Jim Cravens is totally opposed to this and wants to make a fuss about it. What can you do to help shut him up?" Adams asked.

"You leave that lush to me. He's got a five-year old DUI from L.A. when he was still an airline pilot. A second DUI could do him some real harm. So, all I have to do is pick him up when he leaves here after dinner some night."

"And if the kind old Chief is willing to look the other way...," Ben continued.

"Exactly."

"I'll pretend I didn't hear that."

"Yeah, just like I pretended not to know your car was parked outside Mary Kelly's house. All night. And with your wife out of town, too."

"Just what are you saying, Bill?" Ben's voice cracked.

"Just remember how much I know. And how much trouble I can make for you if you don't keep me in mind."

Ben muttered through clenched teeth, "Dammit. You're such a snake."

The Chief stood up and casually stretched as he asked, "Anything else?" He wanted to get home. It had been a long day.

"One other potential problem is brewing, Mr. Fixit," Ben said, having regained his composure. "The Tran case is set for trial in November. That plaintiff lawyer who lives here in Vista subpoenaed the town's financial records going back to 2003, which is the last time we had an outside audit. That's five years ago. Things will not look pretty if we don't make this lawsuit go away. Any thoughts?"

"Jesus. You see what I mean? You can't run this city without me," Riley said, shaking his head in disgust. "I know the lawyer and his wife, but I've got nothing on him. From my observations, he gets up in the morning, drives his kid to school and then goes to SLO Town to work. He comes home in the evening. I've been watching, expecting something like this might come up."

"So, that's it. Nothing?"

"That's it for him, I said. *She*, however, is a different story. Comes from a well-to-do Pasadena family. SC graduate. She and her husband had an on and off romance in college. Worked in Hollywood as an aspiring writer after graduation. Supposed to have done well with a good future but ran into some legal troubles with coke. Recovered in rehab and community service. She got back together with her boyfriend, now hubby, but has a lingering alcohol problem. Some of the guys have stopped her before, but they let her go since she's the wife of a big shot lawyer suing the city. Doesn't look good to be harassing her."

"So, how is that supposed to help us?" Ben asked, not hiding his exasperation.

"We can get her on a DUI and then have Cal run a story on her past history. Wouldn't look good for the pending trial. Might force old David Chase into settling."

"From what I hear, he doesn't need the money."

"I expect not. But he did move out of So. Cal. mostly to get away from the Hollywood crowd who continued to lure his wife. There must be a lot of love there."

"Well, he laughed at the insurance limit the City had and wants nothing less than a million dollars. That means, in order to put this away, we'll need to come up with 800 hundred thousand dollars."

"It would seem to me that Richland, along with Schroeder, could help. It's in their best interest to get this behind them."

"It's in the works. There's property the city can sell to Richland, which should cover it. But you need to push ole David to the table."

The Chief didn't answer and only stared at the mayor. Was it worth all he was doing just to improve his retirement plan?

Ben looked at him for several moments before saying, "I know what you're thinking. I talked to Schroeder already, and Richland is amenable to giving you a security consultant fee the day ground is broken for the new resort and housing development. A nice fee, if I do say so myself."

"That's a start," the Chief said, as he ended their conversation with a perfunctory wave goodbye.

Chapter Seven

On Tuesday morning, Debbie awoke to the sound of the pounding surf. She had missed those sounds living in her condominium. The temperature was mild and there was a slight breeze coming in from the ocean. She showered, dressed in gardening work clothes, and went down to make coffee. It was no surprise when she discovered the coffee was already made. There was a note from her Dad wishing her good morning and that he would be doing surgery most of the day. She fixed herself an omelet and debated about calling Margo. It was eight o'clock and her partner was probably just getting out of the shower. *No, not a good time to call.* Besides, she knew Margo would call her as soon as she knew something.

After breakfast, Debbie stepped out of the house onto a pathway hedged with manicured bay leaf shrubs. The pathway led to "The Garden," which her father, grandfather and great grandfather had worked on diligently for generations. It had been her great grandfather's dream to create a garden that resembled ones in his native Italy. The garden, two acres in size and overlooking the ocean, was designed after ancient Persian gardens with four pathways leading to a central point. Each pathway symbolically represented a river flowing to a collecting area in the center. The pathways were eight feet wide and made of decomposed granite with Belgium stone set into the ground lining them. A large fountain was in the middle. Debbie strolled along the central path and watched the water shimmer in the morning sunlight as it cascaded down the fountain.

Scattered throughout the garden were elevated beds made of gray, flat stones and bursting with vegetables and flowers. Along the outer border were rose bushes of many vibrant colors that were neatly trimmed and dead-headed. The sight was magnificent and had changed so much since she had last been there a year ago. She had grown up playing in this garden with Dolores's children Antonio and Adrianna. Dolores showed her when vegetables were ready to be picked and which herb or hot pepper was best used with them. Later, her foster mother would make them into delicious Mexican or Italian meals for her father. Under Dolores' watchful eye, Debbie had started to cook for her dad when she was in junior high school.

Beyond the fountain was the other half of the garden, which consisted of two large areas covered with St. Augustine grass. There was also a topiary display similar to those in European gardens. These were either individual trees or bushes scattered along the edge of the grass. Lining the entire garden were mature, tall, Italian cypress trees to provide just enough light and shade throughout the day. After Debbie recovered from her visual ecstasy and nostalgia, she began to spot the warts. There were weeds growing around the tomato plants. There were dead leaves and overripe squash on the zucchini plants. She plopped down a barrel she had retrieved from a storage area by the house and began plucking weeds. Soon she had filled the barrel and headed back for a second one.

A few hours flew by while Debbie worked, lost in a trance. All thoughts of the funeral tomorrow had been pushed aside while she methodically pulled weeds and enjoyed the warm sun on her skin. Her trance was broken, however, when she heard two men speaking in Spanish somewhere beyond the garden. She got up and followed their voices until she found herself at the family burial area where her great grandparents, several of their offspring, her grandparents, and her mother were all buried. The graveyard was surrounded by a picket fence and shielded from the beach below by an outside row of trimmed cypress trees. Through the trees she could see two men digging a single grave. It had been Dolores' and Hector's wish to be buried together in the same grave and that wish had been granted a long time ago by her grandfather.

The two men stopped working once they saw Debbie enter the garden. She waved to them, but they ignored the greeting and immediately went back to digging. They were conversing excitedly in Spanish while stealing glances at their new female visitor.

Debbie was quite familiar with this whole scene. It had happened to her a million times before, and she had learned how to handle it. She walked up to the men and introduced herself in perfect Spanish. They were doubly surprised since, not only did she speak flawless Spanish, she did so with an undetectable accent. She waited a few minutes for them to register her fluency before she told them that, despite her clothes, she was the daughter of the owner. She also reminded them that this was a graveyard and references about her female anatomy were not appreciated in this sacred place. Blushing and embarrassed, the two began to bow and scrape while they apologized. Debbie waved her hand in dismissal and walked back to the garden.

She returned to her weeding and pruning for another hour before she decided to break for lunch. Gardening had been a pleasant interlude away from the nagging questions she had about the arson and death of Hector and Dolores. When she entered the kitchen, the message light on the phone was blinking. Debbie listened to a message from Margo, who told her, in a rather urgent voice, to call back right away. She knew Margo would be at lunch so she tried her cell. There was an immediate response.

Debbie skipped the pleasantries and asked, "So, what's up?"

"I've got the labs back on your stuff. The DNA on the straw is an identical match to one of the test strips and the semen. The other strip was a totally different DNA and it was female. I had them both tested for the diabetic gene. So, unless I miss my guess, it looks like two teenage, juvenile diabetics out for fun."

"Ouch. That doesn't sound like a good idea. Two juvenile diabetics cohabitating. Can you date when they both were there?"

"Not on the semen, since the male used a spermicidal condom. The blood, however, shows to be within the past five days."

"So, Sean Casey was there with a female juvenile diabetic. At least they were practicing safe sex."

"He didn't admit to any of that, I suppose?"

"No," Debbie said, "but he had a purple tongue on Saturday and was fishy- eyed."

"Does fishy-eyed hold up in court?"

"Not a prayer. I'll have to go back and talk to him. He probably doesn't want his mother to know. She works for the police chief here. I met her the other day and I couldn't read her reaction. She knew I interviewed her son, but she didn't know why. She didn't seem all that pissed off at me."

"Didn't you say that your dad saved her kid's life when he was in a diabetic coma?"

"Yes. But I think it was more than that. Almost as if she wanted to say something to me but couldn't."

"Is that woman's intuition or cop suspicion?"

Debbie laughed and said, "Both. And no, it will not hold up in court. Thanks for the info. Did you bill my dad's credit card?"

"To the tune of two thousand dollars. Be warned the next time his visa bill arrives."

"Margo, if we can get to the bottom of what happened then it's a small price to pay."

"Amen. Oops, I have a call coming in. Gotta go."

After Debbie hung up, she started thinking. Now, why did Sean Casey speed away the other night? And who was with him? Did he and his companion see something? Debbie needed answers.

Chapter Eight

Debbie went to her father's den and opened a manila folder that contained her prepared notes of the investigation. She found Sean's personal number and dialed it. The grandfather clock behind her clanged out a dozen gongs, reminding her that he might not be home at this time. But, school wasn't back in session until after labor day, which was next Monday. Suddenly, there was a bored voice saying, "Hello."

"Sean, it's Debbie Miceli."

"Oh God. What do you want now? Didn't the Chief speak to you?" he asked, surly as only a teenage boy can be.

"Yes, he did. And he gave me permission to snoop around. I thought we had an agreement to keep our conversation between us?"

"We did. But that snoop Briggs working behind the counter at McDonald's called my mom. Said she had seen me with Debbie Miceli. She somehow knew who you were and what you did for a living."

"Hey, I grew up here just like you. I wasted many hours in there just like any other teenager. I thought I recognized the lady running the show. She was doing it when I was here."

"Mary Briggs is the town gossip. Anyway, I didn't tell anyone, like I promised. My mom tried to get answers from me but I put her off. She didn't believe my story that we just 'happened' to meet. So she called the Chief. Now, when he asks you a question, you better tell the truth. That guy scares me."

"What did you tell him?"

"Nothing really. I said I didn't know nothin' about the fire or eating grapes with some one else. You know, just like I told you."

"That's your story and you are sticking by it. Is that it?"

"Pretty much."

"What if I were to say that I have DNA from a condom, and a glucose test strip that indicates you were there? Not only that, you were there with someone else. A girl. And she also happens to be a diabetic."

The silence was palpable and Debbie could hear more rapid breathing on the other end. "Oh, I get it. Yeah. You got jack. How'd you know it was my DNA? I watch CSI like everybody else."

"Well, you got me there, except for one thing. I saved the straw you sucked on Saturday and sent it off with the other things to a very respectable lab in L.A. Now, you know and I know that you were there that night. It's time we sat down with your female companion and had a heart to heart," she said, emphasizing the word female.

Silence again. Then in a lower voice Sean said, "My mom can't find out about this. And you're wrong about there being someone there. I was alone."

"Sean, the Chief hasn't officially opened an investigation. If he does open one then I have to turn all this evidence over to him. If he doesn't then I'll just sit on it. If you don't cooperate with me, I will turn over my findings. Then you'll have to deal with him. And let me tell you, I'm a picnic compared to the Chief."

"Shit. Is this what they teach at LAPD? Grab the guy by the balls? Okay, forget that. Yeah, I was there with my girlfriend Tiffany. My ma didn't know we went to a rock concert in SLO Town. She can't find out about that or what I was doing with Tiffany or I'd be toast. She would totally take away my motorcycle."

"Hopefully it won't come to that. I assure you, I don't think you had anything to do with the fire. I just need to know what you saw? Then you and I are going to talk with Tiffany."

"You got me. What can I say? Let's meet where there's no snoops around so my old lady doesn't find out."

"Fine. How about I drive over to your place and we talk on the way to meeting Tiffany?"

"That sounds okay. But Tiffany doesn't live in Vista. She's up the road in Sandy Beach. I know she's home cause I just got off the phone with her. I'll call her back."

"No problem. I know my way to Sandy Beach. Been there a thousand times back when I was your age. You call her and we'll meet in Ryan park."

"Okay. But, we have to be careful. If Tiffany's Mom finds out about this she'll be grounded for life."

Debbie hung up, hopeful that the investigation would get off the ground after she questioned the two teenagers.

She agreed to meet Sean in ten minutes on the corner of his street. Debbie had just enough time to race upstairs and change her clothes. Interviewing two hormonal teenagers in a halter top with no bra was not a good way to start. She threw on a bra and blue tee shirt, tucked the shirt into her jeans, grabbed her purse and raced off.

Twelve minutes later, she arrived to see Sean standing on the corner. He climbed into her car and they left heading north for Sandy Beach. Sean said, "Pretty good. You were only two minutes late."

"I had to change."

Sean stared at her for a little too long. Debbie was used to dealing with teenage boys and understood that their brains were filled with two thoughts: food and sex. Rather than prick his bubble, so to speak, she decided to keep her sexual orientation to herself.

"Tell me what you saw Sean? Every detail."

He went through the whole evening and how he had not planned to stop at the vineyard. It was his diabetes acting up that forced him to pull over. There was nothing unusual going on until he had suddenly heard a swooshing sound. Then he saw the fire.

Debbie went over the times with him, pinpointing as close as possible the time the fire started. She asked several questions along the way but, for the most part, she let him talk. She left the issue about the condom alone.

Their conversation made the trip to Sandy Beach go by quickly.

Sandy Beach was a small seaside town about fifteen miles north of Vista Del Mar. It was tucked on a cliff that overlooked the ocean. At the bottom of the cliff, there was a narrow sandy beach accessed by wooden stairs placed at various locations between houses or businesses. There was no center of town. Across the highway was Ryan Park. It was located in a wooded area and consisted of a substantial lawn of well-maintained grass, park benches, and stone barbecue pits. The park was named after a World War II hero who fought at Normandy. He had been born and raised in Sandy Beach. A statue of him with a plaque was displayed at the entrance to the park. The plaque indicated his combat awards, which included a silver star and a Congressional Medal of Honor. Debbie stood and read the plaque as she waited for Melody to show. Although she had read the plaque before, the significance of it had not sunk in until now. Being a civilian police officer and putting your life on the line on a daily basis was one thing. Doing it during a brutal war was quite another.

Debbie was aroused from her thoughts by the arrival of a small, foreign import car in decent condition. She watched the young driver step from the car, and Debbie was immediately struck by how thin she was. She was also struck by how attractive the girl was, in a teenage sort of way. Ponytail, lip gloss, tee shirt, and spandex shorts. Debbie was standing by the statue and watched as Sean met up with the girl. There was no one else at the park, and they kissed lightly and hugged. Debbie walked over and introduced herself.

"I'm sorry to have interrupted your day. Thank you for coming and agreeing to talk to me," Debbie said, shaking Tiffany's hand. Tiffany appeared younger than seventeen, but she had the maturity of someone older.

"What's Sean gone and done now?" She laughed as she asked the question.

"Nothing. He's been very cooperative, with a little urging, of course," Debbie said smiling at Sean.

"Can we get on with it. I've gotta get back home," Sean whined.

"Sean! Don't be so rude," Tiffany said. "Sean can be such a bore. Ask me anything you want. Sean told me you're the daughter of the doctor whose caretaker's house was burned down. I'm really sorry about the two people who died. It was awful to hear the lady scream. We heard it all the way up to the road." Tiffany genuinely looked saddened. "I know you are an LAPD officer, so I have no problem with that. My dad's a cop. My mom and dad split up last year. I still see him down in San Luis Obispo on weekends. He's always telling me to keep my eyes and ears open. Especially after 9/11."

Sean had sprawled on a park bench close enough to hear but not close enough to be a part of the conversation. He adopted a well-practiced, bored demeanor. Debbie and Tiffany were standing, but Tiffany followed Debbie's lead and sat down at the picnic table next to Sean's.

"All I want is for you to tell me what you saw and heard."

"Do you want to know what we almost did, too?" Tiffany giggled.

Sean groaned. He was certain that girls were more open about their sexual escapades than guys.

"It's up to you. But, I would like the whole story."

"Well, we had decided to go to a rock concert in SLO Town. My mother thought we were going to a movie in Vista. So, she can't hear about any of this, okay?" Tiffany paused and Debbie nodded. She continued. "Anyway, on the way back Sean got low on his sugar. No surprise, the way he drank beer." She glanced over at him with a half scornful look. "Anyhow, we pulled off the road and parked next to a vineyard."

"Do you remember the time?" Debbie asked.

"We told mom I'd be home at midnight. So, we checked the time right after we parked and it was 11:15. Sean climbed over the fence to get grapes for his low sugar. We had to drive back to Vista and get my car. I parked there so my mom didn't see us driving on the motorcycle. She hates them. So does my dad."

"So, you drove from Sandy Beach to Vista in your car. Then the two of you went out on the motorcycle?"

"Sounds dumb, doesn't it? But that's what we did. I got home about a quarter after midnight. Of course, my mom was awake."

"Go on."

"Well, Sean and I were getting ready to have, you know, sex and stuff when all of a sudden there was a huge ball of fire, crackling noise, and then a scream. It was awful. I asked Sean if we should go help, but he said there was nothing we could do. After that, we gathered our stuff and got the hell outta there."

Tiffany fell silent. Debbie waited, hoping she would add more details, but none came. It sounded like this was a dead end.

Finally, Debbie asked, "Anything else?"

"No. We didn't see anyone or nothing like that. Did somebody start the fire?"

"That's what I'm trying to find out. You've been very helpful. But remember, this is between us."

Tiffany turned and looked at Sean as if to ask him if there was anything else. Sean shook his head. She smiled at Debbie and the three headed for their cars.

As Tiffany was walking past Sean, he said in an angry whisper, "Thanks for bringing up the sex thing. If our parents find out about that, I can kiss my motorcycle goodbye. And you'd be kicked out of the house."

"Lighten up. You were the one with the hot pants. I'll keep what you said in mind the next time we go out." Sean slinked off, defeated once again by a girl.

Tiffany got into her car and started the engine. While she was pulling out, she thought of something Sean said and it jogged her memory. She saw Debbie ahead of her, so she honked her horn.

Debbie hit the brakes and waited while Tiffany got out of her car and came to the driver's window. "I forget to tell you," she said, "the reason I was nervous about, uh, sex, was that when we pulled onto the side road there was a car parked in the bushes just off the entrance road to the vineyard. We parked about 100 yards from it and didn't hear or see anything."

Excited that there might be something after all, Debbie said, "Go on." She knew better not to ask leading questions to a witness. It was always better to leave your questions short and let the witness do all the talking.

"Let me see, it was four days ago, but I do remember some things. The car was green and on the trunk there was a word that started with C. But it wasn't an American car and it didn't have a California plate. The plates had one of those tall cactuses on the left and a sun."

"Anything else?" Debbie asked.

Tiffany was silent while she tried to recall the picture of the car in her head. The more she tried to think about it, however, the more distant the image became. Clearly frustrated, she said, "The only other thing I can remember for certain is that it wasn't an American car. I'm sorry, but that's all I can recall about it."

"Wait a minute," Sean blurted out. He had crept up alongside Tiffany and was listening to her description when he remembered something. "When we left, you said the car wasn't there anymore."

"You're right. That's right. Thanks for reminding me."

"If I got some pictures of cars and license plates could you identify them?"

"I'm pretty sure I could," she said to Debbie.

"Was it a sports car?" asked Debbie.

"No. It was like a station wagon. Four doors, but not like an SUV. It was weird. I don't think I've seen a car like it before."

"Thank you, Tiffany. You did a great job."

The car ride back to Vista del Mar was silent. Debbie let Sean off on the corner of his block and sped home. She was anxious to get on the computer and check out her new leads.

Chapter Nine

On Wednesday morning, Dan greeted Hector's brother, Carlos, and his crew of ten workers who had driven down from Fresno. They piled out of three cars and were not standing around for more than a few minutes before Carlos had them settled into their work for the day. Although Carlos worked at a vineyard that grew table and raisin grapes, he was familiar with wineries, particularly the winery at Vista. He had learned a lot about winemaking while helping his brother with the annual pinot harvest. Carlos was two years older than his brother, but at age 62 he looked strong and fit.

"Where's Juanita?" Dan asked, noticing that Carlos' wife wasn't among the caravan.

"She is ill, Señor Miceli. She could not make it," Carlos said this while removing his hat.

"I'm sorry to hear that, Carlos. I hope she gets better soon," he said. Dan knew better than to dwell on the point. He had learned over the years that Mexican men take pride in keeping their families safe and healthy, and he didn't want to embarrass Carlos by calling attention to an illness in the family.

Carlos nodded and then quickly deflected attention away from himself by saying, "Señor Miceli, we are here to help. I'll stay as long as it takes to get the grapes into the vats. I owe that to Hector and to you, who have been so good to our family."

Dan had also been around Mexicans long enough to appreciate their loyalty to both friends and family. Loyalty was a characteristic he valued highest in people, and it was not one he came across too often in his own circle of acquaintances.

"You don't owe me anything Carlos. It is I who have benefited from your hard work and expertise. Would you come to the house with me and have coffee? Debbie would love to say hello, and she has some questions for you about Hector."

"Si, Señor Miceli. I'll be right there."

"Bring your bags. I have a room for you upstairs."

"Gracias mi amigo. You are very kind."

Dan waited for Carlos to grab his bag and then led him back to the house. Debbie greeted Carlos with a big hug and told him to put his bag in the room at the top of the stairs.

"I'll have coffee ready when you get back," she added.

A few minutes later, Carlos entered the kitchen and Debbie gestured for him to take a seat at the table. She placed a steaming mug of coffee in front of him, along with a carafe of cream and a sugar bowl. She didn't wait for him to settle in before she started talking about his brother and the fire.

"There is some suggestion that the fire that killed Hector and Dolores was started deliberately," she began. "Did Hector give any indication to you that he was threatened by anyone? Was there any reason for anyone to threaten him?"

Carlos ladled a spoonful of sugar in his coffee and stirred it thoughtfully. He slowly shook his head and said, "How could anyone want to hurt such nice people? He never mentioned anything to me. The only thing he told me was that Señor Dan had trouble with the newspaper man, the one who wanted to close the vineyard. Hector was very worried about that. He said the newspaper man was always stopping him in Vista and asking questions about the vineyard."

"What kind of questions?" Debbie asked.

Carlos took a sip of coffee while he thought about it. "How many bottles of wine did the vineyard sell? How much money did Señor Dan pay him? How much money does the vineyard make? Does Señor Dan treat his worker's okay? He wanted to find out bad things so he could put them in the newspaper."

"What did Hector tell him?"

"Hector despised him. The newspaper man was a hippy and Hector had enough of that during the Vietnam war. He called him a traitor and gutless. Never served his country. Hector told me that when that pinche oyo was at Berkeley he donated blood for the North Vietnamese."

"Anything else?"

"He did tell me that a lot of people were asking him when he was going to Fresno. I mean, they were asking him more often than usual. Hector got the feeling people wanted him to leave permanently."

"Did he talk to the police chief about this? About leaving, I mean," Debbie asked.

"He said he talked to the chief of police. It only came up when Hector mentioned he wouldn't be mowing the baseball field on Sunday. He never missed doing that."

Dan said, "He would have left last Friday, but he had carburetor trouble with his truck. If it weren't for that damn carburetor, we wouldn't be having a funeral today."

While Dan was talking, a car pulled up outside and moments later there was a knock at the door. It was Hector's eldest son Antonio, his wife, and two children. They had driven over from Las Vegas yesterday and spent the night in San Luis Obispo. When Antonio saw Debbie in the kitchen, he breezed over and gave her a big hug. They were like brother and sister to each other, and they immediately began reminiscing about their childhood days at the vineyard. While the two talked about old times, Carlos took Antonio's wife and kids around the garden. As she had done with Carlos, Debbie launched into her questioning about Hector's last days. She asked Antonio if Hector had told him about any conversations regarding the vineyard or if he mentioned any threats directed at him.

"He didn't mention anything to me about the vineyard. Threats? What do you mean?" Antonio asked, his tone becoming more serious.

"This fire may not have been an accident," Debbie said.

Antonio took the news in silence, but his concern was written all over his face. "I hadn't spoken to dad for a week or so before he died," he mumbled to himself. He was obviously deep in thought trying to process this new, disturbing information about his father.

They were interrupted by Dan, who announced that it was time for everyone to start gathering at the family plot. Other family members of both Hector and Delores had been gathering outside, and now they all headed to the burial site. A funeral home in San Luis Obispo had brought the caskets in a black limousine. Two attendants were standing by to lower the caskets when given notice. Father Nuygen from St. Norbert's church gave a blessing. Then Dan stood to give his farewell to his two longtime friends.

"Hector came from Mexico to Texas by way of the Rio Grande at 16. He arrived here in California and not long afterwards joined his brother, Carlos, in Fresno. They worked hard in the vineyards for two years, but Hector had bigger plans in mind for himself. He wanted to step out from the shadows and become an American citizen, so he joined the Marines. For Hector, this was not only an opportunity to serve his new country that had given him a second chance, but it was also a sure pathway to becoming a citizen. He learned to speak English in the Marines, but he also learned about the ugliness of war. He did two tours in Vietnam where he excelled, rising in rank to become a platoon sergeant. His honorable and brave service won him many commendations, including two bronze stars and a purple heart. Before he was discharged in 1972 he fulfilled his dream of becoming a U.S. citizen."

At this point, Dan stopped and looked at the crowd of relatives and close friends. He spotted the Police Chief, who was standing in the back, in full VDMPD uniform.

"It was by chance that Hector came to Vista Del Mar. He had seen an advertisement for workers and applied. It took my father a split second to decide that this young man was perfect. He hired him and showed him how to grow grapes and make wine. When my father died and I inherited the land, Hector continued to run the vineyard; I was at least smart enough to stay out of the way. But, the work that Hector and Delores did at the vineyard cannot compare to the work they did for the community. Every Sunday, Hector mowed the grass at the little league field so the kids, including his Antonio and Adrianna, could play in the best conditions. He always wanted everything right not only for his own children but all the children in the community."

Dan had held his emotions in check during the whole speech, but when he went on to praise Dolores and the job she did raising Debbie, he felt himself choking up a bit. Fortunately, he was wise to leave the toughest part of the speech at the end, where he could finish speaking and recompose himself. Once his eulogy ended, the caskets were lowered side by side into the same grave. Father Nuygen gave a closing prayer and the group returned to the house for refreshments catered by *The Fun Thymes* restaurant. Dan thanked the funeral workers and gave them a generous tip for their service. As he turned to leave, he noticed the Chief and Debbie standing together, out of earshot of the workers.

"That was nice Doc," the chief said, "This has been a great tragedy and it will take a long time for the town to recover. I appreciate you allowing me to attend the funeral."

Dan nodded. The chief waited a beat before he said, "I have a few things to tell you and Debbie."

"Here or in my office?" Dan asked.

"Well, just so no one overhears or gets the wrong idea. Here would be better."

"Go ahead," Dan said.

"I received a phone call from the arson investigator on Monday. It's her feeling that the fire should be treated as arson. Last night she faxed me her final report with her boss's signature. Let me say, I'm not convinced. I'm not going to open a formal investigation, but I will interview the three full time workers here to see if they know anything."

"For what it's worth, Chief, I already did that," Debbie chimed in. "And I saved you some trouble since their English isn't so good. That is, unless you too are fluent in Spanish?" she looked at him with mock innocence and then went on, "They are devastated by the deaths, and you can see they were in attendance today as part of the burial detail. In fact, there they are filling in the grave." She pointed to the men working their shovels into the earth and unceremoniously throwing it into the hole.

The chief reddened. He straightened up a little and eyed Debbie. His last recollections of her, except for Monday's meeting, was that of a serious high school student wrapped up in books and sports. Somehow the vision of her being an LAPD gang investigator had not settled into his cerebral cortex.

"Of course," he said tersely, "I said for you to poke around and let me know if you find anything. I guess that fits. Thanks, but I'll bring an interpreter out here and see if this old tired dog can find out anything."

Dan, seeing that he should break the dangerous direction this conversation was going, asked, "Would you like to come to the house and have some refreshments… with the family? I know they are dying to ask you questions."

The chief glanced in the direction of the house. He was silent for a moment as he considered what that scene might look like. He answered. "No, I don't think that will be a good idea. You can extend my sympathies. Tell them, as far as I'm concerned, it's still under investigation as a possible arson."

"Very well. If there is nothing further I think we should get inside." Dan shook his hand and Debbie smiled at the chief.

The chief gave her a serious look in return and said, "Good luck on your problems with the LAPD." This was certainly a tacky parting shot by the chief. Debbie felt the chief must have something to hide based on his attitude toward her. *Unlike his previous green light for me to snoop around, I really think he wants me to mind my own business.*

The chief pushed ahead and left through the garden. After he departed, Dan turned to his daughter and said, "He seems a bit defensive. Why didn't you tell him about your conversation with Sean Casey and his girlfriend? What's her name?"

"Tiffany. She's way more mature than Sean but a bit too lonely I fear. Her mom and dad separated a year ago. I get the feeling she would rather be living with her dad," Debbie said absently.

Dan noted that she did not answer his question, but he let it go. "Living with her dad. That sounds very mature," while poking his daughter playfully with his elbow. Not getting a playful response back, he went on, "You told me her dad is a SLO Town cop, probably taught her how to be observant and aware of her surroundings at all times."

"Yes. I would like to have more eye witnesses like her."

"Ok, but you didn't answer my question. Why are you keeping the chief in the dark about those two teenagers?"

Debbie stopped and they were standing next to the back door. She gazed up toward the winery before she answered. "Did mom have what you call women's intuition? I mean did she get feelings about situations or people that later proved to be true?"

"All the time. I always asked her about people and situations. She seemed to know more about them than I did simply by observation."

"Well, I've been told by my fellow officers that I have a heavy dose of women's intuition. I seem to be able to tell if someone is lying…. in either Spanish or English. For example, I knew Sean was lying to me when we first met. The second time he was telling the truth. Of course, I have been wrong but not often. Anyhow, I have a feeling the chief, for whatever reason, does not want to make this a homicide case. Is he lazy? I don't think so. Is it because he hasn't had a murder here for years and doesn't want it to spoil his record? Or is he part of the cabal that's trying to move you out of here? Is he trying to avoid any negative publicity for the town?" she finished by opening the back door and stepping onto the porch.

Dan followed her in and said, "As I've said before, the chief runs the town. He's head of the local chapter of the public worker's union. Of course, he wants this vineyard for the city to use for economic development. Or should I say, a tax revenue enhancement," Dan finished with a bitter tone to his voice.

"I'm sorry, Dad. But that will not happen. I'm with you all the way on that one. This has been a part of our family for ninety years. We can't give it up without a fight." They entered the kitchen where Dan noticed a blinking red light on the phone.

As he passed out of the kitchen, he saw the mourners were in the living room with a few more scattered on the front porch. It was a somber crowd; nothing like the Irish wake he had attended in college. Wakes were riotous affairs, much like the Irish themselves. Mexicans and Italians were different, preferring a solemn atmosphere while respecting the dead. As Dan passed his office, he again saw the blinking light on the phone. Afraid of what might be waiting for him, he hesitantly stepped into his office and pressed the button. He hoped it wasn't a call from a patient and was glad to hear the voice of Lieutenant Hernandez at the LAPD requesting that Debbie call him right away.

He passed on the news and watched as Debbie dialed her boss. "I wonder if this is going to be bad?" she asked herself as she dialed. After listening to several prerecorded prompts, she finally reached him.

"Debbie, I'm glad I got you. I have good news. This morning IA met and tossed out your complaint. Totally bogus. If it wasn't for that damn Consent Decree the feds shoved down our throats, this would never have gone this far."

The Consent Decree was handed to the LAPD after a scandal with the Ramparts Division, such as two cops conspiring to murder a gang banger, among other crimes. The scandal was thought to be widespread, but it later proved to be limited to just two rogue cops, both of whom were subsequently imprisoned. But, the Justice Department assumed that this was a departmental epidemic and made the LAPD into a bureaucracy of full-time documenters instead of police officers. Not only that, the decree was further extended three years by an overzealous judge. Other officers, who were implicated, fought their case in court and collected over seven million dollars from the city for wrongful termination.

Any supposed complaint by one officer or officers about another had to be thoroughly investigated regardless of the nature of the complaint. Debbie had been caught up in this bureaucratic morass and was relieved and angry at the same time. "I suppose I should be happy," she said, "but somehow I'm not."

"You know I support you one hundred percent, as does most everyone else here. We only have to put up with this Consent Decree for one more year."

"Do you know what made them toss out the complaint?" Debbie asked.

"When you voluntarily submitted your income tax, bank records, and brokerage account statements to IA; it went a long way to closing this down. You were clean as a whistle. Unfortunately, for your accusers, they didn't agree to submitting their financial records."

"Why not?"

"That's what IA asked. There's a move afoot by the department to make all people in the gang and drug units submit their yearly income tax reports. We'll see how far that goes. Anyway, welcome back, you've been restored to active status with no access restrictions."

"You mean I can get into computers and do some searching?" she asked with more enthusiasm.

"Of course. It's been done. When are you coming back?"

"I'd like to extend my vacation a week or so? I'm in the middle of family business and my Dad needs help." Debbie didn't want to go into detail with her boss about investigating possible homicides.

"Consider it done. I'll expect you back by the 24th. Okay?"

"That should to it."

"By the way, I have to inform you that you have the right to make a counter complaint on the officers that pegged you. Part of the Consent Decree."

Debbie heaved a sigh before saying, "All I want is to work with someone else. They can go their own way. The only thing I would suggest is that they learn how to speak Spanish." Debbie felt good getting in that final dig. Lieutenant Hernandez would not argue with her request.

"I'll see what I can do on all counts Ms. ME-chel-lee," he laughed. "Italian and Spanish are about the same. See you on the 24th."

Debbie hung up and, after some thought, was pleased. It felt good that she stood up to the charges and was vindicated. Maybe things weren't so bad after all. Now she just had to deal with the problems at home, and those seemed to be growing. She went out to console her adopted family.

Chapter Ten

While the mourners were departing the vineyard late Wednesday afternoon, David Chase was driving home from his office in San Luis Obispo. It had been a beautiful, balmy day with warm breezes blowing in from the ocean. He rode with his car window down thinking about a call he had received earlier from the Vista city attorney. He had dealt with Jack Holmes through most of the discovery process and wasn't too impressed with his skills. In fact, he found the Vista attorney not much of a challenge at all. But, if things came to trial, Holmes would have to bow out and let a more experienced attorney defend the city. Holmes was authorized by the city council to offer a settlement of eight hundred thousand dollars. Although the sum seemed tempting to him, David felt the price was too low. He knew something was hidden somewhere in the city's coffers because when he subpoenaed the city's financial records, Holmes made a motion to quash it. He would fight that motion in court next week and felt confident he'd come out on top.

Chase arrived home a little before five o'clock. He entered the house through the kitchen and noticed an open bottle of chardonnay on the counter. Too early, he thought. He also noticed that dinner tonight would be take-out Chinese. He didn't blame Elaine for wanting a no-fuss meal. He'd been out of town for several days, arriving back home late last night, and they hadn't had a moment to catch up. He knew she needed to tell him some story about a dust up with Dr.Miceli.

He stepped out onto the deck of his expensive home that overlooked the Pacific Ocean. The sun was just beginning to set and its bright orange hue was mesmerizing. The temperature was ten degrees lower than inland and he welcomed the difference. In a half hour or so, he'd have to put on a sweater. He walked over to a wicker couch with fluffy cushions, leaned down, and kissed his wife. She had been staring at the ocean with a half filled glass of wine in her hand.

"Starting early?" he asked lightly. He didn't want to begin an argument about her drinking. He had other things he wished to discuss. "Where's Davis?"

"In his room, and it's five o'clock so I'm allowed," she said in a raspy voice. A holdover from her smoking days.

"I'll join you in a moment. Tell me what happened at the doctor's office that got you so riled the other day."

"Oh, it was nothing. I tried to persuade Dr. Miceli, for the sake of the town, to sell his property. He got very defensive and wondered if lawsuits weren't part of the problem. He mentioned you. I don't think he likes lawyers."

"I'm not sure I like lawyers either. We do seem to bring out the worst in people sometimes," he waited for an encouraging response from his wife, but none came.

He added, "Somebody has to do the job of keeping people within the white lines. But, enough of that. My concern is for Dr. Miceli."

"Why?" Elaine asked, somewhat surprised at his sympathies.

"One of the reasons I moved here was because it was a peaceful, seaside town. The Miceli vineyard has been here for nearly ninety years. Their pinot is consistently in the top ten for California."

"So? Times change. Things move on. There are plenty of vineyards in California. It seems a shame to waste that space when it could be put to better use."

Rather than dispute the point, David left his wife with the last word. He got up and went back into the house. He climbed the stairs to his son's room, calling out his name before he reached the top. Davis greeted his Dad like a long lost buddy and they spent a few minutes catching up.

David went back into the kitchen and poured himself a glass of Miceli's Pinot Noir Reserve. He felt he worked hard enough and deserved to drink a twenty-five dollar bottle of wine. He grabbed a can of almonds and returned to the deck. He sat down next to his wife, who hadn't taken a sip of her wine since he had arrived.

"Some almonds?"

"No, thank you. I heard you and Davis in there. Is everything okay? I mean, did I do a good job of taking care of him while you were gone?"

David wasn't going to bite on that bait. Their marriage, for the most part, had been a happy one. Her drinking had put a strain on things, but moving out of the rat race of Southern California had been a restorative measure that seemed to be working fairly well.

"We probably should have discussed this Miceli business sooner. I am totally opposed to this trumped up eminent domain takeover of property for private development. How would you like it if your father's property in Pasadena was taken over to build a hotel?"

"That's different. That would never happen. He has too much political clout."

"Precisely. Everyone in town seems to like the idea of Dr. Miceli, but not his actual personality. He socializes very little, he's not politically motivated, keeps to himself, and uses accountants, insurance agents, legal, investment, and other services outside of Vista. It's as if he doesn't want people to know him that well, and that rubs this community the wrong way."

Elaine considered what her husband was saying. His description of Dr. Miceli sounded just like her own father. The big difference between the two men was that her father had a wife while Miceli didn't. Elaine recalled her mother with admiration. She was an outgoing and socially adept woman who never got the proper attention she deserved from her husband. Elaine herself never felt the love from her father and continued to blame him for her substance abuse problems. While she had at first resisted David's suggestion to move to Vista, she now knew that getting away from her domineering father was the right decision. She was drinking less, despite her husband's opinion, and she never even thought about drugs anymore. In fact, she had been drug free for nearly thirteen years. Well, that wasn't counting the few prescription drugs she took to get over the rough spots.

David was waiting for a response. "Hello, are you still here?" he asked.

"Of course I am. I've decided that it was a good idea to move here. You should call Dr. Miceli and apologize for me. Maybe we could have him over for dinner."

"Now you're sounding like your mother, which is much better than sounding like your father. He would have called the guy an asshole and ended the conversation there." He stopped to think for a moment about her suggestion and then added, "I like that idea. After all, he is our son's surgeon, and a good one at that. A double USC grad trained at Big County." Big County was the name used to describe L.A. County USC Medical Center. It was, without argument, one of the best medical training facilities in the world. David Chase was always impressed by big names, even when he had no idea what work went into earning that name.

"He got a big write up in our alumni journal a while back. That's why I chose him to do Davis' surgery," he said.

"You know, most physicians have plaques all over their walls touting their background and accomplishments, but he doesn't have any hanging on his walls. He only has pictures of his wife and daughter. Oh, and he also has pictures of those two Mexicans who were killed last Friday. That's a little weird, don't you think?"

"Let's just say Doc Miceli is happy in his own skin. I'll call him tomorrow."

They both sat in silence for a minute before David said, "By the way, next Wednesday the city council meets to vote on the eminent domain issue. So far two people have signed up to speak out against the motion and ten have signed on to support it. I'm one of the two arguing against it."

"Are you sure that's a good idea? I mean, with the lawsuit and everything?" she asked.

"I might get a few sour looks, but I'm used to that," he chuckled at his own joke and then quickly turned serious again, "And I think the lawsuit is a separate issue. I want to tweak the council members about the city's budget. They're trying to block me from seeing the city's financial paper work."

"Why?"

"I don't know, but there hasn't been an outside audit since 2003. That's five years!"

"Sounds like you should first talk this over with Dr. Miceli, just to be safe. He may regard your support as a negative. I know what! You're a self proclaimed wine connoisseur. Why don't you invite yourself over to his place Saturday. You've been itching to see the vineyard."

"What about you? You don't want to come?"

"I'll be down in San Luis Obispo with Davis most of the afternoon. Riding lessons."

David looked at his wife. He hadn't seen her this animated in a long time. "Sounds like a good plan." He looked out at the ocean and finished his glass of wine. "I assume dinner is Chinese takeout."

"You are correct. Davis wanted it. Remember when that was our go-to meal when things weren't so good? I'll cook something real nice tomorrow for dinner. I promise."

"Chinese is no problem. Let's go get Davis and eat."

The funeral was over and the mourners had left. It was 9 o'clock when Dan finally trudged up the stairs to his room. Both Debbie and Carlos had turned in earlier. Dan didn't blame Carlos for wanting to hit the sack early, since he and his crew were set to pick grapes tomorrow all day. He was thankful that Carlos was able to help, and Dan would make sure his temporary vineyard foreman received a sizable bonus. He was also thankful there were two people staying at the house. He had forgotten how lonely the place had become. It was a big house, but everything had shrunk down to just the spaces he used: the bedroom, the den, and the kitchen. The rest of the house might as well not exist.

It had been different when Darlene was alive. When Darlene was alive there never seemed a space big enough to hold her warmth and energy. Even though she had been dead for twenty years, she still occupied most of the space in his heart. He jokingly referred to her as his wife by his first marriage, since most people he knew were on their second and third wives. He could never bring himself to marry again.

Dan stepped into his bedroom thinking of Darlene when he suddenly realized that his birthday was in two weeks. He shuddered at the memory of past birthdays. He tried to put the memories out of his mind as he undressed, brushed his teeth, and crawled into bed.

"What, no candles?" Dan asked. "It's my thirty-third birthday. What gives?" he good-naturedly teased his wife while his four year old daughter, Debbie, looked on. It was four in the afternoon and he had come home early to celebrate. Darlene had baked his favorite carrot cake.

"You would bring that up," she laughed. "I was hoping you didn't notice," she said playfully. "Debbie, take daddy out to the garden and show him the new winter vegetables we planted today." Debbie grabbed her daddy's hand and ran out the door.

Dan played the scene over and over again in his mind. He imagined Darlene kicking herself for not getting the candles. He pictured her writing a note and placing it next to the cake. Then she slipped outside and got into her car, carefully waiting until he and Debbie were well into the garden before starting up the engine. She drove up the road leading out of the vineyard, probably with a smile on her face because she knew she was being very sneaky. Once she was at the intersection of Highway One, she looked both ways and then turned left. From there, Dan shifted his memory to the sound of bending metal and screeching tires. He heard it from the garden. He raced into the house to have Darlene call 911 when he saw the note. He called the emergency number and then grabbed Debbie and raced up the hill to the road. When he saw the bent car with the driver's side t-boned by a pickup truck, he froze. He knew right away his wife was gone. Tears immediately formed in his eyes and Debbie, sensing something terrible, began screaming for her mother.

By now, Dan was in a cold sweat. He was shocked to see the clock showed midnight. He had been laying in bed for almost three hours. He must have fallen asleep or at least been in and out of consciousness. He had not had such a vivid recollection of that day for years; he had done a good job up until now suppressing all memories of Darlene's death. Why did he think about it tonight? Was it because of the deaths, the funeral, or the fact that he had recalled his upcoming birthday just before he went to bed? Or was it Debbie's slight hostilities toward him? It was no surprise that she might resent him a little bit. He remembered her screaming, shortly after learning that her mother was dead, "Why did you make her get candles Daddy?! I hate you!" He was sure she did not remember that day in any vivid terms, but somewhere, deep in her sub-conscious, he knew that she blamed him for her mother's death. "Why did you make her get candles Daddy? I hate you!" she said between loud sobs as she pounded on his chest.

Chapter Eleven

Dan lay awake in bed the next morning when he heard Carlos get up and walk down the stairs. It was five a.m., and he had spent most of the night tossing and turning. He decided he might as well start his day early, too. He was thankful he had clinic and was not scheduled for a long day in the operating room. After he showered and dressed, he headed downstairs to grab a banana before heading out the door. When he stepped out of the house, he noticed the men working the vineyards. There was a skip loader already full of grapes chugging toward the preparation area. Dan shook his head in amazement and gratitude, wondering what he would do without Carlos.

He drove to his small hospital in Vista and made rounds on ten patients. Some were recovering from serious breast surgery, others from laproscopic cholecystectomy, and still others from abdominal exploratory procedures. After he had discharged most of the patients, he went to his office to see five more new patients. When there was a lull, Marilyn buzzed his phone.

He picked up to hear her say, "I hope it's nothing, but Davis Chase's father called. He didn't say why he was calling."

"Great. That's all I need right now: an angry attorney because I got into a dispirited discussion with the ice queen. Get him on the line." He hung up.

Moments later his phone buzzed again. He picked up and said, "Dr.Miceli speaking."

"Doctor. David Chase. Davis' father. How are you today?"

Short of a personal call from someone he knew closely, Dan never told people how he was really feeling. Instead he said, "Excellent. What can I do for you?"

"Several things. First, let me say what a nice job you did on Davis. I can barely see a scar. Second, I want to apologize for my wife's behavior the other day. She tells me she was out of line and hopes you will forgive her."

Dan had not expected a mea culpa from Mrs. Davis, considering her demeanor when she left the office on Monday. "I guess we were both a little touchy. Tell her all is forgiven."

"Yes, these are stressful times. I'll let her know. Thank you," David paused, but he heard only silence on the other end, so he went on, "Now, why I really called is to invite you over for dinner. Just the wife and I and you."

Dan managed to hide his shock at this unexpected invitation by responding without hesitation, "That sounds wonderful. But it will have to be after the grape harvest and fermentation period."

"I understand. I'm sure that's a moving target. Well, you just let us know what works for you. We'll be looking forward to it."

"I'll give you a call when things settle down."

"Great. Oh, and another thing I wanted to ask. Would it be possible for me to get a tour of the vineyard on Saturday? Elaine is going to be in San Luis Obispo most of the afternoon, so I figured it was a good opportunity for me to check it out."

Dan's natural defenses kicked in with this new request. He wondered what David Chase had up his sleeve. He never trusted lawyers, and this one's desire to tour his property, especially at this tense time, reeked of something underhanded. But, he figured, it's better to keep the enemy close.

"How about two o'clock?" Dan suggested. "I'll leave the main gate open, so you can just drive down to the house. If I'm not there I'm up at the winery. I'm sure you'll find me."

"Excellent. See you then. Oh, I almost forgot. I've signed up to speak in your favor at the city council meeting on Wednesday" David said.

"Well, I appreciate your support. Thank you."

"No problem. I happen to believe you are in the right. Well, see you Saturday."

After they hung up, Dan was nonplussed. He never would have expected to receive support from such a source. A prominent plaintiff lawyer who is suing the city coming to *my* aid? Something didn't seem right. And he wondered if David Chase's support would be a help or a hindrance.

When the lawyer arrived at Miceli's vineyard on Saturday, he knocked on the back door, waited for less than a minute, then knocked again. After getting no response, he walked in the direction of the winery where he saw men working. He heard the heavy groan of a conveyer belt and saw the workers loading grapes directly onto it by hand from a nearby skip loader. As the grapes climbed upward they were cleaned of any debris or dirt by a gentle spray of water. At the top of the conveyer belt, the grapes dropped into a crusher and stemmer. David was transfixed by the whole process, but his concentration was broken when he felt a tap on his shoulder and turned to see Dan smiling at him.

They shook hands and Dan quickly shouted, "Let's move away from here. It's too loud."

After they traveled for nearly one hundred yards, Dan finally stopped near a row of grapes and said, "That's better, the only place louder is the bottling room."

David smiled and said, "It's nice to meet you. I've been a Miceli fan for years. You don't know how happy I am to finally be at 'the vineyard'."

Dan laughed. He was surprised to find himself liking the guy already. Although he had that lawyer bearing about him---a delicate combination of reserve and calculating gladiator---he seemed relaxed. Dan noticed he was wearing a USC baseball cap and remembered that while he was at USC a number of his classmates went to law school. They all seemed to do well and had that demeanor which said, "I can only be pushed so far." In his experience, lawyers listened carefully to every word as if life was a continuous deposition; whatever you said and how you said it was always being scrutinized, even in the most casual of situations. David Chase was no different.

"Let's start with the grape." Dan walked further into the vineyard and pulled off a stem of grapes. He handed them to David. "Tell me what you think?"

David took a bite of the grape and immediately puckered his lips. "Bitter. Not sweet at all."

"Come up here." Dan led him about a hundred yards further and pulled off another stem of grapes. "Try these."

David warily took a bite. "Hmm, delicious. What a difference. Why?"

"Welcome to wine making 101. All grapes don't mature at the same time. The first grape looked the same as the one you just ate, but it wasn't ready for picking. That's why you have to have experienced pickers and a crew chief like Carlos over there," he pointed to Carlos, who was standing next to the conveyor belt, "he's the brother of the man who was killed in the fire last week. He can tell when a grape has reached that 22% sugar level as well as anybody I know."

David looked around and was amazed. "How many acres of vines do you have?" he asked.

"About 220, more or less. We'll pull about four tons of grapes per acre this year. It's been a mild, misty summer and the grapes are plump, but, oddly enough, that doesn't necessarily translate into a quality wine."

"What makes a quality wine?" David asked.

"It depends on multiple factors. Too many to name here, but we're trying to control things as much as we can," Dan said, realizing he was evading the question.

David looked up toward Highway One and said, "When I come home from San Luis Obispo, I get a great view of the vineyard. Is all that yours? All the way into the foothills?"

Dan nodded, "Yes. Two hundred and twenty acres seems like a Texas cattle ranch when you're picking grapes. As you can see, some areas are picked earlier than others. When the fog and mist roll in at night, it settles in the foothills near the highway. Those are usually the first grapes we pick."

"What are those light stanchions for? They seem to be everywhere."

"Those are halogen lights. I put them in two years ago. It cost me an arm and a leg, but it means we can pick at night."

"What did you do before you had those lights?"

"In the old days, my father used flashlights. Those halogen lights have already paid for themselves in terms of bigger yields and quality."

The two men stood taking in the scene in silence before Dan said, "Let's go to the fermentation building."

They walked into a large room that looked like a barn. There were rows of giant, shiny fermentation tanks. Dan said, "Once the grapes are washed, crushed, and stemmed, they go into the fermentation tanks. This is where you can make or break a good harvest."

"Why?" David asked. He was becoming more and more impressed by how much work went into making a good bottle of wine. He thought about the twenty-five dollar bottle he and Elaine drank last night and wondered if he wasn't actually getting a bargain.

"I won't go into details about that because of trade secrets," Dan laughed. "But you have to mix crushed grapes and whole grape clusters together in the right ratio. Getting that right and keeping on top of the fermentation process is the key to the character of the wine."

He stepped toward a large barrel and slapped it, "When the wine is ready, they go into oak barrels. California oak, I might add. After they sit in the barrels for a year, the wine is bottled and held for another year."

"Running this vineyard is a full time job. How do you do it and be as busy as you are?"

"Well, part of that I owe to the winery," Dan said modestly. "All the profits after expenses go into a foundation that basically runs the financial side of things."

"What foundation?" David asked, clearly shocked to hear that Dan wasn't pocketing all the profits from the winery himself.

"It's called The Dominic Foundation. You probably haven't heard of it because it's low profile, as far as foundations go. It was named after my grandfather Dominic who started the winery."

"What do they do?"

"The foundation donates to multiple charities, scholarship funds, and to the local hospital and clinic. Those donations are what have allowed me to keep the clinic state of the art. We also employ 30 people who mostly live in Vista or surrounding communities."

David stared at Dan in disbelief. "You know, none of that was in the alumni journal article about you several years ago. Does anyone know what you are doing for the town?"

"I don't talk about it much. In fact, few know about the foundation. But now that the city wants to take this land over, it might quell Cal Lacey's criticism that the winery does nothing for the town. I think he mentions that in every one of his editorials on the subject."

David shook his head but didn't say anything. He had to be careful not to say anything about Cal. It might come back to haunt him. The journalist can be scathing when he is fostering a cause.

"Let's go to the bottle storage area," Dan said.

They walked several hundred feet away from the vineyard to a large steel sided building that had a flagstone front. Dan and David walked through wooden double doors inside to a large warehouse cooled to 65 degrees and stacked row after row with boxes of wine. David was again speechless while he tried to grasp the extent of the operation.

"The wine is stored here in bottles for one year before being released. The aging process under these conditions is very favorable for the wine."

"Do you have any idea how many bottles you produce each year?"

"Well, it averages to about 3000 bottles per acre. So, times 220, about 650,000 bottles per year."

Again David was blown away. He did the math in his head and concluded that, at 18 to 25 dollars a bottle, the Miceli vineyard was making some serious "change."

While David was doing the math in his head, Dan called over a young worker who was stacking boxes and said something to him in Spanish. Then the two men left the storage warehouse. David was still shaking his head in disbelief. As they were walking back toward the house, David noted two large plastic Quonset hut type greenhouses. They were about two hundred feet long.

"What are those used for?" he asked, pointing to the arched, plastic covered, steel ribbed structures.

"Let's go over and I'll show you." At the first Quonset hut, Dan opened the door and again they entered an area where the temperature and humidity were controlled. It felt to David like he was experiencing the weather on a tropical island. Inside were two long benches running the entire length of the greenhouse. On the benches were rows and rows of rectangular cardboard boxes, each filled with a single budding grape vine.

"This is our little secret. These are mostly propagated for root stock. We prune the vineyard in February or March…well, we do it all during the growing season, for that matter. During the pruning, we cut the hardwood so there are three or four buds on each. The wood we use is about 1/4" thick. Then the wood is planted with one bud showing. As you can see, they are already budding, some with leaves. These are the cuttings from last March."

"Why do this? There are enough here to start three vineyards," David said as he gazed around the greenhouse.

"We sell each and every one of these. Growers want them for grafting root stock since the vines are *Phylloxera* resistant. They can be used for grafting or be left to grow as pinots."

"Are these the original vines your grandfather started or are they second generation?"

"Some of the original vines, but most are second or third generation."

"Well, that begs the question. Where did he get his vines?"

"My great grandfather used to work in a vineyard in a small town south of Milan. When he came over in 1906 he brought vine cuttings in his suitcase. Don't ask me how he got them past the inspectors at Ellis Island, but he did," Dan chuckled to himself, imagining that scene. "Anyhow," he went on, "he came straight to Sonoma, where one of his relatives owned a small vineyard. He planted the vines and propagated them each year. He soon rose to be the manager and, when his relative died, he inherited the vineyard. In 1918, he sold that vineyard and came here and started this vineyard with offshoots of the original pinots he had brought to the States."

"Amazing, but how do you know the vines' origins? Couldn't he have taken cuttings from the Sonoma vineyard and brought them here?"

"An interesting observation, and you aren't the first to ask. In fact, there have been many lawsuits over vine stealing in the past few years. But, the Italians recently cracked the genetic make up of pinot noir, which, by the way, is the first fruit to be identified so extensively. I have had the DNA of these vines compared to the pinot noirs in the vineyard where my grandfather worked in Italy and it was a perfect match."

"What about the Italian owner? Wasn't he upset to find that his vines had been stolen?"

"No. In fact, he wasn't at all concerned about it. I think he realized that those vines in Italy were brought there by the Greeks before the birth of Christ. No one truly owns them, in the grand scheme of things."

"Wow. I've learned more today about wines and vines then I have in all my years of reading Wine Spectator!"

"Well, I've been doing this since I can remember. I was born here and worked in the vineyards every summer and vacation. It's second nature to me."

"What other vines have been DNA tested?" David asked.

"There is a wine named Wrotham Pinot. A respected Napa wine maker, Dr. Richard Grant Peterson took cuttings from a grape vine growing on a church in Wrotham, England. The vine was rumored to have been brought to England by the Romans 2000 years ago. He propagated the vines into a small vineyard and now makes an award winning pinot noir. The origin of those grapes has also been verified using DNA analysis. At U.C. Davis, they did DNA on the Wrotham vine and showed it to be identical to pinot noir."

"Wrotham's huh? I think I'll get a bottle of it. Knowing the history will make it more fun when I drink it. But listen, I don't want to take up all your time here. Can we take a moment to discuss next Wednesday's city council meeting?"

"Sure. Let's go back to the house and shift gears. How about a beer?'

Chapter Twelve

Back in Dan's den, the two settled into comfortable easy chairs. It was almost 4 o'clock and Dan was through for the day in terms of vineyard oversight. With Carlos in charge, things were moving along better than he had hoped. David looked around the room and his eye caught a number of pictures behind the desk that revealed more about his host than the ones spotted by his wife in the doctor's office. One picture, in particular, got his attention. It was a group of young men in swimming suits with their arms linked at the shoulders. They were holding up a NCAA and a USC banner.

Before David could ask about the picture, Dan asked, "So what year did you graduate from SC, Dave?" Dan usually didn't get this informal so quickly, but he had taken a liking to the attorney sitting across from him.

"'86 undergrad and '89 from the law school. I went to work with a firm in Los Angeles and did well. Of course, it didn't hurt that my father was a senior partner," David joked.

"Well, we've all had breaks provided by our parents. If we're lucky," Dan said, looking around the den.

"May I ask about that picture there? The one with the swimmers standing together?"

Dan turned and looked at the picture. "Sure. When I was a junior, we won the NCAA Championship. I swam the 1,500 meter free."

"You were a swimmer?" David asked. He was constantly being surprised by the unassuming man in front of him.

"Yeah. I guess it makes sense since I grew up swimming in the ocean every day. And I missed the 1968 Olympics by a touch."

Impressed, but wanting to get down to business, David shifted the subject to the lawsuit he had against Vista. He asked, "Are the currents here treacherous for swimmers?"

"They can be. But, as with most things, if you know what you're doing it's not a problem. I'm sure you're asking because you represent the Tran family. He drowned and disappeared on the point out to our left," Dan said, pointing to the left side of the house. "It's very treacherous out there. In fact, when I was young, I never swam beyond the rocks just before the point."

"Am I being unreasonable in carrying this action forward?" David asked in all honesty.

Dan had never heard a lawyer express self-doubt about his own judgment in pursuing a lawsuit.

"Let me say that for years we didn't have signs or lifeguards out there. People swam in the ocean all the time. Sure, we had an occasional drowning, but they were usually visitors to the area. For ten years that beach in front of us has had a posted sign warning swimmers about the currents. But, for the past several summers the city council pulled the lifeguards at this end of the beach to save money. Was that negligence on Vista's part? I guess we'll find out." Dan laughed.

"So, you're saying you aren't sure either?" David asked.

"I don't really have a tidy answer."

David continued scanning the photographs scattered throughout the room. He noticed a picture of a beautiful young lady holding a baby. He assumed it was Dan's wife. He knew she was killed in an auto accident and so refrained from asking about it. However, he did want to ask about a picture of several buff young men in swimming suits holding up a Navy SEAL emblem that caught his eye. They were standing in front of a well-known US Navy SEAL landmark in Coronado.

"Is that you in the center of that picture there?" David asked, pointing to the picture.

Dan looked at the picture in question. "Yes. I joined ROTC in college. I decided to join up after I graduated instead of getting a deferment. I picked the SEALS because swimming was my best sport."

"Were you over there? Vietnam I mean?"

Dan sat a while and looked at David. He hadn't talked about Vietnam for many years. He didn't want to get into it so he said, "Two tours. Search and rescue pilots and helicopter crews."

Dan had talked to this complete stranger far more than he had planned. Was it because he was a fellow Trojan or was he trying to convince David he was worth standing up for? He wanted to change the subject so he said, "Now tell me about what you plan to say on Wednesday and whether I should worry about what you're saying."

David thought for awhile. He wanted to choose his words carefully.

"Basically, I think the whole idea of city government seizing property under the guise of economic development is flawed. If we allow them to take this action then where does it end? I've studied the Kelo decision. The town uprooted all those people then turned the land over to a private development corporation that went belly up. Most of the touted development never happened."

Dan shook his head in disgust and said, "What a waste. All the legal battles that were spawned by the New London, Connecticut city council decision has caused so many ramifications. And, as a result, nine unelected Supreme Court Judges have decided to interpret the Constitution rather than defend it. The Kelo decision was five to four. That means if one person changed their mind the decision would have gone the other way. I don't think the founding fathers planned for the judiciary to be the arbiter of the Constitution, bending it one way then the other. Such things were meant to be decided by the citizens of the country."

"Agreed. But sometimes the judiciary gets it right. The Poletown decision in 1981 by the Michigan supreme court, giving

Wayne county power to seize property and turn it over to private developers, is a similar example. In 2004, they reversed themselves and severely restricted governments such as Wayne County and Detroit from seizing private property to sell to others for economic development."

"I didn't know about that decision. Frankly, the whole process scares me." He shook his head again, adding, "Besides, the compensation package rumored for this vineyard is woefully inadequate. They've got me over a barrel."

"Do you have legal help?" David asked.

"I have legal assistance. I wouldn't quite call it help. The lawyers have written threatening letters, but it hasn't changed a thing. I'm really not looking forward to an expensive, prolonged legal battle," he sighed.

"Well, I plan to make a strong pitch, though I don't know how much good it will do. On the one hand, I'm trying to audit the city's financial records so I can successfully prevail with my legal action against them. And, on the other hand, I'm calling them to task for their proposed takeover of this property to increase the city's tax revenues. It might not sell."

"When's the trial? I mean this thing has dragged on for several years?'

"The legal process is slow. Once I get the city's financial records, it could be any time after that. Oh, there'll be a mandatory settlement conference, but the city wants to settle for too little."

Dan thought about what David had said and whether the attorney should stand up for him. "You speaking on my behalf would be like stealing your neighbor's cow then suing them because the cow couldn't produce milk. But, you know, screw it. I'll take any help I can get. I think you should do it."

Before David could respond to that unfavorable analogy, the kitchen door banged shut and moments later Debbie poked her head into the den. She had just returned from driving to her condo in Glendale for more clothes and her service revolver and badge. She was surprised to see David and shot her Dad a quizzical look.

Dan said, "Debbie, this is David Chase, an attorney in town. He wanted to see the vineyard. David, this is my daughter."

Debbie smiled and entered the room as David stood. "Are you the same David Chase that won a rather large award from the City of Los Angeles on behalf of an injured police officer?"

"The same. How'd you know about that?" he asked with a perplexed look as he shook her hand.

"I'm a police officer with LAPD. You're a hero at work." David looked at Dan, wondering why he failed to mention his beautiful and intelligent daughter before.

"I'm so pleased to meet you, Debbie. We've been so caught up in town politics that your father hasn't had a chance to mention you."

Debbie glanced at her dad and simply shook her head. Finally, she said, "Dad has a lot on his mind right now. He's done so much for this community, now they're rewarding him by taking over his land."

"We're just discussing that," Dan said, "David has offered to speak at the council meeting next Wednesday."

"From what I hear," Debbie said, "you are lucky to have him on your side. By the way, Dad, what's that case of pinot reserve doing on the back porch?"

"That's for David to take home. A little thank-you gift for offering to help. I hope you enjoy it," Dan said looking at David.

"That's way too generous of you. The help comes without strings, but I'll gladly take your wine, anyway," he chuckled and then said, sincerely, "Thank you, really. And I should be running along now. Elaine will be home soon. Nice to meet you, Debbie. Dan, see you on Wednesday." He turned to leave and Dan followed him out to his car. David opened his trunk and carefully placed the wine inside.

Teddy Perkins had been following Elaine Chase's car ever since she left Vista. He followed her to the horse stables and waited on the road outside the fancy entrance until she left. Then he followed her into San Luis Obispo. Again he parked and watched her walk into an upscale restaurant in the revitalized area of the city. He glanced at his watch. Two o'clock. He didn't have to report for regular duty until eleven, so he had plenty of time to get this job done.

This wasn't the first time Chief Riley had enlisted Teddy's off duty help. Sometimes he was paid a generous sum for his services, and sometimes he did it just to give the Chief ammunition for the continuous political battles in Vista. His assignments usually consisted of following errant husbands and wives and catching them in the act. He had once followed a city council member to his girlfriend's house in Sandy Beach and took pictures of them in a passionate embrace on her terrace. After a visit from the Chief, the council member had changed his vote in favor of a pay raise for the police department.

This assignment was a little different. He had to follow Elaine Chase and keep his eye open for any signs of impaired driving. If she showed any sloppy driving, he was supposed to call the officer on duty and have her stopped as she turned off Highway One toward the town.

Officer Perkins sat in his warm car as Elaine enjoyed a late lunch. He hoped it was a wet lunch. Unfortunately for him, however, the warmth of the car lulled him to sleep. Meanwhile, Elaine was in the restaurant's bar drinking an expensive Chardonnay. After her third glass, the world seemed to be a little more settled.

Teddy was shocked awake by a knock on his window. He bolted upright and rubbed his eyes. Slowly he rolled the window down and said, "Hello, officer. I guess I fell asleep."

"License and Registration, please," the burly officer said.

"Actually, I'm on duty under orders from Chief Riley, my boss in Vista."

"I know the man. Let's see your badge," he demanded, not impressed.

Teddy reached around to his back pocket and pulled out his wallet. He flipped it open and flashed his badge. "Does that square things?" he said.

"I'm not real happy you are here on official duty in an unmarked car. But, I won't make a big deal about it. Next time give us a heads up."

With that, the officer waved and walked back to his cruiser. Teddy let out a sigh of relief. *That could have been a mess.* He immediately checked his watch and cursed aloud. It was four o'clock and he'd been sitting there for two hours! He hurriedly looked around the parking lot for Elaine's car and was relieved when he saw it still parked in the same place. He smiled to himself, thinking she must be sucking them down.

Moments later, he saw the door of the restaurant open and Elaine slowly walk out into the sunlight. She put on dark glasses to cut the glare and started down the stairs leading to the parking lot. She kept a firm hand on the railing and took the steps one at a time. Teddy could tell she was lit like a candle. She walked slowly and weaved slightly as she headed to her car. He was tempted to stop her for public drunkenness just to keep her from driving. But, he decided it was better to avoid any face-to-face confrontations. She may, after all, wonder why an off-duty Vista cop happened to be in SLO Town.

No. He would watch and wait. If there was any evidence of danger to her or others she was toast. DUI for sure. But, she seemed to drive just fine as he followed her back to the riding stables. He watched as the boy, talking excitedly, climbed into the car. They went back up the 101 for a short distance then turned onto Highway One. The Chief had told Teddy to call as soon as she was on Highway One. Teddy picked up his cell phone from the seat next to him and speed dialed the Chief's number. The Chief must have been waiting for his call because he picked up after only one ring.

"Yes, Teddy, what's up?" the Chief asked without even saying hello.

"How'd you know it was me?" Teddy asked.

"Caller ID, you knucklehead. Where are you?"

"We just turned onto Highway One. She took the kid to riding school then spent the rest of the afternoon in the bar at a fancy restaurant."

"So, is she impaired or not?"

"That's a positive. What's the saying, drunker than a skunk?"

"Okay. Here's what you do. Call Alvarez. Tell him you spotted the car heading to Vista. He doesn't have to know why you know that. Understood?"

"Mum's the word, boss. You want me to call him now even before she's turned off One?"

"Jesus, Teddy, you scare me sometimes. Just do what you're told," he thought for a second before amending himself, "Okay, you're right. Call Alvarez as soon as she turns off One to Vista. Have him stop her and tell him to call me if he thinks she's juiced. Why call me? Because you think it's someone important and the Chief would want to know. There, I asked and answered your next question."

"Okay, but can't I say I recognized the car from a previous stop and tell him who it is?"

"What did I just say? Follow orders. I don't want this to look like a set-up. Alvarez would ask why you don't stop the driver yourself since you know who it is. Don't tell Alvarez anything more than you have to."

"Ten four boss. Understood."

Just before Elaine turned off Highway One, Teddy called Alvarez and gave him the make, model, and license plate of her car. The on duty cop said he was in the area and would take care of it. He didn't ask any follow-up questions. He was just happy to have some excitement in his day. Once Elaine entered the outskirts of the town, Alvarez was right behind her. She drove slowly, a sure sign of a drunk driver, Alvarez reckoned. He flashed his light and touched the siren just enough to get her attention. She was about three blocks from home.

As he approached the car on the driver side, she rolled down her window.

"Hands where I can see them ma'am. Please."

Elaine put both hands on the steering wheel. "Now, with your right hand reach into your purse and retrieve your license. Then step out of the vehicle and follow me to the back of the car. Young man, we'll be just a minute. Please stay in the car," he said to Davis as he leaned into the car.

Elaine did as she was told. Alvarez took her license and noted her name and address. When they arrived at the back of her car, he informed her that he had suspected she was driving under the influence. He had her do a series of tests: finger to nose, serial 7 subtraction from 100, and walk in a straight line. She flunked gracefully.

"Officer, I had several glasses of wine in San Luis Obispo. That was an hour ago. I feel fine right now," she smiled, trying to make her case.

Alvarez looked at her, slightly perplexed. Knowing who she was, he wondered if he should do a breathalyzer test and risk it being thrown out in court, or should he call the Chief. Alvarez remembered his conversation with Teddy and decided to call the Chief.

"Stay here," he said to Elaine. "I'm going to my car and will be back in a minute." So far, no cars had driven by to gawk at Elaine and she was thankful for that.

Alvarez called from his cell, avoiding the police communication system. When the Chief answered, he explained what had taken place and that he was calling to inform him of the situation, as a courtesy. Secretly, he wanted no part of busting this lady in front of her son.

"Is she being cooperative?" the Chief asked.

"Not a problem. I just wonder how far I should take this. She lives only blocks from here and seems to hold her liquor well. No slurring."

"Do the breathalyzer and then call me back."

Alvarez called Debbie over to the passenger side of the car and gave her a hand held breathalyzer. He instructed her on what she had to do. At first she refused, as any good lawyer's wife would do. But when Alvarez said she failed the field sobriety test and he would have to take her to the station where blood would be drawn, she consented. After three tries, he got an average of .16%, twice the legal limit. He told her to return to the back of her car.

Alvarez got the Chief back on the line and said, "I got her at .16%. That's being generous. It could be higher."

"Okay. Get her husband's telephone number at home. I'll call him and have him meet us there. I'm five minutes away. Have her sit in the car. And take the keys."

"Will do, Chief."

The Chief arrived just before David Chase. The Chief sensed his angst and the two strolled away from the scene while Alvarez and Elaine sat in their vehicles. It was becoming quite a scene and would attract the attention of anyone passing by.

"Let's sit in my car," the Chief said to David.

When they were settled, the Chief said, "I'm sorry about this, but your wife's driving was cause for concern." He stopped to let this information sink in.

"Go on," David said.

"You know, she's been stopped before on several occasions and we've let it go. But this time it's a little different. This time she's with your son. The officer who made the stop was quite concerned."

"What's the bottom line here? Are you going to arrest her?" David asked, trying to convey a sense of control. He was pissed, but not at the Chief. He was pissed at his wife.

"I'll be honest with you, counselor. I've run your wife through our database and I got a lot of info on her. She has a previous DUI and a felony pled to a misdemeanor on a drug violation."

David tried not to wince as he was reminded of his wife's not so glamorous past. "So?" he asked.

"She did two hundred hours of community service to wipe the slate clean. Now, that's a nice deal in L.A., but it wouldn't be a pretty picture in the newspapers around here."

David stiffened his back and stared at the Chief. "Wait a second," he said, "What do the newspapers have to do with any of this?"

"Come on, counselor. You of all people should know that we post all arrests we make in the newspaper every week. This is a small town. Cal Lacey will be on my ass like white on rice to get the rest of the story. He would love to skewer the attorney that's suing the city when we're on the 'financial rocks.'" The Chief threw air quotes around his last statement.

David slid down in his seat, no longer the aggressor. He got the picture and knew this was a shake down. Frustrated he asked, "What do I have to do to keep this buried forever?"

The Chief stared at David, who recognized the look. It was the look of a man who was confidently pissing on his territory.

Finally, the Chief said, "Well, a lot of people work for the city of Vista. Their retirement funds, health care dollars, and workman's compensation are all at stake here. An expensive lawsuit, with the threat of a large judgment, is the last thing these people need."

"I understand," David said. "Is that it?"

"I'd add that it's also important for Vista to expand its economic base with the vineyard."

David's nod was barely perceptible. "How do we get everyone home?"

The Chief opened his door and said, "You drive your son home and I will follow your wife. Alvarez needs to get back to work."

Chapter Thirteen

An old Toyota pick-up truck sped along Interstate 40 heading to Barstow and would soon go north onto Highway 101. Sticking out of the bed of the truck was a beat up surfboard. Inside the cab were three young men in their early twenties sporting baseball caps and some kind of facial hair. They appeared to be surfer dudes heading west to hit the California beaches, but appearances are often deceiving. Not more than eight days ago, two of these same men had been driving a green, biofuel car, instead of a Toyota truck, heading in the same direction. Inside a chrome box attached to the truck bed were three gas driven chain saws, containers of gasoline, and three pairs of night vision goggles.

The three young men had all graduated from American universities, where they had been exposed to a filtered picture of America by liberal, hand-wringing professors. The semblance of balance in political discourse by the professorial elite on American campuses had all but disappeared in the late sixties. As a result of the new, myopic, and biased historical analysis propagated by writers and scholars, Americans were to blame for all the bad things in the world. Most especially, they were guilty of arrogant environmental abuses by not signing the Kyoto treaty and guilty of their failure to recognize the central role humans play in climate change. For the academic elite, the indoctrination into this liberal way of thinking was complete when a student became active in environmental causes. Some students were more active than others. The three in the green truck heading to Vista Del Mar would be considered very active. More precisely, their approach to environmental causes could best be described as zealotry.

In fact, they practiced their environmentalism with such zeal that it was said they belonged to the *religion* of environmentalism. As such, the ends justified the means for them, and sacrifices had to be made for the greater good. For these three, the driver of the truck was their self appointed leader. Although he graduated from a small college in Arizona, he was not an American citizen. He came to America on a student visa from Morocco and never returned back to his home country. The three men didn't like to call themselves terrorists, but, rather, preferred to be identified as environmental freedom fighters. The FBI called them eco-terrorists.

Two occupants in the truck had been quite thrilled with themselves after they burned down Hector and Dolores's garage and house. That is, they were thrilled until they found out about the two dead bodies. The plan was not to harm anyone and the fire was supposed to send a message to the owner. However, the reliable source who told them that the occupants of the house would be in Fresno had obviously been wrong. The leader, Rabat, was most philosophical about the incident and recovered from his guilt quickly. As far as he was concerned, there were two less infidels in the world. Under the guise of saving the environment, he could help destroy Western capitalism and, along with it, kill infidels when necessary. San Diego, his partner, had not been so quick to recover. However, once he considered the possible consequences of being charged with first-degree murder, his concern had rapidly shifted away from the dead people to saving his own skin. The three in the truck felt that going back to the scene of the crime this early seemed risky, but their leader assured them it was necessary.

"I am getting tired of driving," Rabat said to San Diego and Denver. Eco-terrorists were careful not to use their real names, preferring to use the city of their birth.

"I'll take over in Barstow. I know the road well from there to Vista," said San Diego, who was sitting in the passenger seat. He was the smallest of the three, and at 5'9" he did not present an imposing physical presence.

"Okay," Rabat said, then slammed his fist on the steering wheel. "How could I....we...be so stupid to fill gasoline can with corn gas. They are going to trace it so easily."

His comments weren't entirely directed at himself. He also directed them to San Diego, who was with him during the arson. San Diego didn't answer and kept staring straight ahead. Finally, he said, "Relax, you camel jockey. No one is investigating anything at this time. As far as the police department at Vista is concerned, this was an accident."

"But, you said they know about special gas? And don't call me camel jockey again, you infidel!" Rabat was definitely pissed. Of course, his invectives about the Jewish and Christian infidels were hurled all the time without any second thoughts.

"That's easy," said Denver, who wanted to put his two cents into the conversation. "The arson investigators tested for it."

"Exactly. They started already investigating," said Rabat.

"Look, they'll be scratching their heads over how anyone could be so stupid as to use E85. They'll think a bunch of star struck, wannabe ecoterrorist amateurs did this. We've never used anything but regular gasoline before," Denver said.

"If raghead over there stuck to orders and didn't throw the gas on the house, we wouldn't be having this conversation. We were ordered to burn the garage," San Diego quipped. "I'm just sayin' the cops aren't investigating. They think the fire was an accident is all. I got that on good authority."

San Diego was riding in the passenger seat with Denver in the middle. Rabat tried to rap San Diego in the ear for his last comment, but he was stopped by Denver who was by far the biggest of the three. Denver had been an offensive lineman on his college football team.

"Why we doing this anyway?" asked Rabat, settling down after an elbow in the side by Denver. "What does a grape vineyard have to do with improving the environment?"

"The boss wants us do this job because there are beaucoup bucks coming into the till. It well help pay for other jobs that will further our cause. Consider this a fundraiser. Anyway, once we finish tonight we won't see this vineyard again," said San Diego.

The three eco-terrorists seemed somewhat placated now that their mission would soon end and they would earn a lot of money to keep things going. When they arrived in Barstow they gassed up and San Diego took over the driving. It was four o'clock on a Sunday afternoon and the roads weren't that crowded, considering it was Labor Day weekend. As the sun set in the West, Rabat nodded off and Denver kept shoving him toward the door whenever his head rolled onto his shoulder.

Seven hours and one or two more pit stops later, the trio arrived in San Luis Obispo. They turned onto Highway One and headed north. The remainder of the trip to the vineyard in Vista was uneventful and the road was nearly empty. When they arrived at the eastern border of the vineyard, they made a u-turn and parked off the road under a tree. They were at the farthest southern point of the vineyard from Vista Del Mar. The entrance where they had gone the previous week was up the road toward Vista by at least a half mile.

Using latex gloves, San Diego removed the surfboard and stood it upright alongside the tailgate. If anyone drove by, they would think that some crazy surfers were getting a jump on Labor Day. He then opened the tool box and removed the gear inside. Each donned a black sweatshirt, latex gloves, and then blackened their faces. Night vision goggles were strapped to their heads over their baseball hats. They had tested and filled each fuel reservoir in their saws before they left Arizona.

"You get over fence, Denver. I pass you saws," Rabat announced. Because of his worldly airs, having come from outside the United States, Rabat always assumed himself to be in charge.

Denver looked at him, about to say something, then thought better of it. He hopped over the fence and Rabat began passing over the saws and gasoline containers. In the time it took for all the equipment and men to cross onto the property, no cars had driven by. There was plenty of ambient light for the goggles to outline the vines.

"The way to cut the vines is about a foot above the ground. No dogs on this property, so we have free reign. If you see someone, shut down immediately and haul ass to the truck. Understood?" San Diego asked.

"Don't get caught. Do many vines as you can, don't get far from road," Rabat added.

"You know for such a snob, you really are a dumb shit, Rabat," Denver said, unable to contain himself any longer. With that he pulled the cord on his saw and started down a row, slicing the vine's trunks in half as easily as if they were balsa wood. The others followed and the noise sounded like loggers cutting down a forest.

Felipe hadn't been able to sleep. The bunkhouse was warm enough, but he lay awake worrying about his wife, who was about to have a baby in Mexico. He hadn't seen her in two months and was anxiously waiting for her to deliver. He had called earlier in the day and was told she was having cramps. This was going to be their first baby and Felipe was more nervous than his wife seemed to be. He felt like calling again from the cell phone Carlos lent him, but thought he would disturb the other workers. He knew that picking grapes by hand was hard work and that the men needed their rest. He glanced at the illuminated clock on the wall and saw it was after midnight. The worrying about his wife and constant snoring was starting to make him feel claustrophobic, so he decided to go for a walk. He kicked on his boots, grabbed his cell phone, and headed outside.

As he stepped outside he started in the direction of the vineyards away from the winery. The air had a pleasant chill but he was okay with just a tee shirt. As he walked up the rows, he began to hear a noise that repeatedly rose and fell. It almost sounded like the saws he used when he worked as a tree trimmer before he joined Carlos' crew. Curious, he trotted forward toward the eastern edge of the vineyard. Each step brought the sound louder and louder. Finally, he knelt down behind a vine where he was near enough to see some shadows moving and the sparks flying from the saws like fireworks. He could see three hombres dressed in black. This was not good, and he stole away unnoticed. He raced to the main house where Carlos was sleeping.

He banged on the kitchen door and shouted Carlos' name. Moments later, Carlos appeared at the back door shushing him. Carlos thought Felipe's wife had her baby and he was excited. After he calmed him down and found out what was bothering him, Carlos raced upstairs to Dan's room.

"What is it?" Dan asked. He was accustomed to emergency calls and was instantly awake. While he listened to Carlos retell what he heard, he dressed. Debbie, who had heard the loud voices speaking Spanish, was already dressed and waiting in the hallway. She had strapped on her sidearm as a precaution. With Felipe leading the way, the three headed back to the vineyard.

Once outside, Felipe gestured for everyone to stop and listen. They looked at each other as the low buzzing sound was obvious. Dan ran to one of the winery buildings and flipped a switch that turned on all the lights. The vineyard was immediately illuminated, and just as immediately the chain saw noise stopped.

The three followed Felipe to the outer reaches of the vineyard, where he guessed the noise had originated. Felipe suddenly ran ahead and, moments later, shouted out in Spanish, "The vines have been cut." When the three arrived at the outer reaches of the vineyard, they were stunned at what they saw.

Row after row of vines had been cut across their trunk about a foot above the ground. Dan did a quick take and estimated about three acres of vines had been destroyed. Felipe, who had raced forward in hopes of catching the perpetrators, ran back. "Tres hombres!" he shouted, "Green Machina!"

Debbie calmed him down before she asked about what exactly he saw. He told her a green truck had driven away with three men in it. He couldn't name the make of the truck, only that it was a pickup with a big tool box in the back. Debbie hurried forward on her own, keeping her right hand rested on her side arm as she went. When she reached the border of her Dad's property, she gazed out on the road. Along the parking strip under the shadows of a tree was a surfboard. She climbed over and carefully searched the ground around the tree as best she could with the limited light from the vineyard. She found nothing other than multiple tire tracks. She understood the need to return during daylight and make a more thorough search.

When she went to retrieve the surfboard, she noticed a latex glove on the ground next to it. Debbie placed the glove in her pocket and passed the surfboard over the fence. She then scrambled over to the other side where she searched up and down along the fence. She was about to give up when she caught site of a black object in the weeds along the fence. She was about 50 feet further north from where she crossed the fence to retrieve the surfboard.

Debbie was surprised at what she found. She called out, "Dad, over here! I think I found something."

Dan came running up with Carlos not far behind. "What is it?" he asked.

She handed her father a pair of night vision goggles. He turned toward the vineyard lighting to inspect the goggles. After several moments, he said, "These are generation III night vision goggles," he pointed to a small insignia, "See, stamped right here, U.S. Air Force. Way too much for night work to cut grape vines." He turned them over in his hands a little longer and then said, "I wish we had these in Vietnam."

Debbie was surprised. She never heard her father mention Vietnam in the context of his military experience. "What do you make of this?" Debbie asked as she handed over a dark green baseball hat with bold black letters spelling FEN on the front.

Dan inspected the hat while again facing the vineyard lights. "I don't know. Never heard of FEN before. When we get back let's Google it. Anything else?"

"I found a surfboard and a rubber latex glove. The board may have belonged to the perps or it may have been left there accidentally by a surfer. It's a cheap one sold by a shop in Vista Del Mar," she said as she pointed to a sticker identifying the seller as *Shop and Surf.*

"Bring it. No one surfs down on that beach anymore. Especially not locals. I'm guessing it belongs to the assholes that did this."

Dan spent the next twenty minutes inspecting the damage. Fortunately, the grapes had already been picked in what looked like three acres of destruction. He would have Carlos' crew clean it up and save the vines for propagation; the stumps could be grafted and in three years, when the vines matured, he could still harvest here again. But, that fact hardly quelled his anger at the moment. In all his time at the vineyard -- in all the time his family had owned it, for that matter -- nothing even remotely similar to this had ever happened. This was pure vandalism and aimed at getting him to cough up his vineyard. He was sure someone in town was behind this and cynically wondered if anyone there could be trusted.

When they arrived home, Debbie sat at the computer and Carlos went to bed. It was three o'clock in the morning when Dan called the Vista police to notify them of the vandalism. Knowing how Chief Riley handled an obvious arson case, he had no confidence that a thorough investigation of this incident would take place. Still, for the purposes of insurance coverage, he had to report it. The dispatcher at the station said they would send a car some time in the next hour.

Clearly frustrated, Dan asked Debbie if she found anything about FEN on Google.

Debbie smiled and said in a sympathetic tone, "I think I did. Literally, a "fen" is a swamp or marsh, like in Boston. The Red Sox play in Fenway Park near the fens in Boston. But, more than likely, we are dealing with an acronym. I found one organization called Free Earth Now, which is an activist environmental group. I cruised their web site. They are home based in, are you ready for this, Flagstaff Arizona."

"That does sound promising. Any other references to them on the internet?"

Debbie quickly punched in some keys and pulled up a website. She said, "There is one article in a Phoenix newspaper about a fire at a federal wild horse facility in northern Arizona. FEN denied anything to do with that. Here's a quote by Gerald Rains, the leader and founder of FEN, 'We are not an ALF group that destroys. Our mission is educating people on the environment. No follow up articles.'"

"ALF?" Dan queried.

"Animal Liberation Front. They have been active in Oregon and Washington with arson of both private research facilities and federal installations. Some of the members of that group have been caught, convicted, and jailed."

Looking around, Dan said, "We certainly have a lot of physical evidence here. Can we trust turning it over to Riley? He's been sitting on his ass over this up to now."

"We've got flimsy or circumstantial evidence of people from another State involved in this. It could be something the FBI might be interested in. I worked with an agent in Los Angeles on several matters and she might be helpful. She's not your typical territorial fed agent."

As if to forestall her father's doubts, she said, "Cooperation among agencies is much better since Homeland Security and 9/11."

"I've read that, but I didn't believe it. I do want to learn more about these night vision goggles. I think I'll call Fred Lesley. He keeps up with those things."

"Who's Fred?'

"He was in my outfit in the SEALS."

"What's he doing now?" Debbie asked.

"He bummed around a lot after getting out of the service, couldn't keep a job. Several years ago I complained to him about the air service here. Since he was already a commercial pilot, he got some financial help from me and others and started a charter business in San Luis Obispo. It has literally taken off."

"And he knows about night vision goggles?"

"He keeps up with military happenings. Doesn't want to get caught transporting stolen property."

Debbie was silent. She was struck, once again, by how little she knew her father. She was piqued more at herself for not keeping in touch with him than with his lack of communication.

"Do you see him often?"

"We get together about every other month. Have dinner or play golf. That's bad for me because he's a scratch golfer. He was on his college golf team," Dan chuckled. He was lucky to break a hundred and that was on the good days. "He flies me to Los Angeles when I go there. It's great. No fuss. Lands at Burbank, is always there when I want to leave."

Dan looked out the window. He heard a piece of machinery at the winery crank up. The crew was preparing to head out and clean up the mess left by the 'tres hombres.' The fire last week had left a bitter taste in his mouth. And now this. He vowed to fight even harder to find out who was behind these despicable crimes.

Chapter Fourteen

Dan and Debbie had been up for hours, but neither felt like going back to bed. The patrol officer from the VDMPD came by after sunrise to assess the damage and take statements from them. He didn't seem interested in pursuing the investigation and was not willing to concede that the fire a week ago and this episode were connected. The truck would be long gone and, without more complete identification, he wouldn't call the CHP. Since it was Labor Day, he wouldn't bother the Chief unless he himself called in to check up on things.

After he left, Debbie shook her head and threw up her hands in frustration. She walked over to her Dad and hugged him sideways. "Let's have breakfast. Daddy, you make the toast and coffee and I'll cook an omelet."

Dan was pleased that his daughter had warmed to him over the past several days. He had gone from "Father" to "Dad" and now to "Daddy." Maybe this tragedy was bringing them together. Or was she beginning to realize that it was time to get over the past? In either case, it seemed like it was the two of them against the whole town, with the exception of David Davis. He would see on Wednesday the degree of the lawyer's commitment.

Debbie went to the refrigerator and found five eggs, mushrooms, a bell pepper, and onion. Soon she was sautéing the vegetables in a fry pan laced with olive oil. She whisked together, in a separate bowl, five eggs, milk, and a pinch of salt. Delicious aromas filled the kitchen and awakened their sluggish appetites.

They ate their omelets and buttered toast in silence. While they were sipping their second cup of steaming coffe Debbie asked, "Well, where do we go from here?"

Dan looked out the back door and said, "I like your idea of getting the FBI involved but, before we do that, we should do some ground work. We need to find out if the *Shop and Surf* has any records of who bought the surfboard. Should the board be tested for fingerprints? How about testing the goggles? And the hat may have DNA on the sweat band."

"I thought I was the cop here," she laughed. "These guys may be careless, but they're not stupid. Probably didn't leave fingerprints and wore latex gloves. I forgot to tell you I found this by the surfboard." She reached into her pocket and produced the latex glove.

Dan looked at it and said, "We buy these by the box full for the office. Everything we do now is with gloves on. No surprise."

"Just to be safe, I'll give the board a preliminary dusting. If I find anything, maybe SLOPD can look for prints. They don't do any of that here."

"Meanwhile, I'll call Fred Lesley and see if he can shed some light on these goggles. They say U.S. Air force. Maybe they are used for night landings in dangerous places."

Debbie smiled at her dad, "You need this aggravation like a hole in the head. I'll change into something nice then go visit the surf shop. Does old Blinky still run the place?"

Blinky was an Australian surfer who came to Vista twenty years ago after retiring from his successful career in surfing competitions along the California coast and elsewhere. He had been a fixture in the city of Vista and knew everyone by their first name.

"Yes, Blinky is still here and doing great. Other than some skin cancers that pop up occasionally, he's the same as he's always been.

Laid back and still blinking." He got his nickname because he had an ocular tic that resulted in repeated blinking.

Dan went to his office and checked the time. He was sure Fred would be awake at 8:30 and, since he had recently divorced wife number two, he wouldn't be waking up anyone else. He was wrong on both counts.

A sleepy female voice said, "Who is it at this ungodly hour?"

Dan decided he would put on his formal voice and in deep, thoughtful tones said, "Dr. Miceli, is Fred there?"

Dan figured Fred was desperate for companionship because, without covering the phone, the raspy female voice shouted, "Hey Fred, wake up! There's some serious sounding doc on the phone."

After a period of rustling and yawning Fred said, "Doc what in the hell are you calling me in the middle of the night for? I was about to get some sweet loving."

"It didn't sound that way to me. I need your opinion. Okay?"

Shifting the phone in his hands, Fred rubbed his face several times and said, "Shoot. I'm ready."

Dan went on to describe the events that occurred in the middle of the night, including the recovery of the night vision goggles.

When Dan finished, Fred was sitting up in bed wide awake. "That sounds like some serious shit, ol'buddy. The Air Force has all kinds of night vision beside the pilot stuff, which this is not. They use night goggles for dismounted search and rescue, guys looking for downed pilots. Searching crash sites at night or possible aerial targets. Just like we did in Vietnam. Only this stuff is much better. By the way, this technology is restricted to the military and some police agencies. I mean generation III."

"So, how did some pain in the ass lowlifes get their hands on this stuff?' Dan asked.

"Easy. It's sold on the internet. A few Air Force enlistees in Mississippi stole goggles, sold them on the internet. It was easy. They used phony names to set up an account on Pay Pal. The buyer uses a phony name and deposits the money in the Pay Pal account. The stuff is then delivered to a P.O. Box in a private mailbox place. That box is registered to a person who has given a bogus name and identity."

"Then it can be traced to the post office anyway. With some sleuthing they can find the receiver. Can't they?'

"I suppose. The only thing is the goggles were sold to addresses outside the U.S.. Say the Cayman Islands, for example. Then they are shipped back or brought back here. It would be impossible to track down the buyer."

"It would seem to me that the people owning this stuff, or at least acquiring it, are pretty sophisticated. And mean business."

"Sounds like they mean business. Hey, by the way, I've been reading about the fire," Fred said somberly. "I was at your place enough times to have gotten to know Hector and Dolores pretty well. Especially Dolores' cooking. I assume the two events are connected, the fire and now this. Trying to run you out of town. Did we really go to Vietnam to preserve our freedom and end up with this shit?"

"That's a question for another time. How come you know so much about the theft of these goggles?"

"I read the Department of Justice web site. They post their convictions. People are always finding ways to scam you in this charter business. It lets me know what's out there. I don't transport anything unless I see the cargo and meet the sender."

"Well, this has been a big help. I feel more confident that the FBI should be involved. I'll let you get back to whatever you were doing. Don't be a stranger"

Dan hung up just in time for Debbie to walk by on her way into town. He told her about the goggles, but she was not surprised. She said she would call her contact at the FBI on Tuesday.

The drive into town was a welcome relief from the troubled night she had spent. It would be fun to see Blinky again. When she was a freshman in high school, he had been nice to her and helped her pick out her first surfboard. He even taught her how to ride the waves. She turned off Highway One and drove to the main part of town. It was nine o'clock when she arrived and some shops were opening for business, hoping to profit from the Labor Day visitors. Blinky's shop was on the main thoroughfare across the street from the beach. When she pulled up in front, he was dragging out surfboards on racks. She stopped and wrestled the surfboard out of her hatchback. It was almost six feet long.

After finally getting the board out, she looked up and Blinky was staring at her. Along with the eye tic, not much else had changed as far as she could remember. His sandy hair, which was still abundant, topped a tanned wrinkled red face with twinkling blue eyes. In his day he was a girl's dream, and Debbie felt how even now he could still stir some lady's heart.

"It's bloomin' Debbie," he nearly shouted. "Long time no see. We haven't 'ad such a good looking Sheila here in years."

Despite her best efforts, Debbie blushed. "Blinky, you amaze me. How can you remember me? We haven't seen each other for years. Not since I graduated high school."

"Ere, now, how could I forget that lovely face? What are you doing with that old fish board you got there? Sold a lot of them, I did, but stopped selling them a way back. Newer stuff now."

Without going into details, Debbie said it had been lost along the road bordering the vineyard. She wondered, since the name of his shop was on the board, if he know whose it was.

"Let me see it." He took the surfboard into the shop and laid it on a broad counter which was used precisely for that purpose. "This was a great board for this beach. Low rollers. Tame stuff for an expert like myself," he bragged.

"So you sold this one?"

"Quite. I'll show you something. What are you doin' now for your tucker?"

"Tucker?"

"Livin'," he said as he examined the board carefully.

"Now, don't get mad. I'm a cop. LAPD"

"Wish you were the chief of police here. The police will ticket anyone who might be five minutes over the meter. Makes business in town here 'ard. No one wants to park."

"Tickets are a great way to increase the city's revenue. Same stuff goes on in L.A. How's your business?" she asked, looking at the main boulevard that was empty even for a Labor Day weekend.

"Well, since they pulled a lot of the lifeguards and closed the north and south points of the bay we've 'ad a bad go. That's why they're trying to confiscate your dad's property," Blinky said, shaking his head. "Make money for the city. Anyway, I'm going to show you somethin' but keep it a secret."

"Ok. What is it?" she asked her curiosity aroused.

"Years ago people would steal boards off the beach and try to resell them here. So, to fox the bloody arseholes, I started me a numberin' system. I burned a number on 'ere along the rail. Look 'ere." The rail was the outer most portion of the board. "I left me glasses in the back. Can you read that?" he asked, pointing to the side of the board.

Debbie leaned down and read a number. "It's number 107."

Blinky left and went to the back of his store. Minutes later, he returned wearing his glasses and thumbing through a notebook. "Here it is. I sold this to Tad Morrow in 1998. Tad was killed in Fallujah with the Marines three years ago. Family still lives here but 'ave never been the same. Want their address?" Blinky asked with a saddened face.

"Gosh, I knew Tad. He was in the class behind me in high school."

"Great kid. Never gave me any trouble."

Debbie thanked Blinky and worked the surfboard back into the car. She drove down the main street then turned on J Avenue. Soon she turned off onto Spyglass road and stopped at a house that matched the address Blinky had given her. The first thing she noticed was a gold star emblem in the front room window. She shook her head, not relishing a visit on Labor Day to ask about a departed son's surfboard. She thought about leaving when an older woman stepped out on the front stoop and picked up the morning newspaper. She caught Debbie's eye and, rather than drive off, Debbie decided to get out of her car.

"Good morning," she said, "Are you Tad's mom?" she asked.

"Yes I am," she said proudly. "And who might you be?"

Debbie started up the concrete walkway to the front stoop. The pathway was bordered on either side with beds of alternating white and red Begonias. Beyond the beds was well-manicured grass. The house was a small cape cod with aluminum siding. Along the front were white roses all neatly deadheaded.

Debbie waited until she reached the stoop so she didn't have to raise her voice to identify herself. "I'm Debbie Miceli, Mrs. Morrow. I just wanted a moment of your time."

Betty Morrow looked at her and said, "Are you Dr. Miceli's daughter?"

"Yes, I am."

"I'm Betty and you must come in and sit down. My husband had a stroke recently and your dad saved his life. He also took care of my breast cancer. I'm ten years now without a problem. Come on in."

The city government may be up to mischief, she thought, but everyone else she meets is happy with her dad's work. Debbie followed Betty down a small hallway and then left into the living room. She was shown a seat and Betty left to get coffee and freshly baked blueberry muffins. Debbie looked at the gold star in the front window and suddenly realized she was not alone in the room. A man in a wheelchair and an Afghan spread out over his legs and lap was sitting near the window. She could not even hear him breathing, he was so quiet.

Soon Betty came back with a tray and three cups. She placed the tray on a coffee table and poured Debbie a cup. It was welcome after the long night and her post breakfast caffeine levels were dwindling.

When she saw Debbie looking at her husband, she said, "This is Horace. Sorry I didn't introduce you. After his stroke he hasn't talked much, but we communicate just fine. Horace, here's your cup with cream and sugar, just the way you like it."

Horace had not had a paralyzing stroke and took the coffee and smiled at his wife. "Who's this?" he said in a soft, raspy voice while looking at Debbie.

"That's Doctor Miceli's daughter. Your doctor." She turned to Debbie and went on to say, "When Horace had his stroke, your dad did an emergency carotid vein clean out," she said as she pointed to her left neck. He actually had a right carotid endarterectomy. Invariably, non-medical observers call arteries veins and point to the mirror image side of the patient.

They sat and talked awhile. Betty was dismayed at the way the town had turned against her father. She felt the tax revenue they collected was poorly managed, and getting more tax money was like adding fuel to a fire. Debbie wished that more people felt the way Betty did.

Debbie finally got the courage to ask the question she dreaded asking. "Do you remember what happened to Tad's surfboard?" She then went on to explain in limited detail why she was asking the question.

Betty and Horace looked at each other and then at the gold star. Betty cleared her throat. "We've been devastated with Tad's passing. But we know it was for a good cause. He joined the Marines after high school and was killed in Fallujah in 2005. The second time they entered the city. It was an accident really, but Tad's gone just the same. Horace sits and stares at that star all day." She was talking softly while wiping her eye. Debbie let her talk on despite her not answering the question.

Finally, when there seemed to be nothing more for her to say, Debbie asked "And the surfboard?"

By this time, Betty was dabbing both eyes. "I'm sorry," she said, "it's been three years and we haven't gotten over it yet." Finally, taking a deep breath and looking out the window she said, "I don't know. I know he sold it or gave it away at the end of the summer before he was inducted."

Debbie looked over at Horace who was quietly staring at the star. For the first time, she noticed tears in his eyes. Betty walked over to her husband and gave him a comforting hug. She leaned down as he whispered something to her in a soft voice. She stood up and walked back to her chair.

"I'd forgotten. My husband just reminded me what happened to the board. Tad gave it to Everett Riley. The Chief's son. I've lost track of him. He left for college and never came around again. Told Tad he was foolish to join the Marines. There was things that needed to be done at home. Home being the United States."

Chapter Fifteen

The 'tres hombres' were quiet and tired. They were also very worried, and at least one of them was pissed off. After clamoring over the fence and hurriedly reloading the truck, they scooted back down Highway One. The only problem was they had left evidence behind. San Diego was driving and it was difficult wiping off the blackening agent on his face while steering at the same time. He had visions of sitting in prison for the rest of his life for murder and arson as well as property destruction. None of this would have happened if it were not for Rabat, who was sitting in the middle of the cab next to him. He moved a little to his left so he wasn't touching the Moroccan.

Denver asked, "What's the plan now? Straight back to Arizona or do we hole up? I know that Mexican yelling back there saw the truck. Maybe the license plate."

"I know you went to college and played football. I don't know where you went to college, but did you ever graduate? I *told* you we switched out the plates from a guy I know in town. They can't trace us."

"You are ass hole, San Diego. They can trace us to Flagstaff and to your friend's car. FBI is not stupid."

"Blow it out your ass, Rabat. If it weren't for you, we wouldn't be in such deep shit. You're the one that burned the house. Now, you left the surfboard behind *and* the cap *and* the goggles! How long do you think it will be before they figure out who did it? Why didn't you just leave our names and addresses?!," San Diego said, banging the wheel with his open palm.

"Alright, let's settle down," Denver intoned. His physical presence, if nothing else, gave the other two pause. "Let's suppose they did identify the truck. Let's also suppose they called ahead. There may be police or CHP on the lookout for us down the road. What about pulling off the road and waiting a couple of hours? Then maybe turn around and go north and cross to the I-5 at 46. They won't expect that."

San Diego answered his query by doing precisely that. He turned left across the highway to a turnout that led to a picnic area. Fortunately for the three, the grounds were abandoned. When parked away from the road, behind a stand of trees, the three of them stepped out of the truck and stretched.

San Diego wasn't finished with Rabat. "That surfboard you so carelessly left behind was given to me by a high school buddy killed in Fallujah. I'm sure it can be traced to him."

"So? Another infidel killed in Muslim country. No loss."

Denver stepped in between the two before blows were thrown. "I didn't make the trip the first time. You guys are on the docket for that. Still, we are *all* in a pile of shit here. Let's cut the crap and use our heads. What's the next move?" he said, looking back and forth at each of his companions.

"First of all, kill the truck's light. Then we sit here for an hour and go back the way you said. Only, I don't want Rabat sitting next to me," San Diego said as he plunked down on a picnic bench.

Tuesday morning, the day after Labor Day, was as pleasant and mild as the day before. Debbie sat sipping a cup of warm coffee on the front porch. The ocean waves rumbling on the beach were soothing, and she felt relaxed. Off in the distance she could hear the men working at the winery, talking and singing along with songs from the portable radio that always seemed to be blaring away. The music was not intrusive, however, and many of the songs were the same ones she had heard during the years living at home.

Her thoughts turned to the investigation, which had so far turned up no evidence to suggest the fire was a conspiracy generated by some townspeople to scare her dad into selling his property. Tomorrow night, the city council was to meet and vote on the issue of eminent domain. Barring some last minute miracle, she knew how that vote was going to turn out. Only two people had signed on to defend her dad and they were not the city's political heavy hitters by any means. It's a wonder why more people are not on her dad's side, she asked herself. Everyone she ran into once was or is a patient of his and was very thankful for what he did. She had nearly lulled herself to sleep with these thoughts when the phone rang in the office. She raced into the living room down the hallway and got to the phone just before the message machine clicked on.

Nearly out of breath, she said, "Debbie Miceli speaking."

"Good morning, Debbie. This is Lt. Burt Mclemore calling. SLOPD."

"Yes?"

"I'm Tiffany's dad. You met her the other day in Sandy Beach?"

"Of course. I'm sorry. I didn't recognize your name. I didn't know Tiffany's last name. That doesn't sound so good coming from a police officer, does it?"

"Depends. Whatever you did, you made a friend out of her. Especially when you kept her trip to the rock concert a secret. I like Sean. He's been down a few times with her but not on his motorcycle. He knows I wouldn't like that. Anyway, she told me everything, which I appreciate. Her mother, on the other hand, wouldn't be so happy about it. But the reason I'm calling is to follow up on that. She called last night saying that Sean had told her about the vandalism at the vineyard Monday morning. He had heard it from his mother.

I don't know who *she* heard it from, but she does work for the police department there, so your guess is as good as mine."

"I have an idea who told her. But I want you to know that thanks to Tiffany's observations we know a green car, probably with Arizona license plates, was at the fire scene a week ago. The car undoubtedly runs on biofuel, since the fire accelerant was a biofuel. Early Monday morning a green pickup truck was seen leaving the vineyard with three men in it. They left behind physical evidence, but so far nothing that helps identify them."

"Is Riley working on this case?" Burt asked.

"Well, yes and no. He's investigating the fire but very slowly. He hasn't called us about the weekend vandalism. I'm not going to hold my breath on that." Debbie fought to keep the sarcasm out of her voice. She also wasn't ready to part with the information about the surfboard. With the Chief's intransigence about the fire being arson and his son a possible suspect, she wasn't about to be forthcoming.

There was a pause at the other end. "The Chief's a busy man I guess, but the real reason I'm calling is to invite you down here to go over some traffic camera pictures. My thought was that the three could escape north or south. Since they are most likely from Arizona, I figured south."

"What traffic cameras are you talking about? I know there is one at the 101 and 46 crossing, but that's north."

"The city has installed traffic cameras of the finest quality at the first stop light on Highway One just after the 101 turnoff. Lots of traffic there and we've had some collisions due to running red lights and speeding. I got the digital pictures from Sunday night to Monday at six a.m. downloaded on our playback computer. Actually, it's a new deal with DOT (Department of Transportation). They paid for the camera and have it connected in real time to the police and fire. They want to see if first responders get to the scene quicker with maybe better outcomes."

"That's our U.S. Government you're talking about." It wasn't a question but her voice conveyed disbelief. *Am I beginning to think like my dad?*

"The very same. But what's nice is it also helps apprehend hit and run drivers. All in all, it's a win win situation. Most traffic camera data is for ticketing, and that occurs long after the event."

"Sounds too good to be true."

"Doesn't it. The digital pictures are amazing, and since there are four cameras, one at each corner, you can see the car coming and going. Helps to read faces and license plates. You said the pickup truck's green, so we should be able to spot it."

"You don't have to ask me twice. I'm on my way."

"Do you know the address?" he asked.

"No, but I have a GPS in the car. If that doesn't get me there, I'll ask the nearest pedestrian," she laughed. "I went to high school in SLO Town, so I have a pretty good idea where the station is. I'll be there in about forty-five minutes."

Debbie's prediction was off by ten minutes when she noted that it took her thirty-five minutes to travel the twenty miles to the police station. The police department was located in a single story building designed to not look like a police station. It had slanted roofs and open courtyards for hallways. Debbie made her way to the front office and was directed to Lt. Mclemore's office in the back. As soon as she arrived, she was shown into the Lieutenant's office.

Burt Mclemore was tall, lean, and well dressed in a white shirt and red tie. A blue sports coat was draped over the back of his chair. He wore gray, gabardine pants and polished black shoes. Debbie figured he was ex-military. He looked all business and appeared very professional. But the expression on Lt. Mclemore's narrow face made Debbie feel she didn't look like what he had expected. The slight nod of approval and lifting of eyebrows gave her a hint of what he was thinking before she arrived. A dumpy, chunky, female cop with short hair.

After a longer than expected pause, he said, "So, here we are. It's a huge coincidence that we are meeting," he said. "If it wasn't for the fire and my daughter being nearby we would not be here. The random occurrences in life have always fascinated me. Coincidences are either accidental or planned. It's our job to decide which is which."

"Well, our meeting is definitely accidental. By a series of events we are here and hopefully it can lead to something."

"Yes. Come over here and I'll get you started on the search for the green truck. These cameras run continuously, one digital picture every second. That made it nice since we didn't have to tear up the streets placing triggers for the cameras."

The two sat down and he showed her how to advance the images by right clicking on the mouse and pressing "next." The images could be enlarged and/or zoomed in on. He had started with ten p.m. on Sunday night and they went through several minutes of images. The lieutenant then begged off to attend a meeting and said he would be back in two hours.

After he left, Debbie sighed, knowing full well she was in for a boring if not tedious day. She talked herself into believing it would go quickly because a green truck should be easy to spot, and rare.

That didn't happen. It took her over an hour to click through the pictures before she found the truck. It was at 11:09 on Sunday night. A green truck pulled up at the stoplight and stopped. She looked at the other camera images, since there were four at the intersection. After she completed her inspection, she was satisfied that this was the truck seen at the vineyard Sunday night. To her eye it appeared to be a green Toyota two door pickup truck with visible signs of wear. Not a new model. Debbie was excited about the clarity of the license plates, both front and back. She could see they were from Arizona. She printed the pictures and copied the numbers.

Lieutenant Mclemore had not returned yet, so she occupied her time reviewing images of Monday morning from the time the truck left the vineyard until six a.m. She didn't see the truck return through the intersection. She asked herself if the cameras could have missed the vehicle, since the pictures were taken a second at a time. "No, dummy, you've seen plenty of pictures and no car ever made it through the intersection in less than a second," was her mumbled response.

It was past two o'clock when Burt Mclemore breezed back into the office. He seemed cheerful and said his meeting had gone well.

"Did you find anything?" he asked. After she showed him the printout of the license number and truck, he went behind his desk and sat down.

"Unfortunately, I didn't get them returning. I've been through six hours of the after pictures," Debbie said. "Very few vehicles went by at that time of the morning."

"How come they aren't seen coming back? They tore off according to your eyewitness and headed south."

"The only thing I can figure is that they pulled over and waited before turning around and going up to 41 or 46 and crossing over to I-5 south."

Burt nodded his head in agreement. It made sense to do that in case someone called in the description of the truck. "Let me run these plates and see what we've got. I have a sneaking suspicion the plates aren't going to match. These guys seem too clever to mess up that way."

Debbie looked puzzled. "You're not in Arizona. How can you run the plates without going through an agency over there?"

"Easy. I have a website that's top notch for tracking cars in every state. Don't ask me how they do it. It's open to anyone. There are a lot of websites that brag about being able to identify licenses but most of them are useless. This one's great…most of the time."

From his desk computer he logged onto the web site he was touting and punched in the license plate number. Moments later he had a name, address, and make of the vehicle.

"Hah. Just as I thought. The license is bogus. The vehicle is registered to a Fred Simmons of Flagstaff. A Ford Taurus. Here's his telephone number."

Debbie marveled at how much more energetic Lt. Mclemore was about his work compared to Chief Riley. He looked like he was having fun. Moments later he was talking to Mrs. Simmons.

After a brief conversation, he put his hand over the receiver and said, "She's going out to check the car. It's parked behind her garage. Belongs to her son who is out of town. He lives in an apartment above the garage." Suddenly he put the phone back to his ear and listened. He wrote some things down then thanked her and hung up.

"Another coincidence, except this one is planned. Fred Simmons is on a two week retreat with his church group. But a lot of people at his church know he's out of town. I bet if we canvassed the parishioners we could find someone who took advantage of that knowledge. The plates are missing and Fred drives a Ford Taurus."

"At least we know the truck probably came from Flagstaff. I'm sure the person or persons who stole the plates plan to put them back on the car as soon as they can. What day is it? Tuesday," Debbie said, answering her own question. "They've had plenty of time to get back to Flagstaff."

"The night of the fire was the weekend before last. It won't do any good to search the traffic cams looking for the car that Tiffany saw. The cameras were down the night of the fire and on Saturday morning. Can't help you there. It looks like your investigation has to move to Arizona," the Lieutenant said smiling.

Debbie stood and stretched her back. She was tired of looking at the computer and said, "I have to be getting back. I can't tell you how much I appreciate what you've done. As it stands now, I agree that the investigation belongs in Arizona. Since Chief Riley doesn't seem interested, I'll try the FBI. Show them what I have, including these pictures I've printed out."

"Keep them. And the Agency is welcome to look at what we have here anytime. I think that's the smart thing to do. The whole situation is a mystery to me," the Lieutenant said. There was a pause as he appeared to be thinking. Finally, he said, "I haven't had lunch yet. Are you interested in joining me?"

Debbie wasn't about to bite on that. She appreciated what Lt. Mclemore had done, but she wasn't about to mislead him. She smiled and said, "That's awfully kind of you, but I must be getting back. I'll keep you updated. Say hello to Tiffany for me." Not waiting for a response, she waved and left the office.

That evening, after a dinner of roasted vegetables from the garden, jalapeno marinated flank steak, and fresh fruit for dessert, Debbie gathered her notes and sat down in the den with her dad. He was busy at his computer answering e-mails from old college and medical school friends. When she got his attention, he closed out his e-mails and smiled. They had not talked about the investigation during dinner, preferring to enjoy their food and talk afterwards.

"So what do you have? Tomorrow I am presenting my side of the eminent domain issue before the city council. I need ammunition to counter Ben Adams and his band of sycophants on the council. Take that back, there is one councilman supporting me, Jim Cravens."

Debbie looked at her father. She was glad there would be one member supporting his cause, but she didn't think it was enough. The city of Vista Del Mar was riding the wave heading toward taking over her dad's vineyard.

"I hope he stays that way," she said, "I've run into some of your grateful patients who are on your side. They are quiet about it, so don't get your hopes up. You may have to prevail in court when it's all said and done."

Dan looked at his daughter and smiled. She was never one to pull punches. "Let me hear how things have progressed on your end."

Debbie went on and told the whole story from beginning to end. She included the revelation about the surfboard being given to Everett Riley, the misdirection with the license plates, and her research into the FEN organization on the internet. She also summarized what she had learned about the night vision goggles from her father via Fred Lesley.

It took fifteen minutes to tell the story. She used it as an opportunity to polish her presentation in anticipation of the meeting with her FBI contact. When she was through, her father rubbed his chin.

Finally, he said, "This is far more complicated that I had imagined. The concept that someone would drive here from Arizona to damage my home, kill people, and cut down vines is hard to grasp. This isn't some wacko environmental group but a well planned operation to drive me from my property. If I didn't know better, I'd think this was masterminded by Chief Riley. What with that surfboard left behind that may belong to his son."

"Let's go with that scenario," Debbie said. "The Chief told me that he hadn't seen or talked to his son for some time. That doesn't fit. The presence of the surfboard gives strong indication that his son was involved. I doubt he would be acting without some tacit understanding from his dad. The Chief also told me his son was in Oregon the last time he had heard from him. Was he trying to throw me off? I don't know. Everything points to the criminals originating in Arizona. Still, it seems like a hard way to push you into selling your property uncontested."

"Clearly, the Chief has got his axes to grind. He wants this property sold for development. There has to be some hidden reason why this has become so damned important for someone to kill for it."

"I think the fire was supposed to scare you. The arsonists must have been told that Hector and Dolores were out of town. I doubt the Chief would condone any activity that could be potentially lethal. Still, there has to be more than a bunch of overeager city officials behind this. Perhaps the people at Richland International are involved. They stand to gain the most," Debbie said.

Dan thought about what Debbie said. If Richland was involved, then the investigation needed to be expanded. "It's time to get the FBI interested. When are you going to speak to them?"

"I plan to see my contact on Thursday. I'll call tomorrow and arrange a time for Thursday afternoon. Drive back on Friday or Saturday."

"Better yet. Have Fred fly you to Burbank and rent a car. It'll only take about an hour or so to get there and you miss all that traffic going into the city. He can fly you back later in the day. This is official vineyard business, so we'll expense it out," Dan brightened as he sensed something was happening to find the killers of Hector and Dolores.

"That sure would do it. I'll call Fred in the morning. I haven't met him, but I'm sure that won't be a problem since you're paying." Debbie smiled.

Chapter Sixteen

The Vista Del Mar City Council meetings were open to the public. The meeting room was on the first floor of a two story building situated up the street and, therefore, up the hill from the police station. The council meetings were scheduled to start at 7:00 p.m.,which gave everyone interested enough time to get home from work, have dinner, see the kids, and then make it to "city hall." The council members, for their part, routinely gathered for dinner and wine at *The Fun Thymes* to discuss the agenda. Of course, the bill was paid by the city treasury.

Dan was not looking forward to confronting the city's elected officials in an open forum. He had never formally talked to any of them about this issue. Politics was not his strong suit, and he felt it was futile to try and change people's minds. Besides the mayor, he knew there were three district council members who were in favor of the property transfer. Only Jim Cravens, who had called him some time ago, vowed to fight with all his effort to block what he felt was a mockery of the Constitution. Unfortunately, Dan didn't feel Cravens had much political clout since he recently retired to the area and had no business ties in the community. Regardless, he was desperate and could use all the help he could get.

Ordinarily, council meetings drew a dozen or so citizens, but when Dan had to hunt for a parking space down the hill from "city hall," he realized there was going to be a packed house. When he entered the meeting room, all the folded chairs were taken save for one in front, which he could see was being held by Debbie. Wouldn't it be prophetic, he muttered to himself, if he had to stand while being excoriated by the council members. He said hellos to a number of current or former patients. It seemed the whole room was staring at him as he worked his way over to his seat. Debbie was not smiling.

"Thanks for getting here early. I had a suspicion this would be crowded. Something fascinating about watching someone else on the hot seat. Always draws a crowd," Dan said gravely.

"Buck up, Daddy," Debbie said, patting her father on the thigh, "it's only the beginning of a long fight."

"Thanks, I needed to hear that," he chuckled, looking around. "Most of the people here have been patients of mine, but I don't detect any looks of sympathy on their faces. The attitude that doctors make too much money is still alive and well, even in the age of HMOs."

Suddenly, the side door opened and Ben Adams walked in followed by the city council members. Dan could name everyone, since at one time or another he had treated them for something. The only problem was that Jim Cravens was nowhere in sight. He reckoned this could he a bad omen. His eye caught movement at the door and Chief Riley strolled in dressed in full uniform, followed by someone he had never seen before. Immediately, seats became available for the two and they sat down. He looked around the room for David Chase, but he too was nowhere in sight. Dan was gripped with an awful feeling not unlike the feeling he had on his first search and rescue mission in Vietnam. Extreme fear and anticipation.

Ben Adams banged his gavel and the room immediately fell silent. Rev. Edward of the first Baptist Church said a prayer followed by low mumbling. The Mayor banged his gavel again.

"Before we get started, there are a few house-keeping chores and announcements. The sewer pipe leaking on First Street has been fixed at a cost of $90,000. The cost will be apportioned out on the next property tax bill on those people that are hooked to that sewage line." There were loud groans in the audience and Adams raised his gavel but then set it down when the audience quieted.

"The announcements are that Councilman Cravens is sick and will not attend this meeting. If it is necessary for him to cast his vote, he has given me the authority to vote for him. I don't vote on issues before the Council unless there is a tie. Secondly, I am pleased to announce the settlement of the Tran case which, all of you know, has been running for two years and eating up the city treasury with legal costs." Before Ben Adams could go on, there was an eruption of applause from the audience, which by now had swelled to over a 125 people. There was standing room only in the back.

The Mayor held up his hands toward the audience to gain silence. "The amount of the settlement is confidential, but I'll assure you it was highly favorable to the city. The money for the settlement came from selling an abandoned building on a small lot owned by Vista. At this time, I would like to introduce the buyer, Mr. Ted Schroeder, representing Richland International. The company hopes to construct an office building on the property for its own uses as well as for rental purposes. Mr. Schroeder will you please stand?" Ben Adams asked, nodding in the direction of the man sitting next to Chief Riley. There was light applause and then more mumbling. "What was Richland International doing in Vista Del Mar?" people were asking each other. Mr. Schroeder barely got out of his chair before he sat back down. His facial expression indicated that he wasn't pleased with the attention given to him. He glared over at Chief Riley.

What naked arrogance, Dan thought. Bring the people who want to take over his property right into the council meeting where the fate of the vineyard is to be decided.

Dan stood and said, "I thought this meeting was closed to people not living or doing business in Vista. Has that statute also been changed?" Dan asked in a sarcastic tone.

"Well, doctor, that should be evident to you. Mr. Schroeder represents the company that purchased the property. While it is still in escrow, he does have the right to attend meetings. I can refer you to the city's statutes if you'd like." Ben was red in the face, not used to people standing up to him.

Dan said nothing and sat down. "Round one goes to the town," he whispered into Debbie's ear.

"Now, if we can proceed to the main order of business. We are here tonight to discuss and vote on an issue of eminent domain. The city council feels that, because of financial shortcomings, economic development is better than bankruptcy. I have asked Jack Holmes to summarize the background and legal reasons why the city has the authority to use eminent domain laws in this situation. Jack, if you would."

Jack Holmes was the town's part-time legal counsel and as such appeared well dressed with neatly combed hair. He had a commanding, polished voice and his speech was laced with metaphors and analogies so that a lay audience could comprehend what he was saying; similar to what lawyers do when they address juries. If pushed, however, he could disarm any challenges from the floor by simply quoting the law in confusing legal terms.

He stood and said thank you, "The issue before us tonight is this: can the city take over the vineyard owned by Dr. Miceli? To do that in California, in the past, you would have to prove that it was for the public good. For an easement or road, railroad or some such reason. Now, since the U. S. Supreme Court has ruled on the case of Kelo vs. the City of New London, Connecticut, the indications to apply eminent domain have changed. Cities across America can use eminent domain laws more liberally, particularly as it applies to economic development. To meet California statutes to do this has not been easy, but we finally have done everything required."

At this point, he paused for effect. He was in his element. Almost like arguing in front of a jury. Something he was ordinarily not good at because there were those pesky lawyers to challenge him. That's why Jack Holmes did estate planning and contract law when he wasn't working for the city.

Holmes reckoned that no one from this audience would mount a serious challenge to his statements. Earlier, he was pleased when he learned that David Davis wasn't going to be present.

"The main roadblock has been the environmental impact study," he continued. "The study was completed two weeks ago, and I have reviewed it. It has not been given to all the parties involved since it is confidential. We did not get cooperation from Dr. Miceli about his business enterprise, so there *are* some assumptions. The report is based on data from comparable sized vineyards elsewhere."

Ben Adams stood and Jack Holmes sat down.

Adams said, "The environmental impact study clearly shows that development of the land proposed by Richland International would not be detrimental to the environment. Just one example cited in the study is water usage. In a vineyard of this size there is more than twice the water consumption compared to a 250 acre property with 500 homes. So, that alone is favorable since the coastal cities are often on water rations, what with global warming and climate change."

"If we don't know Dr. Miceli's water usage, how can we assume the study will hold up in the event of litigation?" Bill Evans asked, interrupting Adams.

"That is too far in the future and water is only one of the issues. There is electricity, carbon emission from homeowners, golf courses and their impact on the environment. All of that has to be reviewed and studied carefully. That's why the report has not been released. Tonight's vote is whether or not we should go forward. All I can say is the environmental impact study will not be a roadblock no matter what we decide. Now, if we can move on, I would like to introduce members of the audience who wish to speak out. There are ten that have signed up to speak in favor of the proposal and two against. One, of course, is Dr. Miceli and the other is Lila Parker, who as you all know is a native of Vista Del Mar."

"How long do we have to speak?" asked Cal Lacey, who was sitting in the front row.

"Cal, the allotted time is seven minutes for speakers for or against the issue. The exception is Dr. Miceli, who has as much time as he needs to respond to each of the speakers. I am timing you, so you will hear this gavel when your time is up."

"The first speaker will be Blinky McDougal who owns *Shop and Surf.*"

Blinky had parked himself in the middle seat, three rows back from the front and, after some moving and shuffling, he finally made it to the microphone in front of the council members. He cleared his throat and looked around at the people before him. He gave an embarrassed look at Debbie and Dan.

"I'd like to say that business is down. What with the parking tickets bein' tossed out like feathers and the beaches unguarded. Nothing against the Doc and Debbie. They are great people. Known them for a long time. But we need to get the finances in order. I don't know if confiscating someone else's property is the answer. I don't know. All I know is business is bad and something needs doin'." He turned and worked his way back to his chair. It was hardly a ringing endorsement for the proposal, but it was not against it either.

Debbie leaned into her father and whispered, "That's not the impression he gave me the other day. Maybe Riley makes it a point to ticket cars in front of his store to scare him up here."

"Wouldn't surprise me," Dan whispered back.

Ben Adams lightly tapped his gavel and said, "The next speaker will be Cal Lacey, who all of you know owns Vista's only newspaper."

Cal slowly stood up from the front row and dropped a notepad on his chair. He didn't want his speech to appear scripted. He had done enough demonstrating at Berkeley to know how to get a crowd on his side. True to form, he was wearing Birkenstock sandals, but tonight he had put on socks for the big occasion. The remainder of his outfit was straight out of the sixties: drab olive baggy pants and a black collared shirt. He glanced around the room and then focused on the people in front. He wanted to be sure he had their attention for this was going to be the defining speech of the evening, at least according to him.

"Since the unfortunate drowning of a visitor to Vista more than two years ago, this city or town or hamlet or whatever you want to call it has been in turmoil. The appearance from the outside is that we are negligent in not providing safety on our beaches. Is that the case or are we so swamped with commitments for the public good that we cannot even afford lifeguards?"

He had already burned two minutes and so far had said nothing. Ben Adams looked at the Marxist and twirled his index finger indicating for him to speed it up.

Cal nodded and said, "There comes a time when sacrifices for the common good must be made. It's hardly a sacrifice, in this case. A very profitable enterprise has existed in this town for nearly a hundred years. Yet, the town had not benefited from it. Dr. Miceli pays property taxes, alright, but only at Gans-Jarvis tax rates. He has farming subsidies and tax write-offs from the federal and state governments. He does not employ anyone from the town. His refusal to allow the public into his winery, which would attract tourist dollars, is reprehensible. His vineyard, in short, does not help the economic environment of Vista. It needs to be shut down to allow the city to develop the land for the needed replenishment of the public treasury. With that, I will sit down."

"Thanks for those words, Cal. You made it under the wire and gave an excellent summary of the problem and solution. Next, I have several citizens who are not business owners but who, nevertheless, are impacted by the city's financial problems. The next speaker is Beth Truehart. Beth, as you all know, is the elementary and middle school nurse. Beth, go ahead."

If there ever was a stereotypical school nurse it was Beth Truehart. A little overweight, a kind round face and sandy brown hair that ended above her shoulders. She constantly tossed her hair to emphasize her points. Beth was neither attractive nor unattractive. Right in the middle on the looks scale. She had a motherly, school marm tone to her voice.

"Thank you, Mr. Adams," she said as she tossed her hair. "School nursing has been a tradition for many years. School nurses are our children's safety net just as are the life guards at the beach. We see youngsters every day who are sick and should be seen by a doctor to forestall more serious problems later. Sadly, all that we see is not only physical illnesses, but some of our children have social booboos as well." She tossed her hair again.

Dan leaned into Debbie as said, "Here it comes. We need school nurses to advocate for children who come from unhappy homes."

Debbie leaned back into her dad's ear and said, "Don't be such a Neanderthal. There are children who need support outside the family."

"Yes. And that's called growing up." Debbie didn't respond. She looked around and saw people nearby were watching them wondering what they were saying.

Beth went on. "What do I mean by 'social booboos.' Well, I mean child abuse, broken families, alcohol or drugs in the home, parents not paying attention to their children. Without the school nurse, these booboos go untreated and we end up with unhappy youngsters who act out in the school room. Keep the school nurses," she finally said while tossing her hair and pumping her right fist. There was scattered light applause as she sat down.

"I think the school nurse job is safe for now," Ben Adams said as he pointed to the next speaker. It went on that way until all ten of the protagonists spoke. Mercifully, the speeches got shorter and shorter as the subject matter had been picked clean. There were very few revelations that would sway an audience one way or the other. Of course, the council members had already made up their minds anyway. The real purpose of the meeting was to take the community's pulse so that the elected officials didn't lose votes at the next election.

Ben went on, "At this time, there is one person who has signed up to speak against the proposal. There were two people, but David Davis called yesterday to say that he had to take his name off the list because he would be out of town today. Lila Parker is next. Lila and her husband own and operate *The Fun Thymes*. Lila."

Dan was disappointed and shook his head. *Why did I think I could trust Davis to be here?*

Lila was in her early thirties. Pert, attractive and dynamic, she confidently strode to the microphone. "Thank you, Mayor Adams. I've listened to each and every one of the speakers tonight. I won't comment except to disagree about everything that's been said. I am one of those social booboos that Beth talked about. I came from a home with 60's generation parents. Yes, right here in blissful Vista. I grew up here and lived in a home where drugs were freely used. Soon, I became a user and dropped out of high school."

She paused to gather herself while recalling a painful period in her life. "One night I was found on the beach stoned out of my mind. The police dumped me off at the hospital. That's where I met Dr. Miceli. I had no insurance, but he came in the middle of the night and sewed up a laceration on my arm. Don't ask me how I got it." She stopped and wiped a tear from her eye as she hesitated in revealing the events of her early, dreadful life.

"Take your time Lila," Ben said. "Since you're the only speaker for the doctor you can have as long as you like."

"Thank you, Mayor. You're still going to have to pay for your meals." The audience laughed heartily. The humorous moment settled Lila down and she continued.

"After I recovered in the hospital overnight, I was sent home by Dr.Miceli and told when to come back. At an office visit a week later, he talked to me about my life as he took out each suture. What I wanted to do with it and so forth. He must have seen something in me. Maybe a second daughter to his beautiful Debbie over there." She turned and smiled at Debbie, who nodded quietly.

"Anyhow, one thing led to another and he arranged and paid for me to attend a drug rehab program in Arizona, away from my sick family. After getting 'cleaned up,' I finished high school with straight A's. It was Dr. Miceli who came to my graduation, not my parents. After that, I received a scholarship from the Dominic Foundation and had my college tuition paid for. I later became a chef and married one of my classmates in cooking school. Without Dr. Miceli's help, I could not have afforded the restaurant we now own."

Ben Adams was worried about this sanctification of Dr.Miceli. He could tell the audience was enraptured by this young lady's story. He decided to speed up the process. While Lila was gathering herself to go on, he interrupted by saying, "Lila, I think I'm going to go back on my promise and ask you to wrap it up." He smiled like a dad indulging his daughter.

"Certainly," she smiled. "I think it's worth commenting about Cal Lacey's statements. The common good is just a euphemism for control. Now, we all know that Cal is just slightly to the left of Karl Marx. That's his right and we have free speech in this country. It's what allows us to gather here and inspect what our elected officials are doing. This is a wonderful country and we live in the greatest place on earth. Do we really want to see land confiscated from our citizens so arbitrarily? Is this really America? Isn't there another way to accomplish what we need? It would seem that our freedoms are under attack. Cal has been hammering about this in his newspaper for two years now. It's ironic that when he was at Berkeley doing LSD, ranting against his government and donating blood to the Vietcong, he was fighting against Dr. Miceli. Yes, while Cal was acting out in his safe environment of the college campus, Dr. Miceli was a Navy SEAL in Vietnam putting his life on the line for the good of this country. It would be a shame on us and a shame on this country if we thanked his brave efforts by stealing his land."

Lila's last statements had stilled the already quiet audience. They were captivated by this latest revelation. No one had known about Dr.Miceli's service in the Navy, not even the snoopy chief of police. Ben Adams was momentarily at a loss for words. In a matter of seconds, Lila made Cal Lacey look like Stalin and had elevated Dr. Miceli to a savior of the country.

After a rather loud and lengthy applause, Lila sat down. Cal Lacey stood and left the room. He had had enough and would be damned if he'd ever eat at her restaurant again. Of course, that would be stupid since it was far and away the best in town and she advertised in his newspaper. After he thought about it, he decided he would stop short of boycotting *The Fun Thymes*.

Ben Adams rose and watched Lila as she returned to her seat. "Thank you Lila for that emotional appeal. Now, it's time to hear from Dr. Miceli. Doctor, if you please," Ben said pointing toward the mircrophone.

Dan hesitated momentarily, getting all his thoughts together. Rather than address the elected officials, he turned to face the audience. He didn't use the microphone but spoke directly to the people, looking them in the eye.

"The Supreme Court of the United States of America. An unelected body of former lawyers, now jurists, have changed the U.S. Constitution regarding eminent domain. Now cities, towns, local and state governments can seize private property not only for public usage but also for private 'economic development.' Five jurists agreed to this and four did not. In a stroke of the pen, we have gone back to feudalism as it was practiced in 12th century England. In those days, the local lord would decide what you could and could not do with your property. In other words, five jurists have changed the Constitution and all that has evolved over that last hundreds of years."

Dan paused and wondered if he was wasting his time. The blank looks on the faces meant he wasn't getting his point across.

"You have heard tonight that an environmental report was favorable to the city for, of all things, water. Either the council members behind me are ignorant or they are incompetent. My vineyard is maintained by dry irrigation. That was the brilliance of my grandfather. He knew that grapes grown so close to the ocean could be irrigated from the moisture in the air. We have *never* water irrigated our grapes."

Dan heard the people behind him shifting in their chairs.

"Now, let me clarify something Lila mentioned. The Dominic Foundation. Dominic was my grandfather. When I took over the vineyard in 1988, I set up a foundation so that all the profits from the vineyard went to the foundation. That has been successful beyond my wildest expectations. Each year, the foundation distributes over a million dollars in either scholarships or grants to the hospital and clinic I maintain here in Vista. It has bought equipment for the hospital, allowed for the expansion of personnel and space, and kept us able to treat anyone, regardless of their ability to pay."

Now they were listening. The history of eminent domain law he discussed earlier couldn't compare to these revelations.

"We have a very modern hospital that employs nearly forty people. This makes it the largest private employer in Vista. Fully half of our patients come from *outside* Vista. That means we are bringing money to the city in the form of motel usage, restaurants, and other commerce.

"It's interesting that the panel behind me has not proposed cutting the budget instead. A budget, by the way, that has not had an independent audit since 2003. Why not? There are things that can be cut. For example, I have offered to have all sick school children seen in our walk-in clinic at no charge. It's always staffed by a nurse and a family practice doctor. That was met by this panel behind me with a cold shoulder. 'Actually drop a civil service position? No way. The public worker's union wouldn't like it,' our esteemed Mayor Adams said to me. Would they Chief?" Dan looked over at Chief Riley, the leader of the local chapter of the union. Riley turned beet red and said nothing.

"We live in a free and democratic society. But daily it is being challenged in the hope that there is something better down the road. It is up to us, ordinary citizens, to keep it free. Not with guns or bullets but with common sense. Look at the issues, demand what's right and fair from your elected officials or get rid of them. That's all I have to say."

Dan sat down to scattered applause. By no means did he feel like he reached the people. Not a very political presentation, but at least he felt better.

Ben Adams again rose and looked at Dan. "That was a rather scathing speech Doctor," he half chuckled and half frowned. "We are only trying to do what's best for the community."

Dan stood and replied, "Ben, you are doing what's best for Ben Adams. Tell the audience how you have arranged to be the realtor representing Richland International when they put up all those houses they plan to build on my property."

Dan realized, even as the city's leading surgeon, that he hadn't engendered a lot of good will with his quiet personality. He didn't socialize as much as he should and, outside of work, he had few friends. But there was one voice in the back of the room that said, "Well Mayor. Yes or no?"

Ben Adams obviously looked uncomfortable. He glanced in the direction of Chief Riley and Ted Schroeder, but both of them had left after Dan's speech. He was alone now and his answer might break or make the vote. The audience was restless, waiting for his response.

"Arrangements have been made by Richland International to use all the realtors in town to sell property. Not just me. There's Sam Mitchell, Mary Allen, and all the others."

"Wouldn't that be considered a conflict of interest?" Dan asked.

"It's common practice that whenever these eminent domain development issues evolve that the developer use local realtors. It's part of the economic redevelopment process. The money is going back into the community. We live here, eat here, buy our clothes here, so it makes sense for the developer to use us."

"So, let's carry this a little further, shall we? What you mean by 'economic development,' then, is a broader tax base so you can spend money on city government activity. This development doesn't actually bring in a business that produces anything. You want to do away with a profitable vineyard that benefits the town for increased tax revenues. Does that sound about right?"

Dan asked.

"Richland plans to build a resort with a golf course, maybe two, and some surrounding upscale homes. That will benefit the town in terms of jobs as well as revenue from taxes. Now, I think I'm going to call an end to the discussion. It's getting late."

"Mayor, I would like to make a motion to call for a vote," Bill Evans announced.

"I second the motion," said Mary Kelly.

"Okay. All in favor of the motion to pursue the city's right by eminent domain law to engage in the purchase of the Miceli vineyard say 'ay,'" the Mayor ordered. All the council members present said 'ay' and the motion carried. Ben Adams rang the gavel and adjourned the meeting. As Dan filed out with Debbie no one would look him in the eye.

Chapter Seventeen

The next morning, Debbie got up early, showered, and packed her bag with four days of clothing. She placed her service revolver in an outside side pocket of her canvas bag. She could hear her dad downstairs in the kitchen. Soon the smell of coffee was too much and she descended the stairs. They had driven home from the meeting the previous night in separate cars and had not talked when they arrived home, primarily because her dad went directly to his room. His contentious approach to the members of the council wasn't politically astute and it upset Debbie. But, it wasn't a surprise. He wasn't asking for help from the townspeople or the council; he was just informing them of their self indulgence.

Debbie grabbed her bag and purse and headed down the stairs. When she entered the kitchen her dad smiled. "All ready for the trip to L.A.?" he said.

"Yes. Fred is leaving in about two hours. Dad, about last night. I'm really sorry."

"So am I. I know I wasn't tactful, but they'd already made up their minds." He poured her a cup of coffee.

Debbie could see that her dad did not want to talk about the meeting or its consequences.

"I have a meeting with my FBI agent contact at one o'clock. I'll rent a car in Burbank. Hopefully, I'll be back by Saturday. Fred told me to call him and he would fly down whenever. He's sure devoted to you."

"Fred and I go back a long way. We've been through a lot together. Stuff you never forget," he scratched his head, "I guess now it's my little girl who is going out to fight my battles."

"Dad! I'm not your little girl anymore!"

"You'll always be my little girl. Don't you see? That's something between a dad and his daughter. It's special. It's a good thing."

"Alright, for now," Debbie smiled and kissed him on the cheek. She went to the cupboard for a bowl and filled it with Cheerios from the box on the kitchen table. Dan went over to the refrigerator and pulled out a carton of milk and set it on the table.

When Debbie finished eating, she took the bowl to the sink and washed it.

"I did some shopping yesterday and the kitchen is restocked with fresh bread, mozzarella, pancetta and all the things you like. Should take care of your inner man until I'm back," she said while wiping the bowl with a dish rag.

"When you present your findings to the FBI, if they agree there is something to what you have found, what then?"

"The sixty-four thousand dollar question. Ecoterrorism has not been high on the Agency's list since Clinton and Reno were running the show. There was the feeling that since they were not killing people and they were espousing a favorite liberal cause, the environment, they were pretty much not pursued. Not true under the current administration. Since 9/11 everyone gets looked at. We'll see how much looking they're willing to do."

"But you're not part of the Joint Terrorism Task Force are you?"

"No, but I'm assigned to the gang task force which is heavily partnered with the FBI. The agent I've been working with, Denise Weber, is eager to work with the LAPD. It's easy to see it's in their interest to cooperate with local authorities. It shows. Under Bratton, gang violence is down. I won't get any stonewalling on this investigation. It just depends on how interested they are. They have a lot on their plate."

"Do you have all the evidence and photos you've collected?" Dan asked as he stood and brought his cup to the sink.

"Yes, it's all organized and I've gone over the presentation several times."

It was getting close to seven o'clock and Dan was due in surgery at seven-thirty. He looked at his watch and said, "I gotta go. Look, I want you to be careful. Call me tonight and let me know how it went with Agent Weber. Okay?"

"Yes, Dad," she said in her best monotone. "I'm a cop now. Remember? You better get to work."

They hugged briefly then Dan left. Debbie finished packing and placed her suitcase and briefcase in the car. It was quarter to eight and she had to be at the airport in 45 minutes. She was taking a last look around in the house to be sure she hadn't forgotten anything when the phone rang.

"Miceli residence," she said.

"Hello, Debbie? It's Burt Mclemore SLOPD. Got a call from that family who had their son's license plate stolen. The mother said she was out checking on her son's car yesterday and the license plates are back. I don't know what it means, but I thought you'd like to know,"

"Well, that clinches it as far as I'm concerned. This is a crime that crosses state lines. It'll help me convince the FBI to get involved. Thanks Lieutenant. That's kind of you to keep me informed."

"No problem. Where are you going to meet with the FBI? You know they have agents in Santa Maria. The LA office has jurisdiction up here in SLO County."

"I know. Thanks. But I'm meeting with an agent in LA this afternoon."

"Then you better stop talking to me and get on the road."

"I'm on the road as soon as I hang up, but I'm driving only as far as SLO Town. Catching a plane with Fred Lesley."

"How'd you arrange that in such short notice? He's always booked up weeks ahead. He runs a great service. I'd fly with him anytime."

"My dad's an old friend. They were SEALS together in Vietnam. Don't ask me what they did there, but they're as tight as two people can get."

The Lieutenant paused. Then said in a low soft voice, "I'm sure there's a lot there that we'll never know about. You better get going."

Debbie hung up. *Male bonding! It's everywhere. They're worse than women.*

The flight to Burbank was as flawless as the clear weather. Debbie sat in the copilot seat and talked with Fred the entire trip. He proved to be a fountain of information about the FBI. He had plenty of contact with them in his current line of business and previously when he flew for the Coast Guard. When she arrived at the airport, she went to the Avis car rental counter and rented a Ford four door Escort. With her gear and sidearm in the trunk, she headed down the 405 freeway to Wilshire Boulevard until she came to an office building, which housed the FBI on the 10th -12th floors. She parked in a nearby parking garage and left her weapon in the trunk. After a guard searched her briefcase, she received clearance and rode the elevator to the 11th floor. It was twenty minutes before one o'clock.

She hunted down a machine dispensing sandwiches and chips. She decided on a ham and cheese with corn chips and settled in a lounge area to eat her lunch. At one o'clock, she walked to a warren of offices fronted by a secretary who checked her in. Debbie sat down in the waiting area and soon Denise appeared wearing blue slacks and a white, collared shirt with a plastic I.D. holder slung around her neck. Her auburn hair was pulled back with a clip. She wore lip gloss and no other makeup. Denise, like Debbie, had muscular arms, which were the result of intense weight training. At age thirty-six she was attractive with smooth, wrinkle free skin and bright blue eyes. Made up and out of uniform, Denise would sparkle at any party.

"Debbie, so good to see you," she said with a thin smile as the two hugged. "Sounds like you have had some troubles. Let's go into my office where we can talk."

They walked through a maze of small cubicles. If you stood up, you could be seen from across the large room. Once they reached Denise's cubicle, Debbie sat in the only other chair. She pulled out of a slender briefcase the material she had brought and began her story. Denise listened quietly, asking only an occasional question.

Debbie covered the story from beginning to end, including the latest information about the return of the license plates in Arizona.

"Well, it certainly sounds like you have some bad actors but little to go on. From what you say, it appears that someone is harassing your dad over the property issue. It doesn't smack of environmental terrorism. Why would they burn down a garage and a caretaker's house? There's no message there. The cap that was left behind during the second incident is an environmental group unknown to me. Let me check with the terror task force group and see what they have on it."

Debbie was disappointed. Instead of being excited over the information she had brought forward, Denise was as lukewarm as hour old coffee.

"When can I find out about the FEN organization?" Debbie asked.

"I'll have to chase down an agent who knows all about that stuff. I checked before you came, he's out of the office today. Back tomorrow. Why don't I speak to him and find out what he has. Where will you be staying?"

"I live in Glendale. Here's my number." Debbie reached into her briefcase and pulled out a card with her name and cell number on it. She jotted down her home telephone number and gave it to Denise.

"We don't have enough to go on to call it arson terrorism," Denise said sympathetically, sensing Debbie's disappointment. "Things could change if this FEN group, or whatever it may be, is on our watch list. For now, this appears to be a homicide handled locally. No need yet for us to get involved."

Debbie stood. It was nearly two-thirty and she had taken up a lot of Agent Weber's time. "Thanks Denise for making time. I'll be home tomorrow waiting for your call."

They said goodbye and Debbie headed to her car and then drove home. She fortunately beat the traffic to Glendale. When she arrived and opened the door to her condominium she suddenly realized how narrow and cramped her life had become compared to the open spaces of the vineyard. She left her bag and briefcase in the hallway, picked up the mail and went to the kitchen. She poured herself a glass of white wine and then plopped down on the sofa in her living room. The only letter that got her attention was the one from her boss, Lieutenant Hernandez, reminding her that she was expected back on duty on the 24th.

Debbie put the letter down and took a sip of wine. The clock on the desk said five o'clock. She looked around her small living room. She wondered if this was going to be it. Spend the rest of her life as an L.A. cop and live in a space bought and paid for by her father. The only family outside of her dad had been Hector and Dolores. Even their children, who were her closest friends growing up, were living their own lives. The emotion she experienced was not so much being lonely as it was being alone.

She shivered over the latter thought, got up, and walked to the kitchen where she poured the remaining wine down the sink. She wasn't in the mood to get mellow drinking fermented grape juice. *Would I rather be here or up at the vineyard trying to make a life in a quiet town?* She had to admit the life of a cop was exciting and had its rewards. A life as a lesbian cop in a male dominated atmosphere, however, did not appeal to her. *How many more dustups am I going to have with fellow officers over this issue?* She loved Margo like a sister, but some sort of long-term commitment was foolish.

Debbie was beginning to feel as though it was a mistake to have Margo move in with her. At the time, it was an in-your-face move directed at the people around her at work. Now, that decision appeared to Debbie to be stupid and as thoughtless as her dad's approach to politics.

She picked up her bag and went into the bedroom. The first thing she noted was an envelope on the bed resting against her pillow. Debbie walked over and picked it up. It was unsealed. The letter inside came as a total shock. Margo had decided that moving in with her and their relationship, in general, were causing problems at work. She said she loved Debbie but felt they should split up. Debbie checked in Margo's closet and shuddered when she say the empty coat rack. She was alone. Debbie sat down on the bed and wept.

Chapter Eighteen

Debbie woke up the next morning still wearing the clothes from yesterday. She had cried herself to sleep. Her first thoughts were that she had skipped dinner and was hungry. A night's sleep had changed her perspective on the situation with Margo. She felt it was best for both of them to go their separate ways, and she would call Margo later in the morning. Debbie stood, stretched, and walked into the bathroom where she undressed and took a long, hot shower. She shampooed her hair and came out feeling refreshed. Soon she was cooking bacon and eggs while she drank a freshly brewed cup of coffee.

After breakfast, she booted up her computer and scanned her e-mail. There was a message from Denise Weber. It simply told her that the head of the JTTF was due in the office at eight a.m. and she would see him right away. Debbie noted the time. It was nine o'clock and, if things went according to plan, Denise would be calling before long. She responded to her other e-mails but deleted most of them. She went to the FEN website to get the name of the director. Gerald Rains. She copied down his business address and telephone number.

Debbie then googled his name and clicked on a site that said "Rains Bio."

Rains graduated from a small school in Washington State where he was active in environmental issues. He graduated in 1994 and worked for the U.S. Forestry service for three years. For three years after that he consulted with several lumber companies on forest restoration projects. Then there was a blank in his resume for two years, and in 2002 he started FEN in Flagstaff, Arizona. Debbie looked at some more hits but found nothing of interest except for the quote in the Phoenix newspaper she had previously seen. Two unaccounted years of his resume puzzled Debbie.

Debbie closed down the computer and looked at the clock. It was eleven o'clock and Denise hadn't called. *How time flies when you're surfing the internet.* The phone rang and Debbie nearly jumped out of her skin. She had become accustomed to the quiet now that Margo was gone.

She picked up and said, "Hello."

"Deb, it's Denise. How are you? Did you rest last night? You looked tired yesterday."

"Great sleep. Rarin' to go. What have you found out?" she asked.

"Quite a bit, actually. The terrorism expert here was quite interested when I mentioned FEN as a possible player in the incidents at your father's vineyard. Apparently, they've had a successful investigation of an environmental activist who worked as a clerk at the University of Northern Arizona. It's in Flagstaff. She was indicted in 2006 with the outcome pending. Anyway, she has been photographed at various protests with Gerald Rains caught in the same pictures."

"Does that mean FEN has been under investigation?"

"Well, not really. It's just a front for collecting money from environmentalist, but it's not a 501(c) organization."

"You'll have to explain."

"Donations to FEN are not tax deductible for the donor. Meaning FEN earnings are subject to IRS taxes, which means they don't have to reveal their donors. They sponsor things like peaceful sit-ins, literature, campus lectures, carbon credit exchange, that sort of thing. Most ecoterrorist groups aren't structured like FEN. We have indicted at least 12 individuals for destructive acts in Washington,

Oregon, Arizona, and Colorado, and they're all independent of each other. Only thing that holds them together are their beliefs."

"What about Rains? We have stolen license plates and a truck involved in destruction at the vineyard traced back to Flagstaff. Wouldn't Rains be a starting point? Talk to the lady whose son had the plates stolen off his car. Work from there."

"That makes sense, but resources are strained. At least for the terrorist unit. It's on the 'to do' list but not high."

Debbie was struck with an idea and said, "What's to prevent me from going over there and snooping around. Can't I do that since I'm on the Joint Task Force for gangs?"

"It's a free country. You can snoop around all you want. Just don't say you're FBI. If you dig up anything, it may help when we get cranked up."

"Pardon my asking, Denise, but you're not married are you?"

There was a pause. Finally, Denise said quietly, "I was. To another agent. But we divorced several years ago. Why do you ask?"

"I'd hate to drive out there alone. Could use some company. We could be back late Sunday night. Having an FBI badge could speed up the investigation."

"Or slow it down. I'm due for a long weekend. I'll check with my boss and see if I can get off at twelve. Call you back."

Since Debbie had not unpacked her bag from last night, she was already to go. She plugged in her cell phone to charge it and dug around her desk to find another spare battery. She seemed all prepared except she needed to call her dad. She found him at his office seeing patients.

When he picked up she said, "Busy as usual, Marilyn says."

"Always this way on a Friday. What's up? How was the flight? Fred treat you right?"

"The flight was easy. Fred was great. I'm going to Flagstaff in the rent-a-car. Is that alright?"

"Of course. Why Flagstaff?" Dan asked, flustered over the content and speed of her response.

"I presented the evidence to Denise, the FBI agent I work with on the gang task force. Her superiors were interested but put the investigation on hold. They're swamped. So I'm going out there to run down some leads. Act as an unofficial extension of the FBI."

"Is that safe? I mean, these guys have murdered two people. They find you digging around you might get hurt."

"Dad! Some week you should take time off and ride with me. I face extreme danger every time I go on patrol. But you're right in a way. I have no back- up except Denise, who might go with me. I'm waiting to hear from her."

Worried, Dan asked, "Can you at least let me know where you are during the weekend, how things are going?"

"I can do better than that. My cell has GPS capability. You can go to mapquestfindme.com and see where I am whenever I turn my phone on. Let me give you my number." She gave her dad the cell number and promised to be careful.

Just as she was getting ready to dial Margo at work, the phone rang. Denise had gotten approval and Debbie agreed to pick her up at her apartment in Burbank. It would take seven or eight hours to drive to Flagstaff and she would have to arrange to meet Gerald Rains on Saturday.

She put off the call to Margo and, thinking out loud, she asked herself, "Do I call his office and say I'm an LAPD cop investigating an arson murder or do I pretend I'm a newspaper reporter covering environmental issues?" The risk of using her real name, she realized, was that it could arouse suspicion if Rains was involved. She chose to use the name Deborah Michaels, which was close and easy to remember. *God I hate the name Deborah.*

She dialed the number she had copied off the FEN website and there was an almost immediate response.

"Hello, this is the office of Gerald Rains, April Rains speaking."

April Rains? You got to be kidding. "Hi, this is Deborah Michaels, an officer with the LAPD. I plan to be in the area tomorrow and would like to meet with Gerald Rains. I realize tomorrow's Saturday, but it's important."

"May I ask what this is about?"

"Yes. I'm investigating, along with the FBI, an arson murder in California that may tie into environmental activists in Flagstaff. I would appreciate interviewing Mr. Rains in connection with this.

He is not a suspect by any means, but he may be helpful in pointing us in the right direction."

"Wait just a moment while I put you on hold."

Gerald Rains was in his office surfing the internet looking for donor foundations which might be willing to contribute. He had not held a real job since he quit his forestry service job eleven years ago. While April was petite and somewhat well groomed, Gerald was sloppy with a week's worth of beard and uncombed hair that went to his shoulders. He had a large nose, shifty eyes, and a slightly under slung jaw. "What is it?" he barked into the phone when his wife buzzed him.

April Rains was used to her husband's grumpy moods, but it seemed that in the last week he was worse than ever. Rather than act upset, she kept a professional tone to her voice and said, "There's a call from an LAPD cop who wants to meet with you tomorrow. It's about an arson murder. She's just looking for information."

Gerald slowly reached over and shut off his computer. This is the very last thing he wanted to hear. He cursed the stooges he had sent to do a man's job. Better not arouse any suspicions with his wife, who was totally out of the loop. "What do we have going on tomorrow," he said in an uncharacteristic high-pitched voice.

"At eight o'clock you have a meeting with the Brooks Foundation representative. You remember them. They want to contribute in return for a series of lectures on global warming. High school students in Arizona. About twenty lectures, they will pay your expenses to and from, plus a thousand dollar."

"Well, let's be sure the representative doesn't see the officer in the waiting room, so make it ten thirty. Tell him I must be out of here by 11:30."

"Her. The officer is a woman."

"Damn it, the world's upside down. Then tell *her*. Thank you April."

Moments later, April clicked onto Debbie's line and confirmed the meeting along with the particulars. It was fine with Debbie since, after the long trip, she would welcome sleeping late in the morning. She thanked April and hung up.

The trip to Flagstaff was uneventful. The route Debbie chose was Interstate 10 and then the 40 to Barstow. They were just ahead of the Friday afternoon traffic that was building up behind them. In Flagstaff, they found a motel and dropped off their bags. At a nearby McDonald's, they ate a yummy breakfast burrito for dinner. It was after midnight when they hit the sack, too tired to talk.

At ten o'clock the next morning, Debbie and Denise piled into the rental and headed for FEN's office about one mile away. Breakfast had consisted of the motel's continental cuisine, cold cereal, yogurt, and a banana. They both had several cups of coffee, which turned out to be good. Feeling pumped by the caffeine, they were ready for what the day might bring. Over their burritos the night before they had decided that Denise should take the lead, since she had jurisdiction.

The FEN office was simply a store front office located in a small mall. When they got out of the car, Debbie noted a green Japanese hybrid parked in front. The glass front door was propped open by a painted green brick. Inside, they could see a youngish, petite woman on the phone. When they entered, the woman placed her hand over the receiver and mouthed "go right in" pointing to the back of the office. They walked down a short, narrow corridor and entered an office that was cluttered with boxes filled with banners, tee shirts, baseball caps, and neckties. A large man, whose back was turned to them, was seated behind an oak desk. He was working the keys of a computer.

Debbie cleared her throat and the man turned and smiled at them. He waved them to two chairs in front of the desk. Then he closed down his computer and swiveled his chair to face them. He didn't bother to stand to greet his visitors. For this appointment and the one prior, Gerald had trimmed his beard and shortened his hair. He had on a clean, green dress shirt and a matching tie with FEN printed across it.

"Good morning ladies. I thought there was only one police officer visiting me this morning?"

"This is FBI Agent Denise Weber who is heading up the investigation. I'm Deborah Michaels. I'm the one who talked to April yesterday. I'm keeping her company. Thanks for seeing us."

"FBI?" Gerald stammered. "You said you were from the LAPD," Gerald said, looking at Debbie.

"I am. But the FBI has jurisdiction here. I work in conjunction with Denise in Los Angeles and am merely here to keep her company."

"Are you her secretary, too?" Gerald asked, pointing at Debbie. "Why did you make the appointment to see me?" Gerald wasn't happy feeling he had been tricked into being interviewed by an FBI agent.

"I'm truly sorry. I should've explained it to April. I was just trying to help out since Denise was very busy yesterday. She asked me to call. It was my day off, so I tried to help out."

Gerald eyed one then the other with his beady eyes. He had a hard time believing that story, but challenging it would only arouse suspicion. He decided to drop it.

"Very well. How long are you staying?" Gerald asked in an upbeat tone.

"Until tomorrow. Then we head back."

Gerald looked at Denise, who had remained silent. "By the way, Ms. Michaels, where are you staying?" Gerald asked looking back at Debbie. Gerald noted the puzzled look on her face that seemed to ask "why do you need to know?" "Excuse me, in case I need to contact you if I remember something important to the investigation."

"We're staying at the Sandman Motel," Denise answered. "I have a few questions, then we'll be out of your hair. I know you're busy today."

Gerald Rains, who was not noted for his tact, said, "Well today is inconvenient for me but go ahead. You have until 11:30."

Denise went on to explain about the arson murder, but she did not go into specifics as to where or how the arson took place. She explained that a FEN hat had been found at the scene, but she did not say which scene. She told Gerald that a vehicle involved in the crime was traced to Flagstaff. The story was not entirely candid, but enough detail was provided to paint a picture for the founder of FEN.

Gerald struggled to control himself. How stupid of his dumb ass acolytes to validate the theft by returning the plates revealing where the truck had originated. He knew the story Denise was weaving was inaccurate. He knew the details she was carefully leaving out. He had to be careful how he answered her questions and not let her know he knew.

"That's a tragic story. How can I help you? FEN is strictly an educational organization to combat global warming and the rape of the environment by capitalistic logging companies. We don't deal in acts of violence or destruction."

"I understand that," Denise said looking around the office. "Do you sell a lot of your merchandise right from here?"

"We sell a lot of this stuff on the internet. All of it originates here. The hat you found has been sold in every state. In large numbers. So are our T-shirts."

"Do you keep a record of who buys the hats?" Debbie asked. Gerald looked at her with narrowed eyes. Her tone and manner had changed and she appeared to be more than just a companion to the FBI agent.

"Somewhere in my computer there are thousands of names. Of course, that's confidential information and I can't release it to you."

"For now, we would only be interested in the names of people who purchased the hat in, let's say, Flagstaff," Debbie said.

"No can do. Besides, people walk right up to our office here and purchase hats, neckties, shirts, and we don't know who they are or where they live."

Denise could see that this was getting nowhere and decided to shift gears. "I see on your website that you sell carbon credits. How does that help fight global warming?"

Gerald leaned back and laced his fingers behind his head. This was a question up his alley. "Carbon offsets or credits allow someone to make a carbon footprint and then erase it by buying credits. They are given a certificate when they buy the credit. The money that is collected is then used to plant trees or some other project that helps the environment."

"Who plants the trees? Denise asked.

"I do. Or we do. Nine years ago when I started FEN, a concerned patron willed her ten acre property to FEN. Essentially an old farm. It's out of town several miles, with an old house and land ideal for growing trees. So, FEN has a tree farm that grows pines, poplars, aspens, you name it. The person buying the credits gets to decide."

"Do you live there? I mean, who cares for the trees?" Debbie questioned.

"Simple. I have a small crew of environmentally concerned citizens who live there and keep the farm running. They also have other jobs in town here because I can only pay them a small stipend. But they get room and board free."

"How do you monitor that? I mean, it would seem that it's a perfect set-up for fraud. How does the person buying the credit know where their money is going?" Denise asked.

"A frequently asked question, Denise," Gerald answered. "May I call you Denise?" Denise nodded. "Denise, our clients are given a yearly update on the projects that are underway and how their money was spent. April sends a picture of their tree and a note. All done with digital cameras and e-mail of course. Saves on our overhead and is eco-friendly. We've been audited on that very issue and have passed each time it's been done. That's also true of FEN's tree farms in Oregon and Washington."

"You have three tree farms?" Debbie was astonished.

"Yes. And more on the way," Gerald said proudly.

Getting back on point, Denise asked, "Who does the audit?"

Gerald suddenly realized how stupid he was to allow these snoops into his office. *No wonder people don't like to be questioned by cops without an attorney present.*

"There's an organization of dedicated, certified accountants who give up their time freely to do this. They go all over the country auditing carbon credit organizations so as to avoid what you are worried about."

"I've heard that planting trees is done as an offset, but many of them die because they are planted then not cared for. Does this show up in your audit?" asked Denise.

"Yes, some trees do die but most live, so it balances out. This isn't a unique idea. Countries like Norway buy or lease land in places like Africa and plant forests to earn their offsets. They are very careful to care for the trees. So it's more complicated than just a bozo like me planting tress," Gerald laughed.

"I've heard that carbon emissions occur instantaneously but trees store carbon slowly over time. Later on, when they die or get burned up in a fire, they give back the carbon to the atmosphere. So where's the benefit?" Denise asked.

Gerald wasn't about to get into it with the skeptical FBI agent. Having to constantly defend himself against global warming skeptics taught him when to back off.

"Please, there are a lot of questions about carbon offsets, but I don't have time to go into it now. I have a lecture to give at the University and must get going."

"Thank you for your time. I just have one more question before we go. In your cv, I see a blank for the years 2000-2002. Were you on a sabbatical?" Debbie asked.

"No. I attended a UN meeting in Marrakech, Morocco where a committee on the Kyoto agreement met to work out banking carbon credits. It was Conference of the Parties or COP 7 meeting. I also lived there while I helped establish a carbon credit program between France and Morocco. French travelers to Morocco could buy offsets by traveling there other than in an airplane. It's still going on."

"Why isn't that in your resume? Seems to me its part of your work." Denise asked.

"It's a long story and I don't have time now. That's all in the past. Now, if you'll excuse me."

Debbie stared at Denise as Gerald Rains strode out of his own office, leaving them sitting there. They gathered up their belongings and walked out. April was sitting at the desk and the hybrid parked outside was gone.

"I'm sorry Gerald had to leave in a rush, but he is late for a lecture. Is there anything I can do to help?"

"How about you? How are you getting home?" Denise asked.

"Oh, we're open on Saturdays until three, so my husband will pick me up after the lecture."

"Goodbye then, and thank you for your help." Debbie said. They both waved and went to their car.

When they were in the car and heading out of the parking lot, Denise said, "I don't know about you, but that guy is ripe for investigating. Carbon credits my eye. He's up to more than that. Sounds like a racket to me."

"I got the feeling he was uncomfortable when you asked him questions. He definitely has something to hide," Debbie said.

"Where to next?" Denise asked.

"How about lunch? I saw a Taco Bell on the way here. I have a craving for another burrito."

"Lead the way."

After lunch they drove to Leta Simmon's house, which was not far from the FEN office. They pulled up to a single story, white stucco ranch home with a shingled roof located in a moderately upscale neighborhood. In the front garden, bordering the house, an older woman was dead heading roses. She was dressed in khaki shorts, clogs with white socks, a blue blouse, and straw hat. Debbie and Denise stepped out of the car just as the woman looked up.

"Good afternoon," she said, "may I help you?" And she sounded as though she meant it.

Debbie and Denise walked up the pathway toward the house and Debbie quietly said, "I am Deborah Michaels, Los Angeles Police Department, and this is Denise Weber, FBI. Are you Mrs. Simmons?"

"Yes," she said as she peeled off her gloves and shook their hands. "My goodness, FBI. What can I do for you? I suspect I know. It's about Fred's license plates isn't it?"

"Well, yes, but we'd like to talk to you and see his car, if that's possible," Debbie said. Denise was happy with Debbie leading the way. She seemed more able to establish rapport. When people heard FBI invariably they became more cautious about answering questions.

"We can talk but only if it's inside over lemonade and cookies," Leta Simmons smiled. She had a kindly face with remarkably few wrinkles considering the sunny climate.

"That's a deal," Debbie said. When they were settled in the living room sipping lemonade and nibbling at cookies, Debbie asked, "Who are the young men in the photograph's on the piano?"

Neatly arranged on the grand piano were pictures of three boys from babyhood to adult. One was dressed in an army uniform with a rakish beret.

"Well, the oldest is Tim. He's in Iraq with Special Forces. Bobby is in law school at Brigham Young and Fred is going to college locally. His car is the one that had the plates stolen."

"Before we look at the car, I'd like to ask a few questions," Debbie said.

"Go ahead. More cookies?" Leta asked, holding out a plate of freshly baked oatmeal and raisin cookies. After her guests each took a cookie, Leta set down the plate and brushed a strand of hair behind her ear. "My husband is playing golf this afternoon. He might know some things I don't."

"We would like to hear what you have to say. By the way, the cookies are heavenly." Denise nodded in agreement. "I understand Fred is away at a church retreat. We'd like to know who else is aware of that? It might help find the person who stole the plates," Debbie said.

Leta sighed and slapped her thighs before she answered. "Fred lives above the garage and keeps to himself. He hardly ever brings friends over for us to meet. He's different than the other boys in that regard. The others were always dragging people in for me to feed," she laughed. "As far as knowing people who knew he was on retreat, well that would include the whole church."

Debbie nodded her head in understanding. Then she asked, "Does Fred have a job?"

"Part time. He works the three to eleven shift at the new biofuel gas station on Hardy Road, about a mile from here. He was, is, a nut about the environment and believes global warming is man made. Tom, my husband, scoffs at that, of course. Tom's an engineer with the electric company and you have to prove things to him. Fred was never able to do that. Anyhow, Fred got caught up in this environment thing. He loves going to lectures by this guy Rains who started the Free Earth Now or FEN organization."

Debbie nodded her head and said, "Yes, we just met Mr. Rains and his wife. They seem passionate about what they're doing."

"Tom says what they are involved in is fraud. 'Carbon credits my ass,' he always says in front of Fred, who storms out when he hears it. Other than that, Fred keeps to himself. He's a good student, but he likes to live at home while he goes to college. He's deeply religious and never has given us a moments worry. Like drugs or getting girls pregnant."

"Did he ever mention any names in conjunction with the church, his job, or FEN, that you can remember?" Denise finally asked.

After giving it some thought, Leta said, "He does talk about a middle eastern young man that comes into the gas station. It was kind of ironic, too, since he drives a biofuel car. I mean, not buying regular gas that comes from the Middle East!" Leta said with a laugh.

"Did he ever mention his name or describe him to you?" Denise asked.

Leta thought. "Yes. It was Achmed and he also was a member of FEN. At least, he bought into the global warming thing. This also caught Fred's attention. He didn't think that Middle Easterners cared about the environment. You know, it's hot there and they survive by selling oil to the West. But he said this guy was into it. He never described him or said his full name."

Debbie and Denise were not sure how this might fit in but thanked Mrs. Simmons for her time. They went out back behind the garage and inspected Fred's vehicle. The house and garage were backed up to an alley. Fred's car was hidden from the house and parked in a makeshift carport abutting the alley. The license plates were on and it looked like they had never been disturbed. Debbie could not understand why, if someone stole the plates, would they bother to return them. She assumed the thieves had no idea their truck was identified and they were never stopped. So, as far as they were concerned, the license plates went missing for several days and no one was the wiser.

The two debated whether they should ask Mrs. Simmons to inspect Fred's room but decided not to push their luck with this kindly mother. Denise and Debbie agreed, if they uncovered further evidence that the son might have been inadvertently involved, they would come back.

"To the biofuel station?" Denise asked.

"Sounds like a plan." They drove to the station on Hardy Street as described by Leta Simmons. It was after two o'clock in the afternoon when they arrived and only one attendant was on duty.

"Good afternoon," Debbie said as she introduced herself to the clerk behind the counter. There was a small section next to the counter for purchase of newspapers, coffee, candy, and microwaveable hot dogs. No one else was in the room or out buying gas.

"What can I do for you?" asked the young man at the counter.

"I'm Debbie Miceli, LAPD and this is Denise Weber, FBI. Is the manager around?"

The clerk looked from one then to the other with his lower jaw hanging open. "He's at home; I just talked to him. What do you want with him?'

The young man was trying to be professional, on the one hand, but looked nervous on the other. Something was afoot for representatives of two distinguished agencies to be in the gas station asking for the manager.

"We want to ask him some questions about an employee of his. Also about a murder investigation we are involved in." Debbie thought the latter would get the manager's attention and speed up the process.

"Just a moment." The young man disappeared into a small office off the mechanics bay and soon returned. "He'll be right down. He lives close. Can I get you anything?"

Debbie shook her head and did not say anything further. Ten minutes later, a car pulled up and a middle-aged man with thin, brown hair and a red face got out. The manager introduced himself and invited the two into his office. Once seated, Debbie briefly explained they were investigating a homicide in California and asked if he knew anything about a Middle Eastern male who was a friend of Fred Simmons.

"Not off hand. There's a number of Middle Eastern men and women who use the station. Fred works in the evenings. I'm generally gone when he comes on duty."

"I noticed a sign out front that said you used video surveillance. Would you have any of those available to us?" Denise asked.

As before, when Denise asked a question it seemed to invite a wary response. "Why do you ask?" the manager said defensively.

Debbie decided to step in and said, "I haven't given you the whole story, but there is arson involved and an accelerant was used. The arson investigators say it's E85 gasoline. The car may have come from Flagstaff."

Middle Eastern males, FBI, arson, all added up to possible terrorism in the eyes of the manager. He wasn't about to impede an investigation into something as serious as that and suddenly he became cooperative. He ran a gas station that sold regular gasoline and, oh by the way, 'green gas.' That was about as political as it got for him.

"Yes, we have the videos. I keep them for a month and then download them onto a disc. They take a digital picture every second, so it's not a video like you see on TV."

"We understand. We would be interested in the images around 14 to 18 days ago," Debbie said.

The manger flipped on his computer and after several strokes on the keyboard they were looking at digital pictures dated three days before the arson. The manager excused himself to attend to a young woman who had come to the mechanic's bay looking for help. Debbie and Denise settled in and began to look at the digital images. They sat close together in the cramped office allowing them both to gaze at the monitor. The manager returned several times and asked if there were any problems.

Debbie had not appreciated how many people stopped for gas in a single day. After two hours they finally saw something that piqued their interest. The date stamp on the digital image was the day before the arson and the time was 9:30 P.M. A dark, foreign car, with two men seated in the front seat pulled up to the E85 pump. The passenger door opened and a man in a baseball hat stepped out. He glanced upward then waved at the office. A moment later he lifted the handle on the E85 pump and began filling the fuel tank. When he was through, the driver popped the trunk and the passenger took out a five gallon gasoline can. He filled it with the E85 gasoline and put it back in the trunk. The images were in black and white, so Debbie couldn't identify the color of the car. All she could say was that it was a dark color. The passenger pulled out his wallet and began counting bills before he left the picture. Minutes later he returned and the car drove off.

"Paid in cash," Debbie said.

What caught Debbie's attention was when the passenger looked up. The digital camera caught his face and baseball hat which had FEN stenciled across it. He had a thin wraparound beard that went from one ear, then along the jaw line to the other ear. Denise noted it as well and along with other features identified the man as Middle Eastern. They asked the manager if they could print the picture of his face. The manager agreed and said he did not know the young man on the screen. They looked at more images and finally at five o'clock thanked the manager and called it day.

Chapter Nineteen

Gerald Rains was clearly worried when he left his office. Deborah, the LAPD cop, was definitely the smarter of the two. But the other one, the FBI agent, was more experienced and older. "FBI. Shit. How could I have let those two investigators grill me?" he muttered to himself. Gerald spent a great deal of effort keeping a low profile as far as the authorities were concerned. The last thing he wanted and feared was to spend time in jail. He doubted the two female investigators were satisfied with his flimsy story about why he went to Morocco. Gerald reckoned they must have really pored over his past history to pick up on that. *Well, I'll have to do something to throw them off course.* He couldn't have these two spoil what he had planned for America. Namely, eco-activist cells in every state fighting capitalists who were profiting while defiling the environment.

Of course, it was capital that got him into his current mess. Selling T-shirts, hats, and carbon credits didn't do it for him. The real money was in donations. He needed big bucks, and that's when the mystery man called him. Two years ago. All he knew about the man was his cell phone number. Gerald had never actually seen him, but he did talk to him once in person. The man sounded ex-military because he used military jargon like "collateral damage," "taking out," "assets," "casualties," and "losses." Until the vineyard fiasco, Gerald had done five arsons for the mystery man and had been paid handsomely in cash.

Ironically, the one time I trust someone else to do a simple job, all hell breaks loose. He knew his main problem now was damage control and what to do with the three idiots working at his tree farm.

After his lecture to a group of eager students, Gerald headed home. He wasn't going to call the man from his office but would instead use his cell phone in his den. It was early Saturday afternoon and he was confident his contact would be available to take the call. The one in-person meeting with the man had been artfully arranged so that Gerald couldn't see who was talking. The mystery man was hidden behind a screen and used an electronic scrambler to disguise his voice. The five "missions" he had completed for the man bore no relationship to environmental causes. They were done to force people into doing something they didn't want to do. Gerald rationalized that since he needed the money, the monetary reward out weighed the risks.

He pulled into his driveway, parked, and entered his house through the kitchen. He grabbed a bottle of V-8 juice from the refrigerator and headed into his den. He flipped his cell phone open and dialed the number written on a slip of paper taped to the back of his desk's bottom drawer. Each time he talked to the man he was given a new cell number for the next call. Gerald was certain the man used throwaway phones. After he dialed, there was one ring. This was only the second time he had called in a year, so he didn't know what to expect. Most of the time, he was on the receiving end of calls listening to orders for a new job.

A voice which sounded like it was in an echo chamber asked, "Who's calling?"

No hello or how may I help you from this guy.

"It's me. Arizona. I have a problem."

"I'm aware of that. Your personnel are amateurs. Other than that, what's the reason for the call? This is a secure line so you can keep your remarks on point."

This guy isn't the warm and fuzzy type. "A female cop and female FBI agent were in my office today. They were asking questions about FEN in reference to an arson murder. They didn't mention where the arson took place. But I'm sure it's the one in Vista."

"Are they still there?" he asked.

"They are. They leave tomorrow."

"Where are they staying?"

"Sandman motel."

The contact was silent. He was thinking about the next step and weighing his options. "I'm coming there. We'll meet at the same location we met two years ago. Six o'clock. Don't bring anyone with you. But I want your team, such as it is, standing by."

"Roger that. They're up at the tree farm ready to go."

"What's the tree farm?"

"It's ten acres we're planting trees in. To improve the environment. About three miles out of town. The guys working for me live there."

"Give me the location."

Gerald gave him the general location of the farm and also referred him to the FEN website for details.

Before Gerald could say anything more, the phone clicked dead. He slowly pressed the end button on his phone and closed it. Gerald called April and told her to catch a cab home. He was going to be busy.

The FEN tree farm was located about three miles north of Flagstaff on a road that ultimately led to the Grand Canyon. The house Gerald had referred to earlier was situated back from the highway about 100 yards. The trees in front of the house had grown to the point where the house was not visible from the road. Inside the house, San Diego sat engrossed in a football game on TV. The fall college football season had started and he was watching a game between USC and Florida. It was a close game and, when the phone rang, he wasn't eager to pick up. Denver was outside sunning himself. He played football in college but rarely watched it. Rabat was in the backyard chicken coop cutting off chicken heads.

Finally, after the third ring, he picked up the phone and in an annoyed voice said, "Who is it?" he snapped.

"It's Rains, you asshole. I'm trying to run a business and you're answering the phone like you're in a fraternity. Are you doing anything useful?" he asked sarcastically.

"S…sorry Mr. Rains. I'm watching a football game," San Diego stammered as he hit the volume button on the remote.

"What are the other two doing?" he asked in a nicer voice. He liked San Diego best of the three, but it wasn't by much.

"Rabat is cutting off chicken heads, Denver's on the porch."

"Cutting off chicken heads? What the hell is that all about?" Gerald asked, astonished.

"He's killing and cleaning them for dinner. He also says it's great practice for the day when he gets to do it to the infidels."

"Oh God. What have I got myself into? I recruited that guy for environmental activism. I met him in Morocco when he was a high school senior and helped him get a student visa," he said quietly, almost to himself.

"My opinion, he's a nut case. He scares me. The Vista job was his doing. I don't want to take the heat for that. No pun intended. I'm here because I believe in the cause. Not for some religious reason," San Diego said earnestly.

"Listen up. There's a cop and an FBI agent snooping around. They may try to come out and look the place over. So, I want you guys near the house in case I call. No pussy hunting or bar hopping tonight. Be ready to move out if you have to. You got the dog outside?" Gerald asked.

"No sir. He's right next to me here in the living room."

"He's a great watch dog. So chain him up outside and sit by the phone. Let the others know." With that, Gerald hung up.

San Diego stood up and looked out the window onto the porch. Denver was lying on a lounge asleep with his shirt off. He heard some screeching from the chicken coop. He walked onto the porch and shook Denver awake. He told him about the phone call. Denver waved him away and fell back to sleep. San Diego shrugged his shoulders and went out to the chicken coop.

When he walked inside, he was aghast. On the ground amongst feathers, chicken shit, and wood chips were eight dead chickens. Rabat was standing with a machete raised to the sky in the middle of the coop. There was blood everywhere, including on Rabat's white T-shirt. San Diego drew back. He was in no position to challenge the Moroccan who appeared to be praying or mumbling something about Allah with his eyes closed while his head was tilted skyward.

Finally, Rabat brought the machete down to his side and opened his eyes. He saw San Diego looking at him in disbelief. Rabat had a menacing look in his eye but soon turned away. He started collecting the chicken carcasses. San Diego took the opportunity to speak to him and said, "I just got a call from Rains. He wants us in the house ready to leave on a moments notice."

"Good. Maybe he got job for us. You help clean chicken," he said with a satisfied look on his face. "Or are you too squeamish like all Americans?"

San Diego didn't mind poking a skunk, but this was not the time to give it back to Rabat. He seemed to be in a dream like state where killing someone was part of the dream.

"No," he said then turned and left.

Debbie and Denise stopped at a supermarket and bought dinner consisting of turkey sandwiches, green salads, diet Pepsis, and half a decadent chocolate cake. They were hungry and when they finished eating, there was barely enough chocolate cake left to snack on later. The sandwich wrappers and salad containers were stuffed into the plastic bag from the grocery store. The bag was shoved into the waste basket. Denise sat down at a small table and plugged her lap top into the LAN line. She logged onto the secure FBI website and entered Gerald Rains into the search box. Soon, she was looking at pictures of the environmental activist. She read his profile and activity for the past twenty years.

"Well, this is certainly more complete than your Google search. We looked at FEN when I was talking to the terrorist guys but didn't get into Rains. He caught the attention of the FBI in 1988 when he was arrested at a sit-in in Seattle. They were protesting world capitalism, particularly the US. Demonstrators threw chicken blood at the cops. He was arrested and fined. Misdemeanor count only."

"That certainly wasn't on Google," Debbie said.

"It was sealed because of his age and first offense. Let's see, he went to college in Washington, after graduation entered the U.S. Forestry service for three years. What's this? He was arrested three times in 1999 demonstrating outside logging camps. All misdemeanor charges of obstructing legal commerce by lying in front of logging trucks."

"Passive aggressive behavior I'd say. What else?"

"This is where it gets interesting. I don't know how our guys missed this. Traveled to France, then Morocco. Was active in the carbon trading business and helped set up a scheme for French tourists to go to Morocco over land and earn carbon credits by doing that."

"Just like he told us. He's been at this carbon credit thing for some time. Sounds like he's making environmentalism a business. Anything else there?" Debbie asked while she reclined on her bed and flipped through a magazine touting Flagstaff's tourist attractions.

"I'm going to the State Department's secure website and look at Gerald's passport." There was silence as Denise pounded the keys of her laptop.

"This is interesting," she finally said. "He went to Afghanistan, Saudi Arabia, and Pakistan all before 9/11."

"Were there restrictions to travel when he did it?" Debbie asked as she sat up more interested in what she was hearing.

"No, but it seems odd that he would go to the places that have become hot spots in the war on terror."

Debbie let her mind wander. Clearly she didn't get the impression that Rains was interested in bringing down his country with some kind of jihad. But he was interested in all the anti-capitalism issues of the day. Oil, SUV's, carbon emissions, biofuels—the whole basket of issues on the environmentalist's agenda. Debbie tried to put together all the things she had learned about Rains and his Moroccan connection. It came to her that the individual on the gas station's video surveillance appeared Middle Eastern. Suppose he was recruiting Middle Easterners for his tree farms; people who were dedicated to the environment but also willing to carry out illegal acts in America. It would be perfect. They wouldn't be working to establish some 7th century paradise like radical, fundamental Islamists. Instead, they'd be saving the environment. That would keep them below the FBI radar.

"Did Rains ever sponsor students from Middle Eastern countries to enter the US on student visas?" Debbie asked. "I'm just trying to put all this together. The picture of the man at the gas station, the travel to the middle east, the carbon credits in Morocco..."

"That's thinking, Deb. But the State Department gives out thousands of student visas a year. It's maddening. They don't even know who they let in. It's a big bone of contention. The students come here and get lost in the shuffle. They could be anywhere in the country. It's better than before 9/11 but not that much better," Denise said as she logged off and closed down her computer.

"Okay. So Gerald has found a rich place to recruit soldiers for his battle to save the environment. Soldiers who would do as they are ordered and, as a side benefit, would be sticking it in the eye of America. Hurting us economically. It seems to me, if that holds water, then we must make a trip to the tree farm tomorrow. See if the gas station mystery man is working for Rains," Debbie summed up.

"I agree," Denise said.

Chapter Twenty

At five-thirty, Gerald kissed April on the cheek and told her he might be gone for several hours. After the cab ride home, she prepared dinner but he said he would eat when he returned. April wasn't worried about Gerald stepping out on her because he was hopelessly in love with her. He treated her with respect and never gave any hint of being unhappy in their marriage. He had met her at one of his seminars fours years prior and it was love at first sight. At least as far as he was concerned. April was a perfect match for him because she shared all of his enthusiasm for environmental issues. However, he kept the dark side of his business away from her and she never gave any indication that she was interested or knew about the "other" things he did. When he said he would be gone for several hours, she never thought to ask where he was going.

As he was getting ready to leave, the phone rang. He picked up and said, "Hello."

"Gerald, it's Joe Pitts at Green Gas."

"Hey Joe, what's up?" It was Joe who Gerald had convinced to get into the green gas business. It turned his dying gas station around and he was grateful.

"I don't know if it's something you wanted to know or not. But there were two cops here today. Went through my surveillance tapes and picked out that Arab you got up at the tree farm. They copied his picture and were asking questions. Wanted to know if Fred Simmons knew the guy."

"Moroccan, Joe," Rains corrected, "Arab is something else. What did you tell them?" Gerald asked. He tried to sound nonchalant but his gut was churning.

"I told them I didn't know the guy. But they were investigating arson with E85, so I thought you better know."

"Don't know anything about it but thanks."

He hung up and felt like vomiting. They were closer to learning about his operation than he had imagined. He was going to have to be careful about what he said to the man he was going to meet.

He drove to the same hotel in town where he had met his benefactor several years ago. Gerald never understood how the man he was to meet again had learned of FEN. Before that encounter with him, Gerald was told by the mystery man that he was interested in making a substantial contribution to his cause. After that meeting, however, his whole life changed. He took the donation alright, along with all the heavy strings that were attached. Now he was in deeper than he wanted. Up to the Vista affair he was guilty of random acts of vandalism. Some of them significant, like the huge warehouse in Baltimore he torched. He had personally overseen that effort with Rabat and was handsomely rewarded. All cash no records.

He pulled into the hotel's parking lot and parked his car. He went through the lobby and climbed the stairs to the second floor. The door to the room he had entered before was unmarked. He twisted the knob then pushed the door open, entered the room, and quietly closed the door behind him. The room was a suite and there was a screen across the door leading to the sleeping area. He resisted the urge to knock the screen down and see who was on the other side.

"Sit down, Mr. Rains," said a distorted voice that again was filtered through an electronic laryngeal device.

Despite the filtered voice, there was something about the way he spoke that made Gerald willingly comply with the speaker's command. He cursed himself for his cowardice.

Once he was seated, the voice said, "Until recently, you've done everything I have asked efficiently and without question. Of course, you've been paid well. What bothers me is the absolute stupidity you've shown on a simple task, burning a garage and ordinary property damage. I take it you weren't directly involved in those operations?"

"No. I went over the operation with two of my people several times. We waited until the occupants of the house were out of town. So no slip-ups. One of the men assigned to the task took it upon himself to enlarge the mission." Gerald was pleased that he was using military terminology and keeping the details sketchy.

"Except the occupants weren't out of town. Tell me about today."

"As I said on the phone, two investigators showed up and began asking questions. The cop was the smarter of the two. They had recovered a FEN hat from the second operation as well as a license plate number. The number was stolen from another car. Again, this was done without my knowledge. The plates were from a car belonging to someone they knew. Then, beyond belief, they replaced the plates thinking that no one would be the wiser. Now, the investigators know the truck they were looking for is back here in Flagstaff."

There was a long period of silence during which Gerald began to fidget. Finally, the voice said, "Both operations were botched. You are a fool. You've some cleaning up to do. Your team and the two investigators are compromising the operation."

Gerald was not sure what he meant by "cleaning up." He had no stomach for violence. At least he thought he didn't. Did the voice want him to kill five people? Angered, he rapidly rose and headed for the screen when suddenly he noticed a red dot on his chest. It was a laser light.

"One step further and you're history."

Gerald stopped in his tracks then sat back down. He had to be cool here. But he was taking all the chances. *What difference would five more people make?* If he was caught for the other crimes he had committed he would spend the rest of his life rotting in jail or worse, get the needle. It was only a matter of time before he was found out by the two snoops from California. He had dealt with the FBI before. If one of their agents should disappear, they would be relentless in looking for her killer or killers. *Same for the LAPD.* His cause to save the environment was noble and necessary. There were bound to be casualties along the way. He had thought about it before but had not faced it until now. It was time to move on and put this bump in the road behind him.

"You are awfully quiet, Gerald. Questions for me?"

"Yes. What's your part in this? Am I alone or what?"

The voice was silent again for a long enough time to make Gerald anxious. Finally, the voice said, "It makes no difference to me how you solve this problem. I'm untraceable but not unaware of your activities. You must solve the problem ahead of you since you're on the docket for the crimes committed. It's too bad about your last efforts. There is no compensation for incompetence. This will be the last time we shall meet or talk. All contact numbers you've used in the past were to disposable cell phones."

"That's a hell of a shit sandwich you've given me."

"Life is about decisions. You've made yours. What you do from here on in is about your future. Good luck. You may leave now."

As he stood, Gerald again resisted the urge to charge through the screen separating him from the voice. When the pesky red dot appeared on his chest for a second time, he again gave up any thought of physical confrontation. Looking down at the dot, Gerald shook his head. He left angry and frustrated. He had to think and come up with a plan.

He walked out to his car and started it up. He pounded the steering wheel. Slowly, he placed the car in gear and left the hotel's parking lot. As he drove, a plan began to form in his mind. He sat up straighter after he thought about it. It was a plan that he could carry out without violence. If necessary, however, it could be altered but it could get ugly. Instead of going home he drove out to the tree farm to meet with his team.

Absorbed with his dilemmas, Gerald was unaware of the car that followed him to the tree farm. When he pulled into the farm's entrance the car sped past. It was still twilight when he pulled up to the house, which was situated in a clearing surrounded by trees and invisible from the road. The house was a three story wood sided structure elevated off the ground by a four foot wall of large river stones. Periodically, there were windows in the stone foundation allowing light into the basement which contained multiple stalls for cold storage. In the past, root crops such as summer squash, onions, turnips, and potatoes were stored there during the cold winters.

Gerald parked his car and mounted the steps to the porch that nearly surrounded the house. The building's rough hewn, dark brown wooden sidings gave the structure the feel of a mountain cabin. Gerald always liked coming here and silently thanked the old lady who donated her farm to FEN. He dreamed of retiring here someday when the house would be in the middle of a forest. He pushed any thought about retirement out of his mind by trying to focus on the present. His job was to make sure his retirement wasn't spent in Leavenworth.

Gerald could hear the television blaring and he walked into the family room. The German Shepard watchdog jumped up and ran to his master with his tail wagging. Gerald reached down and petted the dog. His three charges were eating fried chicken, mashed potatoes with gravy, and biscuits. They were watching a game show and shouting out answers before the contestants did. Gerald walked over to the television and turned it off. Silence fell as each of the three stopped chewing and quickly glanced at each other.

"Get rid of the food. Meet me in the dining room." The three stood and quietly filed out of the family room. Gerald went to the dining room and sat down at the head of a very old but elegant table. It could easily seat twelve people. He dreamed of someday having environmental seminars at the tree farm and then relaxing afterwards around the dinner table. When Rabat, Denver, and San Diego quietly entered the room they seated themselves as far away from Gerald as possible.

Gerald looked at San Diego and said, "I thought I told you to put the dog outside."

"I did. I only brought him in so he could eat the chicken bones," San Diego said nervously.

"Put him outside after I'm through. We have a problem. Two investigators came to town today snooping around. One's an FBI agent, the other's an LAPD cop. Both females and they know what they're doing. They already discovered that Rabat is a suspect in the Vista fire." Gerald paused. The group was very silent and looked intently at Gerald.

"It won't be long before they find who Rabat is and who he works for." He paused and looked around at the young men sitting at the other end of the table.

Finally, San Diego asked in a subdued voice, "What are we going to do Mr. Rains?"

"I've given it a lot of thought. So far they haven't linked any of you to this tree farm. But they learned about it today. Instead of them coming out here and spying on us I plan to invite them here tomorrow. But we need to do some things. First I want Denver to take the truck used in the grape vine raid and drive to the Oregon tree farm. The group there is planning a demonstration against a logging company next week. I want you to leave tonight. I have cash for you. Eight hundred dollars."

"Where in Oregon? It'll take me two days to drive there." Denver said.

"Outside Salem. I'll draw you a map before you leave. Go upstairs and pack. I want every single belonging you have here in that truck. Boots, shoes, underwear, the whole lot. *Comprende.*"

"Yeah *amigo,* but why me?" he asked belligerently.

"Chill pal. So far you're totally clean. You weren't in on the first job and there is no evidence left behind that points to you in the second. No sense in getting you involved. Let's keep it as uncomplicated as possible."

"Thanks, I guess. But I'm still committed to the cause so don't dump me," Denver said more contritely.

"No one's dumping you. You'll find plenty to do in Oregon and I'll let you know when to come back. Now go."

Gerald turned to Rabat after Denver left. "Well, my friend, you've been made. If those two agents see you here it's *adios amigo.*

In the slammer for you for a long, long time. I want you hidden in the attic on the third floor. Door locked. Clear all the stuff out of your room on the second floor. That means prayer rugs and all that other crap you have"

"You scare me. I no want prison. Maybe I fly back to Rabat."

"Sorry pal. This isn't the Morocco secret police here. Chances are they've got your picture on a watch list already. They'll be looking for you on every international flight before tomorrow."

"I never go to American prison. Become nigger's boy."

"If you're lucky. Chances are, you wouldn't make it out alive. No. You hide in the attic. When we get rid of these two we're sneaking you into Mexico. Then you can get to Rabat. That's the safest route."

"I no like this. Not what I expected. I'm eco-terrorist. Not criminal."

"You dumb shit. If you hadn't gone cowboy on me and burned that house down, we wouldn't be sitting here."

"But you said no one home. I only try to make job better."

"Rabat, I'm sorry things turned out the way they did. Let's not discuss this further. It's best you do as I say. We'll get you home," Gerald said in a placating voice. He didn't want the Moroccan taking things into his own hands.

"I hate home. Live like pig. No jobs. I like it here at tree farm."

Gerald sat staring at the young Middle Easterner. He was a smart kid who was immature and bedeviled with a short fuse. He was his own main problem and he didn't want him arrested by the FBI. Rabat was weak and he would willingly spill his guts. Maybe disposing of him permanently was the best approach. He could drive him to the Mexican border and, on the way there, dispose of him in the vast desert.

"Let's think about it later. I'm sure we can work something out. For now, do what I say and let's get past these two cops."

Rabat glared at Gerald as he stood up and slowly left the room. San Diego sat anxiously looking at his boss wondering what was in store for him.

"Well, that leaves you," Gerald said as he sat looking at San Diego. "You'll stay here with me. I plan to spend the night, help you sanitize this place."

"Sanitize?"

"Yeah. Make it look like three slobs weren't living here. We'll start up on the second floor as soon as those two have cleared out. I don't want the dog running around barking or leaping on our guests. In the morning, lock him up in the barn with the Saab. Understood?"

"Yes, Mr. Rains."

"Would you please stop calling me Mr. Rains? Gerald or Gerry is just fine. You can start by cleaning your room. Make it look like you're a monk living in a monastery. Remember, we're environmental activists. Make sure the light bulb in the lamp by your bedside is neon. You get the idea?"

"Yes, Gerry," San Diego said as he stood and quickly left the room.

Gerald shook his head. *What a sorry ass group.* He flipped open his telephone and dialed the number of the Sandman Motel. He had put the number in his phone when he was waiting to meet with the mystery man. He waited while the desk clerk connected him to Denise and Debbie's room.

Denise was closest to the phone and when it rang she reached over and picked up. The small electric clock by the phone showed the time to be eight o'clock.

"Hello, Denise Weber speaking."

"Ms. Weber," Gerald said in his most friendly voice, "this is Gerald Rains. How are you this evening?"

Denise mouthed to Debbie Gerald's name then said, "We're just fine. Had dinner, now watching the local news channel."

"That'll put you to sleep. Nothing exciting happens in Flagstaff. I suppose that's good. Why I'm calling is to apologize for my quick exit today. I had to give a seminar and was running late." Gerald was very adept at shading the truth, a skill he honed while pushing the man made global warming hoax.

"That's quite alright. We found our way out and have spent a very productive day," Denise said, hoping to stir things up.

"Oh? How so?"

"I think we found some leads on the fire we talked about and are pursuing them. Since it has nothing to do with you, I won't go into detail. How can we help you?"

Gerald didn't like the coy way Denise was playing him but he had to be careful. "You two are going back to LA tomorrow. Before you go, I want to show you my tree farm. It'll take about an hour. How about coming around nine o'clock? Give you plenty of time to drive home."

Denise put her hand over the phone and said to Debbie, "He wants us to tour the tree farm for about an hour. Tomorrow at nine."

"Why not. Can't hurt. I say yes." Denise nodded in agreement.

"That will be fine, Mr. Rains. Nine o'clock tomorrow. How do we get there?"

"Please call me Gerald or Gerry." Gerald went on to explain in detail the route to the tree farm while Denise busily wrote down the instructions. It wasn't complicated and when she hung up she looked at Debbie with palms open as if to say, "what gives".

"That's one weird dude," Debbie said. "I wonder what he has up his sleeve. I don't trust him. Let's go but be on the alert. I'm sure this is about more than showing us his tree farm. Call me cynical, but there's something about him that's not right."

"Hey, you've been a cop for three years. I've been at this a lot longer and he makes my skin crawl. I think one of us should carry."

"Definitely. I don't think he'd do anything dumb but you never know. Is he trying to throw us off or is he a concerned environmentalist? If we find someone out there that looks like the picture from the gas station, what do we do?"

"Good question."

Chapter Twenty-One

Sunday morning was one of those days often described in travel brochures. The air was crisp as fall was nascent and the sky crystal clear. Not a cloud to be seen. Gerald made coffee from beans organically grown in Kona, Hawaii. It was his own private stash that he kept locked up for his personal use when he visited the farm. He strolled out onto the front porch and looked over his developing forest. Trees were spread out before him in all stages of growth. When he inherited the property several years before there were only a few trees growing on the acreage. Now, nearly eighty per cent of the land was taken up by trees. Most were saplings, but some of the older trees had grown as high as twenty feet tall. He insisted that the trees be planted randomly, not in rows, like a Christmas tree farm. He'd started planting at the front of the property first and worked toward the back end. Soon there would be no more room for his beloved trees. He would have to see about acquiring more property.

He sighed as he thought about the cost of that and how little money he really had. Running three tree farms for carbon credits was expensive and donations were on the decline now that the economy was tanking.

He felt something stirring beside him and he turned to find San Diego admiring the landscape with the dog on a leash. He wondered how he was going to introduce his young acolyte to the cops. He can't say, "Good morning, this is San Diego." He asked himself if he should use a phony name. No, "this is the FBI" was his answer. That would be dumb and when they found out he was lying then there would be more suspicion. He made up his mind.

"Good morning, Everett," he said pleasantly. "Sleep well?" he asked as he reached down to pet the German Shepard. The dog playfully nipped at his hand and he pulled it away. "The dog is jumpy this morning. He knows something is up."

Ignoring his assessment of the dog's mental state, San Diego turned quickly, not believing what he was hearing. Except for the first time they had met, Gerald had never used his real name.

Finally he said, "Good morning. Are we using real names now?"

"'Fraid so. At least today while we entertain these pain-in-the-ass-cops. As soon as they leave, it's back to the old routine. You're going to put the dog in the barn." It wasn't a question.

"Yes. The car's in there already. I covered it with an old tarp out there."

"Good. I don't want the dog barking and he won't if you leave him water and food. See to it. It's almost nine o'clock. Come back, we have more cleaning to do."

Everett gave a mock salute and hurried down the stairs and turned left, heading to the back of the house. The barn was about a hundred yards from the back door and the walk was slightly up hill. After he had settled the dog in the barn, he padlocked the door and pocketed the key. When he walked back, he went by the garage and looked in to see that the green Toyota truck was gone. Denver had taken off late last night without saying goodbye to anyone. He wondered if he would ever see him again. Not that it mattered. He had lived with the ex-football player for almost a year and knew next to nothing about him.

Everett entered the house by the back door and walked into the kitchen.

Rabat was pouring a cup of Gerald's special blend to take to the attic.

"Gerald sees you doin' that he'll cut your balls off."

"You mind your business. I take care of Gerald if he pisses me off."

"You're an unpleasant person, Rabat. Be sure not to show your ugly face today. These cops are smart and will pull you out of here faster than you can say Islam."

"You are bad person. You get yours," Rabat said sourly over his shoulder as he left to climb the stairs to the attic.

Everett shrugged and wondered if Rabat would ever lighten up. He certainly didn't understand American humor. He opened the pantry door and pulled two cans of dog food off the shelf. He opened them by yanking on the pull-top, picked up the dog's water and food bowl from the back porch, and headed back to the barn.

At nine o'clock sharp, Gerald heard through the open windows in the living room the crunching sound of gravel as a car pulled slowly up the driveway. He was sweeping the last pile of dirt in the living room. He quickly scooped it up with a dust pan and threw the debris in the fire place.

Earlier in the morning, Debbie and Denise had packed their belongings and placed them in the trunk of the rental car, ate breakfast, and then checked out of the motel. Denise decided she should carry, since Debbie didn't have any standing in Arizona. She placed her Glock in a fanny pack and rotated it to the front where it was covered with a loose fitting shirt. Expecting they would do some hiking, both dressed in sneakers and jeans. Debbie drove, following the directions Rains had given Denise the night before.

When they arrived at the tree farm, Debbie drove past the entrance for half a mile then turned around. The drive was up hill, so they could look down on the farm from the highway. They saw the barn, garage, and house.

"Looks quiet down there," Debbie said.

"Sure does. Let's get this over with and head back home."

Debbie put the car in gear and drove back to the farm's entrance. Neither of the two noted the car hidden in the brush across the road from the entrance.

As they drove up the driveway, Debbie said, "This place is creepy. There isn't anyone around." As soon as they cleared the trees fronting the property, and were able to see the house, Debbie stopped.

"We don't have any backup here, is this smart?" Denise asked.

"No, so let's just act like interested tourists and don't make waves. If he's hiding something it's well hidden. Let's be fascinated with global warming," Debbie said as she inched the car up to the house.

"Warming! I've got chills right now." As she said this, she felt the Glock in her fanny pack. Somewhat reassured she said, "What about calling your dad? Let him know where we are."

"Good idea." She picked up her cell phone and speed dialed her father's number. All she got was the answering machine. Frustrated, she said, "Dad, it's Debbie. We're at a tree farm owned by Rains. Outside Flagstaff. I'm leaving the cell phone on under the seat so you can trace us if need be."

"Look," Denise said, "There's somebody walking down from the barn."

"I see him."

Suddenly, the front door opened and Gerald bounded down the stairs, anxious to greet his guests. Debbie looked to her left and saw Gerald striding toward her car with a big smile on his face.

"Show time," she said to Denise and cracked the door open.

"Ladies, I'm so glad you could make it. Please join me for a cup of coffee in the dining room." Gerald was careful not to overdo it by reaching out and offering his hand to help Debbie out of the car. Debbie got out and closed the car. She glanced back up the driveway where she had seen the man approaching the house, but he was no longer there. She made note that there were at least two people at the farm.

"Good morning, Gerry," Debbie said and offered her hand. Gerald shook it and then turned to Denise who merely said hello. Gerald dropped his hand and guided the two up the stairs to the front hallway.

Debbie looked around and said, "Rustic, but very charming. I hope you didn't clean up on our account," she smiled at Gerald.

"Well, truth be told, the place was a bit dirty yesterday and we've done some sweeping. Come into the dining room and have a cup. I'll give you the ten minute lecture I give everyone who visits FEN Farm."

"Fen Farm. That's catchy" Denise said, cracking a wry smile.

"I agree. Here, sit down at the table while I get the coffee." Gerald walked through the swinging door into the kitchen.

Denise and Debbie sat down on opposite sides of the venerable table and looked at each other. Debbie rolled her eyes skyward.

Moments later Gerald returned with a wooden tray loaded with three mugs of steaming coffee and a bowl of sugar. "Sorry, no cream that's not sour." He offered the cups to Debbie and Denise.

"Forgive the mugs, but it's all we have here," Gerald said as he passed the sugar to Debbie.

"Is there anything besides a mug?" Denise joked.

"Of course, of course. FBI and LAPD. I couldn't imagine a cup and saucer in that environment. Well, I guess that's a great lead in. I'll keep it short. FEN Farm is a UN sanctioned project to fight global warming. That means we can sell carbon credits to individuals or companies who want to erase their carbon footprints." Gerald stopped and looked at his two guests. They seemed to be listening. "Scientists have determined, with a high degree of probability, that carbon dioxide in the atmosphere is the principle cause of global warming."

"This coffee is surprisingly delicious," Debbie said, interrupting Gerald. Denise nodded her head in agreement.

"Kona organic coffee," he smiled. "Got to stay organic. Anyhow, what are the sources of carbon dioxide? Nature. Decaying trees and decomposing creatures such as animals and man. Volcanoes, forest fires, and, of course, humans burning fossil fuels."

"Where do humans quantitatively rank in order of all the things that produce carbon dioxide?" Debbie asked.

"Well, that's a question often asked by skeptics of global warming. Human endeavors are about sixth or seventh on the list, but rising. It just happens that that's the one part of the carbon environment crisis we can control. Or at least attempt to control. Computer models developed by scientists at MIT have shown that by a certain time the earth will heat up to the point of self destruction. This was depicted in Al Gore's movie, *An Inconvenient Truth.*"

"How do you explain that the average global temperature hasn't risen since 1998? Almost ten years?" asked Denise.

"There will be periods of cooling. Nature does this. There are more white caps in the ocean believed to be affecting the temperature."

Suddenly, the sound of running water and clanking dishes came from the kitchen. "Is there someone else here? Denise asked. She instinctively reached down for her Glock.

"Yes. A part-time worker who lives here and manages the farm. Let me introduce you to him," Gerald said. "Everett can you come into the dining room," he called out.

Debbie immediately tensed. Was this the person she had seen earlier walking down the hill from the barn to the house? She had seen something vaguely familiar but dismissed it. The swinging door to the kitchen opened and Everett Riley entered the room. He stopped short when he saw Debbie, but his eyes caught the subtle shake of her head. Debbie worried that Gerald had caught the silent communication between the two old high school classmates.

"Denise and Deborah, this is Everett Riley. Everett this is Denise Weber and Deborah Michaels. Denise is FBI and Deborah is LAPD," Gerald said, not giving any hint that he suspected something passed between the two old acquaintances.

Everett smiled and said, "Glad to meet you. Sorry about the noise in the kitchen. Just cleaning up."

"Gerry tells us you are a part time worker here. What do you do?" Denise asked.

"Dig holes mostly. We have a tractor with an auger attachment. I also make sure the trees get watered when it's real dry. Other than cleaning up and keeping this place tidy, that's it. I also work part time in the operating room at the main hospital in town. Night shift. I'm a scrub tech."

"Don't you get lonely out here? No one around," Denise asked.

"Not really. I keep busy and hardly notice it." So far Gerald was pleased with Everett's humble answers but he wanted to end the inquisition.

"Everett, why don't you finish the dishes. When I'm through with my dog and pony show I'll take the ladies around." Everett smiled, nodded at Debbie and Denise, and returned to the kitchen.

"Let's see. I was talking about Al Gore and his outstanding movie when we were interrupted. This movie is being shown in classrooms all across America and hopefully we'll have a new generation of people passionate about the environment."

"Hasn't it been shown that some of the scenes in that movie weren't real? They were computer generated. Also, the stuff about the polar bears was baloney," Denise said. She was a real skeptic whereas Debbie had more or less bought into the idea that global warming was man made.

"Yes. But only to make a point. Sure, there was poetic license in that movie, but the basic facts are not disputed. The world is getting warmer and green house gases are rising. These gases trap the suns radiation and prevent their dissipation. Hence, more warming."

Gerald, although an average student in college, always felt he was the smartest man in the room. So much so that he was bold enough to invite these two investigators to his farm, believing they couldn't possibly outsmart him.

"Carbon dioxide is essential for our survival. Photosynthesis produces oxygen and we live. As there are more people and oxygen consuming organisms on the earth, won't we need more carbon dioxide? How can we be sure carbon dioxide levels will remain at sustainable levels?" Denise asked.

"You're a doubter aren't you, Denise?" Gerald asked condescendingly. "What's it going to take to convince you that the earth is in a crisis? A flood, tidal wave, what? No, there will always be enough carbon dioxide without burning fossil fuels. Well, let's have a look around. I know you're anxious to get on the road."

Denise looked on Gerald as a fanatic. He was unable or unwilling to discuss the science of global warming without the interference of his own personal feelings. He wasn't interested in the truth, merely exploiting a possible myth for his own gain. She would ask him no more questions and get through this tour and be on the road. This looked like a dead end anyway and she had to be at work tomorrow by 7:00 a.m.

As they strolled up a dirt road in back of the house and passed the barn, the trio heard a growl.

"Quiet, Bingo. That's our watchdog. A little too playful to let loose with guests around."

"What is he?" Debbie asked.

"German Shepard. Now let's see, where was I? Oh yes. As I was saying, we hope to go public with this farm concept next year," Gerald said as they trudged up the dirt road beyond the barn.

"Public?" Debbie asked.

"Yes. For example," he said "there are securities firms in London that sell credits in the industrialized world to companies who need carbon offsets. The money raised is then used to invest in clean air projects in poorer nations. Unfortunately, these firms have had a bad time this year. They were funding companies not approved by the UN as legitimate clean air projects. The UN cracked down and their stock tumbled mightily. Thanks to my work with the UN, they have approved FEN Farm as a legitimate clean air project," he said proudly while he extended his arms forward as if to encompass the farm in his grasp.

"We mostly plant aspens, ponderosa pines, and maple trees. As you can see, the land beside our property is filled with older trees. There's some change of colors already but, in a month, it will be spectacular."

They walked up to a knoll and turned around to look behind them. The view was much the same as the one Debbie and Denise had seen earlier from the road off to their right. It was a beautiful sight and even the burgeoning tree farm looked picturesque with the older, maturing trees adding texture and definition.

To get back to what Gerald had just iterated, Denise said, "So, what you're saying is the richer, industrialized nations must pay a tax to fund poorer nations. Not a bad wealth redistribution scheme. Tax our already overtaxed businesses and damage our economy while the rest of the world benefits."

Gerald eyed Denise. He didn't like her or her insightful observations. He decided it was best get these people on their way.

He was interrupted from his thoughts when Debbie asked, "What's in the barn besides the dog?" The barn was about three hundred yards back down the slope they had just hiked. "On the way up here, I saw it was padlocked."

She turned and looked at Gerald waiting for her answer. Gerald was beginning to realize that inviting these curious investigators was maybe not such a good idea after all. He smiled and said, "Equipment. Shovels, tractor, trees ready to be planted. Tree farm stuff."

"Why is the barn padlocked?" Denise asked as she carefully eyed Gerald.

"Everett lives out here. Alone. But he works at night. We've had stuff stolen from the barn in the past, so we padlocked it. Now, I think it's time that you guys got on the road," he said over his shoulder as he turned and started the walk back to the house.

Denise didn't like the way Gerald was acting. His sudden abruptness made her suspicious.

"Are all these trees bought and paid for on carbon credit donations? I mean, the entire ten acres is nearly filled with trees," Debbie asked without moving.

Gerald stopped walking and looked back at Debbie. *Anymore questions and they'll be putting handcuffs on me.* "It's 80 percent filled with trees. No, I'm planting the trees now. I don't wait until someone buys a tree. They are already in the ground when they're purchased. Only about a third of the trees are sold."

"So, the trees in the front of the property that are older and taller are sold. The smaller saplings which we mostly see are unsold. Is that about it?" Denise asked.

"More or less," Gerald said.

"In other words, business could be better?" Debbie asked as she started walking back, trailing Gerald.

"Yes. But the whole global warming movement is in it's infancy. As soon as new laws are passed by Congress regulating carbon footprints and offsets, I expect to be sold out. I have to hang on until then." Gerald's answers were becoming more clipped as he tired of the questions.

"The auditors that you talked about yesterday would focus on the sales. Make sure that trees are not double sold." Debbie said. It was not a question.

Here Gerald thought he was finally on solid ground and said, "If I ever did anything like that it would be the end of this project. The UN would find out and pull my approval."

They continued walking past the barn toward their car. Between the barn and the house was a garage. Debbie looked inside and could see a red beat up pick up truck and Gerald's hybrid parked there. She decided there was nothing suspicious to see there, but what she really wanted do is look in the barn.

When they arrived at their car, Everett came out of the house to say goodbye. Debbie and Denise thanked Gerald for his hospitality, waved to Everett, got in their car, and backed down the driveway. Debbie was driving and she turned the car around and headed toward the entrance.

"Impressions?" Debbie asked as she drove slowly to the highway.

"It's a crock of shit. A scam. Just another scheme to make money off the man made global warming hoax."

"You should meet my dad. You two would get along real well. He feels the same as you. Besides that, what about the barn? Wouldn't you like to look inside?"

"Hell yes."

"That guy working there was the guy who got the surfboard from his friend who was killed in Iraq."

"What! Are you kidding me? You know that guy?" Denise asked shocked.

"Yeah. He's the police chief's son I was telling you about. I didn't get a chance to talk to him, but he's got some s'plaining to do," Debbie said à la Desi Arnez.

"This has definitely been worthwhile. Coming out here. I wasn't so sure just minutes ago, but Everett casts a different light. I'll write up a report tomorrow, turn it over to the terrorist guys. They will have to bump up their interest in Mr. Rains. At least I hope so."

Debbie came to the entrance and stopped. She looked right and left and could see that the tree growth was dense enough to hide her car from the house. She turned right and headed up the road where they had gone when they first arrived.

"Whoa. Where are you going?" Denise asked.

"They can't see us, the trees will hide the car if I park it along the road. I could sneak over, get a look in that barn. There was a wall ladder to the loft and the loft doors were ajar. I noticed that on the way down the hill."

"That's crazy. It's breaking and entering. If they catch you, what's your excuse? What about the watch dog chained up in there?" Denise asked.

"There's no breaking. Loft doors are open. I don't plan to get caught. I'm in and out before they know what's happened. I'm up wind from the dog and I'll be real quiet." She pulled the car off the road as far as possible. She could see the top of the barn about two hundred yards to her right. She stepped out of the car and came to the passenger window.

"You stay here. Give me my cell, it's under the seat."

Denise reached down and fished around until she felt the open cell phone. She grabbed it with her finger tips and brought it up. She handed it to Debbie, who snapped it closed.

"Turn your cell on. I'll call if there's any problem. Oh, here, put my wallet in the glove compartment." Debbie handed Denise her wallet. "I don't want to lose it crawling up there."

"Take your Glock. I'd feel better."

Debbie shook her head no and said, "I don't plan on any rough stuff. There's only two of them there, they didn't looked armed to me." Without waiting any longer she waved at Denise and headed into the brush below the growing trees.

Down the road, the man who had been watching the entrance was puzzled by the car that went to his left rather than to his right. He called on his cell phone, which was answered on one ring. "What now?" the voice asked.

"Those two cops didn't head back to town. They went up the road and pulled over. One got out, headed into the bushes."

"She was taking a leak for Chris'sake."

"No. Been gone too long."

"Ok. Keep me posted. If they haven't departed the area in a half hour let me know. They may be having a look see."

"Roger."

Debbie zigzagged over to the edge of the tree line and came to the path she had just walked with Gerald. The back of the barn was just ahead of her. She looked down the path all the way to the house and could see no one. Quickly, she scurried across the pathway and then flattened herself against the barn's wall. She heard nothing and inched over to the ladder which was simply slats of wood nailed to the wall. Looking up, she confirmed that the hay loft's double doors were ajar. The hinges were on the outside and she correctly surmised the doors must swing outward. It was about a fifteen foot climb, but she made it without slipping on the narrow rungs. The doors were made of wooden panels and there were no handles to grab. Gradually, she was able to slip her fingers into the crack between the doors, but they didn't budge. They had been in this position so long they were frozen in place.

She looked around on the ground and saw a rusted tree stake lying in the weeds. She climbed down and retrieved it. Fortunately, it looked narrow enough to slip into the open space between the two doors. After she climbed back up, she balanced herself while she slipped the end of the stake into the opening between the doors. Quietly as possible, she jacked the stake to her left while the door on her right gradually moved outward. She dropped the metal stake to the ground and grasped the door on her left and pulled it open. It took all of her strength, but finally the door swung outward without any creaking or moaning. When they were wide enough for her to crawl up, she entered the loft. She lay flat, fully expecting a quick retreat if the dog barked. Fortunately, there was no sound coming from the front of the barn.

Once inside, there was ample light for her to look around. She crawled to the edge of the loft and looked down. Below her, lining both sides of the barn, stood stalls used in days gone by for tethering and feeding livestock. The loft, which ran the full length of the barn, was filled with rotting bales of hay that gave off a musty odor. Instead of animals, the stalls were filled with tools, hoses, and young trees with root balls wrapped in burlap. This was just as Gerald had told her. Directly below her and to her right was a small tractor. The barn was about 100 feet long and had a dirt floor covered with rotting straw. To her left was a ladder nailed to a supporting stanchion. It was similar to the one she climbed to get into the loft. She looked toward the front of the barn and could see Bingo chained in a stall, sleeping.

Debbie listened for any sound that might indicate someone was outside. There was none. She decided to make a quick run down the ladder. If she found nothing suspicious within two minutes, she was going home. The wooden ladder wasn't nearly as sturdy as the one she climbed up on and she had to be careful as well as quiet. At the last rung, she jumped silently to the floor and remained in a crouched position. Quickly she looked around and saw nothing that interested her. Next to the tractor on her right in a larger stall was a series of trees stacked around an old army surplus tarpaulin. She stood up and tiptoed over to the tarp and carefully pulled several trees away from it. She lifted the edge of the tarpaulin and was shocked to see a shiny, green car. The trunk had the word CONCEPT imprinted in bold letters above the latch. She remembered that Melody McClemore had seen a dark car with Arizona plates and the letter C on the trunk. The car appeared to be European and small. Raised, silvery letters on the trunk said Saab. Surprised and delighted she had made the decision to enter the barn she blurted out loud, "This must be the car Melody saw!"

Suddenly, there was loud barking and growling from the front of the barn. Her outburst had awakened Bingo. He was straining hard and making a racket. Debbie threw the tarp down and replaced the trees then quickly climbed the ladder, but at the top rung the rotting wooden slat pulled out of the stanchion as she grabbed for it. Her fall was partially broken by the straw on the ground; she was dazed nonetheless. Her first thought was to hide but getting herself to move was not so easy. Gradually her head cleared and she sat up. Just then the barn door swung open and she saw Gerald, Everett and another man enter.

Everett told the dog to shut up. Gerald approached Debbie and said, "Well what do we have here? A prowler has broken into our barn. Should we call the police? Oh yeah, they're already here," Gerald said sarcastically.

"No apologies, Gerald," Debbie said, "you're a fraud and you're going to answer for it." She didn't feel as bold as she sounded but knew the best defense in this situation was an aggressive offense.

Gerald stared at her then looked at the tarp. "So you've found my precious car. Nice work. Where's you're partner in crime?" he asked, kicking her in the shin.

"Hey, take it easy," Everett said as he approached Gerald. "That's no way to behave. I'm sure there's an explanation."

"You're naïve, San Diego. She has done her job and either we deal with this or go to jail…. for a long time. What's your choice?" Gerald said, staring at his impudent acolyte like a professor does when challenged by a student.

Everett remained silent but Rabat spoke and said, "This is problem. She knows about car. Gas station picture too. She can't leave or we dead."

"Precisely, Rabat. That's why I hired you. Your world view is much more realistic than your whimpering partner there. Help me get her up. San Diego get those cable ties off the counter over there and bring them here."

Everett returned with the ties, which were long enough to bind wrists and ankles.

"You see, I am very familiar with these since you cops use them for crowd control during demos. In fact, I've been bound with them myself."

He reached down and lifted Debbie to her feet and then pulled her arms around to her back. Holding her wrists with one hand he was able to guide the tapered end of the tie through the square shaped locking mechanism on the other. He slipped the plastic O around her wrists and pulled it snugly but not tightly. He didn't want to leave telltale marks indicating she had been restrained. Debbie winced when she heard the zipper sound of the plastic strap as it was pulled through the lock.

"I would be remiss if I didn't search you wouldn't I, Deborah?" Gerald asked when he finished binding her wrists.

"C'mon, Mr. Rains, we can't do this. She's a cop." Everett said in less than his usual reverential tones.

"And a damn snoopy one at that. So far, all I've done is apprehend a common burglar who has broken into my barn. Now search her, be sure she doesn't have a weapon. I want to see identification. How do we know she's a cop?"

Everett went over and patted Debbie's ankles, then her pants at hip level and finally under her arm pits. He also looked for a fanny pack like he had seen her partner wearing earlier. He missed the razor thin cell phone deep in the front pocket of her jeans.

"No wallet. No ID. She still is unidentified. Take her to the basement. Bind her ankles Rabat. We'll close up here. Unchain the dog, hook him up at the back of the house," Gerald said, looking at Everett.

Everett watched as Rabat shoved Debbie ahead of him. "This is dumb, Gerry. Why make it worse? They got us dead to rights. Blame it on Rabat, he's the loose cannon around here."

Gerald noted the quick change in Everett's attitude toward him. There was no "Mr. Rains" anymore. Maybe he wasn't so naïve after all. "I hate to tell you, but we're all in this together. You put the incendiary device together. You set the timer."

"Yes. But our intent was not to kill anyone. You know that. We got verification that no one was home. It was that crazy Arab that threw the gas on the house."

"You mean you got verification. From whom?" Gerald asked. "We went forward based on your information. So who's culpable here?" Gerald asked, staring at him. "By the way, Everett, we're using our real names from now on. The Arab you call Rabat is Achmed. Achmed is a Moroccan not an Arab. A real distinction. So get your facts straight. When I first met him he was a starry eyed young man who loved America. He wanted to come here and get educated. It was the hate spewed by anti-America professors at the university who gave him second thoughts about the U.S., not some Imam. Understood?"

"Yes."

"Now close this up and padlock it. Go around back, close those hayloft doors. Then meet me in the dining room. Oh, and one more thing, Everett. You call the cops and everyone here dies," Gerald said, flashing a .38 pistol stashed in his waist band.

Chapter Twenty-Two

Denise looked at her watch. It had been over 30 minutes since Debbie left and she began to worry. She wondered if her partner had fallen getting into the hayloft or, worse yet, fallen inside and impaled herself on a tool or piece of machinery. She came up with two options. Wait for five minutes more and then go find out or go now. She decided on the latter. It was nearly 11:00 AM and time to head home. Denise cracked the passenger door and stepped outside. It was a cool, breezy fall day but she was dressed warmly. Her Glock was in her pack. She took the car's keys along with her cell and put them in her pocket.

Denise followed Debbie's trail through the trees and brush until she came up to the path they had taken earlier. The hayloft doors were pushed nearly all the way back to the barn's walls. This didn't look good. She looked down toward the house and saw that the coast was clear. She ran, crouched over to the barn and flattened herself against it. Hearing nothing, she hurried to the ladder and climbed up to the loft. Once inside she heard a voice. She crawled to the loft's edge and looked down toward the barn doors. One door was partially opened and she could see Everett talking on a cell phone.

He was holding the dog's chain in his left hand. She couldn't make out the words but Everett was talking hurriedly, in hushed tones.

Debbie was nowhere in sight. She looked down at the ladder leading to the floor of the barn. She noted the rotted top slat was missing and she could see it lying on the floor. *Debbie must have fallen.* Quietly she slid back to the loft opening and descended the ladder. After peeking around the corner of the barn, she hurried back to her car.

While Denise was getting into her car, Achmed entered the dining room where Gerry was seated staring straight ahead. He slid the razor thin phone over to Gerry as he sat down next to him.

"What's this?" Gerry asked.

"What it look like? Phone in cop's pants. San Diego missed it. He dumb shit."

"His name is Everett. No more false names. We're in deep shit here so we might as well get to know each other. That clear?"

"Very clear. Does not mean I like him."

Gerry flipped open the phone and scrolled through Debbie's phone book. He saw Denise's number and pushed it hoping it would connect to her. To his surprise, she answered immediately.

Before Gerald could say anything, Denise assumed the caller was Debbie and said, "Where have you been? I've been worried."

"Sorry Agent Weber, but this is Gerald Rains. Debbie fell in the barn and is injured. She's lying on the couch as we speak." Sort of true.

Denise's tone softened as she asked, "May I talk to her?"

"Yes, when she wakes up. Right now she has a big knot on her forehead. She's not really conscious yet."

"I'll be right there, but it sounds like the paramedics need to be involved."

This is easy, Gerald thought as he said, "They're on their way."

Denise hung up and started the car. It seemed to the FBI agent that the weekend has been like a yo-yo. Promising leads one minute and misfortune the next. Down is how she felt as she sped past the man sitting in his car watching events unfold. The man couldn't figure out what was going on, so he decided to gather more intelligence before he contacted his boss. He returned to listening to music on his iPod.

When Chief Peter Riley received the call from his son it was Sunday before noon. That meant he was parked in front of his TV watching professional football. His beloved Raiders were losing their opening game against the Giants in the Meadowlands. This did not make him feel like taking a call, but he picked up anyway after the third ring.

"Riley," he said gruffly.

In an excited voice he heard his son say, "Dad, we're in deep shit."

The Chief couldn't be sure what his son said so he hit the mute button on the remote. "Say again. Who's this?" he asked.

In hushed tones Everett said, "It's me. Everett. I'm at the tree farm. All shit's breaking loose. Debbie Miceli came here with an FBI agent. They've gone too far. She broke into the barn here. Rains caught her."

This was definitely not good news. The Chief shut off the TV. "What do you mean *caught?*"

"Caught as in *caught*. Rains caught her in the barn. He's got her hogtied in the basement. The FBI agent is still out here somewhere," Everett said excitedly, his voice rising in pitch.

"Now calm down, son. What's Rains planning? I mean there's not many options."

"That crazy Arab is here running around cutting off chicken heads. He sounds like one of those Al-Qaeda loonies. I think he wants to cut her head off."

Chief Riley sighed. *How did things for Everett spiral so out of control?* His son's involvement in what was supposed to be a routine harassment has turned into arson, murder and now further violence. It wasn't supposed to have been this way, he thought. Riley felt that his culpability in the deaths of Dolores and Hector was non-existent since he gave Everett information about Hector and Dolores' whereabouts unaware of his son's intention. But now he had been willfully hindering an investigation, so problems here on forward could give him big legal troubles. Despite this, his first obligation was to his son, who desperately needed his help.

"How the hell did Debbie Miceli make Rains? Does he know that you know her?"

"I don't know and no. So far he knows nothing about us. Debbie was careful that didn't happen when Rains introduced us today. But Dad, I'm worried. He's going crazy on me. I may be next. I think he'd do anything to save his butt. He warned me that if I called the cops we're all going to die."

"He's a nut job alright. Stay put. I'm flying out there right now. Should be there within two hours."

"Hurry!"

Everett closed his cell phone and slowly put it in his pocket. He had to be calm and act confident. He walked out of the barn and decided to leave the hayloft doors as they were. Instead, he brought the dog to the back of the house near the outside cellar doors and hooked him to his post. Looking around, he didn't see anyone outside or staring out through the kitchen windows. He pulled open one side of the cellar double doors and descended the steps. He closed the door and inched his way into the middle of the darkened room. He saw Debbie on her knees. Wrists and ankles bound with a pillow cover over her head. Everett shuddered as images of beheadings from Middle East television flashed through his head.

"Debbie, it's me, Everett," he said in a whisper.

The pillowcase, which had been bent forward, straightened up and moved from side to side as Debbie tried to orient herself to the sound. "Everett?" she asked in a whisper.

"Yeah. It's me. Don't talk loud, sound carries in this madhouse."

"I'm scared," she said, choking back a sob. "That Achmed guy scares me. He was rough with me."

"He's a first class asshole and dangerous. I'm going to try and talk some sense into these guys, so hold tight. I haven't much time or they'll suspect something."

"You have to warn Denise somehow. She's in the car on the road north of the farm near the barn," Debbie said slowly, trying to control her voice.

"Hang tight. I gotta go or they'll start looking for me."

Pete Riley clicked off from his son and spent a moment thinking about the situation. He was in deep trouble, but so was his son and Debbie Miceli. If he had been straight with her, she wouldn't be in her current predicament. Conspiracy to commit arson was one thing, but knowing what he knew and not acting on it was another. He could get the local Flagstaff police involved, but Everett's warning about Rains' threat made him cautious. Besides, he could manage the damage to both himself and Everett better without a nosy local police department asking questions. He decided to fly out there as quickly as he could. In fact, Fred Lesley had flown him out to Flagstaff two years ago when he had visited Everett at the tree farm.

These thoughts and memories led him to think of Dan Miceli. He had never warmed up to the doctor even though he respected him. *Shit, what's he going to say if he finds out I was involved in arson murder?* He pegged the guy as a classic loner who didn't flaunt his military experience as a SEAL. There's more to this guy than he figured. He picked up the phone and dialed Dan's number. When there was no answer, he left a short message on his answering machine along with a request to call him. He left his cell number and home number. Then he called Fred Lesley on the pilot's emergency line.

He found him at the golf course. Without getting too specific, he was able to convince Fred to drop the sticks and get over to the airport. The Chief promised he would be there within the hour.

Everett quietly left the basement through the outside access and walked into the house through the kitchen. His throat was dry and he stopped for a glass of water. He then pushed through the dining room door and sat down at the table with Achmed and Gerald. He could barely look at either one of them and wished he had never met them. Environmental activism sounded glamorous on the campus but sucked in real life. He vowed to himself he would do everything possible to protect the two who had stumbled into the mess he had created.

"The dog chained up? We got the FBI agent on the way. You didn't search the police officer very well," Gerald said, holding up her phone.

"Yeah, the dog's chained, and I was just trying to be careful. Who found it?" Everett asked.

"I did. Search pockets like anyone would," Achmed said.

"I bet you were real cool about it," Everett sneered.

"That's enough guys. Achmed, you can't be here when the agent gets here. Beat it up stairs. I'll let you know when to come down."

Achmed sulked out of the room and climbed the stairs to the attic.

Turning toward Everett, Gerald said, "I know you don't like the situation we're in. But it's jail for a long time or these two. What's it gonna be?"

"If you think you can silence these two without someone finding out, you're dumber than I thought."

"It depends on how they get silenced. For example, there are plenty of places to drive off the road around here, end up in a canyon. Wouldn't be the first time someone unfamiliar with the roads has ended up at the bottom."

"Count me out."

Gerald put his index finger to his lips, indicating silence, while he turned his head. "She's here. Go into the kitchen if you're too squeamish to save your butt," Gerald said. He stood and pushed his chair back. When he turned to go to the front door, Everett noted the revolver flashed earlier by Gerald was stuck in his back waistband. He shook his head and headed for the kitchen.

Moments later there was a knock at the door and Gerald went over and slowly opened it. He saw Denise standing well back from the door, her right hand resting on her waistline pack.

"Hi Denise. Come in. Debbie's waking up on the couch in the TV room. I think she's okay," Gerald said sympathetically. "She took a bad tumble off the ladder."

Denise was still wary but she approached the door cautiously and kept her hand on her pack. She knew where the TV room was, thanks to the earlier tour she had taken courtesy of Rains. She passed a little too close to Gerald who towered over her and, before she knew it, her right arm was pinned behind her back. She tried to struggle but he was exceedingly strong and unyielding. However, after kicking him several times in the shin, she was able to break free. Suddenly, she was grabbed from behind. It was a bear hug pinning her arms to her side. She was held in this position while Gerald removed the Glock from her pack.

"Good work, Achmed. Hang on to her. I've got cable ties in the kitchen." Gerald disappeared but quickly returned with the ties. A concerned Everett followed him back to the main hallway. Denise was clearly angry.

"Do you have any idea what you're doing?" she blurted out while Gerald was securing her wrists behind her back. Again, he was careful not to create wrist burns which might later indicate she had been held captive.

"You two broke into my barn. That's against the law. The property is posted and you trespassed. So, we're making a citizen's arrest," he laughed. "Take her down stairs, Achmed. Just like the other one. Search her and do not bind her ankles tightly. Understood?"

Without warning, Everett ran directly at Achmed and tackled him, sending the three of them (Denise included) to the floor. Everett was in great shape from the work on the farm. He was wiry and almost as tall as Achmed but not as strong. Soon the Moroccan was gaining the advantage over his attacker by grabbing him in a headlock while they rolled around on the floor. Denise stood up and with her arms bound behind her began kicking Achmed in an attempt to give Everett an advantage.

Gerald stood back and drew his .38 revolver. It looked like a water pistol in his meaty hands. He walked over and pulled Denise away with his left hand while holding the firearm to her ear with his right. She got the message and backed off.

"That's enough," Gerald bellowed, but it did no good. The two continued to roll back and forth slugging each other at will. The animosity between the two dated back to the day Achmed arrived. Almost immediately, Everett took offense to his arrogant, American-bashing attitude. Achmed, for his part, was put off by Everett's stereotypical comments about terrorists and Islam.

Gerald saw this interruption as potentially dangerous. If Everett bloodied up Achmed enough to make him useless, then he'd have no more muscle left in his fight against the authorities. Without giving it a second thought, he fired his pistol into the ceiling and the fighting stopped immediately.

"You two dirt bags stop this shit. Everett, get off Achmed and stand back. Achmed, go to the kitchen and clean up. Then take Denise downstairs."

Achmed's nose had been bloodied and he was pissed at Everett. He glared at him as he went into the kitchen. When Gerald could hear water running, he turned to Everett.

"Your ass is in a sling," he said, pointing the gun at Everett.

Dan had spent the morning walking the vineyard and swimming in the ocean. The weather was still holding and it was a warm September Sunday. After a quick shower with the backyard garden hose, he dried himself off on the back porch.

He went to the kitchen refrigerator food hunting, but wasn't quite sure what he wanted. He grabbed a container of yogurt, an apple, and a spoon from the kitchen counter and headed for the den. He was hoping to find Debbie was on her way home by checking her GPS rigged phone. He clicked onto the appropriate web site but couldn't get a recent location. There had been no change for two hours. The previous location identified a position about three miles north of Flagstaff. *No new updates for two hours?* He put down his yogurt and spoon and began to search the site when he noted the red light blinking on his phone. He glanced at the clock. It was 20 minutes after twelve.

He punched the new message button and heard the automated voice tell him there were two new messages. One was from Debbie, giving him an update on her location. The other was from Riley who said, "Doc, this is Pete Riley. It's after eleven on Sunday morning. Got a call from Everett about some trouble out in Arizona where he works. Debbie's involved too. I'm on my way there with Lesley." He then gave his cell and home phone number.

Dan dialed Riley, but got no answer at home. Frustrated, he began to dream up all kinds of scenarios involving his daughter. He told himself to calm down while he dialed the Chief's cell. There was an immediate response.

"Riley. Is that you doc?" he asked tersely.

"What's going on Chief? It sounds serious"

Riley was in his car and about ten minutes from the airport. "That's affirmative," he said, defaulting to his military persona, "Everett tells me Debbie is being held against her will. The nut job who's doing this says any police interference and everyone dies. I think he includes himself in that."

Dan couldn't believe what he was hearing. "When's Fred leaving? I'm going too," he said forcefully.

"As soon as I'm on site. But I'd prefer you come along, given what I've learned this week about your past experience."

"That goes for Fred, too. We were together a long time. Give me half an hour to get my stuff together and call Fred. If I don't get him, let him know I'm on my way. Does he know the details?" Dan asked.

"Not exactly. I was vague. I only told him it was urgent. Because time's an issue, I'm sending one of my guys to meet you at your gate. An escort is in order here."

Dan clicked off and dialed Fred's number. He reached him immediately at the airport and explained the details Riley had left out. Fred was very concerned and said he needed to go back home and get additional gear. After Dan hung up, he raced upstairs and climbed into black chinos and donned a black shirt as well as a dark windbreaker. He pulled on his heavy hiking boots and strapped a hunting knife to his ankle. He raced downstairs to the den and unlocked the door to his arsenal. "Thank God for the second amendment" he mumbled to himself. He picked out his favorite, a Beretta semi automatic 9 mm. with a muzzled tip, and also grabbed six ammunition clips.

Outside he met Carlos, who was walking in from the winery. Dan told him he would be gone the rest of the day and to hang around the house for calls. He gave him his cell phone number and then jumped into his pick up truck.

He raced up the hill to Highway One where a police cruiser was waiting with its siren lights sweeping back and forth. The cruiser took off without a second look back, and they were speeding to the San Luis Obispo airport.

Chapter Twenty-Three

Gerald Rains was born in a small western Washington town in 1968. His mother, Lilly, was a product of the 60's generation upheaval and never quit being a protesting, college dropout. While perfectly able to work, she chose to live on welfare. Because of chronic LSD usage damaging her psyche, she felt the world owed her a living. Lilly lived at home with her parents in a small garage apartment. Lilly wasn't sure who Gerald's father was until she saw how big Gerald had grown in junior high school. If her suspicions were correct, she didn't want anything to do with the man. Lilly never had time for her son and left the necessary parenting to her mom and dad. Gerald's granddad was an outdoorsman and a retired US Forest Ranger. Her grandmother was a grammar schoolteacher who loved Gerald but hated the way her daughter had turned out. The two were more than willing to help the young man grow up under their watchful eye to make up for their disastrous Lilly.

In junior high school it was clear that Gerald was little better than average in his school work and above average in his size and athletic ability. He played football and after high school received an athletic scholarship from a small, western Washington college. It was perfect for him because he wanted to follow in his granddad's footsteps and become a forest ranger. This occupation seemed to suit his personality, which could be best described as introverted. Consequently, despite his success on the football field as an offensive lineman, he made few friends and was considered a loner. Before he graduated, he was devastated when his grandparents were killed in an auto accident and, shortly after that, his mother committed suicide. This left him bitter and depressed, but he finished college and passed the test to become a US Forest Ranger.

Somewhere along the way he became an environmental activist as he witnessed lumber companies clearing trees from the mountainsides near where he lived. The incompetent attempts by the logging companies to reforest the land made him angry. On several occasions, his anger was such that he felt like getting a gun and using loggers for target practice. He didn't think the government was putting enough effort into regulating the logging companies. After three years in the ranger service he was sufficiently disillusioned to quit and do odd jobs to survive. It wasn't long before he was strongly supporting political causes involving the environment, anti-capitalism, and the harassment of logging companies.

"The ties aren't going to make marks?" he asked Achmed when he returned.

"I careful. No need to tell me twice, not like San Diego." Gerald was sitting at the dining table after Achmed had taken Denise to the cellar and bound her ankles. Using more cable ties, he had linked her ankles to her wrists while she was in a kneeling position.

Everett was sitting at the table. He looked up but did not respond to Achmed's comments. His chances for a long-term future were in serious jeopardy and he was in no position to fight back. Gerald, who had worked hard to get where he was, had the memories of living with a dysfunctional mother to remind him how far he had come. He owned three tree farms and had a loyal following of environmentalists who backed FEN. He wasn't going to toss that away without a fight. Gerald held a gun on Everett but talked to Achmed.

"Go in the kitchen and get some latex gloves. They're in the pantry. Put them on, go search the car. A pair for me too. Look in the trunk, under the front seat, glove compartment, everywhere. Bring what you find in here ASAP."

Achmed stood, scurried into the kitchen, and found the gloves exactly where Gerald had said they were. He donned them, picked up a pair for his boss, and dropped them off on the way out to the car. He returned with two overnight bags, papers, and two wallets fifteen minutes later.

"Did you find anything when you searched the agent?" Gerald asked, having forgotten to ask him prior to the car search.

"Other than gun in pack, no. It is here," he said, pointing to the pack lying on the table. He slid the pack over to Gerald so it was out of Everett's reach.

Gerald donned his gloves, being careful to keep an eye on Everett. He opened up Denise's wallet first and took everything out. He slowly went over the material and carefully replaced each item as he had found it. He then went through her overnight bag where he found her laptop computer. *Fat chance I'll find anything important in there that's not protected by passwords.* After he finished with Denise's wallet he picked up Debbie's and pulled out her California Driver's license. He was stunned when he saw her real name was Miceli. That was the name of the winery his inept team had vandalized. It took him two seconds to realize that, since Everett was from Vista Del Mar and his dad was a cop, he would know Deborah Miceli.

"I thought I saw something pass between you and that cop this morning," he said, glaring at Everett. "You know her, you dumb shit."

"So what? I know a lot of people, I actually work for a living," Everett sneered.

"Where's that obsequious Everett that used to address me as 'Mr. Rains'? You're in a bad position. You should be kissing my ass."

"That's what you'll be doing in Leavenworth. There's no way you're getting out of this."

"Maybe you didn't understand me. One goes, we all go. I mean, no one's leaving here alive if the cops get involved. Now, shut it. In fact, Achmed, let's take the boy scout down to the basement so he can be with his friends."

With that, Gerald stood keeping his gun pointed at Everett. "Come around here Achmed and pin his arms so I can snap on some ties."

In a flash, Achmed was standing behind Everett pulling his arms behind him. Everett didn't resist with the gun trained on him. Gerald looked loony to him and he had no doubt he would shoot.

"Take him down the stairs, rig him up like the girls, pillowcase and all. You didn't duct tape them, did you?"

"No. They're whispering. I checked when you searched bags."

"Good, I don't want marks on them. Nothing to show they've been tied up. They can talk all they want. Yell if they want. No one's going to hear. Understood?"

"Yes boss."

Achmed jerked Everett to his feet and pushed him toward the basement door. Achmed was tempted to throw him down the stairs but he wanted him awake when he departed earth. In the basement, he directed Everett to a stall next to Debbie and Denise. With the noise of people descending the stairs, the two held up their covered heads, turned, and listened. Suddenly, Achmed kicked Everett on the legs from behind, forcing him onto his knees. When Everett's knees struck the cement floor, he cried out. The two other captives quietly shook their heads as Everett's ankles were bound with ties. They could hear the zipping noise as the ties were pulled tightly, linking his ankles with his wrists.

Achmed placed a pillowcase over Everett's head and then gave him a swift kick in the groin. Everett cried out again when the rush of pain hit him. Achmed spit at him before going back upstairs.

Dan, Fred, and Chief Riley stood next to the Cessna Citation that was prepared to fly them to Flagstaff. The jet was fueled and ready to go. Chief Riley looked at his watch and shook his head. It was nearly three o'clock. The one o'clock departure time had long since passed. Fred had gone home for "additional gear" and he was reviewing what he was "bringing to the party." He was also dressed in dark clothes.

The Chief, however, was dressed in blue jeans, a red windbreaker, and white T-shirt. The black baseball cap on his head had the initials VDMPD stenciled in front.

"Chief, that red jacket and white tee shirt are beacons. I don't have anything you can wear instead. Now, here's what I do have," Fred said to the group as he opened a Nike gym bag. "Flash bangs for entry, night vision goggles, flashlights, black knit stocking caps, bottled water, face paint, and my own 9mm Beretta with six clips. Sorry, no vests. What about you, Dan?"

"I've got my Beretta, six clips, and a knife, that's all. But I gotta ask you, where did you get this stuff? I mean flashbangs, night vision goggles?"

"That ain't the half of it, Doc. You can get this stuff off the internet. I'm prepared at home."

Dan shook his head in wonderment and then asked "Chief?"

"My side arm. Glock. Four clips of ammo. Should be enough. Flashbangs are easy to get. Fred's right."

"What laws are we breaking bringing this stuff into Arizona?" Dan asked.

"I'm familiar with that," Riley chimed in, "Arizona has virtually no restriction on carrying an unregistered firearm as long as the weapon is not concealed. We couldn't be going to a better place for doing what we have to do."

"Okay. What about the target area? We might as well do this now. It won't be easy talking on the plane," Dan said, looking at Riley.

"Everett lives at this old three story farmhouse. It has a basement with access through outside doors. In the back, by the kitchen. We could enter there if necessary. Most likely the women will be held in the basement."

Fred tossed his Nike bag onto the plane. "How far is the location out of town?" he asked Riley.

"Three miles. I've been there. You flew me to Flagstaff when I visited Everett several years ago. Remember?'

"Yeah, now I do. Dan any more thoughts," Fred asked.

"No," Dan said with a puzzled look. "I haven't heard the story about how the Chief and Everett got involved in this. Save it for later. Let's get moving."

The three climbed aboard and soon were heading southeast for Flagstaff. At four-thirty, the plane landed and they loaded their gear into a dark Chevy Tahoe that Fred had ordered while in the air. It was still light, but the sun was setting in the West as they drove from the airport. Fred was driving when he suddenly braked the car.

"Look over there in that hangar. A Citation like mine getting a wash. Wonder who owns that?" Fred mused out loud. "That's twenty million dollars of airplane." He looked around at the other two and they seemed uninterested and anxious for Fred to get moving.

He had been watching the entrance to the tree farm from across the road for nearly twenty-four hours. Bottled water, oranges, peanuts, raisins and string cheese were all he had to eat. He had seen the FBI agent return in her car but had not seen the car leave the farm. Earlier, he thought he had heard a gun shot when he was outside the car taking a leak. Only one shot from a low caliber firearm. At the time, he decided not to call his boss, but now that the sun was setting he felt it was time to make contact. He reached over and grabbed his cell phone and speed dialed the boss's number.

"Yeah, what now?" was the response.

"No real excitement except the two females are still there. About two hours ago one drove back into the farm. That's been it."

"What happened to the other one that left the vehicle earlier?" the boss asked.

"Got me. She never came back. Only the agent drove back to the farm alone."

"Nothing else?"

"I did hear a single gunshot coming from the house up there."

"What! When?"

"About two hours ago," the lookout said.

"Jesus. Why didn't you tell me?"

"I wasn't sure where the shot came from. But yeah, should'a called."

"Ok. It's four-thirty. Sun's going down. I'll be there in half an hour."

The conversation ended there. The lookout shook his head wondering to himself how he got involved with his old skipper. So far, his hands had been clean, but he didn't like the smell of this. He put the iPod plugs in his ear and cued on his favorite music.

Gerald had called April and told her he was going to be at the tree farm an additional night. She wished him well and was looking forward to seeing him in the office Monday morning. *Ah, the perfect wife. No dumb questions.* He was munching on a peanut butter and jelly sandwich while he tried to break into Debbie's computer. Other than some boring, unclassified correspondences in her Word documents, he found nothing. Everything else was password protected. He toyed with the idea of forcing her to tell him, but that would involve physical injury. He was sure that pre-mortem markings on either of them would be discovered by even an incompetent coroner. No, he was going to wait until it was dark so there was no chance an unannounced tourist drove in and looked around. The farm stayed open for visitors and potential buyers until five on Sunday. He gazed out to his left and through the window he could see the sun sinking in the West. It would soon get dark very quickly, aided by the Arizona's irregular terrain and cover from the trees surrounding the house. Then he would take care of business.

He had turned it over in his mind a dozen times and was convinced he had no other choice. First, it would be Everett. Then, repack the car and drive up the road with the ladies in back. He had picked out a perfect spot in his mind: a turn in the road where there was no guardrail and a deep gorge over the side. He and Achmed would put them in the front and hold the door on either side and, with the engine running, push the car over the side. They wouldn't be found for months. Perfect.

"What you thinking, boss?" Achmed asked. He had been upstairs saying his prayers in Arabic. The sounds could be heard all over the house and they had a chilling ring to them.

Gerald jumped as the Moroccan had quietly descended the stairs and entered the dining room without a sound. "You startled me. I guess I was deep in thought. Nothing. We got some work to do."

"I know. I take care of Everett then we do girls."

"Take care of Everett? What did you have in mind?" Gerald asked, having not given much thought to how he was going to dispatch of Everett.

"He should pay. How you say, 'big time.' He say many nasty things about Arabs and Islam. Quran says off with his head."

"Is that humane? I mean, he's not a bad kid. A little mouthy at times." Gerald said.

"I not care about that. Best way to do it. Shoot with gun make noise. I practice on chickens. Can do it quickly. Chop, chop the head comes off,"

"Are you sure? That Jewish college student who was beheaded in Iraq took three swings of the blade. The video was awful and he yelled during the first two chops until they cut his wind pipe. No, it's brutal. I don't know if I could sit through that."

"I better than Iraq. You wait upstairs here. I do it, you not see. Allah has condemned the infidel," Achmed said in a soft voice trying to persuade Gerald that this was more a religious rite than an execution.

"Shit. Oh, I suppose so. Make sure your blade is sharp. It gives me the creeps. But, so does being in jail for the rest of my life. I'll let you know when. You get ready."

"How soon?" Achmed asked.

Gerald looked at his watch. "It's five o'clock. In half an hour. I'm going down and close the entrance gate and padlock it so no nosy asshole drives in here. I'll be back before the fireworks start."

Chief Riley cursed himself for wearing a white T-shirt. The best he could do was zip up his windbreaker to the top. Dan insisted that the small part of the shirt that was still visible be smeared with face paint, and as much of the red jacket as possible. The ex-SEAL was very particular and it was clear that in this group he was in charge. They had driven to within two hundred yards of the farm's entrance and pulled into dense brush along the road. Despite the bushes surrounding the Tahoe, they could still catch a glimpse of the tree farm's entrance. While they waited for the sun to disappear, they blackened their faces and loaded their weapons. All three wore the dark knit stocking caps. They sat sipping water in order to hydrate themselves after the flight.

"Tell me the layout again, Chief," Dan said.

"Everett has been volunteering here for room and board for at least two years. I've visited here once. The house is about a hundred yards up the road from the entrance, which you can barely see from here. It's an old style house. Three stories with an attic and basement. Wood siding. The basement windows are built into the rock foundation. There's an entrance to the basement next to the back porch stairs."

"Is the basement door one of those double door things built on a slant?"

"Exactly, Doc," the Chief said.

"Any thoughts, Fred?" Dan asked.

"How many people are there? We know about Debbie and Everett. Who else?"

"Debbie came out with an FBI agent named Denise Weber. I assume she has been detained. There's Rains, I don't know who else," Dan said.

"I've not seen any of these people. Description?" Fred asked Riley.

"Well, Rains is a big guy. Over six feet five, I guess. Has long hair and sports a mountain man beard. At least he did last time I saw him. Everett is shorter. Under six feet. Thin and wiry," the Chief said.

"That's four, but I can't see Rains holding three people by himself. There must be more than him." Fred said.

"Let's assume five plus. We caught three white males on traffic tape before the vineyard incident. So let's assume four males and two females. At least three are assumed to be the enemy. Males, one tall, and two other possibles of unknown identity," Dan said.

"What traffic tape?" Riley asked annoyed.

"It's a long story, Chief. Your officer who came to the house after the vineyard destruction was not helpful. We'll talk about it later," Dan replied.

The Chief pulled back and realized he had better be careful and not make an issue of this bit of news. He was hardly in a position to be critical.

Returning to the problem at hand Riley said, "When I saw Everett he didn't say much about others working at the farm. Only that there were people there. No one was around the day I visited. I met Rains briefly. He wasn't too friendly when he heard I was a cop," Riley added. "Shit. Speak of the devil. There's Rains now. He's closing the front gate. Ugly son of a bitch."

"I can barely see him," Fred said, "but he's big alright."

"We'll have to assume nothing's gone down yet. Not likely to do anything with the gate open," Dan said.

It was just after five and the sunset to his left was gradually being blocked by the trees across the road.

"Well, I guess that answers one question. We walk in. It'll be dark when we get there, let's go," Dan said. The three donned their night vision goggles and packed their side arms. Dan was startled when a car cruised by slowly and turned left off the road near the entrance to the farm.

"What now?" Dan asked.

"I don't think the driver spotted us," Fred said.

"That car is stopped up there. We'll get out on the right side and make our way up through the trees to the house. Agreed?" Dan asked.

The other two nodded. "Chief, you've been there, you lead. I'll flank left and Fred on the right. Stay close. These trees are crowded."

The lookout spotted his boss's arrival and watched as he turned the car around and backed up so he was nose out. The boss rolled down his window and motioned to his lookout to do the same.

"Right on time. Rains was just down closing the gate. The women haven't left, something's going down."

"You got those aerials of the area?" the boss asked.

"Yep. Not much up there except house, barn and garage. Here we are," the lookout said while pointing to their position and handing the aerial photographs to the boss. The pictures had been copied off Google map after the boss's conversation with Rains the day before.

"The entrance is across the road. The gate was closed and secured by mountain man moments ago. There's no surrounding fence, so you could walk up to the house through the trees dead ahead. House iss over a hundred yards or so."

"You're through here. Good job. Get back to the airport, check out the aircraft. Make sure it's clean and refueled. I plan to be here only a short time so we'll be heading back around nine. Here, take these photographs and get rid of them," the boss ordered as he handed them back to the lookout.

"Can I give you a hand?" the lookout asked, taking the printed photographs.

"No. I'm just an observer here. There shouldn't be any heavy stuff. Take off."

When the lookout had left, the boss stepped out of his car and locked it. He was dressed in black sneakers, dark denim pants, a black T-shirt and windbreaker, and a plain, black baseball cap. Holstered inside his jacket was a silenced 9 mm Beretta. *Have I thought of everything?* His main goal was to be sure that there was no evidence or person traceable back to him. He acknowledged it didn't take a genius to realize that the two female investigators had made great headway by pinpointing Rains. *Could they connect Rains to me?* Rains didn't know the boss from Adam, but there had been direct contact between the two on more than one occasion.

The boss crossed the road. He looked right and left before he did and saw nothing. He entered the tree line and headed straight ahead. There was just enough light to avoid the trees and when he had traveled 150 paces he stopped and listened. The silence was deafening. *What have I forgotten?*

It was nearly five-thirty when Gerald entered the house and shut the front door. Standing, waiting for him was Achmed, dressed in black with a white head band. He held a large machete in his right hand and looked at Gerald with eyelids at half-mast. The color of his eyes was ordinarily brown but they seemed darker to Gerald.

"Holy shit, Achmed. You're scarin' the shit out of me."

"Ready to take care of San Diego," he muttered softly."

"It's not five thirty yet and it's still not dark enough. Turn out all the lights upstairs, I'll get the ones here."

"How we see?"

"Good question. Do the lights. I got candles in the kitchen. I don't want anybody looking in here."

Gerald went to the kitchen and found two candles and two holders. He lit the candles then turned out the lights when Achmed returned.

Debbie remained quiet while Everett was being abused by the Moroccan, who was the one she had seen on the gas station video. The car in the barn was just as Melody had described it to her. She had no doubt that the deaths of Hector and Dolores were traced to these psychos. *But why would they do such a thing?* The idea that Everett and maybe his dad were involved sent shivers down her spine.

When Everett had quieted down and Achmed was gone, she whispered, "Everett are you all right?"

Trying to control the sob in his voice, Everett waited before he answered, "Yeah. I'm okay. But I'm scared shitless. That loony tunes upstairs wants to cut my head off." He began to sob quietly.

Debbie waited until he quit before she asked, "How did you get involved in this?" She hoped to distract him from his pain by talking.

"I met Rains at one of his environmental conferences. Like a wide-eyed college student I fell for it. I thought the guy was for real. He's not. He's a hustler. Global warming is his religion, but he's out to make a buck."

"Okay. So far that's okay. Your intentions were good. But what happened?"

"First off, he brought in that fucking Arab...Moroccan... whatever... who worried me from the beginning. Since 9/11 I don't trust any of them. Say one thing and mean another." Everett fell silent and Debbie waited.

Finally, she asked, "Go on. There's more isn't there?"

"Rains did some things that the Arab bragged about. Burned down a warehouse in Baltimore, torched a multimillion dollar house on a Florida beach. Weird stuff. But somebody was paying him. Then one day he asked if we were interested in burning down a garage."

"I'll assume that was my dad's, right?"

"I guess you can call this a death bed declaration. Yours and mine. Yes, it was. But I was assured that Dolores and Hector were out of town. My dad told me, but he didn't know anything about why I asked. Rains was going to make it 'worth our while.' The Arab got carried away and soaked the house."

"So, Rains was behind it?" Denise asked. She had been silent but now felt compelled to be part of the discussion.

"That you, Denise?" Everett asked.

"Yes. I'm really sorry we got you into this," she said, realizing if they had gone home without barn hopping they would be in Los Angeles by now.

"You didn't get me into anything. I brought this on my self. I'm afraid he has plans for you two. Maybe not cut your heads off, but something else."

"That's comforting. Any ideas about getting out of here?" asked Debbie.

"There's one hope. When Rains left me in the barn to bring the dog in, I called my dad. He's on his way."

"Why didn't you call the police? A lot quicker," Denise asked, being careful not to vocalize her disbelief at such a stupid decision.

"That was my first choice until Rains said if anyone called the police we were all dead. I've known him long enough to know he hates the idea of prison. The several time's he's been arrested because of demonstrations has convinced him of that much."

After hearing that, Denise was glad she had not been openly critical of Everett's decision.

Then Debbie asked, "Did you tell your dad to call mine?"

"No. I told him they had detained you. I could be next. What good could your dad do anyway?" he asked skeptically.

"My dad's an ex-SEAL. He's in great shape, target practice twice a week. Did two tours in Vietnam and he was not sitting on his butt."

"Jesus. I never knew that. If I did I would've called him first, maybe skipped my dad," he said half seriously. Just then they heard the basement door open.

"Chief, I gotta tell you I've counted out two hundred paces from the car. Where are we?" Dan asked.

"It's near here. They must have turned out all the lights in the house. I know my bearings are right," the Chief said as he searched the area in front of him with his night vision goggles. The Chief took off his goggles and looked skyward hoping to see the North Star. When he couldn't, he replaced his goggles.

"We're in deep shit if we can't find it. Excuse me, I should say Debbie and Everett are in deep shit," Fred said.

"Wait," Dan said. "There's a compass on the end of my blade." He reached down and unsheathed his hunting knife. He took his flashlight and aimed it at the compass. "East is straight ahead. North is to our left. We're off course. We need to go to our left." They turned and headed north. Several minutes later they heard loud, continuous barking dead ahead.

Chapter Twenty-Four

The boss remembered what he had forgotten. It was his electronic larynx, which he always carried with him when he went out. He'd left it in the car but he wasn't sure he really needed it. The battery-operated hand held device, which was placed near the larynx, worked by changing speech vibrations into sound. As a consequence, his true voice was rendered unrecognizable. He had a laryngeal injury during the first Gulf war when a piece of shrapnel struck him in the neck. After a partial laryngectomy, he used the device while rehabilitating his speech. Although his natural voice, albeit high pitched and distinctive, was perfectly acceptable in conversation, he chose to use the electronic larynx whenever he wanted to disguise his speech.

He convinced himself not to go back and get the voice device since no one in the house would ever again see the light of day. As he approached the dark shadow of the house, he moved to the left and passed a basement window. To his surprise, he saw a flicker of light in the window and heard what sounded like Islamic prayers. He had had his belly full of that in the Middle East and he could recognize the character of the chanting a mile away. He looked in the window and was aghast when he saw a figure, dressed in black and wearing a white head band, preparing to behead someone with a pillow case on his head.

In the basement, Everett was begging for his life. This appeal fell on deaf ears as Gerald stood idly by while Achmed rattled away. He wasn't going to stop the Moroccan who was in another zone. The only way to stop him was to shoot him. He would save that for later. Besides, he needed Achmed to help him dispose of the snoopy broads. He also heard appeals from the women and he told them to shut up. "Your turn is coming," he said. His main concern right now was how to dispose of Everett's body. A headless corpse dumped along a road somewhere was bound to create a stir. The cops and FBI would be here in minutes asking questions. He knew that Everett's dad, whom he met one time, would be like any good cop and not rest until he found his son's killer.

Finally, his thoughts were too much for him and he said, "Hold on. This is going to be messy. Get a couple of blankets under him to soak up the blood. We don't need to leave evidence all over the place."

"I ready. Do quick. He die quick."

"You're an animal, Rains," Denise blurted out. "You have no decency. You're a piece of shit."

"Tut tut, young lady. You're in no position to say that. If it wasn't for your nosy partner, this wouldn't be necessary"

Meanwhile, Achmed was rummaging in the corner and came out with six or seven old produce burlap bags. He made Everett move while he placed them under the hapless captive. He couldn't help wincing from the odor of sweat, urine, and feces emanating from his captive. When he finished he looked at Rains, who nodded his approval.

Suddenly, the dog barked several times and there were two pfsst sounds of muzzled gunshots. The boss threw open the basement doors and came down the stairs so rapidly that Gerald didn't get a chance to respond.

"Hold on, Rains. Don't turn around," the squeaky voice said. "Have you ever seen one of these? I mean there's blood everywhere. Ever hear of the heart or aorta?"

Gerald was tempted to turn around and put a face to the voice since he assumed it was the same person he had talked to yesterday at the hotel. The man was in the shadows beyond the stairs behind him. He also doubted he could make an identification with only two flickering candles providing illumination. Wisely, he heeded the warning and stayed standing with his hands in a half surrender position facing Achmed. Achmed, who stood in front of him with bowed head, was mumbling prayers.

"I kill quickly. Hood over head will catch blood. Why it's there."

"I saw enough of your type in Kuwait. You can't wait. It's a badge of honor for you sick rag heads," said the high pitched voice behind Gerald.

"Gerald, tell him no need to talk like that. This is humane."

The boss pondered the situation and concluded that if Achmed beheads him he could always say he came on to the scene and shot the perpetrator. He could also claim a gunfight with Rains started and the girls got caught in the crossfire.

When Dan heard the dog bark and recognized the sound of a silenced weapon, he made a beeline in that direction. He came to the house, which was completely dark. He also noticed a faint, flickering light in the basement window near the front of the house and moved toward it. Riley and Fred followed, and the trio collectively gasped when they looked into the cellar. It was a macabre scene with the girls hog tied and hooded, and Everett on his knees. Rains was talking to someone over his shoulder while his hands were in a half surrender position.

"We've got no time to waste here. Someone else is in the shadows back there," Dan said nodding in the diagonal direction of the basement's far corner.

"Must have come down the outside stairs. Ran into the dog. No more dog,"

Fred said.

"Shit. I should have told you Rains has a big, mean German Shepard," Riley added.

"It's of no consequence now. In fact, the dog helped us locate the house. One for us. Chief, work your way around the front to the back of the house, cover the cellar entrance. Don't enter. Fred, you toss a flashbang through this window in exactly 45 seconds. It looks like something is getting ready to happen. That Arab is beginning to chant and swing his blade. Lets go."

Dan quietly climbed the stairs to the porch. Fifteen seconds until the flashbang. He tried the front door and it was locked. "Shit," he muttered to himself. He decided to wait for the flashbang before busting in the door. He knew all hell was going to break loose as soon as the grenade went off.

In the basement, the boss had made up his mind. *Let the rag head have his jollies then kill him.* "Go ahead, Gerald, have the camel jockey do his thing," he said, loud enough so Rains could hear what he was saying over the chanting Achmed.

"Achmed, go ahead. Be quick," Gerald said. Of course, Everett heard everything and was praying to a God, but it wasn't Allah. Condemning himself for getting involved with these crazies, he began to sob.

"Rains, you bastard. You'll burn in hell," Denise shouted. Debbie was too grief stricken to say anything.

The twirling machete and chanting stopped while Achmed reached back with both hands on the handle of the blade. At the top of the swing there was a pause, not unlike a golf swing, while Achmed gathered himself. Everett could sense what was happening and shouted in a high pitched, sobbing voice, "Dad, help meee!"

Just then, there was a shattering of glass. The window broke and the room turned stark white, followed by a 180 decibel, ear splitting bang. It was the equivalent of a cherry bomb going off next to one's ear. The grenade known as a noise, flash, diversion, or flashbang, for short, did its job. The noise caused disorientation and vertigo. The flash, which freezes the eye receptors for five seconds, burns on the brain the image that was present just before the flash. Achmed, instead of finishing his swing, came off plane and decelerated, hitting Everett on the end of the collar bone. The blade bounced off the bone and severed a neck muscle and partially cut the internal jugular vein.

Dan was ten feet from the door when he heard Everett's heart wrenching "help meee." Seconds later, the ground around him turned white as the flashbang went off. He sprinted to the door and leaped at it with both feet; it easily crashed open. Not relying on his night vision goggles anymore, he turned on his flashlight and raced straight ahead. He knew the flashbangs were good for less than ten seconds before personnel would recover and start running for the exits. He heard two suppressed gunshots from the backyard and a voice cried out. He found the basement door, opened it, tossed a flashbang down the stairs, and shut the door. For a brief moment before he threw the grenade, he saw a dark figure heading up the stairs. The flash and bang was again ear shattering and someone cried out as they tumbled down the stairs.

Dan opened the cellar door but kept his flashlight off and used the night vision goggles. He could see the figure of a large man sprawled on the floor. *Rains.* He descended several more stairs when he felt something behind him. It was Fred, eager to get into the action. Off to his left he heard shuffling and could see the faint outline of a figure standing over a crumpled body. The figure was staggering, but at the same time he could see the arms rise in a ritualistic way as the figure gazed upward. *Shit, the Arab's going to kill Everett twice.* Dan had no choice and put two in his chest rather than miss with a head shot. Achmed staggered backwards and fell against the stone wall, dead before he hit the ground. Dan raced down the stairs and kicked Rains aside. Then he heard a moan in the direction of Everett.

"Fred, give me some light," he called out. Dan rolled Everett over and saw the black blood and location of the wound. He pulled off the hood and jammed it into the wound and pushed firmly. He pushed enough to easily stop the bleeding and, noting the dark color of the blood, reckoned the carotid artery was not involved. Everett was alive, but he needed to be in the operating room.

"Fred, get my knife out. Cut these God damned cable ties. I can't lay him back."

Within seconds, Fred had the bindings loose and they were able to lay Everett flat. "Look around for something to elevate his legs."

Fred rummaged in the corner and came back with an old wooden chair. "Strong work. Place his feet on it then go check the Chief." With his legs elevated, Dan knew that venous return to his heart would improve, giving a much needed transfusion. He estimated from the volume of blood on the floor that Everett was already in deep shock.

"No need for that," the Chief said in a hoarse whisper. "That son of a bitch got me in the ear. He took off. I didn't get a look at him, it happened so fast. He was out the door as soon as he heard the glass break."

In their eagerness to save Everett, the improvised hostage rescue team had forgotten about Debbie and Denise. They were lying on their sides dazed and nearly incoherent. Fred went over and cut their ties and removed their hoods.

"Remind me to give you guys a big kiss," Denise muttered as she sat on her haunches.

"Me too," echoed Debbie. "What a close call. We owe Everett for calling when he did," she said, shaking her head.

"We'll talk about that later," Dan said, "right now we need the paramedics. Chief, you mentioned Everett worked in a hospital in town. What's the name?"

"St.Francis. It's the biggest hospital with a great emergency room. It's also the designated trauma center."

"When the paramedics arrive, I'm going to insist we go there. No dumping us off at the nearest facility. You need to back me."

Chapter Twenty-Five

Fred called 911 on his cell and told the dispatcher their location and that the front gate was padlocked. The dispatcher said the gate was no problem since a rescue truck would be accompanying the medics. It seemed like forever, but in twenty minutes two young medics and an older fireman descended the stairs with a giant tackle box and portable gurney in tow.

The lead paramedic asked, "Where's the victim?" He looked down at Gerald, unconscious on the floor, and then saw Achmed sprawled against the wall. Fred had found a light switch and a single 75 watt light hanging from a cord, barely illuminating the basement.

"Right over here," Dan said, not looking at the paramedics. One rushed to the left side of Everett and was applying a blood pressure cuff while the other was standing staring at Dan.

"Please step aside, we'll take over now," the second paramedic said in an authoritative voice.

"I'm Dan Miceli. I'm a surgeon, and under no circumstance am I turning over the care of this patient to anyone. Understood?"

Without answering his question, the lead paramedic said, "We're in charge now. We're under control of the base station doctor. So please step aside!"

Dan looked over at Fred who was standing behind the paramedic and said, "Fred, call Tom Vessey's exchange. We trained together at 'Big County,' he works primarily at St. Francis. Tell him the situation. Have him meet us in the emergency room, get the O.R. ready. Everett has a transected jugular vein." Dan turned back to Everett and ignored the paramedics order.

Denise had roused sufficiently to hear the exchange between Dan and the paramedic. It sounded like a bureaucratic turf battle, except the stakes were higher than usual.

"Sir," the paramedic, whose name tag said P. Swanson, more loudly said, "I have no choice but to call the police to restrain you. We're in charge." He reached for his radio to contact the dispatcher.

The older accompanying fireman was senior to both the paramedics and felt like saying something to Swanson but held his tongue.

Denise stood and gathered herself. She was wobbly but oriented. "Son, this location is a crime scene. I'm FBI Agent Denise Weber. I'm in charge. Don't make this worse. This young man's life is at stake,"

The Chief, while holding a soiled rag up to his right ear, said, "I'm Chief Riley, Chief of Police for the city of Vista Del Mar. This is my son. The doc's in charge. So lose the attitude, get to work."

Paramedic Swanson was beginning to wither but held his ground. "We'll see about that."

The other paramedic, who was busy getting a blood pressure said, "I've got audible and palpable 80. Monitor pulse 120. His color is not good but breath sounds are clear. We need an IV, then we'll transport."

Fred came back from where he had moved to get optimal reception and said, "Swanson. Doctor Starkson's on the line." Fred handed his cell to Swanson.

"Hello," the young paramedic said into the phone. Moments later he reddened and said, "Yessir." He had apparently been put in his place by the doctor on the other line. He snapped the phone shut and went around to Everett's left side and prepared to start an intravenous of normal saline.

Minutes later, they were carrying the gurney out through the basement's outside access. The lone rescue truck fireman, who had accompanied the medics, called for a back up unit to transport Rains. After that call, he notified the Flagstaff police that there was a crime scene at the FEN tree farm.

At the hospital Dan met Neil Starkson, who was Vessey's partner. Neil was covering for Vessey, who was at a meeting in Texas. The two hit it off well and soon they were in the operating room. The Chief, who had ridden along to the trauma center, was treated for the gunshot wound to his right ear. After the wound was debrided and dressed, Riley went to the doctor's lounge to await the outcome of his son's surgery.

After a backup paramedic unit and the police arrived at the farm, Rains was transported to St. Francis hospital under police escort. After listening to Denise, the officer in charge arrested Rains for kidnap and murder with other charges pending. Early reports from the emergency room indicated Rains had a serious if not lethal head injury.

The operation on Everett went smoothly. The operating room crew was personally involved since a popular Everett worked there at night. "Never said no to work," said one of the circulating nurses in the room with Dan. When Everett was asleep, intubated, and blood running, Dan gently removed the bloody pillow case and got his first look at the wound. It was deep, and the machete had nearly cut the white, glistening collar bone in half. Dan was thankful for Fred's timely flashbang, since the full force of the blow landed short of the neck's soft tissue. There was enough congealing of blood in and around the wound that bleeding was minimal. Dan gingerly prepped the skin and chest to avoid dislodging clots then left to scrub.

At the sink, he watched Everett's wound through the window to be sure there was no sudden release of blood while the scrub nurse applied sterile drapes. Satisfied, he began washing his hands.

"Do you mind if I do this. He's from our hometown in California. I know I don't have privileges here," he said to Dr. Starkson, who was scrubbing along side of him.

"Who says so? I'm the president of the medical staff, I can grant emergency privileges any time," Starkson said, "and yes, you do the surgery, I'll assist."

"By the way what did you say to that paramedic on the phone? The sudden change in his attitude helped," Dan asked.

"You know, we do most of the trauma for this region. I see Swanson all the time. He's a capable guy but very territorial. He was an army medic in Iraq and goes by the book. This isn't the first time he's overstepped his boundaries. I told him that Vessey and you go back a long ways. Vessey never shuts up about you, I might add. Anyhow, Vessey runs the medic training program in town, certified Swanson. I told him that you were an ex-SEAL, knew what you were doing. Also told him if Vessey finds out the trouble he, Swanson, was causing, Vessey would kick his ass."

Dan laughed, "It seemed to work."

"I'm done here. There's a small favor I'd like to ask since you got me out on a Sunday evening," Starkson said as he kicked his water off.

Dan kicked his water off and shook his arms over the sink to dry them.

"Why do I get the feeling my pocket's being picked. What can I do for you?"

As he entered the operating room Starkson looked back and said, "A case of Miceli's reserve Pinot."

"Consider it done."

Chapter Twenty-Six

The Flagstaff police department went into high gear once they received a call from the fire chief at the scene. Soon, cops were swarming around the house and in the basement. After a quick consultation with Denise, Rains had been arrested and accompanied to the hospital with several police officers. Crime scene investigators were in action collecting evidence and taking pictures. Debbie and Denise were moved upstairs and separated, with Debbie in the dining room and Denise in the living room. From the rescue truck a fireman brought blankets and steaming cups of coffee.

Debbie kept shaking her head in disgust about her decision to enter the barn. On the plus side, though, she reasoned her actions had brought the investigation to a head. While in the dining room, the uniform in charge returned her cell phone and other belongings he had discovered on the sideboard. She turned on her cell in hopes her dad would call with news concerning the status of Everett. Once she stopped shivering from the cold night and fear, she gathered herself together in preparation for an interview with a Lt. Perez.

The latter was a homicide detective for the FPD and currently was talking to Denise in the living room.

Not paying attention to her surroundings she was startled when there was a light tap on her shoulder. She looked around and stared at the detective who was a medium built, middle-aged man with dark, black hair graying at the temples. He had a disarming smile and appeared to be more Indian than Mexican. He was dressed in an open collared white shirt with a gray sports jacket and blue chinos. His face was round with dark brown, totally wrinkle free skin. Debbie thought Lt. Perez looked like a detective straight out of a Tony Hillerman novel.

He introduced himself in perfect English by saying, "I'm Detective Perez, FPD. Are you up to talking?" The sympathetic tone in his voice was not lost on Debbie.

She gave a wan, thin smile of thanks and said, "It hasn't been a fun day, but I'm ready."

"Good. I've heard some of the story from the uniforms, what can you tell me? Take your time, I'm a patient listener," he said. He sat down in the chair next to her.

Debbie appreciated the open-ended question free of any judgmental bias.

"I work for the LAPD gang division. I was called home to Vista Del Mar, that's in California, because of an arson murder on our property." She then went on to explain that she came here with Denise Weber, an FBI agent, because of evidence uncovered during the investigation of the murders. She described her interview with Rains and how he had invited them to his tree farm. She also explained that she was suspicious of the way he was acting and took it on her own to enter the barn, where Rains caught her.

While she was talking, Perez took notes and only interrupted her once to have Debbie go over what Everett told her in the basement regarding the arson.

When she finished, he clicked his pen closed, stood and said, "We've had our suspicions about Rains. Nothing solid, just seemed to be around whenever an anti-war or environmental demo got out of hand. I won't make a big deal about you being out of jurisdiction or entering the barn. Rains can file a complaint if he survives. It'll be hard to do that from prison," he chuckled.

"Thanks for that," Debbie said, glad that Perez seemed to have the big picture.

"One more thing. Did you hear or see another person down in the basement?" Perez asked looking, directly into her eyes.

Debbie looked pensive trying to pull back into her consciousness something that had happened only several hours beforehand. "Not really. I heard the dog bark then there was a commotion. Seemed Rains was doing the talking. Could've been talking to someone else besides Everett or the Moroccan. I'm not sure."

The detective waited patiently, hoping Debbie remembered more, but finally said, "For the most part your story checks with Ms.Weber's so you're free to go. But I do have to talk to Rambo."

"Rambo?" Debbie asked looking into the detectives twinkling eyes.

"That's your dad's nick name. A fireman on scene said it's the best description he could give. Tell him to call us the next time he comes to Flagstaff. We can help," he said, laughing again.

Debbie was glad somebody was getting a laugh out of the tragic affair she seemed to have started. She looked up at the wall clock over the sideboard to see the hands were at eleven. She jumped when suddenly her cell phone went off.

She pushed the receive button and said, "Dad?"

"It's me," Dan said softly. "Where are you?"

"Dad! I'm so glad to hear your voice. I'm in Rains' dining room, how's Everett?"

"Good 'ol Debbie, worrying about someone else. He'll do fine. We repaired his jugular vein. He's waking up now, Riley's with him, bad ear and all."

"What happened to his ear?" Debbie asked concerned.

"Long story, but there was someone else in the basement. Shot the Chief when he escaped. Don't have a clue who it was. Is there a detective Perez there?"

"Yes. He just finished taking a statement from me. He's waiting for you. Called you Rambo."

"Rambo! I'm no Rambo. We were a team. It was a well coordinated effort." Changing the subject, he said, "There's a uniformed officer outside wants to drive me to the farm. Perez is anxious to take a statement from me."

""Don't worry. I think he's okay with what went down. Just a bit miffed they weren't called is all," Debbie said.

"I guess I've got some explaining to do. Is Fred nearby? I got to get back to Vista. I have cases tomorrow afternoon."

"Hold on. You could take the day off," Debbie scolded into the phone as she stood up, not waiting for a reply, and walked into the living room. Fred was sitting on the couch talking to Denise. She interrupted them to tell Fred her dad was on the phone. Fred took the phone placing a finger in one ear and the phone next to the other as he stood and walked into the hallway.

"How's the kid, partner?" he asked.

"Doing well, thanks to you. You brought the right stuff, the timing was perfect or near perfect," Dan said as he thought about the injuries Everett had suffered.

"I'm getting too old for this shit. My heart's still racing. When're we headin' back? I've got eight fly fisherman flying to Montana on Tuesday."

"I say I come back there, give my statement to Perez then we take Debbie and Denise back to town in their car. We'll sleep at some motel and take off in the morning. How's that?"

"Sounds Great. Give my best to the Chief and Everett," Fred said as he clicked off.

At three a.m. the four of them fell into beds at the same motel Debbie and Denise stayed in earlier. Detective Perez took Dan's statement and was convinced that another individual, identity unknown, had escaped from the basement. The local FBI agent in Flagstaff arrived just before they left the farm. Debbie and Denise gave a brief statement to him, but they were so exhausted that he delayed further interrogation until after they got some rest. He insisted Denise stay in Flagstaff until he could complete his report.

At ten a.m. the three of them arrived at the airport where Debbie and Dan boarded the airplane. Fred stayed outside talking to one of the ground crew who was going through a flight check and weather report. The efficient young man had a crew cut and Fred pegged him as ex-military.

When the briefing was completed Fred asked, "When did that Citation leave? The one in the hangar over there. Saw it getting a wash yesterday."

The young man checked his records and said, "Last night around nine. Pilot and one passenger."

"Names?" Fred asked.

"Sorry, no can do. Confidential."

"Did you ever see them?" Fred asked.

"No, but when I came on shift Sunday morning the guy I relieved saw them arrive. They drove off in an SUV and spent no time on site."

"Plane been here before?" Fred asked.

"Oh yeah. It's a Richland plane. You know, the big resort company. They own a pricey hotel and golf course in town. Their planes fly in and out of here all the time. Well, everything checks out. Have a safe trip," the crewman said as he waved Fred up the stairs. Soon the plane was winging its way back to San Luis Obispo.

Chapter Twenty-Seven

Two weeks after Dan had returned from his adventure in Arizona, things were settling down. Because of his son's revelations in Flagstaff, Chief Riley recused himself from the arson investigation and turned over jurisdiction to the FBI. The day after the events in Arizona were over, Denise gave her statement to the FBI agent then drove Debbie's rental car back to L.A. She spent several days answering questions from her superiors, but in the end they thanked her for her efforts. However, she was temporarily assigned to administrative duties while a more thorough investigation was completed.

It didn't take long for the FBI to secure evidence by airport video that Gerald Rains and Achmed Razzuk were in Baltimore the day before a warehouse fire. Also, similar discoveries were made in a Florida fire. After each one of these fires, the land was condemned by the city and sold to PDI, who then sold them to Richland International. Both condemned sites had then been turned into luxury hotels. Further activity concerning Mr. Rains' fraudulent activity was also uncovered in Oregon and Colorado. As a result, the fire in Vista Del Mar appeared to be part of a larger conspiracy and an investigative team was assembled, headed up by Denise.

Although enough evidence had been uncovered to suggest that the fire at the vineyard was the work of Gerald Rains, the city council saw no need to stop their quest to acquire the vineyard property. Richland had not been implicated in the fire and as far as Ben Adams was concerned, the Vista's purchase of the vineyard property was on track. Dan had been notified through his attorney's that, unless he was prepared for a long, drawn out, expensive legal battle, he best get used to the idea of losing the vineyard. He was told to devote his energy and resources to fight for as big a settlement with the city as he could.

It was Saturday afternoon in early October when the phone rang while Dan was watching a football game. The caller identified himself as David Chase, but Dan wasn't sure he wanted to talk to the lawyer. Finally, after a longer than usual pause, he said, "Yes, David, what can I do for you?"

"First of all, we haven't spoken in a while. I'm sorry about not appearing at the council meeting. The settlement process with the city precluded me from supporting you. It's complicated. Bottom line, the negotiations fell through when the family balked on the agreement."

"So the lawsuit is on? What does that have to do with me?" Dan asked in an disinterested tone.

Dan's cool demeanor wasn't lost on the attorney who said, "Again, I'm sorry about the meeting. Nothing directly to do with you. But I did subpoena the city's budget and financial records for the last five years. Riley and Adams are complicit in pension fraud. I met with the U.S. Attorney for this district yesterday. He was very interested."

"Is this going to put an end to the land grab?"

"I can't say. But those two, in time, will have to step down from their positions. May make it easier for you to fight 'city hall,'" David said.

He had paused, and then added, "Just to let you know, Riley strong armed me into not appearing on your behalf. He muzzled me by threatening to arrest my wife for her third D.U.I. if I appeared. She's at the Betty Ford now. I'm not proud of what I did." Chase didn't feel compelled to tell Dan about the other half of the threat, namely, settle the lawsuit with the city.

Dan was taken aback by the lawyer's candor. He would never have expected such a revelation from an attorney. *Maybe the guy is trying to mend fences. Maybe I've gotten too cynical.* Dan decided to back off.

"I'm sorry to hear about your wife," he said in a sympathetic voice.

"Basically, Riley's heart's in the right place, he's just a typical hard ass Irishman when it comes to politics. He saved my daughter's life getting me involved in her capture. I'll reserve judgment."

"Very well. Just thought I'd bring you up to date. Maybe we'll be seeing each other again when this is all over. Goodbye."

Dan hung up and mulled over what he had just heard. Riley was just too close to the arson. He didn't arrange it, but he knew about the details after it happened. While recovering from his injuries and, under arrest in Arizona, Everett had confessed to the arson. He also iterated that he had told his dad about the fire after it was over. Furthermore, he swore in an affidavit that his dad was not in any way involved in the fire itself.

The statement from Chase about possible fraud by the Mayor and Chief was interesting. It gave him hope but it was completely out of his hands.

He had Denise Weber's home and cell number. He called her home and when there was no response, he tried her cell.

"I'm on my way home," she said, "if we lose each other I'll be there in ten minutes."

"I won't take up much of your time." Dan went on to explain what he had just learned from Chase.

When he had finished, Denise said, "Hey, you can call me anytime day or night. Thanks to you I'm even breathing. You're a legend down at the office. Gave the 'old guys' a boost. Excuse me, I didn't mean to imply you're old, you behave like a twenty year old," she laughed. "Bottom line, we don't think Riley knew about the plans to burn your caretaker's garage. As far as Vista's budget issue, pension fraud is all too common. The Justice Department will handle that. But it goes to motive. Some city official, other than Riley, must be complicit."

"If not Riley, who?" Dan asked.

"Don't know. Adams is a likely candidate but so far nothing has turned up. Outside of Vista, we're taking a hard look at Richland International. They've benefited from fires before. I'm interviewing the president in Palm Springs on Monday. Debbie's going with me. She's off Monday after a working weekend. Talk to her when we get back."

"Thanks. I'll do that. Give my best to my daughter when you see her. I didn't want to be a bother while she's on duty. Thanks for taking my call." Dan hung up. It sounded like the FBI was very involved and he was glad Denise was leading the investigation. At least he had an inside track to keep abreast of what progress, if any, was being made.

Monday morning Denise picked up Debbie at her condo and they drove Interstate 10 east. The meeting was to take place at the Richland Country Club near LaQuinta. The president of Richland International was John Richland. He told Denise when she was making the arrangements that Monday morning was his time to play golf. He would meet her in the Club's executive office at 11:30. From Denise's investigation she discovered that Richland played collegiate golf at a University in Texas. In his senior year he was a scratch golfer and captain of the golf team. After graduation and an MBA from Harvard, he got into the golf course business and from there built his empire. He owned the third largest international hotel chain in the world and had just turned fifty-five. Described as a family man with down home qualities, he was said to be very charming but ruthless when it came to business decisions.

They drove to the guarded front gate and flashed their ID's. As they drove away, Debbie noticed the guard picked up the phone. They parked at the rambling clubhouse that looked more like a three storied Italian Villa. The walls were a yellow-brown colored stucco with green shuttered windows, and the roof was red tile. Once they had entered the clubhouse lobby, an attractive young lady showed them to the executive suites. They were offered coffee or a beverage of choice when they were seated in the waiting area. Exactly at 11:30 John Richland emerged from his office to greet them.

"How y'all doin'?" he said in his Texas drawl, "com'on into the office and set a spell." John Richland was just under six feet, was slightly overweight, and had brown hair that was graying at the temples. His round face had a Palm Springs tan and he was average looking. His outward manner was polite but his attitude was "this better be important; you're taking up my time."

The large third story office looked out onto the golf course and the rug was a deep red and exquisitely textured with a thick nap. The walls, which were paneled with rich Mahogany wood, were hung with pictures of professional golfers whose identity was known by anyone who had even the slightest interest in golf. All the pictures were autographed to 'John Richland the greatest….. etc. in the world.'

After they sat down, Denise said, "We've talked briefly on the phone. There are some questions I felt best asked in your presence. By the way, this is Debbie Miceli of the LAPD. I told you it was her father's vineyard where the fire took place."

Richland looked at her and said sympathetically, "I'm sorry for your loss. I understand your closeness to the two people who died. Now how may I help y'all," he said in a more businesslike tone. It didn't bother him in the least that the young lady sitting in front of him was the daughter of the vineyard's owner.

"As I said before, it has come to our attention that your company has been involved in the acquisition of condemned properties, sometimes after fires that were later shown to be arson. I assume this is a coincidence, but what can you tell me about it?"

"Everything. I've nothin' to hide. Since eminent domain laws have changed with a looser interpretation of the Constitution, it's been easier to acquire prime property. It's easy and legal. There's a website where cities advertise potential property for development. Usually cities with financial problems."

"I've not heard of that. What's the website?" Denise asked as she sat poised with her pen and pad.

"It's not as well publicized as you might expect. WWW. Citiesintrouble.com. I have my people monitorin' that site ever day. We're lookin' for property to develop all the time," Richland said with a big smile on his face. "I'm conservative by nature but when liberals get ahold of somethin' then ya gotta go along. It's a shame but y'all got to go with the flow."

"So you call the cities and they offer you a price?" Denise asked skeptically.

"Nope. Dudn't work thataway. There's a company called Property Development Inc. PDI for short. It buys the property from the city then resells it to the highest bidder. That way there's no direct acquisition by the developer from the city."

Denise couldn't believe what she was hearing. Eminent domain was now a business.

"Where's this company located? Who are the owners?" Debbie asked.

"*That* I don't know. They're registered in the Cayman Islands. I do all of the bidding on the internet. So far so good. We're a cash cow here at Richland. Sorta fits, dudn't it? *Rich*land?" he said, staring at the two. There was no response to his pun so he went on, "We let the cities know we're interested up front, even help 'em. But the acquisition process has to be at arm's length. Why we have PDI."

Denise silently shook her head. Five judges, unelected officials, have given us this mess. Inwardly she said, "America's exceptionalism lost by activist judges."

"There is one more issue and then we'll be gone. A Richland jet was in Flagstaff several weekends ago. We discussed it on the phone. We need to know who was on that plane. What were they doing in Flagstaff?"

"What if I don't tell you?" Richland asked with a smirk on his face. There was a slight change in the friendly attitude.

"I suppose we could subpoena your flight records, but since you have 'nothing to hide' we shouldn't have to go that route."

"Just joshin' y'all," Richland said laughing. "Here's the records you're lookin' for." He handed over several pieces of paper to Denise. "As you can see there was a pilot and two passengers. They were flown to Las Vegas for a working-pleasure weekend. We have a new hotel going in there. The plane then went onto Flagstaff were it was serviced and cleaned. The pilot also had a girl friend there he visited."

Denise didn't know what the statement 'had a girlfriend there' meant. Was she no longer a girlfriend or had the pilot quit working for Richland. "We'll need to speak to him," she said as she glanced at the copy of the flight log. "That would be Mark Best." She looked up and stared at Richland.

Richland sadly shook his head. "I'm sorry to say it's a little late for that. We're bummed out here. Mark took a tumble in Palm Springs canyon last week. He loved to hike in there. Fell and broke his neck. He survived the first Gulf War. Flew recon planes, then this had to happen."

Denise couldn't believe what she was hearing. She had an eyewitness who swears that the pilot and an unidentified passenger deplaned in Flagstaff the day before the incident at Rains' tree farm. She sat unable to get to the next question.

"I know what you're thinking. What about the two who went to Las Vegas? Was there a third passenger? Well, I have a sworn statement signed by both of 'em sayin' no one else was on the plane." He handed over a sheet of paper and then stared out the window, indicating that the meeting was effectively over.

Debbie wasn't intimidated by the self-absorbed idiot in front of her and wanted to ask her own questions. She said, "By the way, there was a representative of your company at several meetings in Vista. Most notably at the council meeting when the city voted to take over dad's property. I believe his name is Ted Schroeder. I'm interested in his relationship to Chief Riley. They seemed to know each other quite well."

Richland stared at her. Nosy cops, he thought. "Well, young lady, that's not quite right. Mr. Schroeder does not work for me. He works for PDI. He may represent us at meetin's, get the ball rolling so to speak, but he's PDI. Now, I'll leave it up to you as to how you can contact him. As I said, PDI is a Cayman Islands corporation, so there's where you'll have to start."

"You mean you two never talk? You don't have a phone number or e-mail?" Denise asked, suddenly interested in a name she had not heard before.

"He's called me occasionally but prefers to communicate mostly on the internet. As I said, you can get his whereabouts and contact info from PDI. I'm afraid the people runnin' the show in Vista Del Mar misrepresented the relationship between Ted and Richland International."

Debbie took in the scene playing out in front of her. It was clear that their trip to Palm Springs had been unrewarding. She had empathy for her dad going up against this ruthless business type. Doctors, at least the one's she knew, weren't cut out for this kind of warfare. With all of Richland's resources, her dad was going to be buried in an expensive legal process. She caught Denise's eye while Richland returned to staring out the window and gave a look which said "let's get the hell out of here."

Denise agreed and when Richland turned back to them she said, "Thanks for your time. I think we have covered all the issues that are open here. May I call you again if anything more comes up?"

"Darlin,' you certainly may," Richland boomed as he stood up. He pressed a button and his attractive greeter magically appeared. "Show these two lovely ladies out, will you Ariana. And if you want" Richland said, looking at Denise and Debbie, "there's lunch in the club house downstairs. Just tell Manuel it's on me."

The duo decided to skip lunch and head back to L.A. on Interstate 10. After a long period of silence, Denise shook her head and asked, "Does something smell fishy to you or is it just me?"

"I wouldn't trust that guy as far as I could kick him. What an asshole. He's rich and full of himself," Debbie replied. "It's convenient that his pilot dies in an accident. I know a guy in the Palm Springs PD. I'll see if he can shed some light."

John Richland stood up and stared out the window at the parking lot to his left. He saw Denise and Debbie drive away after skipping his lunch offer. When the guard at the gate confirmed they had left the premises, he walked through a door into the smaller office next to his. Ted Schroeder was sitting at his desk reading some papers when Richland walked in unannounced.

"I'm glad I told you to stay put. Those were two nosy bitches."

"I nearly had them in Flagstaff. Wise ass father, ex-SEAL. A bunch of swimming sissies," Schroeder squeaked in his characteristic voice.

"Seemed to handle you alright. Maybe Special Forces aren't so special."

"Stick it John. This isn't high school where I bailed your sorry golfing ass out of trouble. More than once I might add." Schoreder said with a smirk. "Oh shit. What's the bottom line here? They got nothing on me. Rains can't identify me. He's gorked anyway. What's the big sweat?"

"Hey, we're solid here. We go back a long ways and I'm grateful. But we're talking the FBI in my office! They've got resources and time on their side. Whatever possessed you to use that bunch of amateurs in Arizona? You told me you had it covered. How'd y'all find out about Rains? Refresh my memory."

"Lemme see. I was contacted at PDI by Riley a couple years ago. When you were bidding online for the vineyard. We met and during the conversation he told about his lefty, tree hugging son working for a radical group in Flagstaff. I checked on the guy. Saw he had a record, including suspicions of arson, the rest is history."

"So Riley is not directly involved in any of the pranks your amateurs pulled in Vista?"

"Nope. Now, the son may have told his dad after the fact. The idea to stir up trouble came from here, remember? I think it was you who first mentioned it. Said you had a contact in Vista who brought up the idea. You were pleased by the way the Baltimore and Florida gig worked out."

"Shit. I'd never admit to that. You're on your own, high school or not. I think it would be best if you skedaddled to the Islands. Lay low. I'll contact you when things smooth over. I'm still going to get that Vista property. One way or t'other. It's primo," Richland said.

"I'm outta here. I could use some down time," Schroeder squeaked.

"Take one of the jets. They're all here."

"Shit, I miss Mark. It'll seem strange flying without him."

"Yeah. Mark was good people," Richland said absently while gazing out the window.

"Convenient for you he took a tumble when he did," Schroeder sneered.

"For you, too. You're not implying I had anything to do with his fallin' in the Canyon, are you?" Richland asked with piercing eyes.

"Kiss my ass, John. You hike up there all the time. I've never even been in there. You iced a great soldier, patriot and one of the good guys. It better be worth it."

Richland eyed his old high school and college chum. Maybe he had gone too far this time. He made a mental note to keep a close tab on Schroeder.

"Have a safe trip. I'll be in touch."

Chapter Twenty-Eight

Late Monday afternoon Debbie spoke to a lieutenant in the Palm Springs Police department. The two had met a year earlier when the lieutenant was investigating a gang homicide in Cathedral city. The perpetrator was found to be living with a cousin in Los Angeles and not in Mexico, as was rumored. Debbie had hit it off with the lieutenant after they captured the suspect, and they traded phone calls several times during the course of further investigations.

From information that was faxed to her from the Palm Springs' Lieutenant, she learned that the accident in the canyon was studied thoroughly and that nothing suspicious was uncovered. There were no identifiable witnesses; however, a park ranger reported she had spotted another hiker in the area of the accident. Her description was too vague to be helpful. "Mr. Best had allegedly been hiking by himself, and, at one point, slipped on a rock and plunged fifty feet to his death," the Lieutenant told Debbie.

She also learned that Best had served ten years in the military and flew reconnaissance for Special Forces during Gulf War I. He was unmarried and his only relative was a sister living in Maryland. He was buried there, near his home town of Cumberland. After she dug through his records, she discovered that he had been flying jets for Richland for five years. She also had a copy of his service record faxed to her from the Military Personnel Records Center in St. Louis. Sticking out was an evaluation of Best by one Major Ted Schroeder, Best's commanding officer in Saudi Arabia. What a coincidence, she thought. Schroeder and Best were in the same unit in the Army.

Tuesday morning. Debbie sat in front of her computer reviewing what she had learned in the past twenty-four hours. She had arrived at work early and was using her own time to continue the investigation before going on patrol. The effort to pin the blame of her father's problems and the deaths of Hector and Dolores on someone was beginning to consume most of her time and energy. The episode at Rains' tree farm while she was waiting to be shot or worse yet, decapitated, kept creeping back into her mind. *Can I ever blank that out?*

When she again called St. Louis, this time for the military file of Ted Schroeder, she was told there was no access to that file. It was listed as unavailable. Despite talking to several more people up the chain, the answer was the same. Schroeder's file was off limits to anyone.

Strange, she thought, as she dialed Denise's cell. "I'm at work early too," the FBI agent said when she answered. Debbie told her what she had found out about Best and the stonewalling from the Army's personnel file center in St. Louis.

"Must be he did some behind the scenes work. We get that on occasion during investigations. Never had any luck in cracking that though. Even the Director can't get them to budge," Denise said.

"Too bad," Debbie said, "I've got the feeling he's somebody important. At least get a bio on him. The only thing on Google is that he works for PDI, an executive officer. That business is registered in the Caymans Islands. No luck in finding the owners or other officers."

"His past has been scrubbed. Probably ex-CIA or military intelligence," Denise said, sounding certain she was right. "Did you know there are more American businesses registered in the Caymans than there are people on the Islands. The only way to find out anything about PDI is you must show proof of illegal activity. But you have to wait in line. They do things on a case by case basis. It's very slow."

"Well, we don't have anything to show them regarding illegal activity. We're investigating," Debbie said.

"You know what they say down there, don't you?"

"No."

"Come to the Caymans and fish, but we do not allow fishing expeditions. Or something akin to that."

"Got it. What's next then? We have an untraceable business with an untraceable employee."

"Well, if Schroeder is living there, I have access to his passport. I'll see what comes up. Call you back on your cell."

Debbie looked at the clock on the wall and saw that it was nearly time to leave on patrol. Her partner would be downstairs ready and eager to go. She definitely couldn't be late after her recent suspension. She was nervously tapping her fingers when her cell phone sang. Denise told her that access to his passport was classified, and she wasn't likely to change that situation. Debbie told Denise she would call her later and hung up. "Back to the real life on the mean streets in Los Angeles," she said out loud.

Since his talk with David Chase on the weekend, Dan had spent Monday and Tuesday bouncing between patients, surgery, and his lawyers. The news on the latter was not good. He learned that the government had the power to take his property for "public" use as well for private development, and there were few options available. He could either fight the city council in court and lose, or hold out for as big a price as he could get. At the present time he didn't even want to think about it; the property was his whole life. Worse yet, he learned that the city had the right to take his property before the parties had agreed on just compensation. The city could deposit the money it felt was "just compensation" then set about taking the property in several months. *Where would the city get money to do that?*

"They had quoted a low ball of only twenty-five million dollars," he mused out loud. "Could they get the money from Richland?" he had asked his attorney. If they did, his lawyer assured him he could challenge that in court.

Late Wednesday evening, after three glasses of Pinot Noir, he found himself in stage three wallowing. He finally decided feeling sorry for himself wasn't healthy or useful. In a rare moment of self help, he called Debbie. She answered immediately, but she sounded as down as her dad.

"I had a terrible day. Arrested some illegals, gang bangers, took a swat on the chin for my efforts. It hurts. This job sucks. How was your day?" she asked with a small laugh.

"Nothing broken I hope?" Dan asked with concern. "My day was not much better," he said despondently. He was looking for consolation from his daughter, who was also feeling sorry for herself. Dan decided to stop the wallowing and more sharply asked, "Have you learned anything more about Richland and what he's up to?"

"Denise told me you knew about our trip to Palm Springs. What a dirt ball Richland is. All smooth on the outside but mean underneath. We tried to chase down Ted Schroeder but couldn't find him. Turns out, at least from preliminary investigations, that he doesn't work for Richland. A company called Property Development Inc.. Registered in the Caymans."

"Wait a minute. You mean that guy sitting next to Riley at the council meeting?"

"The very same. His name is Ted Schroeder and he works for PDI. He's a 'facilitator,' according to Richland. Helps close deals. PDI finds potential buyers then they purchase the property and resell it to their clients. You bid online for the property, the winner gets access à la Ted Schroeder'."

"That legal?' Dan asked.

"As far as we know. Oversight is an issue. They're outside American law to a certain extent. Probably most of the business, except for Schroeder, is done online. They could do that from the moon or anywhere else in between. They're impossible to track down."

"How do the cities and PDI get hooked up?"

"Simple. There's a website where cities can register potential properties for development. Then there's a link to PDI if someone is interested in bidding on the property. The winner gets Ted Schroeder."

"How tight are Schroeder and Richland?"

"The answer Richland gave me was they rarely talk...e-mails, mostly. But I got the feeling that was a crock. If you ask me, they're tighter than two Irishmen on St. Patrick's Day."

Dan understood the meaning his daughter was trying to convey. It was clear he was up against a wealthy, ruthless opponent in Richland, and he had doubts that his resources, emotional and financial, were enough to fight the man. He found himself drifting back into despondency. He had no cadre of friends except Fred to help him get through this. His daughter was his only immediate family and she had troubles of her own.

"Let's suppose you find this guy Schroeder. So what? What good is that going to do me at this stage? The city wants this property and that's that."

"Well, if he was the guy running Rains and we could connect Richland to him then that'd put an end to Richland."

"But it sounds like PDI would just find another bidder and that's that. I'm cooked no matter what. It pisses me off. I'd like to take a gun and put a bullet in Adams' head."

"Dad! You almost sound human. Good going. You need to fight back and get out of your negative state. There are many Richland's out there. Your problem is the city council and Adams. You need to put pressure on the U.S. Attorney to haul Adams and Riley to court over their pension fraud. Bug Chase. Get him on your side."

Dan said goodbye to Debbie and decided she was right. Lawyers weren't doing him any good. Despite his ambivalence toward Riley, he had to put on pressure to have those two indicted. He would call Chase tomorrow and catch up on the status of the investigation into the council members handling of city revenues.

Chapter Twenty-Nine

Dan spent a restless night in bed. At 6:00 a.m. he finally gave up. It was a beautiful day outside, the ocean was a deep blue and the surf was pounding. Not so bad, he thought. He climbed out of bed, jumped in the shower, dressed and went downstairs. Again he was overcome with loneliness. No one around to share his thoughts. Only work and the vineyard to keep him occupied. He made coffee, scrambled a couple of eggs, and popped two pieces of bread into the toaster. When he finished eating breakfast, it was nearly seven o'clock. He walked into his office and turned on the computer. Soon he was typing in thoughts about strategies he had mulled over during his fitful night's sleep. At eight o'clock he dialed his secretary, Marilyn.

"To what do I owe the early call?" she asked.

"I'm turning over a new leaf. A new Dan Miceli. Instead of fighting city hall I'm going to change city hall. That's between you and me by the way."

"Gotcha."

"I'm not coming in today. Apologize to Jim and Bill for me, then have them see my patients. Don't cancel any appointments. If anyone asks, tell them a family business issue popped up. Okay?"

"Got it. What else?"

"If you need me, use my cell. I'll be home mostly, but bouncing around."

"Just to let you know, I stopped searching for my replacement. I got word late yesterday that all jobs have been frozen. The town is out of money, and it doesn't look like it's going to get better any time soon."

"That's good news for me. Sounds like the lawsuit over the lifeguard fiasco is going forward."

"That's what everybody's saying. I guess the lawyer and family weren't happy with the settlement."

Dan said goodbye and smiled to himself. Sounds like pressure is mounting on the incompetent assholes who run the city government. Can't hurt, he thought. He reached over for the yellow pages and got the telephone number of Jack Holmes, the part-time city attorney. *No way he'd be in his office this early.* Dan decided to wait until later and, in the meantime, he'd called Fred Lesley, hoping the pilot was in town.

Fred answered. His voice was breaking up, "Can you hear me?" Dan asked when he thought the static had cleared.

"Loud and clear. Doing a hop to Vegas. What's up?"

"I need your help. Are you willing?"

"More trips to Flagstaff?" he asked, laughing into the phone.

"Not quite. The story Lacey wrote for his paper makes Riley look like a hero. We were there to support him. Do you know anybody over there in the paper at SLO Town?"

"Only the owner. I take him on fishing trips to Montana. Why?"

"Since almost everyone in Vista gets that paper, I'd like the story redone with the facts. Tell your contact they can interview the FBI agent involved and Debbie. I need to get out that Riley's kid was involved and Riley knew it during his investigation."

"That's a shit load of stuff. I'll be left hanging with ol' Riley."

"He made his decisions and he's not backing off on the town acquiring my property. What d'ya say?"

"Consider it done. Will call Jesse tonight and get the ball rolling. Gotta go, ready to land."

Dan had a brief moment of regret over exposing Riley, but it was the right thing to do. It was Riley's kid that did the arson, and whether it was supposed to be prankish or not, people did die. Riley hadn't been going to bat with him over the issue of eminent domain. It's just business. Nothing personal, he rationalized.

Dan grabbed another cup of coffee from the kitchen and waited until 9:30 when he called Jack Holmes, the city attorney. His secretary put him through right away.

"Jack, I hope I'm not disturbing you. Our talking may be a conflict of interest," Dan said.

"Not anymore. Yesterday I resigned as city attorney. I sat through the mandatory settlement conference on Monday. Chase has a great case and Adams, Evans, and Riley may go to jail. I had no idea what was going on. So talk away."

"I want you to take over my foundation's legal matters as well as my estate. I've heard nothing but good things about your work so this is no bribe. I'm tired of going to L.A. just to speak face to face with my lawyers."

Like most lawyers, what they are thinking and what they express do not necessarily coincide. "Well, this is a surprise," Jack said quietly. Inside he was doing cartwheels.

"That's not all. I'm making some changes here at the vineyard and legal advice will be necessary. Are you up for that too?"

"Of course. When should we meet to talk about particulars?"

"Sometime in the near future. But first, I'm calling my lawyer today with the news. I'll have him contact you to arrange transfer of documents. When that's all done, then we'll meet."

"Can I ask what brought about this change? Don't get me wrong, I appreciate the business, but what's behind it?"

"I've been meaning to do this for years. Now seems like the right time. I can't tell you anything further. Before you go I need to know the procedures involved in recalling city council members."

"I'll fax a summation over to you. But that may not be necessary with what I heard on Monday."

"Maybe so. But it's one more thing to bug Adams, Riley, and Evans. Fax it to my home."

Dan gave Holmes his fax number, home and cell numbers, and then hung up. He put a check after the third thing on the 'to-do' list he had composed earlier. "Politics are local" his father had warned him years ago when the elder Miceli fought the city over an easement issue. His dad finally won his case when he actively worked to get the townspeople on his side.

Although Dan was well known in town, he felt he had been so preoccupied with his practice and the vineyard that he was not really in touch with the townspeople. He decided it was time to change his image, learn from his dad's mistakes, and become part of the community rather than just a busy, eccentric surgeon. He needed to be seen and heard. He opened a box he kept in his desk drawer and pulled out a stack of old letters. The letters were requests from tour companies to open his vineyard to visitors. He placed the correspondences into a manila folder and stood up.

Dan walked into the kitchen, turned off the coffee maker and washed his cup. He went outside, got into his truck, and soon he was on Highway One heading for Vista. When he arrived in town he drove to the *Sea and Surf* motel. There were three major motels in Vista and "the Surf" was the only one locally owned and operated. Ned and Betty Baker, salt-of-the-earth and long time owners, were patients of Dan's. He didn't need to call ahead to tell them he was coming because he knew they would be on the job.

He found Ned sweeping out the front office when he walked in and said hello. He was happy and surprised by Dan's sudden visit.

"It's good to see you, Dan," Ned said, laying the broom aside.

"Ned, I see you are still working hard," Dan held out his hand and gave the motel owner a hearty handshake.

"What brings you here?" Ned asked.

"Well, I wondered if I could have a word with you and Betty?"

"Of course. Of course," Ned waved Dan to follow him to the office in the back where Betty sat typing on a desktop computer. She greeted Dan with equal surprise and pleasure.

Once they were seated in the back office, Dan said, "I'm going to open the vineyard to limited tours. Weekends only. I want you two to run the operation. I have letters from interested tour companies." Dan handed over the manila folder to Betty. "There's also a list of other vineyards in the area who want to join in. I was thinking of a day tour going to four or five vineyards. That way, the tourists can spend the whole day in Vista and stay at your clean motel."

Betty looked skeptical. She was the business brains of the operation and never took anything on face value. "What's in it for you? How much is it going to cost us?" she asked warily.

"For now, it will cost you nothing. I plan to open a tasting room. From there, I'll recover costs of liability insurance, taxes, business expenses. In the future, if the venture is successful, I can't say. I'm sure you will do well. I've been bugged many times over the years to do this. Now's the time."

"This doesn't have anything to do with Riley's land grab, does it? We're against that one hundred percent," Betty said earnestly.

"Why didn't you speak up at the council meeting?"

"Riley implied that if we did we might find it harder to do business," Ned added, pounding his fist into his hand.

"Well Riley may not be the Chief too much longer, from what I hear. If you have any legal questions setting this up call Jack Holmes. Use Bob's Travel on High Street to help you with the arrangements."

Dan left knowing that Ned and Betty would get the ball rolling. His next task was to talk to an interior decorator about fixing up the pathetic, rarely used tasting room at the vineyard. He drove to one of the local decorator's office and set up an on site meeting to go over plans.

The next thing on his list was to visit the local Wachovia broker. He knew the broker well and his reputation was impeccable. The firm could handle all of his Foundation's needs. After he met with the broker, the paper work transferring the assets from a brokerage in Los Angeles to Vista was started.

When Dan left the broker's office he had three things remaining on his "to-do" list. First, he drove to *The Fun Thymes* restaurant and found Lila Parker in the kitchen going over the dinner menu with her chef. She smiled when she saw Dan and gave him a big hug.

"What brings the mighty surgeon to my humble kitchen?" she kidded.

"It's the other way around. The humble surgeon to your booming enterprise. Can we talk in your office?"

Lila nodded to the chef, indicating she would be right back. Once settled into her cramped office, which was filled with invoices, folders, and recipe books, Dan said, "I want to have a dinner for fifty couples at the vineyard. In two weeks, on a Friday."

Lila took out her notebook and began to jot down notes. "I assume this will be outside in your yummy garden."

"Yes. I'll get a tent and heaters, if necessary. I want a buffet. Wine of your choosing. Fax the menu to me, but I'm leaving it in your hands. You know what people eat better than I do."

Lila stopped writing and looked up and said, "Might I ask what's the occasion? We're not announcing anything are we?" she asked with a coy smile.

"Yes. But it's not what you think. Keep it under your hat, I'm running for mayor. But I'm asking the invited guests to help me get a recall going to unseat Adams and maybe Evans, too."

"I've heard the same rumors you have. A little sleight of hand with the budget. The upcoming lawsuit doesn't look so good for the city."

"Let's just say I'm applying pressure. The guests will be people I've known for years. Not closely, mind you. Some may even be supporters of Adams. Once the truth comes out, people will side with me."

They shook hands and Dan left. He didn't ask for a budget, knowing full well Lila would give him a fair price. The second to last thing on the list could be done from home. He was hungry, and when he arrived back at the vineyard he immediately made a peanut butter, jelly, and banana sandwich. After he devoured his lunch in the fashion he learned as a medical student, he settled into his den. It was nearly two o'clock when he dialed a Santa Barbara number and Jane Lawson answered.

"Jane. Dan Miceli. How have you been?"

"From what I read in Lacey's paper, better than you. Are they really going to take over your vineyard?" she asked sympathetically.

"They'd do it in a heartbeat if they could. But I'm fighting that. You've been bugging me for years about wanting to write a story about the vineyard. Well, I'm ready," Dan said.

"I'm sure *Sunset* will be happy. When can we do it?" Jane asked.

"This weekend. Some things you need to know first: the city council tried to justify the grab based on environmental impact. They were so off the mark when they claimed water usage was an issue."

"Well, isn't it? It sure is in Santa Barbara."

"The vineyard is maintained with dry irrigation. We use much less water than the average vineyard of this size. Some members of the city council are about to be indicted for fraud and misuse of public funds. There's a wrongful death lawsuit pending, trial due to begin in two weeks. It should be interesting."

"What time Saturday?" she asked. She was excited to start on what could turn out to be a juicy strory.

When Dan hung up, he looked at his list. So far, nearly one hundred percent completed, with only one item left. The last item had been in his thoughts more frequently since Dolores and Hector died. He realized that his down moods were related to missing his two closest friends. He talked to Dolores everyday and he now realized she had become his surrogate companion. Dan convinced himself it was time to move ahead.

He had dated sporadically after his wife died, but none of his companions seemed to spark his interest. Dan had fallen into the surgeon's trap of letting medicine become his primary interest in life. Recently, however, a former floor nurse at his small hospital had crept into his thoughts. Maureen Collins had dark hair and piercing blue eyes. She was spirited with laughter that made those around her happy. He had never known her to be down or cross.

More than once, the thought of dating her crossed his mind. But he had built up excuses. Her husband had been a patient and died with pancreatic cancer two years before. It would be unseemly to date a former patient's wife, particularly one who worked for him. Then Maureen left the hospital and took over her husband's plumbing business. He had not seen her often after that but, when he made a point of stopping by her store, she looked and acted the same.

Dare I, he asked himself, while he nervously stared at the phone. Finally, he picked up the phone and dialed the number of the plumbing store.

A young male voice answered the phone. Still not sure of himself, Dan cleared his throat and asked, "Is Maureen there?"

"Just a minute," the voice said and Dan could hear rustling then a muffled "Mom, line one."

"Hello, this is Maureen," she said, in a business voice.

"Maureen, this is Dan Miceli. How have you been? Is that your son who answered the phone?"

"Dan! Good to hear from you." Dan always insisted that the people working for him call him by his first name. It seemed to have stuck even after they left his employment. "That's Jeff. He's taking a year off from business school. He's been a great help. We're busy as heck."

"That's wonderful," Dan said, with the tension inside him building. He felt calmer during the assault at Rains' farm. Asking someone out on a date conjured up images of his high schools days when he feared rejection. "The reason I'm calling is to see if you're interested in dinner Monday night." He held his breath waiting for an answer.

"Are you asking me out on a date? Did I hear that right?" Maureen laughed.

"Call it what you will. I've been meaning to do it for awhile. Now seems like a good time." Dan was encouraged with her playful laugh and thankful it wasn't a snicker.

"I'd love to. What time? We'll be eating here in Vista?"

"I'll pick you up at 7:30, dinner at *The Fun Thymes.*"

"That sounds great. See you then. You know where I live?"

"I'll find it," Dan said. He hung up and said "yes" out loud as he punched his fist into in to the air. He wadded up his "to-do" list and threw it in the waste basket next to his desk. Dan stood, stretched and headed out the door to the vineyard looking for Carlos.

Chapter Thirty

On Monday night Dan was excited over the prospect of going out to dinner with Maureen. He picked her up as planned and they drove to *The Fun Thymes* restaurant. Maureen was dressed in a simple, green cotton dress and had a string of white pearls around her neck. Her dark brown hair was brushed straight back and held in place with a barrette. Her face was lightly made up and she appeared vibrant. At the restaurant, Lila met them and brought them to a table that overlooked the bay. Already prepared and sitting on a small serving dish was a slice of cantaloupe wrapped with prosciutto. Dan thanked Lila as they seated themselves.

"Wow, what service. The boss no less. Do you have pull?" Maureen asked in a conspiratorial tone while leaning forward.

"You bet. Lila and I go back a long way." Dan took a bite and then looked around. He was glad he selected Monday night for a dinner date because the restaurant was not busy. He did nod to a couple who were staring at him.

Maureen noticed and giggled when she said, "Are you going to get into trouble being out to dinner with a former employee?"

"To be honest, I've wanted to do this for a long time but was afraid of the fallout from the tongue waggers. The couple over there are old time patients who don't even live in town. So, here's to your health," Dan said as he raised a glass of Sicilian red wine."

"That wine complements the appetizer perfectly. Did you also think of that?" Maureen asked, taking a second sip.

"Yes, I did. This dinner has been well planned out in advance."

"You did that to impress me?" Maureen asked with a twinkle in her eye.

Of course," Dan smiled, "but no kissing on the first date," he laughed.

The second course was carrot soup followed by an orange salad. The fourth course was shrimp with zucchini julienned to look like spaghetti. They talked about the town, their respective off springs and what they were doing. Maureen told Dan about her four children and, at age forty-eight, was glad to have them out of the house, except for her son, who was helping in the shop.

"I was quite impressed with the story about your raid in Arizona. Sounds like Chief Riley put his military background to use."

Dan put down his fork after tasting the fifth course of rosemary seasoned lamb chops on top of butternut squash risotto. He put down his fork and forced himself not to demean Riley and make it look like sour grapes.

"Riley was a big help," he explained. "But the events that unfolded were not quite as they were presented in the paper. Tomorrow's SLO Town paper will have a more accurate and detailed account."

Maureen sensed in Dan's voice less than wholehearted endorsement of Riley.

"Between you and me," she said, "Riley does his job okay, but he's a little heavy-handed. The day before the town meeting several weeks ago, which, by the way, I didn't attend, Riley came to my shop. He was talking casually about the vineyard while pretending to shop. He said it was important that the town council pass the proposal for the city to acquire your property."

"He actually came out and said that?" Dan asked, not shocked but clearly disappointed.

"Yes. And he said that the town's future depended on it and what did I feel about it?"

"What did you tell him?" Dan asked.

"I asked him who was next on the list. Surely it won't stop with one property. The council could make major shifts in the town's demographics and people would be helpless. They'd be unable to fight back with the legal costs and time involved."

Dan sat back and took a sip of wine. Maureen had given it back to Riley. Two people of Irish descent had gone head to head. Both were descendants of beleaguered immigrants who came to this country to escape oppression. Now, each had a different perspective on the role of government in their lives. It was amazing to Dan how history is forgotten, or maybe it was never learned. Regardless of his biased observations, Dan had a wonderful time with Maureen and felt a spark ignite within him.

The story in the SLO Town paper appeared the day after Dan's dinner date with Maureen. The article contained quotes from Denise Weber and Lieutenant Perez of the Flagstaff PD. The article implied that Riley, shortly after the fire, had been told by his son of the latter's culpability in the arson at the Miceli vineyard. It also noted Riley's secondary role in the actual assault, hinting that the story by Cal Lacey was misleading. There was a side story on Rains and the carbon swap scheme he had arranged through the UN. The story was factual and not filled with anecdotes from unknown sources. Dan was pleased with Fred's efforts and made a note to call and thank him. When he arrived at the office later that morning, Marilyn gave him a thumb's up.

"When's Riley going to retire?" she asked, skipping a discussion of the article.

Dan didn't answer and set about happily seeing patients. His thoughts, however, were on the wonderful evening he had spent with Maureen. He couldn't remember when he had such a good time talking to someone as nice as her. He was particularly pleased when she agreed to be his guest at the shindig planned for a week from Friday. He couldn't wait and secretly hoped their relationship would blossom.

The party at the vineyard was well planned. Dan arranged for the guests to be picked up by a bus at Ned's motel, where they could also park. There were fifty couples who enjoyed a sumptuous dinner of either poached salmon on wild rice with steamed vegetables or prime rib cooked to perfection. Accompanying the main course, there was artisan bread, stuffed baked potatoes, and dumplings. Dessert was a choice of chocolate mousse or ice cream with homemade Macadamia nut cookies.

Sitting at Dan's table was Debbie and Denise Weber, Maureen, David Chase and his wife Elaine, who was nursing a glass of water, and Jim Cravens and his wife. The evening had started out with wine sampling, including many of the wines from local vineyards. The wine was displayed at four sites throughout the garden, but the most popular site was the one overlooking the ocean. Dan had rented a large tent, which was positioned on the grass portion of his formal two acre garden. The garden was pristine with the rose bushes and boxwoods meticulously trimmed. Guests were allowed to roam and see as much of the vineyard and winery as they wanted.

At Dan's table he noticed Denise and David Davis were enjoying themselves in an animated conversation about Los Angeles. Jim Cravens was talking to Elaine Davis quite openly about their alcohol related problems involving Riley. Maureen and Debbie were reminiscing about the old days in Vista. Dan talked with Mrs. Cravens, who also had graduated from USC. Dan could tell from the general noise level and laughter in the tent that everyone was having a good time. He shuddered when he thought of the wine bill, but that was business.

Finally, around ten o'clock, when dessert dishes were removed and coffee served, Dan stood and clinked his glass for attention. It took awhile for the talkative, well-lubricated crowd to focus.

When the shh's were over, Dan said, "I want to thank you all for coming tonight. This is the first time there's ever been a party of this magnitude at the vineyard and I'm quite pleased that you came. I hope you enjoyed the wine and food."

There was a hearty applause followed by further talking.

When the noise settled down Dan went on, "You are all aware of the issues that I have confronted lately. I want to pose to you a question: what if we lived in a country whose laws were handed down by a body of unelected men in black robes? You'd say that couldn't happen. After all, this isn't Iran where the Mullahs do just that. No, we live in America, the land of the free, and freedom according to our forefathers is a gift from God. But sadly, that gift is gradually being taken away from us. Nine justices, by one vote, have decided to change the Constitution by allowing government to take over private property and sell it for private development. It was Thomas Jefferson who said, 'The Constitution....is a mere thing of wax in the hands of the judiciary which they may twist and shape into any form they please'.

Dan paused to let the words sink in. The crowd was listening attentively.

"American exceptionalism is being challenged daily. What do I mean by that. Because of our freedoms, America is an exceptional country--not perfect, but human endeavor is never perfect. My grandparents came to America from a small village near Milan, Italy. My granddad packed vine cuttings from the vineyard he grew up tending. He brought those cutting to Napa Valley, planted them there and then brought them here. The wine we drank tonight came to this country in an immigrant's suitcase. That's a uniquely American story."

"Now the city council wants to turn this land into a resort. Why? To enlarge their tax base and pay off the debt they have incurred from incompetent management of the city's funds. Tonight, I'm asking for your help. We've all heard the saying 'you can't fight city hall.' Well, that may be true. But I don't want to fight city hall. I want to run city hall!"

A wave of hushed voices rippled across the tables. This was certainly an unexpected announcement from their host.

Dan raised his hands, nodding, while he spoke again over the noise of his surprised guests, "I need a thousand signatures from citizens of Vista to force a recall of Mayor Adams."

A thunder of clapping erupted. The clapping was louder and longer that Dan expected. He was sure there were people in the audience who favored the city's move to take over the property, but they were being drowned out by the rest. He needed to win over the reluctant few, however, and again clinked his glass to get the attention of the excited crowd.

When there was silence, Dan said, "You may have thought that the large cards in front of you with your names on them were your place cards. Actually, I would like you to use them for another purpose. There is room on each of your cards for ten signatures below your name. If every one of you signs the card and gets nine more signatures, then we can have a recall. The serving staff will begin handing out pens to anyone who needs one. Let me thank you all again for coming tonight, and I hope you will stay as long as you like. The buses will be available until everyone has gone home."

Dan started to walk back to his seat as people shifted around to grab their cards and sign their names.

David Davis pulled Dan aside and said, "So, there's a politician inside you after all. I just wanted you to know we begin jury selection next week. There was no settlement with the city. Adams may well have to resign when this trial is over. Save you the trouble of recall."

"Thanks Dave. Whether Adams quits or shoots himself in the head, I'm running for mayor. I used to think local politics was a joke, but times have changed. Did you sign your card yet?"

"I don't know," he said in his best courtroom voice. "You were kind of tough on the lawyers and court system. But, it's not altogether without some foundation."

"Maybe I was a little over the top with that speech, but you answered my question with a double negative. So, is that a yes? Counselor?"

"There's a conflict of interest in my case." He laughed and said, "Of course."

Chapter Thirty-One

By Monday afternoon a thousand signatures had been turned into the city's part-time elections supervisor. She promised that the petition would be referred to Jim Cravens, the chairman of the council's election committee, without delay. He had been given that position by Adams, who felt the job to be politically unimportant at the time. On Tuesday, the committee met and worked into the early hours, verifying the signatures. When the task was completed, Cravens immediately set a date for the recall vote in six weeks.

Adams read over the city charter in his real estate office hoping to find a legal loophole. There wasn't any to be found and the gathering of recall signatures was done according to the statutes. This would never do, he thought. The rumors about Vista's troubled liability had grown to over ten million dollars. City workers were calling Adams on a frequent basis wondering about their pension plan. Shorting a bloated pension fund to pay for routine city services didn't sit well with the employees. In desperation, Ben Adams decided to call John Richland.

Richland was in his office when he picked up the phone. "What's happening in Vista? Must be important or y'all wouldn't be calling," he said in his best Texas drawl.

"Trouble. I'm being recalled. That asshole Miceli pulled a fast one on me. He's got enough signatures to do it. The town's pissed over the mishandling of public funds. I may be indicted by the U.S. Attorney," he whined.

"Shucks, that sounds bad. What're you goin' to do about it?" he asked.

Adams, sensing Richland's tone, said, "Now wait a sec. I've been busting my balls for you on this property deal. It's about ready to go. I need help from you."

"You need help alright, but not from me. Sounds like any deals with you could make me an accessory to whatever you an' your cronies have been hatchin'. What with arson, murder, and shootouts in Arizona."

"That's bullshit and you know it. Do I have to remind you of our arrangement? I keep quiet and you help. Remember? How will it look when people find out the great John Richland knocked up my sister in college and then ditched her to raise your love child. Sure would scare away those politicians you buy off."

"Now hold on. You shouldn't be sayin' those things over the phone. I took care of your sister," Richland said indignantly as he reached over and erased the tape on a telephone recorder that had been documenting their conversation.

"Quietly, when she threatened a large paternity suit after you got richer than Solomon. It's time you stepped up and helped me. In case you've forgotten, I arranged that little settlement."

"I haven't forgotten that it was you who called me two years ago about land in your city. You're the one who called me later with the idea of burnin' down the Doc's vineyard to speed things up." Richland restarted the recorder.

Ben thought about what he said and decided it was a standoff. He considered throwing another punch, but then thought better of it. The only way to get Richland is to show him the upside.

Finally, Adams said calmly, "The fire was just an idea. I had nothing to do with it. Riley's kid was involved. If I had a twenty-five million dollar loan, we could do a quick takeover. It's in the law. City's can do that. We could sell the property to you in two months."

"Now that sounds downright interestin'. Who's payin' the interest on the loan? Your city is broke."

"I'd be counting on you to arrange an off shore loan. Interest free. One of those banks in the Caymans I hear you secretly own."

"Possible. How much for the land?" Richland asked.

"Fifty million would cover all the city's problems, get me off the hook."

"What's goin' on with that lawsuit you been fussin' about? Doesn't sound so good."

"We're going to lose big time. Could be huge. I hope we can settle for six million." Adams sounded down as he went on and enumerated the troubles he was facing. Civil trials, possible indictments with jail time, legal costs, and an election recall.

After he finished, Richland said, "You've given me a plateful of grits. I'll have to think it over." There was a long pause before he added, "By the way, just to let you know, I record my phone conversations with you, as I am doing right now. So we have a Mexican standoff here, don't we?"

"You bastard. I'm sorry I ever met you. Get it done or else," Adams said, angrily hanging up the phone.

Richland chuckled to himself. He derived a perverse pleasure in watching scumbags squirm, even though he was well aware that many would place him in that same category. He stood up and walked next door. Ted Schroeder was back from the Cayman Islands looking fit and tan. Richland knew he was in a bind with Adams, and Schroeder was critical in his plans for damage control.

"Was that you I heard shouting through the door? Who's the poor bastard on the other end?" Schroeder asked in his distinctive high-pitched voice.

"Guess? He's a mayor of a small, seaside town in California," Richland grumbled.

"He's small potatoes. What's he done now?" Schroeder asked.

"The guy is as incompetent as a Texas politician. He's gone and got himself in trouble with the U.S. Attorney over pension shenanigans.

City's broke and that doc up there, the one you couldn't handle, has got him on a recall vote."

Schroeder leaned back in his chair while keeping his eyes locked hard on Richland. Finally, he said, "What is it about you I don't like? Oh, yeah, I know what it is. You're a pain the ass."

"Alright, alright. You're doin' a fine job. So far you're clean as a whistle. As long as the FBI doesn't figure out who you are," Richland said almost apologetically.

"Cut him loose. Deal with the doc directly. Everyone has their price," Schroeder said, as if the thought had not crossed Richland's mind.

"Thought about that. Only trouble is he's got somethin' on me." Richland paused while Schroeder waited expectantly for him to go on.

"Well, are you going to tell me what it is or do we sit here and pout?"

"Okay. Here it is. I shoulda' told ya'll a long time ago. It's no big deal now. I mean it's water under the bridge, at this point. But, one night in college, I got real drunk and screwed Adam's sister. You'd have to be drunk to screw that bitch, believe me. Nine months later I got this note sayin' she was having a baby. Which she did. A little boy."

Schroeder tried to control himself, but he burst out laughing. When he quieted down he asked, "How do you know you're the father?"

"It ain't funny," Richland said, glaring at Schroeder, "shit, I don't know. But Adams had me cornered. Eighteen years ago he threatened a paternity suit. His mama wanted to send him to a fancy school but couldn't afford it. My best choice was to pay them off and not take a chance DNA would bail me out."

"Well, there you go. He's not such an incompetent politician after all. Look, I see the picture. He wants you to get him out of trouble. Buy that grape farm and put the city in the black. Save his butt. The question is: you going to do it?" Schroeder said. He shook his head in disbelief.

"Ya'll are enjoying this, aren't you?" Richland looked down at his hands and muttered, "Bastard. Hell, I don't know. The choice is bail him out or buy the property myself. At this point in my life, what's a scandal?"

"Could be serious. What about all those politicians who get their picture taken with you? What about all the professional golfers you hang around? They are a conservative group, wouldn't go for those antics. And what about the churches and mission you sponsor to give that clean-cut image?" Schroeder asked more seriously.

"That could be a problem, but I don't think he'd say a word. I got him on tape recommending that vineyard be burned down—not just a house, but the whole damn place. He was as serious as a cowpoke fleeing a mad bull when he said it."

"I suppose he could meet with an untimely accident. But I'm sure he has the info on you stored, to be released should something unexpected happen to him. Maybe his sister has it."

"Don't make him out to be smarter than he is, damnit. You're makin' my stomach churn worse than a Texas tumbleweed."

"You know, I didn't grow up in Texas. I was only was there for three years in high school, but I don't remember anyone speaking like you do. Where did you get all those metaphors, anyhow?"

"They's as common as flies on a dead horse," Richland said, laughing. "At home we'd never say meta-whatevers you said. They's just sayin's," he said with his best Texas drawl. Suddenly he slapped his chair and said, "I think I got it."

"Got what? So far this is the best entertainment I've had in a long time."

"Listen up. You meet with Miceli and make him an offer he can't refuse, as his people might say. I'll be willing to go up to 150 million. He can keep the house and some property. If he doesn't accept that, tell him there's banks willin' to loan the city money to close the deal. Adams is talking about 25 million."

"Why don't you go that way first? Cheaper and a sure choice. Avoid Adam's big mouth."

"Hell. He's so sure that depositing money in an account and closing the purchase in two months is such a sure deal. I'm not so sure. Been through this before. Some smartass lawyer gets a hold of it and it could tie us up faster than a cowboy in a calf roping contest. I want that land *now*."

"Is that another sayin'?" Schroeder asked with a mock drawl. But Richland didn't think it was so funny. "Okay, I'll start working on it. It'll all be done through PDI as soon as ten percent of the price is deposited in PDI's account."

"I'll do it now."

Chapter Thirty-Two

The recall vote was scheduled for the first Tuesday in December, and the news for Adams had only gotten worse. During the ongoing Tran trial, David Davis presented evidence showing that the city council had cut lifeguard coverage a year before the drowning. While arguing that this cut was in response to a mounting budget deficit, he emphasized the fact that, at the same time, the pension plan was funded well beyond the necessary limits because of increased retirement benefits to Adams, Riley, Evans and others. Furthermore, he presented to the jury that the following years, in order to make up for further deficits and avoid public outcry, the council voted to cut the retirement funding to sixty-percent of what was required by federal law.

In short, the evidence against the city was overwhelming. The high-powered lawyers representing the defendants pleaded with Davis to settle the case before it went to the jury. They knew their case was weak enough, but the testimony of Adams and Riley would only make matters worse. Davis, of course, was having none of it; he knew he could get a large judgment against the city and was happy to let the jury have the case. The jury was excused the day before Thanksgiving and the trial was continued the following week.

Ted Schroeder followed the course of the trial, which was chronicled daily at the SLO Town newspaper's website. The money he needed to make an offer was in PDI's account and Richland was pushing Schroeder to get going on it. Ted felt that a big judgment against the city would hurt their cause in the event that Dan said no to their generous offer. It would be hard for the city to 'borrow' for a precipitous purchase of the property if they were staring at a possible multi-million dollar judgment. The day before Thanksgiving, Schroeder telephoned Dan, who was in his office finishing up paper work before the holiday.

"Dan," Marilyn called from her desk, "there's a Mr. Schroeder to speak to you on line one."

Dan almost told her to tell the PDI agent he was busy, but he decided instead to face this demon now.

Dan punched the blinking light on his phone and said, "Dr. Miceli speaking."

"Doctor Miceli, this is Ted Schroeder," he squeaked, "we've not formally met, but I saw you at the city council meeting awhile back. My firm is very interested in the sale of your property. Is there a possibility we can meet as soon as tomorrow to discuss some of your options?"

"The property's not for sale. Not now, not ever."

"I understand that. But the city council, as you know, can force the sale. I have a client who would rather not go through the legal process of obtaining the property, but he will if it becomes necessary. If you could hear what I propose, it might sway your thinking."

Dan wasn't sure what he was up against. Judging from the events of the past several months, he knew he was facing some shrewd and unscrupulous characters who would stop at nothing to achieve their goals. The details of the conspiracy to scare him into relinquishing his property without a fight were still unknown. Denise, while she was at Dan's backyard bash several weeks beforehand, had admitted that Schroeder was someone she would like to question.

He made up his mind. "Alright. Tomorrow's Thanksgiving. I'll be at home all day. Let's meet at my place around 10:00 a.m. I assume you know how to get there?"

"Yes, I know how to get there and I'll be there at ten," Schroeder promised and hung up before Dan could change his mind.

Dan twiddled his thumbs while he mulled over the call. Debbie was arriving later in the evening and Denise tomorrow morning. Debbie had invited Denise because she knew the agent was going to be all alone for the holiday. Denise he had clearly enjoyed herself at the dinner party in the garden, and Debbie thought she would enjoy spending more time with her and her Dad at the vineyard.

Later that evening, when Debbie arrived, she saw her dad's truck parked next to the back porch and decided to park her car inside the garage, out of the salty air. When she entered the house, she found her Dad sitting in the office reading.

"Hi, Dad," she said as she entered the room. Dan stood, and the two hugged each other. Dan was happy his daughter was going to stay for the long weekend.

As they pulled apart, Dan said, "I left my truck out so you could park in the garage. With this wind picking up, the sand and salt air will eat it alive."

"Thanks. I figured that's what you wanted."

"Before you dash upstairs, I had an interesting call today. Ted Schroeder, the so-called broker trying to put together this property steal, said he wanted to meet with a possible offer on the vineyard."

Debbie stood back, looking amazed. "How weird that he called! He's a hard man to find, even harder to talk to. Both Denise and I tried to track him down. It's as if he didn't exist."

"Well, he's coming at ten o'clock in the morning. If you're up, you can meet him. What did my two favorite peace officers want to talk to him about?" Dan asked.

"Thanks for putting me on the list. We still don't know who the man was that got off the Richland plane in Flagstaff. John Richland told me and Denise that there was no one on the plane except the pilot."

"That's simple. Talk to the pilot. Why should he lie?" Dan asked, puzzled.

"Can't. He's dead. Took a tumble in Palm Springs canyon," she said, putting air quotes around the word tumble. She went on, "He's dead and buried in Maryland. It's suspicious because it came a day after Denise had called Richland and asked about the unidentified airplane passenger."

"Let me guess. You think the passenger was Ted Schroeder and he's the mystery man in the cellar. Correct?"

"I wouldn't go that far just yet. Why is Richland trying to hide the identity of the passenger or even deny there was one there? Fred Lesley said the ground crew guy was very reliable. The worker was interviewed again by another FBI agent who agrees with Fred's story. Denise would be very interested in talking to him. Since this is now an FBI case, I have no standing, but that doesn't mean I wouldn't love to talk to him."

"When is she getting here tomorrow?" Dan asked.

"She plans to leave at six a.m. so about 10:30 or eleven. Should I call her and let her know he's coming?" Debbie asked.

"Can't hurt."

The next morning, Dan showered, dressed and tiptoed downstairs. It was Thanksgiving and Dan had a turkey, mashed potatoes, green beans, and a pumpkin pie he had ordered from *The Fun Thymes* waiting in the refrigerator. They wouldn't be eating until four or five, so he prepared a hearty breakfast to keep him satisfied until then. He made coffee, fried two eggs, and toasted some bread. After breakfast he walked to the main gate and opened it. Then he crossed over to the vineyard and met with Carlos. The foreman informed him that the fermenting process was going well and he predicted a good vintage. Dan was pleased by the news and whistled as he continued surveying. He walked past the area where the vines had been vandalized and noted the stumps had already been grafted with new shoots from the green house. Dan reminded himself to tell Carlos how much he appreciated all his hard work.

It was just before ten when he returned to the kitchen and poured a second cup of coffee. As he was savoring the brew's aroma, there was a knock at the back door.

"Anybody home?" a high-pitched, squeaky voice asked.

Dan knew it was Schroeder. *Right on time.* He took another swig of coffee to fortify himself and went to the back door to let Schroeder in. Ted Schroeder was an inch or two shorter than Dan. He was wiry and not the typical Hollywood image of a muscular Special Forces soldier. Of course, the Hollywood image of a Special Forces soldier wasn't entirely accurate since members of that elite squad were not selected because of their physical size or strength but more for their cunning, intelligence, and endurance.

"I parked up by the road. Thanks for having the gate open." Schroeder said as he stepped into the house. "I'm Ted Schroeder by the way," the PDI representative said as he extended his right hand while the left held an expensive, black leather briefcase.

Dan shook his hand and said, "Dan Miceli. Come on in. Coffee?'

"I'm glad you asked. Black. Thanks."

Dan went over to the counter and pulled down a mug from the cupboard and poured. He gave the mug to Schroeder and gestured for him to sit down at the kitchen table. Schroeder sat down placing the briefcase on the table. He rubbed a scar on his neck that ran from below his right ear to his Adam's apple.

Once seated, the two looked at each other in silence. Dan widened his eyebrows and raised his hands as if to say, "what's on your mind?"

Schroeder took a sip of his coffee and smiled. "Coffee's great. I can see your love affair with the house and property," he said, looking around the rustic kitchen with its tile countertops and tall oak cabinets. Contributing to the ambiance was the sound of the surf pounding in the background.

"It's easy to love this place," Dan said. Unable to control his curiosity any further, he dramatically changed the subject when he said, "Tell me about that scar on your neck?"

Schroeder again reached up and rubbed the scar. "Gulf War One. Shrapnel to part of the voice box. I'm lucky I can talk at all. Special Forces Recon. I know you were in the SEALS. My hats off to the 'swimmers.' They were a great help in the Gulf."

Dan acknowledged their common military bond with a nod and said, "Let's talk about the vineyard. I told you yesterday it wasn't for sale. But last night it came to me that I'm all alone here. Maybe I could think about an offer. Who do you represent, exactly?"

"PDI. Property Development Inc. It's home based in the Caymans…and that's *not* because we're trying to hide anything from the government. But American banking laws have not kept up with the times. It's much easier to do business in the Caymans. To everybody's advantage, including the government's."

"I see. How did you and Richland hook up? He doesn't own PDI does he?" Dan asked.

"He owns a resort in the Caymans but has no connection to PDI, financial or otherwise. Even the Cayman officials would look askance at that. No, we're basically an internet real estate company. All our business is done on the internet. Wire transfers, documents etc."

"I'm curious. How did PDI get involved in my situation?" Dan asked.

Schroeder sat back and gazed at the ceiling as he thought about Dan's question.

"The Vista city council posted your land for possible development. They had pictures of the vineyard on citiesintrouble.com. Richland has people watching that site for deals. Two years ago, when your vineyard was listed, Richland was on it like 'pigs eatin' corn.' Sorry, those are Richland words."

"Why did he e-mail you?" Dan asked.

"We're listed as the broker for citiesintrouble.com and are linked to their website."

"Okay. Let's see if I got this right. The city council, presumably Ben Adams, lists the property on a website. Richland sees it and then e-mails you his interest. That it?"

"Not quite that simple. Once the property is listed, the 'lister,' in this case Ben Adams, gives a minimum allowable bid. For your property it was 25 million dollars. After that, interested buyers can bid the price up over that amount. The bidding period is one month, then the property is taken down."

"I know where he got the 25 million number, but what was the closing bid price?" Dan asked.

"I'm afraid that's confidential."

"Is this legal? You putting other people's property on the market without their permission or prerogative? More or less auctioning if off!" Dan's voice raised in anger.

"Hey, take it easy Doc, I'm just as conservative as you are. It stinks, but it is what it is. That's where we are as a society. I can't change the rules."

Calming down, Dan asked, "How does your company make money?"

"The winning bidder, in this case Richland, must deposit 10 percent of its bid amount in a PDI account. Let's say the city acquires this property from you for twenty five million. Assume Richland's bid for the property is fifty million. PDI buys the property from the city for fifty million minus our 10 percent commission. Then we turn around and sell it to Richland at their bid price, which includes the deposit."

"So, the higher the bid price the more your commission. The city recovers their purchase costs plus the difference between the bid price minus your ten percent commission. So, in your example, the city would recover 45 million or a 20 million dollar profit."

"Correct. Sometimes the profit can be substantial and other times it is virtually breakeven. It depends on what the developers want to pay and whether the property is worth the asking price," Schroeder said.

"What happens if the city goes through the process of you buying the property but then the bidder backs out?"

"Well, then he's out his deposit. It doesn't really hurt us. We can always find a buyer."

"So what exactly is your job?" Dan asked.

"My job is to get the transaction completed. I'm a facilitator, if you will. We're not interested in confrontation. Amazingly, if it's a fair price, most owners are glad to dump their property on the city or state, as the case may be. In your case, Richland informed me last week that Adams told him you were putting up a big fight. Having him recalled. I'm here to make you an offer. Mr. Richland told us he would go well over the final bid price and authorized us to deal directly with you. He wants the land, so he's willing to negotiate."

Dan didn't respond to Schroeder's comments and sat staring out the back porch door. Off in the distance he heard a car door slam shut. He turned to Schroeder. Despite his squeaky voice and military manner, he presented himself as a polished, professional businessman. He was just doing his job,

Dan reckoned, and had skillfully made it clear that Dan was the problem.

Debbie had promised herself that she would sleep in late and let Denise worry about talking to Schroeder. She knew the PDI representative could refuse to answer any of the FBI agent's questions and, judging from his hidden past history, would probably do just that. At about 10:30 she suddenly awoke, shaking and frightened. She had been dreaming about her captivity and the period just before Everett's attempted beheading. The man's voice, the one she couldn't recall immediately after the events at the farm house, came to her clearly in the dream. He had a high pitched squeaking voice and said, "Go ahead, Gerald, have the camel jockey do his thing."

Looking around, she saw she was in her own bed and quickly realized it had only been a dream. Relieved, she slid out of bed and started for the shower. Halfway to the bathroom, she suddenly stopped. She heard voices coming from downstairs: one of them was from her father and the other one she recognized all too well. The voice in her dream a few minutes ago was actually coming from the man now sitting in her Dad's kitchen. Panicked, she nearly called out to her Dad, but decided against doing that. Instead, she quietly got dressed, silently closed the door to her bedroom, and speed dialed Denise's number on her cell phone.

Denise had got out of bed at 5:30, showered and dressed. She was on the road by 6:00, driving faster than she ordinarily would. Debbie's

phone call from the night before telling her that Schroeder was going to be at the farm at 10:00 was all the motivation she needed to get there by at least 10:30. She reemphasized to Debbie not to confront the man since she was not part of the investigation and could jeopardize subsequent questioning.

When she arrived at the entrance to the Miceli vineyard, Debbie noted the Cadillac sedan that was parked along the fence on the frontal road near the entrance. She went over to the car and found a tiny Hertz window sticker. She went back to her car, sat down, and called the main office in L.A. She gave the duty agent, Don Cowlings, a brief history, and the Cadillac's license plate number. The agent was a close colleague who was familiar with the investigation and promised to get her the information as soon as possible.

Ten minutes later, her cell chirped and she answered. "Agent Cowlings returning your call," the voice said. "Sorry it took so long, but it wasn't easy. The car was rented in Palm Springs to Richland Inc. The agent told me Richland keeps a fleet of them on rental for VIP guests. He also said there's no log at Richland indicating who drives the car."

"Thanks for doing that Don," Debbie said, "unfortunately it's not much help."

"There's one more thing. A fax came through during the night addressed to you. FBI forensic lab had completed evaluation of the slugs from the dog killed in Flagstaff as well as the cartridges recovered at the scene. Tool mark analysis showed the handgun used was a Beretta M9. Standard military issue. The casings are consistent with ammo manufactured in the 1990's. Good chance the shooter is ex-military, but without the gun it can't be narrowed any further."

"Well that fits with Schroeder alright. Thanks. Are you on all day?" Debbie asked.

"Yes," Cowlings said, not sounding too happy about it, "I'm gonna miss all the games. Just call if you need anything. You're up at the doctor's vineyard, aren't you?"

"Yes, I'm shutting off my cell now because the batteries are low, but I'll call if I need something."

"Give him our best and be careful. Schroeder sounds like trouble."

Just as Denise was preparing to turn off her cell and plug the charging cord into the cigarette lighter, the phone chirped again.

"Hello, Agent Weber," she said.

"Denise, it's Debbie. I'm under the covers in my room so Schroeder won't hear me. He's downstairs talking with Dad," Debbie said as quietly as she could. "He doesn't know I'm here. Luckily I parked in the garage last night. Dad's pickup truck is out by the back porch."

"I'm headed down there now. I'm at your gate. Why do you sound so worried?"

"I woke this morning with a dream about the events at the tree farm. I heard this voice telling Gerald Rains to 'let the camel jockey do his thing.' But the voice I was hearing was Schroeder's coming from downstairs. It's real scratchy and distinctive. Once you hear it, you'll never forget. I'm certain he's the one who was in the basement and shot Riley when he escaped. He has to be our link to Richland for sure."

"That's incredible. Are you sure? I don't remember anything about another person in the room. I know your dad and the others saw an unidentified man in the shadows just before the rescue. I just got the report of the ballistic analysis from the recovered shells and bullet at Rains' place. The gun used on Riley was a military issue Berretta M9."

"Schroeder has to be the person. It fits. Ex-military. Quick on his feet and got out of there without being identified."

"It fits alright, but I still don't remember a thing about a mystery guest. Obviously hearing his voice while waking up was a subliminal stimulus for you. If I arrest him, you'll need to repeat to him what you just told me. Makes me nervous. I'm heading down there."

Denise hung up and shut off her cell. She didn't want to put Dr. Miceli or Debbie in any danger, but she didn't want to let Schroeder go without at least questioning him as a suspect on Debbie's say so.

While Debbie and Denise were talking, Schroeder picked up his briefcase and placed it on the table. He popped the latches and slipped out an offer to buy contract for Dan to sign. Dan, for his part, kept the negotiations alive in hopes that Denise would arrive and question the broker sitting across from him.

"It beats me why you don't let the city just plop down 25 million and force the takeover."

"That's an option, but Richland is anxious to close this deal and doesn't want to risk a possible lengthy court battle."

Schroeder handed the contract to Dan, who immediately began reading it. He was being offered one hundred million dollars plus the opportunity to keep the house and 10 acres. He had to admit it was an offer he couldn't reject outright. What he didn't know was that Richland was prepared to go even higher on the price. Suddenly, there was a knock on the back door. Dan looked up and saw Denise standing next to the porch's screen door. He immediately stood and greeted her.

When Denise entered the kitchen her eyes shot to Schroeder who, feeling their sting, knew right away who she was. His flat expression didn't change, but his eyes hardened. She looked just like the picture he had seen of her featured in an L.A. Times article about fraudulent carbon offset investments.

Schroeder didn't wait for any formal introduction. "Good day, Agent Weber," he said in his distinctively squeaky voice.

"Mr. Schroeder. Glad to meet you," Debbie said returning the favor of addressing him without an introduction.

How does she know who I am, Schroeder wondered. Did Miceli tell her about the meeting today? *Am I being set up?*

"I hadn't realized there would be others here," Schroeder said. "Perhaps I should go. After all, it's Thanksgiving. I'll leave the papers with you Dan, and we can speak by phone after you've had a chance to look them over some more."

Denise knew her presence had made Schroeder uncomfortable. She could tell he was looking to get out of there and avoid any potential confrontations. Unless she acted now, he would be gone and untraceable. "Just a moment, Mr. Schroeder," she said, " you're a hard man to find and I have a few questions for you."

"I never take questions from police or FBI without a lawyer present. So, if you'll excuse me, I'll be on my way." Schroeder reached down to close his briefcase.

Denise, feeling more confident said, "If you don't want to cooperate the easy way, then I'll be forced to detain you for interrogation. There are many questions you need to answer." She kept her eyes fixed on Schroeder as she spoke. She had already given him a visual search and did not see any evidence that he was armed, at least not with a shoulder holster.

It was only when she saw him reach into his briefcase that she realized her mistake---a realization that came too late. In an instant, Schroeder pulled his Beretta from the case and flashed the laser on Denise's chest.

"Let's be clear about one thing," Schroeder said, "under no circumstances am I being taken into custody. You have no authority to do that nor do you know who I am."

Denise was cursing herself for jumping in without better assessing the situation. Now she had put Dr. Miceli and Debbie in a bind. *Sorry, Debbie,*

she thought to herself, *I guess it's my turn.* It was Debbie who got her and Everett in a bind in Flagstaff and now she was returning the favor.

"Mr. Schroeder," she said, with as much authority in her voice as she could muster, "pulling a handgun and pointing it at an FBI agent is enough to arrest you. Maybe I jumped the gun, so to speak. Let's put the hardware away and we all calm down."

"Too late for calming down. Why does the FBI want to ask me questions? You must know something I don't. As far as the Agency is concerned, I don't exist. With all your resources, you should have been able to find me by now."

"I only wanted to ask you questions. Arresting you was a bit over the top."

Schroeder stared at her, but his expression didn't soften. He had left no trail whatsoever and, other than his dealings with Riley and the city council, he was an unknown entity. The only possibility for this sudden interest in him was that somehow someone had made him as the man in the basement. His brain quickly processed what kind of evidence they could have linking him to the crime. He was aware that he had left ballistic evidence behind, but he considered that a long shot. Still, if they did have something like that, then he was holding the nail in his coffin. He knew he should have gotten rid of the Beretta, but in a moment of lapsed judgment and sentimentality, he had decided to keep it.

Finally, Dan spoke up. He hadn't moved an inch since Schroeder pulled out the gun, but his brain was running a mile a minute. "Ted, I don't know what's going on, but it's time you put the Berretta away. No one's accusing you of anything. She only wants to ask some questions," he said with urgency in his voice.

Schroeder looked at Dan and said, "No can do, Doc. I'm afraid your friend here has tipped her hand. I don't see a future here. Let's all take a walk over to the 'Point'."

"The Point?" Denise asked, genuinely puzzled.

"Vista Point," Dan said. "It's right outside the door. Land juts out into the ocean; the currents are fierce. I think our visitor here has plans for us to go swimming."

"It's not a great day to go swimming, but I can't do anything about the weather. And besides, bullets are so messy. Leave evidence and all that. This way, at least, I'm giving you a chance."

"Fat chance. It's murder all the way," Dan said angrily.

"Cool down, Doc. Anyone else here? Like your daughter, maybe? It's Thanksgiving. Or is the agent here the only guest today?" Schroeder asked in his squeaky voice.

"There's no one else here," Dan lied."

"I've told the agent in L.A. before I came down that your car was here," Denise said.

"All the more reason to clear up this mess and get out of here," Schroeder said. "Now let's have a look around."

Upstairs, Debbie could make out some of the conversation and, based on Schroeder's last comment, she knew he would come looking for her. Panicked, she made her bed and threw all her belongings into her gym bag including her cell and Glock. Quietly, she opened the door and tiptoed along the carpeted hallway, hugging the wall to prevent noise from the floorboards under the rug. Once in her dad's bedroom, she crossed to the closet and opened the door. She stepped inside, closed the door, and then stood on a small safe her dad kept there. This allowed her to barely reach the wooden panel that covered the access to the attic. She pushed it aside then reached down for her bag and carefully shoved it into the attic. After that, she grabbed the edge of the opening and chinned herself up. With her feet on the top of a built in shoe cabinet, she was able to scramble into the attic and quietly replace the access cover.

With Dan leading the way, Schroeder followed while they walked into each of the rooms downstairs. Finding nothing, Schroeder told Dan and Denise to climb the stairs while he followed. With the Beretta trained on his captives, Schroeder opened each bedroom door and examined the rooms and closets. When he got to Dan's bedroom, he herded Denise and Dan against the windows on the other side of the bed while he searched the bathroom and under the bed. When he finished, he opened the sliding door to the closet and looked around. He pushed the clothes on the rack and was about to gaze upward when Dan interrupted him.

"There's no one here. There are several workers at the winery, but they never come into the house. Why don't we drop all this. You go your way and we'll go ours."

Distracted, Schroeder stopped looking in the closet. He was satisfied there was nothing there. He ignored Dan's plea and waved the Beretta so that Dan and Denise got the message it was time to go. They walked down the stairs and when Debbie heard the back door slam shut, she slipped her Glock into her waistband, the cell into her pocket, and climbed down from the attic. She hurried to her bedroom and looked out the window where she saw Schroeder trailing Dan and Denise as they walked through the formal garden heading for Vista Point.

She raced downstairs and ran out the back door along the path leading to the garden. Just as she was about to enter the garden, she saw Schroeder disappear through the Cyprus trees heading toward the path leading to the rocky point. The path they were taking was well worn, used frequently by visitors and beachgoers alike. It was the only practical access to Vista Point since, on the south side of the point, there were steep cliffs and a rocky shoreline. A cold, blustering wind was blowing and the surf was pounding with large rollers smashing on the empty beach.

Instead of cutting through the Cyprus trees and following Schroeder, Debbie continued straight ahead to the end of the garden then out along the rows of vines. To her right were sand dunes, brush, and the ocean shoreline beyond. To her left were rows of vines. The dunes hid her from view as she ran crouched down toward the hill that ended in a rocky point. The hill bordered the vineyard and at its base was a culvert which carried runoff water to tide pools on the beach. She had taken this route often as a child when she wanted to beat her dad to Vista Point. When she reached the culvert, she was winded and bent over to catch her breath. She glanced to her right and could see her father just beginning to pick his way through the rocks leading to the point. To his left was the culvert tightly covered with brush.

Debbie saw Schroeder look around and he seemed satisfied that the threesome was alone. She hurried down to the bottom of the sandy culvert, which contained a small stream of runoff water from the hills to her left. Dodging rocks and branches from the overhanging brush, she made it to a place just before the rocky point. To her dismay, Schroeder had just past her and the three hikers were walking up hill to the tip of Vista Point.

When Dan reached the area where walking further was impossible without taking a plunge, he grabbed Denise's arm and stopped. A cold, blustering wind was blowing hard on top of the point and the waves on the rocky shore line below were crashing like thunder. Dan knew the only choice left for them was to jump into the rocky ocean that was roiling twenty feet below them. The chances were slim that they would survive the fall and chances were slimmer that they would be able to swim through the lethal waters to safety.

Two hundred yards or so directly ahead of them was a large rock that split the incoming waves. As the waves continued to the lee side of the rock they were bent inward, creating confusing, treacherous cross currents. The waters were extremely dangerous and unswimmable, as far as Dan was concerned. Dan also realized, noting the irony, that this was the exact spot where Tran had drowned attempting to swim out to the rock. Denise stood trembling next to him and he grabbed her arm again in an effort to reassure her.

Suddenly there was a loud boom as a large wave hit the wall of rocks below them and sent spray up over their heads. Schroeder was behind them with his gun pointed at their backs. He remained where he was not willing to get any closer to the ex-SEAL, who he knew wouldn't give up without a fight.

As the wave receded Dan loudly whispered in Denise's ear.

"Do exactly what I do. Ten feet directly below us there's an outcropping of rocks forming a tide pool with enough wet sand to break our jump. Beyond that it's a straight drop to the rocks or water, depending on the tide."

Denise nodded and said, "Then what? The next large wave will blow us off our perch or slam us against the rocks. We're goners," she whimpered.

"We got 90 seconds to get off there while the 7th wave builds. The only hope is Schroeder leaves and we scale the ten feet back up here. I did it once in high school on a dare," Dan said, shaking his head at his youthful stupidity. Of course, he left out the part about how his friend with him had to throw a rope and pull him up just before the wave hit. In this moment, however, he felt confident he could at least save Denise by jacking her up to the rocky edge. From there she was on her own.

"That's enough talking." Schroeder yelled, "you can say your good-byes on the way down. Take off all you cloths. Throw them back here."

"Do as he says," Dan said out loud.

The chilly wind was making them shiver as they undressed. As soon as all their cloths were removed, Schroeder walked forward and picked them up.

"When or if they find you it will be death by drowning while swimming. Good luck. Jump after this next big wave hits."

"Fuck you, Schroeder. You're a chicken shit rogue. I'm ashamed you ever served."

As Debbie snuck out of the culvert onto the final approaches to the point she saw her dad and Denise standing naked. There was a sudden big boom as a large wave hit the rocks.

"Jump!" Schroeder yelled.

Debbie didn't stop to think. She aimed her Glock at Schroeder's right leg. When the bullet hit, he did a backward cartwheel into the air and screamed as he fell flat on his back. He was grabbing his right leg. Debbie raced up to him and kicked his handgun away. She hurried to the edge and looked over. She grunted in relief when she saw they had jumped into the natural tide pool framed by rock outcroppings. If they had been three feet further out, they would have dropped straight down.

Debbie yelled down to them and they both looked up. Denise waved frantically and her Dad yelled back, "We need help here! Is there anything to throw over? We have ninety seconds."

Denise looked around and saw some dried seaweed. She raced over and grabbed it, but the weed pulled apart with a mild tug. Panicked, she looked over at Schroeder moaning on the ground. An idea struck her. *Maybe all my weight training will come to good use.* She raced back to the edge of the point and looked down at her dad.

Meanwhile, Dan looked out at the ocean while he waited for Debbie to return. In the distance, he could see a large wave building as smaller waves raced ahead and crashed into the rocky shoreline below him. Four more waves, he thought, then he would be swimming for his life or he'd be dead, smashed against the rocks.

Dan looked back up behind him to see Debbie lean over and yell, "Boost Denise up here. I think I can do it. Be quick."

Dan cupped his hands and Denise put her right foot in the cup and stepped up as Dan raised her. As soon as she could reach the edge Debbie grabbed her hand and pulled her up and over.

Debbie pointed at Schroeder and said, "You grab one ankle and I'll take the other. We'll flop him over and Dad can climb up."

Dan looked over his shoulder as the dreaded seventh wave was building for the big slam. It had been exactly one minute since he had boosted Denise to safety. Suddenly, he was broken from his thoughts when he heard a loud scream. He turned back to see the hapless Schroeder was being unceremoniously dumped over the side. Debbie was holding onto one ankle and Denise the other. They both squatted down and, with biceps bulging, dug their feet into the sand. Dan prayed that the two of them could hold his weight. If not, all of them would tumble into the ocean. He felt a silence then heard a distinctive, soft sound familiar to surfers when they knew a wave was curling and about to break behind them; a sequence of feeling and sound he had experienced many times while visiting Vista Point as a young man. Instinctively, he leaped up and grabbed the screaming Schroeder's pants. He stepped in his crouch and began to shinny upward like a monkey climbing a coconut tree.

Dan heard a loud boom as he reached the rocky edge, but the upward draft created by the wave pushed all of them backwards instead of knocking them into the ocean. Dan landed awkwardly on Denise who gave him a big kiss.

"Two times in one year. That's a first for me," she said relieved.

"Same for me," Dan said as he rolled off the agent, not sure what she meant. He looked at Schroeder disgustedly. "You're a piece of shit. Debbie, call the medics and tell them to come get this guy."

Chapter Thirty-Three

Six months later, in Dan's garden, a crowd stood as the new mayor of Vista Del Mar and his soon to be bride walked down a garland-laden pathway to a makeshift altar. It was May and the garden was spectacular with roses blooming, topiaries trimmed, and beds planted with everything from snapdragons to begonias. Dan had always hoped that his daughter would be married here. He never imagined that he would be the one to do it instead.

They had everything planned to perfection. After a brief ceremony, there would be a gala reception within the confines of the winery. The oak barrel fermentation room was just a short walk away form the garden. Inside, tables had been set with the barrels acting as a backdrop. In the center of the room a temporary dance floor was assembled to accommodate the one hundred and fifty guests.

Dan wanted a short ceremony. He had trouble finding a Catholic priest to do the vows outside of a church, but he did find a Jesuit priest willing to perform the rites. Flanked by his groomsman—Fred Lesley, Carlos, and his two partners—Dan stood confident and eager to begin this new chapter in his life. He and his bride said their vows and then kissed, with a roaring applause from the guests. The recessional music, played by a live string quartet, was softly heard as the newlyweds departed to the area outside the garden where pictures were to be taken.

While the wedding party waited for the photographers to prepare their shots, they mingled amongst themselves and with other guests who wanted to watch the pictures being taken. David Chase was one of those guests. He saw Dan standing apart from the others and took the opportunity to speak to him privately.

"Congratulations," Chase said. He gave Dan a hearty slap on the back. "I guess it's never too late to tie the knot."

"It's not too late," Dan retorted. "I'm going to enjoy every day to make up for the years I've been alone. My blushing bride is perfect for me. I hope she thinks the same."

"I'm sure she does. But, and I hate to bring this up now," Chase said, more seriously, "the U.S. Attorney called me on Friday and said the grand jury has handed down indictments against Ben Adams, Riley, and Evans. The main complaint is pension fraud and mishandling of public funds. I guess you could indict the whole Congress on that charge."

"Well, it has made my job easier. Riley and Evans sent me their letter of resignation yesterday, pleading for help with their legal costs."

Before they could go on with the conversation, the photographer began waving the bride and groom into position for a photo. Dan stood with his bride and smiled sincerely as their pictures were taken. When the photographers were finished, Chase moved back to stand next to Dan as guests lined up to enter the reception area in the barrel room.

"I'm happy the settlement of the Tran case is behind us. Now the council can get to work straightening out the fiscal mess," Dan said to Chase.

"Yes, the Tran family didn't want to go through more legal hoops while the large jury award was appealed. They were happy with the settlement," Chase said. "They want to set up a scholarship fund for needy students from South Vietnam. Two million dollars will go a long way in that regard."

"Hector's and Dolores' kids want to file a wrongful death claim against Richland, Schroeder, Rains and Adams," Dan said. "They've asked me to find an attorney who could handle that. Would you be interested?"

Chase looked around for a moment and was silent. Then, looking at Dan, he smiled and said, "Well, lets see, according to the FBI, all four of those individuals have been arrested and charged with conspiracy to commit arson, murder, and real estate fraud. It would seem that discovery has already been done by the FBI, making it easier for me to bring a civil case against them. Yes, I will be happy to meet with them. I'm sure there are assets aplenty for a decent judgment in their favor."

"They also want to set up scholarship funds in their parents names," Dan said.

Suddenly from behind there was a tap on Dan's shoulder. He turned to face his bride and they hugged lovingly. Pleased with himself Dan turned to Chase and asked, "You've met Denise before, haven't you?"